RC. 8B
oo
MP 519

Katherine Howell is a former ambulance officer. *Frantic*, featuring Detective Ella Marconi, is her first novel, and is about to be published in the United Kingdom, Germany, France, Italy and Russia. Katherine lives on the New South Wales north coast.

Visit the author's website at:
www.katherinehowell.com

FRANTIC

In one terrible moment, paramedic Sophie Phillips's life is ripped apart — her police officer husband, Chris, is shot on their doorstep and her ten-month-old son, Lachlan, is abducted from his bed. Suspicion surrounds Chris as he is tainted with police corruption, but Sophie believes the attack is much more personal, a consequence of her own actions. While Chris is in hospital and the police, led by Detective Ella Marconi, mobilise to find their colleague's child, Sophie's desperation compels her to search for Lachlan herself. She enlists her husband's partner, Angus Arendson, in the hunt for her son, but will the history they share and her raw maternal instinct lead to an even greater tragedy?

KATHERINE HOWELL

FRANTIC

Complete and Unabridged

CHARNWOOD
Leicester

First published in Great Britain in 2008 by
Pan Books, an imprint of
Pan Macmillan Ltd.
London

First Charnwood Edition
published 2009
by arrangement with
Pan Macmillan Ltd.
London

British Library CIP Data

Howell, Katherine.
   Frantic
   1. Allied health personnel- -Australia- -Sydney
(N.S.W.)- -Fiction. 2. Kidnapping- -Fiction.
   3. Police corruption- -Fiction. 4. Suspense fiction.
   5. Large type books.
   I. Title
   823.9′2–dc22

   ISBN 978–1–84782–801–9

Published by
F. A. Thorpe (Publishing)
Anstey, Leicestershire

Set by Words & Graphics Ltd.
Anstey, Leicestershire
Printed and bound in Great Britain by
T. J. International Ltd., Padstow, Cornwall

This book is printed on acid-free paper

For Phil H. and Phil G.

Acknowledgements

Thanks to Graeme Hague for much help over many years.

Thanks to Selwa Anthony and her assistant, Selena Hanet-Hutchins, for advice, belief, and unending encouragement.

Thanks to Cate Paterson and Kylie Mason at Pan Macmillan, and also to Julia Stiles, for fantastic editing and support.

To my friends in the job, thanks for the paramedical, pharmacological, and firearms insights, 'war stories', and, of course, friendship: Col Benstead, Allan Burnett, Jenni and Steve Flanagan, Garry 'Syd' Francis, Warren Leo, Justine Petit, Alan Smith, John Wood, and, in particular, Mel Johnson. Thanks to Adam Asplin and Esther McKay for police procedural advice. All errors and stretching of truths are mine.

Thanks to UQ staff Dr Veny Armanno, Amanda Lohrey, and Jan McKemmish, and to my friends in the MPhil and sf-sassy groups.

Thanks to Varuna — The Writers House: Peter Bishop, Mark Mcleod, Leigh Redhead and Alice Nelson.

Thanks to Tanya and all the great staff at Angus and Robertson, Tweed City.

Thanks to my family, especially my brother.

And — saving the best for last — my most heartfelt thanks to Phil.

1

'Seventy-four to Control.' The paramedic's voice was tight.

Sophie Phillips leaned forward and turned up the volume of the ambulance radio.

'Seventy-four, go ahead,' Control said.

'We've got two children code two, post house fire. Request urgent back-up.'

Sophie grimaced. *Two kids in cardiac arrest. Jesus.*

Seventy-four was a Randwick ambulance and unless the crew were out of their area and somewhere in the CBD it was unlikely she and Mick would be called on to go, thank God. Serious kid jobs were never good. Since she'd had Lachlan ten months ago they were even worse.

Although most people didn't know it, every moment of every day catastrophe slammed its heavy boot into the face of some poor Sydneysider. On a day like this it seemed particularly unfair. The sky was the crisp and endless blue of late autumn. The wind snapped in the flags along Circular Quay and the smell of salt water and fried foods filled the ambulance. They were parked in a bus stop on Alfred Street. Mick was across the road in a Quay takeaway fetching kebabs for a late lunch, listening in on

1

the portable radio in case they got a call. Sophie watched for his return and thought about the parents of the code two children, and the small, still, smoke-stained faces.

'Thirty-one, what's your location?'

Sophie grabbed the microphone. *Not the fire, please.* 'Thirty-one's at the Quay, picking up twenty.'

'Thanks, Thirty-one. I have a person shot at the Civic Bank on George Street. Police are on scene and CPR's in progress.'

Adrenaline jolted her. 'Thirty-one's on the case.' She rehooked the mike and yanked a pair of latex gloves from the box stuffed between the seats. Mick ran back empty-handed from the kebab stand and threw the portable radio into the cabin, then leapt into the driver's seat and cranked the engine. He turned off the hazard lights and hit the beacons and siren as he pulled out of the bus stop. There was a squeal of brakes and the blast of a horn behind them. Mick didn't so much as glance back.

'Bet it's another robbery,' he said.

'Think so?'

They hit the red at Bond and Sophie checked the traffic on her side. 'Clear.' Mick floored it and punched the horn to change the siren from yelp to wail.

'Yeah. Another gang job,' he said.

Another red. 'Clear.' Every time the gang of four struck, the newspapers went nuts over the continued failure of the police to catch them, and Sophie's husband, Chris, took the insult personally. He'd been a police officer in the city for nine years. His shell should have grown harder than a turtle's, but things like this always struck home.

'Chris working today?' Mick said. 'He might be on scene.'

Sophie hoped not. If he was there, his partner, Angus Arendson, would be too. It was only five weeks since Sophie had made The Biggest Mistake Of Her Life, and ever since then, whenever she saw Angus she felt as though she'd forgotten how to arrange her face in a normal expression, how to speak casually like an ordinary person. It was worse when Chris was around. If Chris wasn't so caught up in his PTSD or whatever it was, Sophie felt sure he'd have realised long ago what she'd done. He'd have known that very night.

The closer they got to the bank the more the traffic clogged up. Sophie tried to focus on the case, not the people who might be there. Shootings had become more frequent in the city in the last couple of years but they still couldn't be called commonplace. They translated into scenes of high emotion where you could really do your stuff and make a difference to a person — if the bullet missed vitals and you got there quickly enough. Eight years ago as a trainee she'd been to a shooting where the bullet had lacerated the victim's aorta. The guy was dead inside a minute. She always remembered her senior officer's words: 'If he'd been shot on the operating table, he might just have made it.'

Mick swung onto the wrong side of the road. The siren was on yelp and the headlights on high beam. He leaned on the horn. Cars coming from a side street swerved out of their way. Mick charged down the clear path toward a marked police car parked sideways across the street. He veered around it and to the front of the bank. Police were everywhere. Sophie's hands were sweaty inside her gloves.

'Thirty-one's on location,' Sophie said into the radio microphone. Before Mick had stopped the engine she was out on the roadway. She yanked open the side door into the rear of the ambulance to grab the Oxy-Viva and drug box, and Mick came around from the driver's side to pull out the cardiac monitor and first-aid kit. They hurried across the footpath towards the wide glass doors. A police officer held them open, his face pale, his eyes fixed straight ahead onto the street. 'It's bad.'

The bank was big and marble-floored. Their steps echoed. Four metres inside the door a police officer stood guard over a blood spatter on the floor. Sophie looked around for the patient. 'This one got away,' the officer said. 'That's your man there.'

He lay on the floor at the far end of the roped-off queue area. Three police officers and two bank staff stood around him in a huddle while two more police did CPR.

Sophie's stomach lurched.

Chris was leaning over the guard with his elbows locked, counting loudly with each compression. 'One and two and three and four and breathe.' Angus was kneeling at the guard's head. Neither he nor Chris were wearing gloves.

He bent to blow into the one-way valve on a plastic resuscitation mask he held on the man's face.

Sophie made herself breathe deeply before putting down the equipment and looking over Chris's shoulder.

The guard was dead, that much was clear. The bullet had hit him in the throat and a pool of blood lay like a halo around him. A blood-soaked dressing was taped roughly to his neck. Every time Angus blew into the mask, air bubbled out of the wound.

Mick knelt and attached electrodes to the cardiac monitor's three leads. He reached around Chris's hands and opened the guard's grey uniform shirt. He stuck two electrodes to his upper chest then pulled the shirt out of the guard's black trousers, placing the third electrode over his lower left ribs.

'Keep going?' Angus said, businesslike. His bloody hands gripped the dead man's jaw and his knees were in the halo.

'Stop for a second,' Sophie said. Chris froze, his hands still touching the dead man's chest. Sophie put her hand on his shoulder. 'Raise up a little.' He leaned back so his hands were clear of the guard's shirt front but still maintained their position. Through her gloves and his shirt Sophie felt the warmth of her husband's skin, and she squeezed his shoulder gently. He didn't move, didn't glance around. She guessed he was still angry about that morning's argument.

She exhaled and let him go, then crouched by the body and eased back the guard's eyelids. This was always hard. Not for the dead man — he was long gone — but for the people who'd tried to save him. Sophie knew Chris had struggled with things like this before. The bank staff would take it even harder. She glanced over and saw the blood on their hands was dry. They'd obviously started the resuscitation effort, maybe when the man was still alive and gasping.

The guard's pupils were fixed and dilated. Sophie released his eyelids and took the six second ECG strip Mick printed out. It showed the flat line of asystole, as she'd expected. You checked these things not so much to confirm what you already knew but to make the people involved feel they'd given the man a chance. You couldn't walk in, take one look and say, 'Stuffed.' You might think it but you couldn't say it.

Maybe if he'd been shot on the operating table . . .

She got to her feet. 'I'm very sorry but he's gone.'

The bank staff turned to each other in helpless fright. The three police standing by murmured words of comfort and gently herded them away. One officer carried the guard's gun in an evidence bag. They left behind a little first-aid kit, the top open, and various small dressings scattered about the polished marble floor. A roll of medical tape lay on its side three metres away, covered in bloody fingerprints.

Angus put down the plastic mask. His knees came free of the pool of clotted blood with a small wet sound, and his bloodstained hands hung by his sides as he looked down at the guard. Chris still knelt at Sophie's feet, his hands over the guard's chest.

'You gave him the best possible chance,' she said.

Angus blew out a breath of air, and went to put his hands on his hips then stopped himself. Mick pulled the monitor leads off the electrodes, leaving the electrodes themselves in place and the guard's shirt open. For a non-suspicious death Sophie's next move would be to get a sheet from the ambulance and drape it over the body, but this was a crime scene. Nothing more could be touched.

Chris was motionless at her feet. She picked up the Oxy-Viva and touched the back of his neck. 'Come outside and we'll clean you up.'

George Street was in chaos. The police had sectioned two lanes off and queues of cars, trucks and buses were stuck behind the blue and white tape strung between police cars. Horns blared and people shouted. Flashing red and blue beacons glinted off the windows of shops and banks across the street. Curious workers watched the scene, talking with their arms folded.

At the ambulance Sophie put the Oxy-Viva back into the equipment shelves and took out a bottle of alcohol handwash. 'Hold out your hands,' she told Chris. She squirted it onto his palms. He held them clear of his body as he rubbed. The bloodstained liquid dripped to the roadway.

Mick leaned into the ambulance to radio Control and say the victim was code four.

Sophie turned to Angus and squeezed the bottle over his bare hands. The legs of his blue uniform trousers were dark with blood and the right one was hitched up from sticking to his knee. 'So the guard got one, did he?' Sophie said, trying to sound normal.

'That's what they reckon.' Angus met her eye. 'Shot the guy in the bum. The tellers said he let out a hell of a yelp.'

'More,' Chris said.

Sophie coated his hands again. The alcohol smell was strong. Chris scraped at the edges of his fingernails where the blood had gone deep. Sophie could see his short nails weren't up to the task. 'Here.' She reached for his hands but he pulled back.

'I can do it.'

He still didn't meet her gaze. She lowered her voice. 'What's the matter?'

He shook his head.

She shook hers in return, annoyed but unsurprised at his reticence. Since he'd been assaulted two months ago he'd become silent and moody. It was sometimes hard to shake the thought that it was actually because he knew what she'd done, that Angus must've slipped and said something, but oft-checked logic told her he was moody before that. Shit, it was the reason she'd gone and done it. No, that wasn't fair. It was only partly the reason. A small part. A very small part.

Guilt bubbled in her stomach like gas in a stagnant swamp.

She eyed him. 'Where were your gloves?'

'There was no time,' he said.

'There's always time.'

He didn't answer.

'Make sure you both go to the hospital and get tests done. So should the bank staff.' She'd had to do that once, when a psychotic patient bit her on the arm. Chris's chances of contracting a disease through the unbroken skin of his hands were tiny, but still the security guard was going to be a small and silent ghost in their house for the next three months. More tension. Great. 'You should've worn your gloves.'

More police arrived. They walked past with camera cases and equipment boxes. Behind the police tape a growing crowd of people watched. Some held up mobile phones and took pictures of the gathered police vehicles. Overhead, against the bright blue sky, two news helicopters hovered. The chopping of their blades was a familiar background to much of Sophie's work.

A lanky female detective in a black pants-suit came over. 'Phillips, you were first on scene?'

Chris nodded. 'We were on Broadway when the call came in.'

'See anything?'

'The gang was gone before we arrived,' Angus said. 'All we saw was the guard.'

'Okay,' the detective said. 'Come and find me when you're done here.'

There was a commotion and raised voices in the crowd, then a woman in a grey skirt and white shirt, her red hair tied back in a bun, ducked the police tape at a run. Her face was bloodless. 'My husband,' she gasped. She wrenched open the ambulance's rear door. Chris went to her and she grabbed his arm. 'Where's my husband?'

'Who is your husband?'

'He works security in the bank. They said on the TV he was hurt.' The woman's eyes brimmed with tears. 'Please tell me he's already gone to hospital.'

Chris put his hands on her shoulders. 'I'm sorry.'

'No.'

'We did everything we could.'

'No, no.' She began to weep into his shirt, half collapsing against him. Mick hurried to help, and between them they walked the sobbing woman away from the mesmerised crowd.

Sophie was aware of Angus coming up close behind her. 'Your husband's a good guy,' he said. His breath was warm against her neck.

She turned to face him. He smiled at her. His blond hair shone in the sun. His blue eyes flicked down to her mouth for a second, then up again. 'Don't you reckon?'

'You haven't said anything, have you?' she said.

He made a zipping motion across his lips. 'Never.'

'He's so angry.'

'Depressed,' he said. 'I think it's post-traumatic stress.'

'So do I. I tell him to go and see someone, but he won't listen.'

'It's the culture,' Angus said. She could smell

10

toothpaste and the same cologne she'd inhaled that night.

He took the handwash from her and she watched his broad hands squeeze the plastic bottle.

'It'll take time,' he was saying.

Sophie raised her gaze. She'd promised herself she would stop thinking about it. Wasn't each thought another betrayal?

She felt guilty. She always felt guilty.

Mick came back and said to Angus, 'That detective wants you.'

Angus handed the bottle back to Sophie. It was warm. 'You guys going to the Jungle tonight?'

'Betcha,' said Mick.

'Good,' Angus said. 'I'll see you there.' He walked away.

Sophie had forgotten about the night's fundraiser at the Southern Jungle Bar. She pictured herself sitting at a table, Chris on one side, Angus on the other. Oh Jesus.

'You're still okay to give Jo and me a lift home after, right?' Mick said.

Sophie had been abstinent since That Night. It was the only sensible response, and it came in handy for other people too. 'I guess.'

She tossed her gloves in the ambulance bin. She rinsed her hands then put the almost empty bottle back. Mick climbed into the driver's seat. 'What's that, the fourth robbery?'

'If it is the gang,' Sophie said, 'it's their fifth.'

'And the third person they've shot dead.'

11

'Only the second. The other one's still comatose.'

'Good as.' Mick started the engine.

Sophie picked up the mike. 'Thirty-one is clear the scene.'

'Copy that, Thirty-one,' came the crackling reply. 'You can return for your twenty.'

'Hallelujah.' Mick aimed the ambulance back towards the Quay.

In Alfred Street he parked in the same bus stop, took the portable radio and got out of the ambulance. Alone, Sophie stared at the case sheet and considered what she'd write.

She wanted to make it clear that the police had done everything possible. It was ridiculous, but a defence barrister might suggest that the guard's death had resulted from their ineptitude rather than from the actions of whichever scumbag was paying his bill. Sophie had seen it done before; hell, she'd been accused of similar incompetence herself. No matter how solid she made the case sheet, there was still a chance that accusations would fly, especially with one of the police officers being her husband. She could just imagine it: 'Isn't it true that you are covering for your husband? Isn't that why you pronounced the man deceased right there and then? Because you knew he had no chance, because these officers weren't doing their jobs? Because their mistakes would be picked up if a doctor was able to examine the victim at hospital?'

God forbid they found out about Angus too.

She shook herself and focused on her wording. She scribbled some notes on a scrap of paper and was just starting to write when Mick came back with the food.

He drove them around to their station in The Rocks. The old brick building stood on the corner of George and Gloucester Streets, right under the southern end of the Harbour Bridge. Mick hit the remote to raise the roller door and backed into the narrow plant room. Traffic rumbled overhead on the Bridge as it did twenty-four hours a day, and closing the roller door made no difference to the noise. Taped to the muster room's noticeboard were packets of ear plugs. It was a running joke: on nightshift at The Rocks you were never on station long enough to lie down, let alone fall asleep.

Sophie left the unfinished case sheet on the bench in the muster room and they sat in the lounge to eat.

'That ranks in the top ten worst ways to go.' She spoke through a mouthful of kebab. 'It's got it all. You're in pain, you're going slowly, you can't breathe, and you're totally aware.'

'Did you see his hands were all bloody?'

It was too easy to picture the dying man grabbing at his own throat. 'Number three, I reckon.'

'No, it's worse than the steamroller,' Mick said. 'This guy knew.'

'Didn't we decide the steamroller guy knew too? You get caught legs first, you've got a second or two to figure things out.'

'A second or two is quicker than this guy had,' Mick said. 'Muuuuch quicker.'

'Okay. This goes in at two. The steamroller

goes to three.' Number one was kept vacant for the awful death even they couldn't imagine.

Lettuce fell out of Mick's kebab. He collected it in a pile on the coffee table. 'Mind me asking — you and Chris okay?'

Sophie looked down at her food. Where was this going? Had he guessed something? If he asked her straight out was there something going on between her and Angus, could she look him in the eye and lie? Well, hang on, she thought. There wasn't anything *going on*. There had been one incident. One.

'Chris just seems really down,' Mick said. 'He had tears in his eyes when we were helping that woman.'

Sophie relaxed, just a fraction. 'It's since that assault. I think it's PTSD.'

'He should get some help.'

'We argue about that every day.' Sophie felt tears come into her own eyes. She was grateful when Mick looked away, intent on an OH&S poster on the wall.

After a moment he looked back. 'It'll be okay, Soppers.'

She nodded, not trusting herself to speak.

6.58 pm

Chris was in the kitchen of their Gladesville home when Sophie got in. She dumped her bag on the floor and looked into the living room. Lachlan pulled himself up on the side of his playcot when he saw her, and she went to him

14

and picked him up. 'Hey, my boy, who's my lovely boy?' The sight of him, the feel of him in her arms, took away every bad thing the day had thrown at her.

She carried him into the kitchen. Chris was bent over a dish on the bench. She held Lachlan on her hip and smiled at the child. *My wonderful son*.

'There was a load of washing still in the machine.' Chris's tone brought her back to earth.

'Dammit, I forgot to hang it out this morning before work,' she said. 'Will we put it out now?' She nudged Lachlan's forehead with her nose. 'Will we, huh, will we?' He grinned at her.

'It's done,' Chris said.

'Oh. Thanks.' She raised her eyebrows at Lachlan. 'At least we're speaking.'

Chris didn't look at her. 'When were we not?'

'What would you call it?'

'We were at a job. I had work to do. Things to think about.'

'You've been doing a lot of thinking lately.'

'I told you how busy I am.'

'Yes, I know, and the robberies bother you, and the media pressure, and everything else.' He didn't answer. She wondered at her own behaviour, the way that without even planning to she poked at him with her words, trying to make him talk. Part of her swore it was for his benefit, that if he could talk about what was on his mind, even through provocation, he'd feel better. At the same time another part of her was terrified he'd turn to her one day and say, 'You want to know

15

the truth? The truth is I know what you did!' A small cynical voice suggested maybe she wanted this to happen. She couldn't stand the pressure, the secrecy, the guilt, and needed it in the open in the same way that she wanted his problems out there.

She noticed he was making lasagne. 'Aren't we eating at the Jungle?'

'I don't feel like going,' he said. 'I spent most of the afternoon doing a statement about the bank job and my head's killing me.'

'But it's for Dean.'

'I rang him. He said he didn't mind that we wouldn't be there.'

'I promised Mick and Jo a lift home.'

'You can still go.' He spooned sauce into a baking dish. 'If you want.'

She didn't know what she wanted. Going meant getting out of the house, away from the uncomfortable silences and the awkwardness that now filled the space between them. Being around Angus would feel less weird if Chris wasn't there, and although every time she saw Angus her cheating behaviour slapped her in the face like a cold wet fish, there was something secret and deep inside her that wanted to see him again. Wanted to remember what they'd done.

No. She hugged Lachlan gently to her. *I am not going down that road. It's dangerous. And wrong.*

Chris continued to layer the pasta sheets and the meat. Sophie studied his face. He didn't even glance at her to see if she'd made up her mind.

He doesn't know, or he wouldn't be quite so blasé about letting me go out without him, to a place he knows Angus will be.

'Maybe I will go,' she said.

Chris shrugged. 'Whatever.'

She took Lachlan into the lounge room and sat down. Marriage was a minefield sometimes, and for the past five weeks she'd been stumbling through it blindfolded.

She sighed. At least she had Lachlan. He lay on her chest, still for a rare moment, his head against her neck. She inhaled his sweet baby scent. She'd been living her life flat out, running frantically from one thing to the next, with no time to sit and breathe. Lachlan must feel the same, passed continually between his parents and grandmother, depending on who was working and when. She should try to go part-time, if the mortgage would allow it — no, even if it wouldn't — and make more time for him. She rubbed her cheek against the top of his silken head. He clutched at her throat and she stood him up, facing her, his feet stamping in her lap and his tiny starfish hands reaching for her face. She brought him closer. His fingers groped along her chin and came to rest on her lips. His deep brown eyes stared into hers, unblinking. 'I love you more than anything, and I always will,' she said around his fingers, and his face beamed with joy.

Fifteen minutes later, in the shower upstairs, she squeezed the shampoo bottle hard. Nine weeks ago their house had been a happy place. Coming home had been a delight. She and Chris had willingly shared household tasks and looking after Lachlan. They'd had small disagreements — who didn't? — but they had always made up before the day was out. Then two months ago he had been bashed. Sophie remembered his bruised ribs and throat, his torn uniform shirt, and the story of how he and his mate Dean Rigby had fought with a suspect in a back lane in Surry Hills. Dean came out worse and was permanently off the road now: hence tonight's fundraiser.

Chris had changed that day. He'd become preoccupied. *Much* less communicative. As for their sex life, well. He was quicker to anger, and they fought. Did they ever fight!

The night she'd done The Stupid Thing they'd had a big one. She'd tried again to get him to agree to see a counsellor. He'd said some things couldn't be helped by talking. She challenged him to explain himself but he wouldn't, and she took that to mean that he couldn't. It was a bad move, she knew that now, because next thing he was accusing her of needing to control everything in their life, not just him but Lachlan too, and that their son would grow up under the thumb and hate her for it. She had walked out the door and went to the Southern Jungle, started drinking, and then Angus introduced himself. She'd thought about it a lot since, and sometimes she decided that what she'd done was due partly to alcohol, partly to anger, and partly to her wish to prove that she was not obsessed with control, that she could go with the flow as much as the next person. *See, Chris?* she'd thought, squashed into the back seat of Angus's car, her head bumping the roof. *See how uncontrolled I can be?*

Sometimes she decided even that could not explain it.

It was the worst mistake of her life. *But it was also — No.*

She stepped from the shower and dried herself as though she could wipe the memory from her skin, and turned her thoughts back to her husband. The problem was that the robberies and the assault, on top of all the things Chris had seen and done in his years of service, were piling up around him like a wall he could find no way around. He was so lost he needed someone on the outside waving a big flag, calling in a loud voice, helping him discover the way through. And as his wife, wasn't that her job?

She dressed in jeans and a red shirt then dried her long brown hair and tied it up again. Being on the road was no good for Chris, the way he was. The sooner he got a transfer into the Academy, the better for all of them.

The smell of baking pasta greeted her as she returned downstairs. Chris was perched on the lounge in front of the TV. Lachlan was on the floor nearby, looking at a cardboard book. Sophie stood in the doorway and watched the Police Commissioner speaking about the robbery on the news.

'Secondly, I want to ask every person with medical experience to be aware they may be approached for assistance by this man. Do not accuse him or attempt to apprehend him

19

yourself. He is armed and very dangerous. Call the police immediately.' With all those micro-phones in his face, Commissioner Dudley-Pearson looked like a man being held up himself. 'Finally, I want to assure the city that its police service is working extremely hard to catch the perpetrators of these robberies. And no, I will not be resigning.' His bulldog jowls wobbled as he spoke. 'Now more than ever the service needs strong leadership.'

The newsreader spoke about the victim. The screen displayed a photo of the security guard in happier times. The red-haired woman smiled into the camera over his shoulder. They had twin boys, three years old. 'Tragic,' Sophie said.

Chris jumped.

'Sorry, I didn't mean to scare you.'

'You didn't.' Chris stood up abruptly. 'Mum's coming over. You'd better go before she parks you in.'

'Is that the real reason you're not coming to the Jungle? You should tell her — '

'I'd already decided not to go before I asked her over, okay?'

'Fine.' Sophie crouched to kiss Lachlan's forehead. 'You have a good night too.'

7.50 pm

Sophie drove to Annandale through the autumn night, trying to excuse Chris this latest episode of irritability. Everything else aside, he'd been covered in the guard's blood and couldn't save

20

him. While paramedics were used to fighting in vain for people's lives, she sometimes forgot that for others it wasn't a routine occurrence. She felt bad that she'd been abrupt, too, but you could blame guilt for that, along with the cumulative effect of eight weeks of domestic disharmony.

She found a place to park some distance up Johnston Street and walked back to Parramatta Road. She waited at the lights then crossed to the brick-fronted building with the neon toucan in the window.

The Southern Jungle was a cop bar. Six police injured in the line of duty had pooled their payouts and bought it a few years before. They served the beers; they learned commercial cookery and ran the small kitchen. Police and their friends drank there, and this meant it was a haven. Any time an officer was badly injured on the job, a fundraiser was held. If the worst happened and an officer was killed, the wake was held here too.

She pushed the door open and was accosted by a police officer she recognised from the southern suburbs. 'Door tax,' he said with a smile. He held out a firefighter's helmet half-full of cash. She dropped in a ten dollar note and he gave her three raffle tickets. 'Lucky door prize. It'll be drawn at nine.'

'Thanks.'

The place was packed. She shouldered her way to the bar through the crowd of laughing, cheering people. On the wall behind the bar was a blown-up photo of the man of the hour, Senior Constable Dean Rigby.

'Buy you a drink?'

Sophie turned to see Angus beside her. 'Just mineral water,' she said quickly.

He smiled. 'Of course.'

When he had their drinks they moved to a space near the front window.

'I had my blood tests.' He showed her the bandaid on his arm. 'And my butt's sore from those boosters.'

'It only lasts a week,' she said. 'Kidding. Couple of days.'

The light from the neon toucan turned Angus's blond hair green. Sophie glanced around for Mick, and her gaze fell on the table in the corner where she and Angus had sat and talked for so long on that night. It had all been about work, she remembered, nothing personal was shared at all, but somehow — with a look, a touch — it had developed. She could smell his cologne again now, and the laundry powder he used, the scent rising from his clothes with the heat of his body.

Angus looked at the table too, then back at her.

She said, 'I want us to be clear about something.'

'You don't have to say it.'

'I need to.' She felt a wave of guilt and regret. What a thing she'd done. She blinked back sudden tears. 'It was wrong and I can never do it again.'

'I know,' Angus said. 'I feel the same way.'

'If Chris ever found out — '

'I know,' Angus said again. 'He won't find out

from me.' He touched Sophie's arm lightly, reassuringly. She felt a thrill at the touch, and looked down at his hand, remembering.

She started when there was a loud cheer by the door. Dean Rigby walked in. He wore a soft foam collar round his neck and she could imagine the shiny pink of the recent surgical scars it covered. He was immediately surrounded by well-wishers.

'Where is Chris?' Angus said, his tone casual.

'Felt like a night in,' Sophie said. 'He's babysitting and entertaining his mum.'

'Ah, the lovely Gloria.'

'You know her?'

'Chris and I knew each other when we were kids,' Angus said. 'He didn't tell you?'

Sophie thought back to when Chris had come home from work a few days after the assault and mentioned he had a new partner. Sophie had said, 'Good bloke?' and Chris had shrugged. 'Seems okay.' That had been it.

'Must have slipped his mind.'

'He dated my sister Belinda when they were sixteen,' Angus said. 'It was kind of funny when we met again. He didn't recognise me at first. Only natural, I suppose. I guess I was just a pesky fourteen-year-old brother when he and Bee wanted time alone.' He smiled. 'How well do you get on with Gloria?'

Sophie rolled her eyes.

He started to laugh. 'I see.'

'We have different ideas, about child-raising, motherhood, you name it.' Sophie mashed the lemon in her glass with the straw. 'Plus, she and

Chris have this ongoing thing about his dad.'

'Still?'

'It's as if she feels the bad fathering genes might've been passed down and if she's not vigilant Chris'll do something awful,' Sophie said. 'I think he should stand up to her, tell her to leave him alone, but he'd rather keep the peace.'

'She a matron yet?'

'She quit nursing to tell us how to live our lives,' Sophie said. 'I should be grateful to her, because she looks after Lachlan when we're both at work. And she adores him. But I can't get over her attitude.'

'Hey, Soph!' Mick grabbed her from behind. 'Did you hear, the youngest kid from that fire in Randwick's still hanging in there?'

His wife, Jo, carried glasses of red wine. The contrast between them was stark: Mick's white blond hair and easily sunburned skin looked all the more pale beside Jo's black hair and fine features. The only thing that matched were their blue eyes. Mick introduced Jo to Angus, then swigged half his wine and looked about. 'Deano!' he called and pushed through the crowd to talk to the man of the moment.

At eight-thirty, they shared a jumbo plate of nachos. At nine, Angus's number was drawn out as the lucky door prize winner. The prize, a bottle of Glenfiddich, he immediately donated to the fundraising auction. By closing time Sophie was yawning, Mick was wearing the NSW Blues rugby league jersey he'd successfully outbid six other people for, and Jo was dancing with Angus to the Bee Gees' 'Night Fever'.

'Signed by the current team,' Mick said to Sophie. 'Look.'

'You showed me before,' she said.

'All of them.' Mick stared down at the front of the jersey and ran his finger over the names.

Angus and Jo came back laughing. The barman shouted for last drinks. The four of them stood up to go.

Angus walked them to Sophie's car. 'See you on the streets tomorrow?' Mick asked him.

'Not likely,' Angus said with a smile. 'Few days off for me.'

'Lucky bastard.'

Angus bent to look in Sophie's window. 'Say hi to Gloria.'

'Ha,' Sophie said.

It was only a five-minute drive to Mick and Jo's place in Chippendale but Mick was asleep before they got there. Sophie double-parked and leaned into the back seat to punch him in the leg. He opened his eyes. Jo climbed out of the car and pulled on his arm, and he struggled, grumbling, out onto the footpath.

'Don't you dare ring in sick tomorrow,' Sophie called.

Fifteen minutes later she parked in her own garage and let herself into the house. Lachlan was asleep on his stomach in his cot. She gently rolled him onto his side. He snuffled and made a face then relaxed again. She stroked his head and kissed him.

Chris lay in their bed in the dark. 'Hi.'

'I didn't mean to wake you.'

'It's okay.'

To Sophie's relief he sounded friendly. When she climbed into bed Chris moved close to her and they hugged. 'Sorry about before,' he said.

'Me too.'

'You smell of cigarette smoke,' he said. 'How was it?'

'Good.' She tried to sound casual. 'Angus was there. He told me about your disreputable past with his sister.'

She felt him smile against her cheek and her spirits rose.

Chris answered, 'It was totally innocent.'

'Yeah, right. I remember being sixteen,' she said, smiling herself. 'How was dinner?'

'Same as ever.'

He was quiet. She propped herself on her elbow and ruffled his short dark hair. 'Still thinking about that guard?'

'And his wife. And his kids.' He pressed his head into her hand. His eyes were open and he looked at the ceiling. 'That gang needs stopping.'

'So far they've just been lucky,' she said. 'They've never been spotted stealing or torching their getaway cars, they don't leave their prints, and nobody's come forward to identify the CCTV pictures. But that guard might have done the trick. Your guys will test that blood left behind and, who knows, the DNA might match up. The name will pop out and that huge strike force will absolutely swamp him and his mates.' She ran her hand across his bare stomach then snapped the elastic of his pyjama trousers against his skin, but he kept staring at the ceiling.

26

'Chris?'

'The DNA database isn't that big,' he said. 'Chances are it won't match anyone.'

'But he's been shot, he'll have to get some help, right? He'll turn up at a hospital or doctor's surgery sometime soon. All you guys have to do is wait.'

'Maybe it's not a bad wound though. Maybe the gang will treat it themselves.'

Sophie rolled onto her back. 'Or maybe it's really bad and he dies and you find his body with the bullet still in it, but at least then you'll know who he was and you can start checking out his mates.'

'I just worry.'

His tone made her soften. 'I know you do.' She pressed against him, absorbing his warmth. 'You will catch them.'

'I know.' But there was doubt in his voice and tension in his body, and Sophie wondered what he really thought.

2

Detective Ella Marconi both loved and hated
being on call at night. People thought they could
get away with things in the dark, and there was
always the potential that it would be interesting.
But while someone outside the job might think it
was a fifty-fifty shot that when her pager went off
it would be something decent, something
worthwhile, Ella knew the odds were actually
very different. Boring and stupid beat interesting
almost every single time.

Like this case: a fire in a takeaway shop on
Victoria Road in Gladesville. The passing traffic,
steady even at this hour, meant that it had been
quickly spotted and reported. The fire brigade
had soon had the place covered in water and
foam. The firefighters had told the uniform cops
that there was evidence of a Molotov, and so
Ella's pager had gone buzzing off her bedside
table onto the carpet.

Ella stood on the footpath outside a newsagent
three shops up from the burned takeaway. She
held back a yawn. The fire truck was still on the
scene and fat hoses lay across the wet footpath.
Firefighters walked around, doing Ella couldn't
figure out what. The air stank of burned plastic
and smoke. Every time a car went past the smell
was stirred up even more.

28

So far the owner of the takeaway business had not given Ella any facts she didn't already have from the constables or the firefighters. 'I don't know who would do this,' he said again. His name was Edman Hughes. He was a skinny white guy in a brown T-shirt, dark blue jeans and dirty Dunlop Volleys. His arms were bony and when he talked he scratched one or the other of his elbows.

Ella held her pen over her notebook and looked at him. 'How's business?'

'It's okay.'

'Rent must be high on this stretch.'

He shrugged and glanced along the line of shops. 'It's a tax deduction.'

She said nothing. He scratched his elbow again. 'I don't know what this city's coming to, that somebody would do such a random thing as this,' he said.

The good old Molotov. Such a handy random thing. She flipped the notebook closed. 'I'll need you to come to the station during the day and make a formal statement.'

'Sure, okay.' He took the card she held out. 'Thank you.'

The front windows and door of the shop were smashed. Ella looked in at the blackened dripping mess. A firefighter picked through debris on the floor. The case was such a washout she could feel it sapping her strength already. Paperwork, identification of the accelerant — she was guessing petrol — talk to Edman again, put a little pressure on, but in the end what for? If he admitted to the insurance fraud it'd only mean more paperwork. Days hanging around court waiting for his hearing, which would probably end in a suspended sentence. If he'd been a bad boy before, maybe a few months inside. Whoopee.

Ella watched the firefighters roll up the hoses, and sighed. Where was the big case, the one that would envelop her, the one she could attack with passion and drive? Over the last few months her enthusiasm for the job had leached away like water through Sydney sandstone. She found it hard to know whether she still loved the job or only the potential it held. She sometimes felt a little of the old thrill when she drove in to work, or when she was at home and the pager went off, but lately all the cases were such crap. Stupid people did stupid things to other stupid people and she had to sort it out and clean it up. She was like one of Pavlov's dogs in reverse. When the bell rings but there's no meat, you soon stop salivating.

She heard a thump and looked around to see newspapers being dropped at the newsagent's door. She walked up as a man came out of the shop. A few coins later she was reading about yesterday's bank hold-up and shooting.

Now that was a decent job. Strike Force Gold — so called because the thieves were scoring pots of it, the joke went — was a huge team made up of detectives from the Metropolitan Robbery Squad plus a few from various city stations. They and the other squads in Crime Agencies had everything: resources, money, profile, interesting cases and genuine bad guys.

They never had to deal with assault complaints where Girl A accused Girl B of throwing an avocado at her, while Girl B said Girl A threw it first.

Ella ground her teeth. Over the past three years she'd applied regularly to move into Crime Agencies — preferably Homicide Squad, but she'd take whatever she could get — yet never scored so much as a week's secondment. Forget what her mate Detective Dennis Orchard said about the process being fair; someone was white-anting her.

Oh, it was fine for Dennis. He was already in there. It was easy for him to say nobody remembered the time on her first homicide case when she'd barked at the Assistant Commissioner to get the fuck out of the crime scene before she had him arrested. It wasn't entirely her fault: the man wore civvies and it had been *really* dark at the time. His name was Frank Shakespeare and he was retired now, but it was clear he still had friends in the job.

Ella watched Edman Hughes stare into the ruins of his shop. The world was chock full of weasels like him determined to pull the wool over her eyes, and it would always be so, but she wished it could at least be for a big and juicy reason.

5.05 am

Ella's bank owned half an unrenovated Federation house in Putney, a small suburb sandwiched between Victoria Road and the northern shores of the Parramatta River, and let Ella live in it for an exorbitant amount of money each fortnight. The house was built of dark red brick with a red tile roof, the kind of place where you expected to see a swan made from an old tyre on the front lawn and the lawn itself to be thick and springy and mown once a week right down to the white. The lawn around her house had neither a swan nor springiness. It was thin and weedy and grew rank along the edges where unused garden beds lay like the mounds of simple graves.

She parked the unmarked car on the street, leaving the windows down a bit to let out the smoke smell. Her part of the house was the back. The front was owned by a thin young man by the name of Denzil, who was deaf and worked as a computer programmer from home. He kept hours as odd as hers; even now the light in his study cast a glow on the path down to her door. They had a nodding relationship and kept an eye on each other's places when one went away. Well, she kept an eye on his place when he slid a note under her door saying he was off to another conference. She herself didn't go away. That was what piddling wages and a Sydney mortgage could do to you.

She unlocked her front door and went inside, snicking the deadbolt behind her. She'd bought the place not long before Dennis left Hunters Hill Station for the bigger, brighter world of the Homicide Squad. On one of their last shifts together he'd brought her home after a scumbucket had deliberately vomited on her, and had waited to take her back to work. When she'd come out of her room, freshly showered and in clean clothes, sniffing at herself for any lingering hints of semi-digested hamburger, he'd been all around the place and made a helpful list. 'Your shrubs are too close in the back there.'

'I've bought an axe and a hoe and Dad's booked in for next weekend.'

'The locks on the side windows are flimsy.'

She pulled a plastic bag full of clinking steel out of the pantry to show him.

'The front door — '

'Is not solid core, but will be replaced.'

He'd nodded and flipped his notebook shut. 'Good.'

She'd made coffee. Dennis had talked about what he hoped to achieve in the squad and Ella had felt like a little sister being left behind. The more enthusiastic Dennis had become the darker her emotions had turned. They'd joined the job together, been probationers at Newtown together and helped each other through some pretty tough early days. He'd become a detective before her but that was no reason why his application should have been accepted while hers was turned down. She'd finally jogged the table with her leg to tip over Dennis's coffee and make him shut the hell up.

Ella opened a window and leaned on the sill. The sky over the city turned brighter as sunrise approached. The air was cool and clear, as yet unspoiled by the breath of thousands who would spend their day creating annoying cases for police.

The house was her refuge. After a day spent listening to people bitch and moan it was wonderful to return to the clinking of mast cables on the yachts moored in Kissing Point Bay. With the shrubs gone from the wall no perp could lie in wait or try to jemmy the windows without being seen. The doors were solid and deadlocked, the window frames were equally secure. Even the manhole into the roof space was padlocked from the inside. Her mother said she was paranoid but Ella had seen too many crime scenes to feel comfortable in a house with less security.

Besides, her mother said many things. When would she settle down? How could a nice girl get a man if she was always at work? Perhaps if Ella took a desk job in Traffic or in the courts she'd have time for a family. What her mother couldn't grasp was that Ella was happy with her life. She didn't need a man to make her feel complete. She had no desire for children. Going to work each morning, or night, or whenever her pager went off, and doing the job she'd looked forward to her whole life was plenty.

She picked peeling paint from the windowsill.

Had been plenty.

9.35 am

'Thirty-one, you on the air?'

Sophie scrambled into the ambulance cabin to

grab the radio. 'Thirty-one's clear in Stanmore.'
They'd just delivered an elderly woman to her
nursing home following her discharge from
hospital. Mick leaned on the bonnet, taking a
moment, chin in his hand, face turned into the
sun.

'Wonderful, Thirty-one,' Control said. 'I have a
woman in labour. Waters broken, contractions
less than five minutes apart. She's at 320 Glebe
Point Road, Glebe Point.'

'Thirty-one's on the case.' Sophie banged on
the windscreen.

'What?' Mick said.

'Labour, waters broken.'

He ran for the driver's seat. Sophie was still
yanking on her seatbelt when he gunned the
engine and swung onto the street. They raced
down Percival Road and screeched right through
the green light onto Parramatta Road.

Sophie knew that like many paramedics Mick
was apprehensive of maternity cases. He didn't
have much practice at them. They involved two
patients instead of one, and the potential for
disaster always seemed so great. The whole aim
was to get in and out and to hospital as quickly
as you could before anything happened.

Mick weaved through the traffic, blasting the
horn, then took the angled left into Pyrmont
Bridge Road. The engine revved hard. 'Go, baby,
go,' Mick said.

Sophie, on the other hand, was looking
forward to the case. It would be her first
maternity call since Lachlan's birth, and already
it was bringing back memories of the pain and

euphoria. More than likely the baby wouldn't be born until hours after they got the woman to the hospital, such was people's understandable tendency to ring early rather than late, but she thought through the possibilities anyway, knowing that being prepared equalled staying in control. *Cord around neck — if loose, lift over head; if tight, clamp and cut. Prevent tears by slowing and controlling the delivery. Be sure to suction the baby quickly, clearing the airways. Wrap warmly to prevent heat loss.*

Mick roared left into Glebe Point Road. 'Numbers?'

Sophie looked for letterboxes as she pulled on a pair of gloves. 'Two-ten this side.'

Mick's head bobbed as he drove and searched for a street number on his side of the road. Down at the end of the street Sophie saw a man run waving into the road. 'Starjumper dead ahead.'

'Got him.'

Mick turned the siren off and pulled up outside a two-storey house painted in heritage colours. The man ran past a dark blue BMW parked at the kerb and went up the sandstone steps to the front door of the house. 'Please hurry,' he shouted. 'It's coming!'

Sophie grabbed equipment and hurried to the open front door. The foyer was large and spacious, white walls decorated on one side with an oil painting of the beach and on the other side with framed degrees declaring that Boyd Sawyer was a plastic surgeon and a member of some college. Sophie went by too fast to read any more details.

In the living room the man crouched by a weeping woman. He wore a rumpled white shirt and grey suit pants. 'She's six weeks early. She's booked into RPA and our obstetrician wants her there immediately.'

The woman wore a pink nightdress and lay on her side on the carpet. She clutched her swollen abdomen. The man tried to pull her up by the arm. 'Julie, they're going to take you to hospital now.'

Sophie knelt with them. She introduced herself. 'Is this your first?' She put her hands on Julie's abdomen and felt the tension there.

'Yes.'

'How long have you had pain?'

'About an hour, but they're less than a minute apart now,' Julie wept.

'When did your waters break?'

'Just when we rang you,' the man said. 'Our obstetrician said — '

Julie cried out and clutched between her legs. 'Boyd, it's coming!'

He grabbed Mick's arm. 'Where's your trolley?'

'It's going to be okay, sir,' Mick said.

Sophie raised Julie's sodden nightdress and saw the baby was crowning. Immediately she turned to Mick. 'Open the kit.'

As he tore the top off the maternity kit Julie groaned and the baby's head was born. Sophie supported it while checking that the cord was not around the neck. The shoulders delivered;

then, with a rush of blood and fluid, the slippery purple body was in Sophie's hands. She felt the newborn's wet heat through her thin gloves and smelled the blood and vernix that coated the tiny form, and in a split second was taken back to her own delivery of Lachlan, her first touch of his skin, the feather weight of his body on her chest, the look on Chris's face as he embraced them both. There'd been such magnificent promise in that moment — where had it gone?

'It's a girl!' Mick crowed.

Blinking back tears, Sophie wrapped a sterile blanket around the baby. She glanced at her watch to note the time. 'Congratulations, Julie. She's beautiful.' She laid the baby, still attached by the umbilical cord, on Julie's exposed abdomen. Crying, Boyd Sawyer reached out and stroked the tiny face.

Julie cradled the small form while Mick worked the thin suction tube into the baby's mouth then nose to clear the fluid. Sophie rubbed the little girl vigorously. Her arms and legs jiggled as Sophie massaged her torso with the flannel blanket. Julie tried to sit up. 'Why isn't she crying?'

'She will in a second.' Sophie paused in her rubbing to make sure the baby's pulse was still strong. 'Better bag her,' she said to Mick. He grabbed the paediatric resus bag and fitted the round silicone mask over the baby's face. The little rib cage rose and fell but when he stopped squeezing the bag the baby didn't take a breath for herself. Nor did she move her limbs or open her eyes.

Mick kept bagging while Sophie attached the cardiac monitor. The three electrodes almost covered the baby's tiny chest. Her pulse was fast and the high blips filled the room.

Sophie and Mick exchanged glances. The baby should have taken a breath by now. They'd had no chance to cut the cord and Sophie saw that Julie was bleeding. 'Get back-up,' she said. Mick handed her the bag and pulled the portable radio from his belt.

Sophie felt her chest tighten in the iron grip of her need to control the situation. She struggled to set up an oxygen mask for Julie with one hand while continuing to bag the baby and mentally mapping the new course of the case. Once the baby started breathing she'd still need to monitor her closely in case the tiny girl went apnoeic again. They'd cannulate Julie and pump the fluids in to replace her blood loss, monitor her blood pressure, make sure she was stable. But this was assuming that nature, the universe, whatever, would play its role by having them both respond to treatment. Sophie grimaced as tension pulled her neck and back muscles taut. So far nature was failing. Badly.

Boyd crouched to connect the oxygen tubing for her. He loosened the elastic strap on the mask and slid it gently over his wife's pale face.

'Thanks.' Sophie hesitated. 'You're a surgeon.'

He nodded.

'Would you be comfortable trying for an IV?'

He pulled the drug kit open and found the alcohol swabs and intravenous cannulas. His eyes darted from his wife's pale face and flowing tears to his new baby's motionless body. He clipped a tourniquet around Julie's arm.

'You understand why we had to stay here for the delivery,' Sophie said. 'Even knowing she was premature. At least here we have some room. The back of the ambulance . . . '

Boyd Sawyer's hand holding the cannula trembled over his wife's arm. Sweat hung in beads on his brow. The tight brown curls at the back of his neck were wet.

Mick hurried back in. 'Back-up's three minutes away and Control's notifying RPA.' He followed Sophie's deliberate glance and hastily exchanged the cannula Boyd held for the sealed packet of cord clamps. Boyd moved aside and wiped his eyes on his forearm.

Royal Prince Alfred Hospital was only five minutes away on the siren but at the moment it felt as far as the moon. 'Julie, how are you feeling?' Sophie asked.

'Tired.' Julie hardly opened her eyes. Her face was paler than ever, and sweaty. Mick cannulated her arm and started IV fluids. He took a blood pressure reading. 'Ninety systolic, with pulse of one-ten,' he reported, and opened the clamp on the IV line to let the fluid run in fast.

Boyd clamped and cut the umbilical cord. With the baby separated from Julie, Sophie lifted the little form onto the lounge and wrapped her more firmly in the blanket. New babies lost their heat quickly and there were enough problems to fight without adding hypothermia to the mix.

In a moment the baby was completely encased. Only her face was exposed for the mask. The monitor leads snaked out of the top fold of the blanket. Sophie knelt by the lounge, her forearms either side of the baby, her hands starting to cramp with the continuous effort of rapid bagging. *Come on*, she thought, leaning close over the little girl. *Open your eyes. Look up at me. Scream, and we will know that you are all right.*

Behind her she could hear Mick inflating the BP cuff. 'Eighty-five.'

Boyd clutched his head. 'What are we waiting for? They need to be in hospital.'

Sophie heard a siren in the distance. 'As soon as the other crew arrives we'll get the baby on her way, then we'll take Julie,' she said. 'We're doing everything we can, Mr Sawyer.' She saw tears in his eyes and quickly looked down at the baby. Before she had Lachlan she'd thought she'd known fear, and joy, but holding her newborn son she'd realised she'd known nothing about either.

Mick searched Julie's other arm for a vein without success. The siren stopped outside. Feet pounded up the steps and across the small porch. Two paramedics hurried into the room. Rob Nestor, shaved head and almost two metres tall, kneeled beside Sophie. 'Still apnoeic?'

Sophie nodded. 'Her pulse is strong.' The rest didn't need to be said. One glance showed the baby was unresponsive. She handed the baby and the resuscitation bag over to him. Mick disconnected the monitor as Rob's partner, Dave O'Brien, yanked the oxygen tubing free. The uniform tie he always wore swung madly. The crew rushed the baby outside.

'What's happening?' Boyd said.

'They're taking her to hospital,' Mick replied. Outside, the ambulance motor revved, then the siren began to wail again. 'She needs to be there sooner than we can get Julie ready to move.'

'I wanted them both there from the start,' Boyd said.

Arguing with him gained nothing. Sophie changed her gloves and checked the pad between Julie's legs. It was soaked with blood. The placenta hadn't delivered. 'Julie, do you still have pain?'

Julie nodded slowly without opening her eyes. Her lack of emotion was a bad sign. Sophie took a quick blood pressure. Down to seventy. She replaced the nearly empty fluid bag with a full one and started pumping it in while searching for even the smallest blue vein worthy of a second cannulation attempt. Mick hurried in with the stretcher. They lowered it beside Julie then lifted her onto it. Blood gushed to the floor.

'Oh my God,' Boyd said.

'It's okay,' Mick said. 'It's probably just the placenta delivering.' Sophie hoped her own anxiety was better hidden.

Sophie shoved the Oxy-Viva under the foot of the stretcher mattress to elevate Julie's legs and get blood into her upper body. They loaded the stretcher into the ambulance and Sophie climbed in. Massaging the uterus could help it contract and seal off bleeding vessels. She pressed the heel of her hand onto Julie's lower abdomen and made firm circles. Midwives could give an injection that did the same job but there was no time to call one.

'Julie, I'll follow you in, okay?' Boyd called. Julie murmured something but didn't open her eyes.

About to close the back door, Mick nodded at the cardiac monitor. Julie's heart rate was up to one hundred and forty beats per minute.

'Pedal to the metal.' Sophie made sure the straps across Julie were snug and clipped her own seatbelt into place. She leaned over the stretcher and gripped the stainless-steel frame with one hand, pressing hard into Julie's abdomen with the other. Blood ran off the sides of the stretcher mattress and dripped onto the floor. The siren was loud even in there.

Julie's face was porcelain white, her skin slippery with sweat and cold even through Sophie's gloves. 'Julie, how do you feel?'

She moaned.

'The siren's just to get through traffic, okay? It's busy out there.'

It did no good to tell a person they were dying.

In the ambulance bay of Royal Prince Alfred Hospital a doctor in a gown wrenched the back door open before Mick had completely stopped. 'This is the post-partum haemorrhage?'

Sophie nodded. 'Baby was born at nine fifty-four this morning, six weeks early. The patient's had increasing blood loss since then.'

Mick grabbed the stretcher and pulled it out of the vehicle. Blood had run along the floor and under the back door, and dripped from the back

43

step onto the ground. Sophie jumped down. She continued massaging Julie's abdomen and giving her report to the doctor as they hurried inside. 'First obs after the birth were BP of ninety, pulse one-ten. She's had two litres of Hartmann's. Last obs were beep of seventy, pulse one-forty. Level of consciousness decreasing.'

They hurried along the Emergency Department corridor. Robert and Dave, the paramedics who'd brought in the baby, stood to one side to let them pass. Their stretcher was empty except for a pile of equipment. There was no time to ask about the baby's condition but they weren't smiling.

In the resuscitation room one nurse searched for veins in Julie's pale arms while another took a blood pressure reading. 'Sixty on thirty.'

'She's unconscious,' someone said.

The doctor said, 'Let's intubate, get blood off for cross-matching and get to theatre.'

Sophie felt a touch on her arm. A nurse held a clipboard. 'Do you have her details?'

'Only her name and address.'

'The husband was right behind us,' Mick said. 'He should be at the front desk by now.'

Sophie said to the nurse, 'How's the baby?'

She made a face. 'They were still ventilating her when they came belting through here. She's in the Neonatal Intensive Care Unit. She's critical.'

The doctor said, 'Let's move.' An oxygen cylinder and the cardiac monitor were crammed on the end of Julie's bed. Someone kicked the brakes off. They rushed her out of the room and down the corridor to theatre, leaving Sophie to step carefully over the drops of blood that marked their path.

She walked outside in time to see Rob and Dave's ambulance accelerating out of the hospital driveway. 'They got another case, huh?'

'Yeah. Fall with a fractured leg.' Mick stood at the ambulance's rear door with an armful of towels. Lemon-scented steam rose from a mop bucket labelled 'RPA Hospital Property'. 'Man, look at this.'

The pool of blood on the ambulance floor lay still and smooth. The air was full of its cold butcher's shop smell. Sophie said, 'That must be two litres.'

'I wouldn't be surprised,' Mick said. 'Poor woman.' He gently laid a towel over the centre of the pool and it instantly turned red.

Sophie retrieved the case-sheet folder from the cabin. She needed details about Julie Sawyer but didn't feel like approaching the husband just yet. From the ambulance bay she watched the traffic drone by on Missenden Road, the sound overlaid with the rustle of plastic as Mick lowered sodden towels into a bag. The air was humid. Her shirt clung to her aching back and she realised how much she'd sweated on the case. She was still sweating. There was a sick feeling low down in her stomach. *This job, sometimes* . . . You felt capable, powerful even, then the universe showed you exactly who was boss. She wished it could've waited to show her on some other job and kept a baby out of it.

'Hey.' Mick peered around the side at her. 'Doing okay?'

Sophie let out the breath she hadn't known she'd been holding. Her chest felt sore when she drew in a fresh lungful of air. The iron grip loosened, but only a little. 'Yeah. You?'

He shrugged and nodded at the same time, and kept looking at her.

'What?'

'We should buy that baby something. A soft toy,' he said. 'A pink fluffy rabbit.'

Sophie nodded. The baby might not make it, they both knew that, but they weren't going to say so. You could talk about the likelihood of your adult patients pegging out, but kids were different.

Mick lifted his collar off the back of his neck. 'That second little kid from the fire died.'

Sophie closed her eyes. On Missenden Road a truck ground its gears. Somewhere a siren wailed, distance making the sound small and forlorn.

'And I heard some interesting police news,' Mick said.

'What?' Sophie was relieved by the change of subject.

'A man walked into St Vincent's this morning, weak from blood loss and septicaemia.'

She went to the back of the ambulance. 'Dog bite?'

Most of the blood was cleaned up. Mick stood with his head against the padded vinyl roof and dunked the mop into the bucket then slopped it on the floor. The lemon disinfectant overpowered the meaty metallic smell.

46

'Nope. He has a wound, left lateral hip, looks like a bullet entry. No exit wound. The injury looks maybe a day or so old. The doctor says, 'How'd this happen?' And the guy says, 'I was walking through the city and I got mugged. I was slow giving up my wallet and they shot me.' The doctor says, 'Why didn't you come in straight-away? You could've died. This is the sort of stuff you should call an ambulance for.' The guy goes, 'Yes but I was scared. I was drunk, I was looking for a good time if you know what I mean, and all I could think was that it would all be more ammo for my ex-wife to keep my kid from me.' '

Sophie clutched the case-sheet folder to her chest. The man might not be the one shot in the bank hold-up. He might have been injured in a drug deal gone wrong or in some domestic dispute. The timing was perfect, though, and the story was definitely dodgy. 'Any word on his history? What kind of dead-beat he is?'

'Well, this is the thing,' Mick said. 'He's a cop.'

3

Tuesday 6 May, 10.45 am

Sophie stared at him. 'Are you sure?'

Mick nodded. 'Rob was in the neighbouring cubicle in Vinnie's ED, dropping off a patient, when the guy was telling his story to the doctor.'

The doors to the Emergency Department swung open and a nurse stuck her head out. 'Sophie, your husband's a cop, isn't he? You'd better come and see this.'

She hurried after the nurse while Mick went to clean the mop and put it away.

In the ED staff room the television's sound was loud. Nurses and doctors on their breaks were packed around the table, coffees steaming before them. More staff stood behind them, talking in low voices, and people walking past crammed in for a few seconds, trying for a glimpse of the screen.

' *— an anonymous caller has contacted this and other television stations alleging that all the members of the armed robbery gang are in fact serving police officers.*' The newsreader was pink-cheeked with importance. '*In what he described a 'gesture of good faith', the caller gave the name of the man who presented at St Vincent's Hospital today, claiming to have been shot in a mugging, as Senior Constable Peter Roth. The caller alleged that Roth was the gang*

48

member shot by the guard in yesterday's bank hold-up. Both the Police Service and St Vincent's Hospital are so far refusing to comment.'

'Like you couldn't see this coming.' A slim moustached man spoke knowingly from his seat at the table. He had a shiny black stethoscope slung around his neck and when people in the room turned to look at him he reached up to finger it. Sophie could feel the blood pumping in her face. A medical student. Know-all. He said, 'Well, you think ordinary robbers would be allowed to go on for so long?'

'Shut up,' someone said. The student turned red.

'The caller identificd himself as a police officer and said that he is prepared to give a statement, naming all gang members, once his safety has been assured by senior police management. Police Commissioner Stephen Dudley-Pearson was unavailable for comment but his office has downplayed the allegations, stating that they may be a hoax. They refuse to comment on whether they have been approached by a member of staff with information on the robberies. They also state that as a matter of course the gunshot victim will be interviewed and an examination done of any bullet fragments found during surgery.'

'Sophie,' Mick hissed from the doorway. When she looked over he held up the portable.

In the corridor she said, 'What is it?'

'Everyone's busy. They want us to head into town for cover.'

They walked back through the ED. 'That didn't look good,' Mick said.

Sophie pulled her mobile phone off her belt. You weren't supposed to use them in the department but nobody was looking her way. She raised the phone to her ear, half hiding it behind her hand.

Mick glanced over. 'Who're you calling?'

'Chris.' Her own voice said in her ear, '*Thanks for calling the Phillips house. We're sorry we can't get to the phone but please leave* — '

She cut herself off and dialled Chris's mobile.

'*The mobile you are calling is turned off or not answering.*'

Sophie hit the end button again. 'No answer.'

'Is he working today? He's probably on a job.' They climbed into the lemon-scented ambulance.

'He's home with Lachlan on a day off,' Sophie said. 'He should be answering one phone or the other.'

Mick drove out of the hospital grounds. 'Flat battery in his mobile?'

She shook her head. 'He's obsessive about keeping it charged.'

'Switched it off?'

'He never does. I mean, never. Ever.'

Mick slowed at a crossing for a middle-aged woman walking a black terrier. 'So the problem is . . . what, exactly?'

Chris's state of mind was the problem. Sophie imagined him imagining the news headlines, the media frenzy. It was foul icing on top of the PTSD cake. 'I just wanted to ask if this Roth

50

actually is a cop,' she said. 'If it could really be a hoax.'

The traffic on Broadway was sluggish, full of buses and couriers' trucks trying to squeeze into the CBD. The sky was clouding over and wind whipped scraps of rubbish along the gutters. On the footpath a teenaged boy and girl stood together, the girl screaming at the boy, the boy looking away from her into the shop windows.

After a moment Sophie called Gloria. 'It's me. Is Chris there?'

'Funny you should ask,' her mother-in-law said. 'He dropped Lachlan off this morning and was supposed to be back by now. I've got an art class soon and I have to pay even if I don't turn up.'

'Did he say where he was going?'

'He had to go into town,' Gloria said. 'Something to do with work. Have you tried his mobile?'

'There's no answer.'

'If you do catch him will you tell him I'm waiting on him?'

'How's Lachlan? Is everything okay?'

'Everything's fine. Why?'

'No reason. I'd better go.'

Mick took Eddy Avenue onto Elizabeth Street then stopped at a red light. His window was down and the smell of hot chips from a takeaway shop wafted into the ambulance. Sophie called Chris's mobile again and when the tinny voice started up once more she pressed the end button so hard her thumb hurt.

Mick stuck his head out the open window. 'Looks like rain.'

The wind gusted, rocking the ambulance. Two heavy drops landed on the windscreen.

'That's it for us then.' Mick took his sunglasses off. 'You know I don't work in the rain.'

She smiled half-heartedly.

The airwaves became suddenly busy with ambulances calling mobile to a scene. Mick turned up the volume when the rescue truck dittoed the message. 'Something big's happening. Cross your fingers they want us.'

'I thought you don't work in the rain?'

'It's not really raining yet.'

Control said, 'Thirty-one, what's your location?'

'Yes!' Mick smacked a hand on the steering wheel.

Sophie grabbed the mike. 'Thirty-one's on Elizabeth Street in the city'

'Thanks, Thirty-one. Proceed to Anzac Parade, Kensington, for an MVA, query code nine.'

Mick hit the siren and the beacons and hauled the truck into a U-turn around a set of traffic lights, and Sophie felt the adrenaline start to pump again. She pulled on a fluorescent safety vest, her damp shirt cold against her back, and her hands trembled a little when she yanked on a fresh pair of gloves. Some days were like this in the job — one big case after another — and you soon got used to it, though secretly she would've preferred a cruise around town doing nothing for a while.

'I love a good code nine,' Mick said with a grin.

Usually Sophie enjoyed it too, though she knew how gruesome that could sound. She liked arriving at a scene of chaos to impose order, using all her skills to treat multiple injuries and plan the extrication at the same time. She invariably came out the other end sweaty and tired and feeling for the injured, but exhilarated at doing the job she'd trained so hard for. If she wasn't so anxious about Chris, or wrung out after the birth, she'd be excited.

Mick turned left into Cleveland Street as an ambulance called on scene. The officer was back within a minute with a report. 'Three cars and one small truck. Two people code four, three code nine and one of those unconscious.'

Mick screeched right onto Anzac and swerved around the back end of a braking bus. 'Go you good thing!' The traffic was heavier and he used the horn and the wrong side of the road equally. Sophie moved her shoulders, trying to work the tension from them.

'Here we go,' Mick said, switching off the siren as they approached the crash site. 'What a beauty.'

Sophie assessed the scene quickly. A small glazier's truck stood near a silver Ford sedan. The major damage to both front ends indicated a head-on collision. An old red Subaru was crumpled around a power pole on the side of the road by the golf course. Golfers had left their balls on the green to gather behind the low chain fence and watch. A yellow Daihatsu had been pushed sideways in a lane, damage to the front and back. Glass from the truck lay smashed everywhere on the road. Two ambulances were on scene, their beacons still flashing, and paramedics bent through the windows of the wrecked cars.

The wind seized Sophie's door as she jumped out. She grabbed her equipment and crunched over the glass to Steve Jones, a stocky paramedic in a hard-hat. He was by the driver's door of the truck. Steve's patient was pale, sweaty and moaning. Steve's gloves were covered in blood. Lightning flickered through purple clouds overhead.

'Where do you want us?' Sophie said.

Steve nodded at the silver car. 'Man's code four. Woman's code nine with chest and head injuries. They're all yours.'

Sophie crouched by the silver car. In the driver's seat a heavyset man was slumped with the seatbelt still across his chest and his head resting against the door. Deflated airbags sagged from the steering wheel and the passenger dash.

The woman in the passenger seat said, 'He's dead.'

She couldn't have seen the massive wound to the right side of his head, but it didn't take a genius to understand the half-closed eyes and the motionless chest.

'I'm sorry,' Sophie said.

The woman closed her eyes. Her face was pale.

Mick was by her door. He pulled the handle then tried the rear door. 'The impact's jammed everything,' he said over the roof. Rain started to spit from the sky.

'Same here.' Sophie reached in beside the dead man, her shoulder against his as she fumbled for the rear window winder. The glass rolled down most of the way before jamming. She put her arms and head through the rear window, grabbed the edge of the back seat, and pulled herself inside.

The seat was soft underfoot. The car smelled of vinyl cleaner and blood. Rain spattered on the roof.

The woman was crying. Sophie rubbed her shoulder. 'I'm Sophie, I'm a paramedic, and we're going to get you out of here,' she said. 'What's your name?'

'Marisa Waters.'

'Do you remember what happened?'

'No. Ow.'

'That's sore, is it?' Sophie palpated the wound above Marisa's ear. It felt soft and boggy.

Mick leaned in the open window, shoving the Oxy-Viva, drug box and monitor inside. Sophie said quietly, 'Skull fracture.'

He matched her frown. 'I'll get rescue.'

'Marisa, is your neck sore?' Sophie felt the vertebrae, one by one.

'No.'

Sophie saw Mick by the Subaru. He was talking to a rescue officer who was shaking his head. A paramedic was bent in the driver's window of the red car. He held a mask and resus bag over someone's face. The background was a tarp, sky blue. It was draped around the pole and over the passenger side of the car, hiding the body there from the golfers.

'Marisa, can you take a deep breath?'

'It hurts.'

Sophie wriggled her upper body between the seats so she faced Marisa. 'I'll touch your chest and you tell me where it's sore.'

The ribs moved normally under Sophie's hands until she reached the far side. Marisa flinched. 'I promise I'll be gentle,' Sophie said. This time she recognised the grating sensation of bone end against bone end.

'They'll be here as soon as they can.' Mick handed her a plastic collar. He'd put his raincoat on. It flapped in the wind.

'We've got crepitus in the lateral ribs.' Sophie pressed her stethoscope to the woman's chest. 'Air entry's good though.'

The rain got serious. It struck the cracked windscreen at an angle. It came in the open windows and splashed off the dead man's face. Glancing over at him Sophie noticed the heavy jowls. She paused and studied him a moment longer.

Marisa wasn't wearing any rings but Sophie could see a white line in her tan where one had been. The man's hands were pale and chubby. On his ring finger there was an indentation in the flesh. Sophie said, 'Is this your husband?'

'My friend.'

'What's his name?'

Marisa closed her eyes. 'I want to die.'

'No you don't,' Sophie said. 'We'll have you out of here in a flash.' She put an oxygen mask on Marisa's face, the plastic collar around her neck, and attached the cardiac monitor. When

Mick got back she was deflating the blood pressure cuff. 'Ninety systolic.'

'I want to die,' Marisa repeated.

'You're doing fine.' Sophie scrambled into the back seat and put her head out the rear window into the rain to speak to Mick out of Marisa's hearing. 'Ask one of the police to come over, would you? See if they recognise this guy.'

Mick came back with a young police officer. He bent to peer into the car. Sophie saw his eyes widen and knew she was right. The dead man was Police Commissioner Stephen Dudley-Pearson.

In a moment two older officers were looking grim-faced into the car. There was a lot of gold braid on their epaulettes. One said, 'Hello, Mrs Waters.'

Marisa didn't look at them. She was crying. The police moved away, talking quietly.

Sophie clipped a tourniquet around Marisa's arm and swiftly cannulated a vein. Mick set up a bag of Hartmann's solution and connected the tubing. The fluid was soon running into Marisa's system.

Sophie saw that the police were at the back of the car. She felt the car move a little. There was a pop and the lid of the boot rose, cutting off Sophie's view.

Sophie looked at Marisa but the woman stared out the windscreen. Sophie nudged Mick. 'Go and hassle rescue again, will you?'

When he was gone she squeezed Marisa's hand. 'So where were you headed today?'

'It'll all come out soon enough.'

'What will?'

Marisa simply shook her head.

Mick came back. The hood of his raincoat had slipped off and his white-blond hair was slicked to his scalp. 'They're coming now.'

Sophie checked Marisa's blood pressure again. It was holding steady. 'Doing fine, Marisa.'

The inside of the car darkened as firefighters opened a tarp over it. The rescue crew set up their gear under its shelter. Gloved hands draped a protective sheet over Marisa. Sophie held the sheet off her face and turned her own head away as the metal cutters bit into the B pillar. The tarp made the air warm and still and full of petrol fumes.

'Control's got St Vincent's ready for us.' Mick leaned in the window. Water dripped down his forehead. 'Spineboard and bed're ready to go.'

The crew peeled back Marisa's door. Mick crouched in the space. In the car, Sophie checked the monitor one more time before disconnecting the leads for the extrication.

The rain became heavier. They had to shout to make themselves heard over the pelting on the tarp. Mick yelled at someone to bring the stretcher closer.

Hands reached in to help Marisa onto the spineboard. Crying, she struggled to turn herself. 'Let us do it for you,' Sophie said. She squeezed between the seats, hitting the dead man with her elbow as she wriggled forward, and twisted so she was held there by her hips and could help the rescue crew lift Marisa.

The tarp was carried over them as they took

the board to the stretcher then they crunched across the shattered glass to load the stretcher into the ambulance. Once inside the vehicle Sophie and Mick moved Marisa off the board. Sophie raised the head of the stretcher so Marisa sat upright. 'That's better for your breathing, isn't it?'

Marisa didn't reply. Mick shut the door. The only sounds were the rain on the fibreglass roof and Marisa's ragged breathing.

Sophie reattached Marisa's oxygen mask. She listened to her chest and smiled. 'How are you feeling?'

'Where's Stephen?'

'Someone will bring him to the hospital, and you can see him again there.'

Tears ran from Marisa's closed eyes. Sophie gently wiped her face. 'Everything's going to be okay.'

Mick opened the side door to push the kits into the ambulance and hand Sophie a hastily scribbled note.

'There's $50,000 in the boot and she's the wife of the Director of Public Prosecutions.'

11.50 am

Detective Ella Marconi yawned. She was sitting on her bedroom floor, next to the scanner she kept under the bed. God forbid that anyone at work ever found out she had it, that on her days off she eavesdropped on the radio traffic now and again — well, okay, pretty bloody frequently

— to learn what was happening in her absence. Because, naturally, that was the other time that interesting things happened.

There was certainly something going on today. First allegations about the shot cop and the gang of robbers had been splashed all over the TV, then she'd picked up news of a car crash on the scanner. Two people dead, an officer reported. Three injured and trapped. Rescue at work. Traffic diverted. All normal, normal. But then the tempo of the messages changed in a way that had Ella leaning close to the black box. An officer said in an almost-but-not-quite-panicked voice that he'd get in touch with the radio room on a landline. Shortly after that, hordes of brass called on the air that they were mobile to the scene. Their voices were heavy and serious, and Ella knew at least one of the deadies was somebody important.

Her pager sounded. She grabbed it from her bedside table and saw Detective Dennis Orchard's number. She turned off the scanner and reached for the phone.

'Orchard,' he answered.

'It's me,' she said.

'You've heard about this crash?'

'A bit of it. Who's the toetag?'

'Dudley-Pearson.'

For a second she couldn't speak. 'You're shitting me.'

'That's not all. He had Marisa Waters plus a whole wad of cash with him. They were headed for the airport and had tickets for Thailand.'

'Get out of here.'

'The rumour is,' Dennis lowered his voice, 'that Duds was in on the gang, got scared about this malarky over the possible informant and bailed before it all fell down around his ears.' There was a noise in the background and Dennis said, 'Yeah, okay,' to someone before coming back to Ella. 'I've got to go.'

'Hey, what about this Roth guy?' she said, but Orchard was already gone.

Ella put the phone down. So Duds was dead. Ella had seen more than her share of bodies but found it hard to picture that florid face gone pale and those wobbly jowls still. He'd been commissioner for almost two years, right through the time of the robberies, and he was an idiot, no doubt about it. But corrupt? Though size and shape meant nothing, Ella couldn't imagine the tubby man scheming and conniving. He was like a baby elephant. Then again you didn't get to be commissioner without having some skill for the game.

Marisa Waters was PA to one of the deputy commissioners, and married to the Director of the Department of Public Prosecutions. Robert Waters was quite a looker: a real Ralph Lauren model beside the baby elephant. Sure, looks weren't everything — but still. More amazing was the fact that if Marisa and Duds had been on together it was the best kept secret in the job. The idea of Duds being somehow involved in the gang was beyond that again.

There would be repercussions, of course. A new commissioner would be appointed. Dudley-Pearson wasn't popular with the officers but it was a case of the devil you knew. Although, Ella realised, she knew the most likely replacement as well. Rupert Eagers was the current Assistant Commissioner in charge of Operations. He was a man for whom the job was practically a family gathering. He had uncles, nephews and a father sprinkled about the state, more in high-up positions than not, and all known for their longevity. Dennis had once described the lot of them as harder to shift than a limpet off a rock. In fact, Eagers's paternal grandfather had died at his sergeant's desk while working on station rosters. Eagers was a man with things to prove and a tree to climb. There was little doubt in Ella's mind that if given the chance to step up into the acting position, he'd bust a boiler to make a good impression and persuade the government he was the right man for the job.

Yeah. He probably knew retired Assistant Commissioner Frank Shakespeare too.

3 pm

Sophie switched her mobile on, ignoring the look Mick shot her in the ambulance's rear-view mirror. So what if it was impolite to use a phone while sitting beside a patient? The old lady had dementia, and anyway Sophie felt if she was able to understand what Sophie was doing and why, she wouldn't mind one bit. As it was, the ninety year old lay on the stretcher looking out at the traffic, waving at pedestrians who couldn't see in the tinted windows, her sparse white hair and thin neck giving her the look of a baby bird getting its first view out of the nest.

There were no missed calls. She dialled Chris's mobile. 'Got to find my husband,' she said to the old woman, who smiled widely at her and repeated, 'Husband.'

For once Sophie's call didn't go straight to voicemail. She sat up straighter.

'Hi,' Chris answered.

'At last,' Sophie said. 'I was starting to worry.' She tried to put a note of levity in her voice but she knew he'd have seen how many messages she'd left on both phones.

'I've been a bit busy.'

The old woman started to sing in a high quavery voice. Sophie thought it was a hymn.

'What is that?'

'Patient,' Sophie said. 'So is everything okay?'

'Why wouldn't it be?'

'All this stuff happening.' Sophie gritted her teeth. 'And Gloria didn't know where you were.'

'I had to go in to headquarters,' he said.

'On your day off?'

He gave an irritated sigh. 'I went to see Dean, okay? I went to apologise for not going last night.'

Sophie rolled her eyes at the old lady, who rolled her eyes back. 'And what did Dean say?'

'Dean said it was fine.' Chris mirrored her smart-aleck tone.

'He must've said it slowly.'

Chris said nothing.

'For you to have been in there for so long, I mean.' Even as Sophie said it she regretted it, but couldn't cut the words off. She was hurting and she wanted him to feel a bit of it too.

Chris said, 'You're really funny, you know that?'

Mick was looking at her in the rear-view mirror again. She met his eye reluctantly then saw his gaze shift past her. 'Look out the back,' he said. 'That blue Beemer just hung a U-turn in front of all those cars.'

The old lady hit a high note in her song.

Sophie turned to the rear window to see the traffic behind them in chaos. A bus slewed sideways. Smoke rose from someone's tyres. The BMW careened in the ambulance's wake.

'Is he after us?' Mick slowed down. 'He's flashing his lights. Maybe he's got a sick kid in the car or something.'

Sophie released her seatbelt and knelt up in her seat to watch the car draw closer. She couldn't see anyone other than the driver in the car but someone could be lying down in the back. 'He's blowing his horn too,' she said.

Chris said, 'What?'

Mick pulled to the side of the road. The Beemer screeched to a halt behind the ambulance, half in the next lane. Horns blew as traffic started to queue behind it.

Sophie said, 'I've got to go.'

Chris said, 'Fine,' and hung up. Sophie had just a second to feel angry that he didn't ask what was wrong when the driver of the BMW threw his door open. She recognised him with a start. 'It's the father from this morning.'

'The what?' Mick was still in the driver's seat,

64

looking alternately in the side and rear-view mirrors.

'The father, from the birth. Sawyer.' Sophie tried to read the man's face as he passed close to the rear door. 'He's coming up your side and he looks angry.'

Mick opened his door and got out. The old lady said something to Sophie but Sophie ignored her. She moved forward, leaning between the seats into the cabin to hear what was going on outside.

'You killed my family.'

Sophie gasped. *Julie and the baby died?*

'Sir — ' Mick's words were cut off by a thud. Sophie strained to see him through the open driver's door but only caught a glimpse of Sawyer, bent over. There was another thud and Mick groaned.

Sophie stretched forward into the cabin and grabbed the radio microphone to call in a code one.

'All cars stand by,' Control said. 'Thirty-one, I copy your message. What's your location?'

'You.'

Sawyer was glaring at her. She kept on with her message. 'Thirty-one's on Liverpool Street in the city. Mick's been assaulted. Assailant's still on scene.'

Sawyer stepped over Mick up into the cabin.

'Copy, Thirty-one. Friends are on their way.'

Sawyer's face was red and sweaty. He breathed out a cloud of alcohol fumes. Sophie wasn't scared yet. She'd been in situations like this before and knew that sometimes you could stall or distract the person from hitting you. She didn't need much time either: the police always turned up super fast and in droves when you put in the code one. But she was worried about Mick, and the old lady behind her was calling out in fear.

'I'm so sorry about your wife and baby,' Sophie said. Out on the street a man in a suit approached them, looking to where Mick lay, his hands out in a placating manner, but Sawyer growled and the man backed off. Behind him people stared and got out of their cars in the developing gridlock. In the distance, sirens wailed.

'You killed them.'

Okaaay. Slow down and think. He's drunk, but he's still a doctor. Sophie said, 'We did everything possible. You saw that.'

'You let them die.'

The thought of the cold, still baby blurred her vision. 'We tried to resuscitate your baby and we gave Julie as much fluid as we could.'

'I told you they had to go to hospital.'

'I'm sorry, but I explained at the time why we couldn't move any earlier,' she said. 'Do you remember me saying that?'

He held onto the steering wheel with one hand, the back of the seat with the other. He wore the same grey trousers and white shirt. His eyes were bleary and he looked wobbly, as if she could shove him hard in the chest and make him fall out of the ambulance. But he might land on Mick, and to shove him meant getting within reach of his grasp.

The sirens drew closer.

His fingers dug into the seat cushion. 'You killed them and now I'm going to kill you.'

She'd heard that kind of threat before. 'Look,' she said, then Sawyer disappeared, tackled from behind so suddenly that even Sophie yelped in fright. One second he was there, the next he was gone.

She scrambled through the cabin to get out and saw him kicking on the roadway under three uniformed police officers, shouting, 'She killed them! She killed them!'

More police joined the fracas. Sophie crouched beside Mick on the road. He blinked and tried to see past her. 'Are you okay?' she said.

'I think so.'

There was a bruise and a swelling on his left cheek. She helped him sit up against the wheel and he felt his stomach gingerly. 'I can't believe I let him hit me twice.'

'You were hardly expecting it.' Sophie palpated the back of his neck. 'Any pain or tenderness there?'

He shook his head. 'I'm fine.'

'You were almost knocked out, and it's worker's comp. You should go to hospital.'

He got to his feet. 'It's okay.'

'What if you have a cerebral bleed and die during the night?'

'Jo knows how to dial triple 0.'

'Idiot.'

Mick watched Sawyer being hauled to his feet. His hands were cuffed behind his back and mucus ran from his nose as he sobbed.

One of the police officers came their way. 'Hey, Soph.'

'Allan, this is Mick. Allan works at Wynyard with Chris.'

They nodded at each other. 'Can you come to the station later and give your statement?' Allan asked Mick.

'I don't think I want him charged.'

'Yes you do,' Sophie said. 'People have to know they can't kick us around.'

'The guy's family just died,' Mick said.

'Yeah, and he wilfully got pissed and decided to get us. You can't think it was chance that he saw us,' Sophie said. 'More likely he'd been driving around checking the big red numbers on ambulances for half the afternoon.'

The police stuffed Sawyer into the back of a paddy wagon. He kicked out at the open door. 'He's suffered enough,' Mick said.

Allan looked at Sophie. 'Did he do anything to you?'

'Said I killed them, said he wanted to kill me. That was about it.'

'Do you want to press charges?'

She felt Mick's eyes on her. 'I guess not.'

Allan shrugged. 'We'll still get him for driving under the influence.' He went back to the paddy wagon and Sophie and Mick climbed into the ambulance.

Mick inspected his face in the mirror. 'That was a good thing you did there.'

She didn't want to talk about it. 'Are you sure you're okay to drive?'

'I'm fine. Really.'

Sophie clambered into the back. 'I still think you're being an idiot. If you were a patient of yours, you'd tell yourself to go to hospital.'

He shrugged and started the engine. 'I can't believe that woman and her baby died.'

The old lady on the stretcher looked up and smiled at her. Sophie smiled back and patted her gnarled hand, but in her mind she was seeing the bodies of Julie and her tiny baby growing cold in the morgue.

Was she as blameless as she'd thought? Perhaps there was some way they could have got moving sooner. Maybe she could have started the fluids running into Julie earlier.

But second-guessing was completely useless when she didn't know how they'd died. She had to call the hospital and find out. Only then could she look objectively at how she'd run the case and decide whether anything else could have been done.

But the look in the bereaved father's eyes and his words weren't easy to shake off.

You killed them.

4

The Southern Jungle was so crowded that Ella had trouble pushing the door open. She squeezed between groups of heavy-set cops to reach the bar. Everyone had had the same idea as she had, obviously: come to the real heart of the job and find out the facts.

She'd watched the five then six o'clock news but nothing was reported that she didn't already know. Dudley-Pearson had been killed in the car accident along with a twenty-year-old university student, and injured were a fifty-year-old truck driver, another twenty-year-old uni student, and Mrs Marisa Waters, wife of the Director of Public Prosecutions, Robert Waters QC. No word about the money or why Duds and Mrs Waters were together.

There was no fresh news about Roth or the anonymous caller either. Just a rehash of what they'd been saying in the updates all day, that the robbery gang were alleged to be police, and that police management would be making a statement in the morning.

No self-respecting cop could wait that long to find out what was happening.

Detective Dennis Orchard was already at the bar. He rested his elbows on the bar towel and toyed with a cigarette.

70

'Don't do it,' Ella said.

'I'm not.' He started to get off his stool, gesturing for her to sit, but she shook her head.

'I've done nothing but laze around all day,' she said. 'You've been working.'

He smiled and got back on. There was just enough room for her to belly up to the bar herself. In a moment the barman placed a glass of red wine before her with a wink. 'Thanks, Bob,' she nodded.

Dennis drank some of his beer and looked at the bags of chips hanging on the wall behind the bar. 'You hungry?'

'No.'

He fiddled with the cigarette some more. 'I can't tell you much.'

'Course you can.' Being in the Crime Agencies was like being party to a gossip hotline.

He sniffed the non-filter end. 'Eagers has been harping on about people knowing too much.'

She knew it. 'He's Acting Commissioner.'

'Until everything's sorted,' Dennis said.

'He loves that cone of silence shit,' Ella said. 'But come on, this is me.'

'I know.' Dennis drank more beer.

She didn't want to put him on the spot, but neither did she want to go home knowing nothing. 'Whatever you can, then.'

He studied her for a moment then leaned down to her ear. 'A mate in the Robbery Squad says Roth could be the real deal.'

'So he is a cop.'

'Yeah,' Dennis said. 'So far they've got no witnesses to any of his story. Rumour says the bullet they dug out of him looked like a .45, which is what the guard was carrying. They checked Roth's roster and he was off on all the dates of the previous robberies.'

'I've never heard of him. Where's he from?'

'Padstow for the last five years, and Penrith before that. Did a couple of years plainclothes. Good at it too.' Dennis's breath was warm and beery. 'Apparently he's not saying a word about the gang. Just lies there in his hospital bed with his arms folded, staring out the window. Says he can't remember where the alleged mugging happened or where he'd been drinking before-hand or anything. Hence the trouble finding witnesses.'

'What about the person who rang the telly stations, promising a statement?'

'Roth had no response when he was told about that. And Eagers isn't saying whether he's been contacted or not,' Dennis said. 'But there is a whisper that the call is for real. Don't know who it is, though.'

'Wow.' Ella finished her drink and put down her glass. 'So what about Duds?'

Dennis looked away.

She poked his arm. 'If you clam up now, what can I think except that he is involved?'

He shrugged, his glass to his mouth.

'Jeezus.'

Around them the bar was getting fuller. The words 'Roth' and 'gang' and 'Dudley-Pearson' could be picked out in the buzz of conversation. Someone elbowed Ella in the back and said 'Sorry' but she didn't take her eyes from

Dennis's face. 'Were he and Marisa Waters actually an item?'

'I don't know.'

'You do so,' she said. 'How was it kept so quiet?'

He pulled bits of tobacco out of the end of the cigarette. She grabbed it and threw it over the bar.

'That's not very nice,' he said.

'You're supposed to be quitting.'

'I can still play with them.'

'Who's investigating the crash?'

Dennis tugged at a loose thread on the edge of the bar towel.

'I'll find out soon enough, you know.'

'So find out,' he said. He looked at his watch. 'I have to go. Tim's doing a roast.'

Ella watched him push his way towards the door. His wife, Donna, was a professor of nursing with the wickedest sense of humour Ella had ever known, and their teenage son Tim was a) friendly, b) cheerful and c) an apprentice chef who couldn't get enough of cooking. Ella had a microwave meal in the freezer, half a bottle of flat Coke in the fridge, and a bird cage that she hadn't cleaned since her unnamed canary escaped two months ago. There was also a stack of photos from the fire in the takeaway shop. Case of the year. Hip hip hooray.

Perhaps she'd get another drink and a bag of chips, and just sit here with her ears open.

Sophie and Mick worked overtime, and by the time Sophie finally got home she was wound up tight. Chris had not rung back to ask why she'd had to cut their phone conversation short, whether everything was okay, and the concern and rising guilt that she might be somehow to blame for the deaths of Julie and her baby weighed on her like a forty kilo sandbag, on top of the one she was already carrying over Angus.

She slammed the door as she entered the house.

'How about a bit of quiet?' Chris came hurrying down the stairs. 'Lachlan's asleep.'

Sophie stalked into the kitchen. 'You eaten?'

'Leftovers.'

Sophie yanked the remains of the lasagne from the fridge and threw it in the microwave. 'Interesting thing happened at work today.'

Chris was washing baby bottles and didn't look up.

'Yeah,' Sophie said. 'Got my life threatened. Just after I talked to you.'

'What?'

'What I said.'

'That's not good.'

She almost laughed out loud. 'Never mind my day, how was yours?'

He put the bottles in the steriliser, slowly and deliberately. 'I know you're angry that I didn't answer your calls and didn't ring you back.'

She stared into the microwave. The dish went round and round.

'I went into the city to talk to Dean, not just about missing the party but also about the robbery. The guard. The whole thing.'

Now she looked at him.

'You were right,' he said. 'I needed to talk to someone.'

Light burst over her head. This could be the turning point. She thought again of the promise, the possibility she'd felt when Lachlan was born.

Things could be good again.

'I'm sorry I was nasty before,' she said, 'about how long you'd spent with Dean. I understand it now.'

Chris finished screwing on the steriliser lid before answering. 'I wasn't there all the time. I went for a walk along Mrs Macquarie's Point. Had a bit of a think.'

Or could they?

The microwave pinged. Sophie busied herself opening the door and lifting out the dish.

'Isn't that hot?'

The burning in her fingers was nothing. Mrs Macquarie's Point in Sydney Harbour was where they'd gone on their first date, and where Chris had proposed to her two years later, on New Year's Eve, as fireworks blasted into the sky. If he was going there to walk and think, how could it not be to do with their marriage? She had the sudden image of herself coming home from work one day to an empty house. Lachlan, Chris, everything gone.

As if picking up on her feelings, Lachlan started to cry upstairs. Chris went up to him and Sophie sat at the table with her lasagne.

75

I should ask him if that's what he's planning.

But what if he says yes? And what if he asks me a question in return? Challenges me to tell the truth?

She put her face in her hands.

She looked up when Lachlan's crying subsided. In the silence her pulse beat in her ears. She felt surrounded by trouble, most of which she could do nothing about.

She pushed her plate away and got up to grab the phonebook.

Her friend Danielle Dawes was on duty in Royal Prince Alfred's Emergency Department. Sophie asked if she could find out the cause of death of Julie Sawyer and her baby.

'I'll have to put you on hold while I phone upstairs,' Danielle said.

Sophie sat listening to what sounded like a doorbell version of 'Greensleeves'. Damn Sawyer and his drunken accusations. Being scared that she'd stuffed up was like being new to the job all over again, when patients were a complete mystery and she was constantly terrified that each one had some life-threatening condition she was failing to recognise. Had she missed something here?

'You there?' Danielle said.

Sophie started. 'What did you find out?'

'Looks like the mother died from an amniotic fluid embolism.'

'Oh.' Some of the weight lifted from Sophie's shoulders. On the rare occasions that amniotic fluid crossed into the mother's circulation during the birth it changed her blood so that it wouldn't clot. It could happen in a hospital just as easily as at home, and couldn't be foreseen.

'Yeah,' Danielle said. 'A mate of mine in theatre said they were pumping blood into her as fast as they could but she slipped away.'

'And the baby?'

'She was on a ventilator and just arrested. They couldn't get her back. They're not sure why. PM's planned for the morning.'

It was an ugly thought, the tiny body being autopsied. 'That poor father.' No wonder he'd gotten drunk and tracked them down. 'Thanks, Dani.'

Sophie hung up, glad now that she hadn't made a statement against Sawyer. Impulsive death threats from drunks were nothing new anyway.

Chris came downstairs and poured himself a glass of milk in silence. He glanced at her as he took the carton back to the fridge and she thought she saw wariness in his eyes.

I should make a better effort. He might not leave if things improve.

'So this Roth guy,' she said brightly. 'Is he really a cop? Do you know him?'

'We did a course together once, I think.'

Sophie nibbled at the edge of her lasagne. 'At that car accident, I couldn't believe it when I recognised Dudley-Pearson.'

'Can we not talk about this?'

'What's the matter?'

'I'm sick of hearing about the bad stuff in the job. I have to listen to it all day at work, then when I open a paper or turn on the TV it's there as well.' He drained his glass. 'I don't need it from you too.'

Like I never have a stressful day. She scraped the lasagne into the bin. 'So you can talk to Dean but you can't talk to me.'

'It's not like that,' he said.

'What's it like then?'

'I can't say.'

'You mean you won't.'

He came close to her, anger in his eyes. 'I mean I can't.'

She felt the blood surging in her face. 'What's so important that you can't even tell your wife?'

'Like you never have things you don't tell me?'

By force of will she kept her eyes locked on his, but mentally she backed right off.

Chris stared at her. His dark eyes were flat, unreadable.

If it's going to happen, it'll surely happen now. She held her breath and braced herself.

But Chris only turned to the fridge, poured himself another glass of milk, then went upstairs.

Sophie sagged against the table, tears blurring her vision.

Wednesday 7 May, 11.36 am

Ella flipped dully through the photographs of the ruined takeaway shop then leaned back in her chair with a sigh. She was alone in the detectives' office in Hunters Hill Station. Of the six separate desks in the large room, four belonged to individual detectives and the other two were

78

piled with the various dross that came with police work: forms mostly, and manuals that explained how to do stuff in the PC bureaucrat-speak that had taken over the world. There was also a copy of today's newspaper. It was open to articles about the anonymous caller, Roth, the death of Duds in the crash, and a short piece about the bank guard whose funeral was to be held that afternoon. The statement by police management about all these matters was exactly what Ella expected: vague and brief. Investigations were ongoing, nothing could be confirmed. Blah blah.

Ella rolled up a scrap of paper and flicked it at the ceiling. Fifteen years she'd been in the job. It was funny, really, that she could recall every early step — the application process, starting then finishing at the Academy in Goulburn, her first job on her first shift — but the last four years were a blur. Sure she remembered moving into the detectives, and there had been a couple of decent homicide investigations she'd been part of (and naturally she'd never be allowed to forget the one where she'd told off Assistant Commissioner Shakespeare), but these days she was tired and bored. Whatever life was meant to be, surely it was more than this. Shouldn't she wake up each morning with at least *some* enthusiasm?

She spread the fire photos out and stood over them but found no insight, no breakthrough — just the throb of an incipient headache and the memory of the stink of burned plastic.

One thing that wasn't helping her frame of mind was what she'd overheard in the Jungle the night before. People said that Strike Force Gold was going to be widened in scope to take in the crash that killed Dudley-Pearson. The Homicide Squad would join in. Ella had been hit with the thought that Dennis was the investigating officer. In that light, his reluctance to talk made perfect sense.

The phone rang. 'Detectives, Hunters Hill.'

'Um, Detective Marconi please.'

'Speaking.'

'Hi, it's Edman Hughes, from the fire? I called in yesterday but you were out. I was wondering if I could come in and make my statement today?'

'That sounds fine, Mr Hughes.' Ella checked her watch. It was almost midday. 'How does one o'clock suit you?'

'That'd be good. Thanks.'

'See you then.' Ella put the phone down and reached for a piece of paper. *Steve, had to go out. Do us a favour and grab a statement from this Hughes guy, please? Thanks.*

Detective Steve Clunes ran his life like clockwork. The mornings he spent out, the afternoons in, wherever possible. He liked to finish each day with pages typed out and neatly collated. This morning he'd been to see a witness in hospital and Ella knew he'd be back soon. She left the note on his desk, grabbed her bag and headed out the door. She might not know what she wanted but she knew talking to Edman Hughes was not it.

The phone rang as Sophie walked into the ambulance station. 'The Rocks, hello and good evening.'

'You nightshift? Your partner there?' a stressed voice asked.

Sophie heard noises in the locker room. 'Yep.'

'I've got two people code seventeen, unconscious, query not breathing, in Bourke Street, Woolloomooloo,' the Control officer said. 'It's crazy out there; this is the fifth OD call in the last half-hour.'

'Heroin?'

'Yeah but way strong. People all over are going down and some aren't coming back up.' Phones rang in the background. 'Good luck.'

Sophie banged on the locker-room door. 'The sick of the city await your loving care.'

Mick stuck his head out. The bruise on his cheek was darker. 'Already?'

The roads were thick with evening traffic and when they reached the scene a woman with purple hair screamed in the dusky street, 'Where you been?'

There was no time to explain. Mick and Sophie grabbed the equipment and followed the woman into a narrow alley. There was enough light in the sky for Sophie to see two figures on the ground. Closer up she saw they were two young men, twenty years old if that, both with the dark blue complexion of the non-breathing. They wore dirty ripped jeans and grubby T-shirts, and smelled like they hadn't showered in a while. The one with the scruffy moustache had vomit around his mouth. Sophie yanked her gloves on and reached for his neck. 'Mine's in arrest.'

Mick crouched by the other one. The young man's light brown dreadlocks were spread out around him. 'Mine's still going.'

Sophie looked for the woman but she'd gone. She grabbed the portable radio and called for urgent back-up.

'I'll do my best,' Control said.

Mick injected naloxone, the narcotic antagonist, directly into his patient's veins, while Sophie tore open the dirty T-shirt and slapped the defibrillator pads onto the arrest victim's skinny chest. The screen on the monitor showed the wiggly line of ventricular fibrillation. She charged the machine and hit him with a shock. His body jumped but the monitor showed no change.

Mick rolled his patient on his side and kept an eye on him as he came over to help Sophie. 'Good. My guy's starting to breathe up.'

Sophie charged the machine again. 'Clear?'

Mick let go of the arrest victim's head. 'Clear.'

This time the shock caused the man's heart to go into the flat line of asystole. Mick started one-person CPR while Sophie searched the scarred arms for veins. 'He's all trackmarks.'

Mick paused in his CPR to poke his patient in the ribs. 'How you doing?'

There was no reply. Mick watched him closely for a few seconds. 'His resps are falling,' he said.

'How strong is this shit? I'm going to have to hit him again.'

Sophie found a tiny vein and quickly cannulated it. She injected adrenaline and took over CPR while Mick gave another shot of naloxone to his patient. Sirens sounded in the distance. People wearing suits and carrying briefcases walked past the end of the alley, looked in and kept going. Sophie envied them the end of their working day when hers was just beginning. She compressed the skinny man's chest. His ribs were bony, his skin thin. His head lolled. The vomit on his face was drying. The chances of getting him back were slim, but he was so young. They had to try.

'There you go,' Mick said. His patient coughed and tried to get up. 'Relax for a moment, mate. Just sit tight.'

The man shoved Mick's hands away. 'Fuck off.'

'Listen, mate, you were almost dead.'

'Bullshit.' The man staggered to his feet and headed out of the alley. The sirens drew closer.

Mick followed him. 'What'd you take?'

'Nothing.'

'That's good,' Mick said. 'The Narcan won't have any effect then.'

'You din't give me that shit? Aww.' The man threw a punch at the brick wall as he lurched along. 'Fuckin' bastards.'

'What about your friend?' Sophie shouted but the man turned the corner into the street and was gone. Sophie shook her head as she compressed her patient's chest. Addicts hated

Narcan. They didn't care that it saved their lives; it ruined their high and meant they had to go out and beg, borrow or steal enough to buy another hit.

Mick took over squeezing the bag, inflating the arrest victim's lungs. Sophie paused in her compressions to inject another bolus of adrenaline. They were watching the monitor screen, hoping for a reaction, when the back-up crew arrived.

They took the man to St Vincent's, where he was declared dead on arrival. A nurse searched his clothes but found no wallet or identification. He was logged in as 'Unknown male'.

In the ambulance bay Sophie found Mick restocking the drug kit. He said, 'That crew was saying there's been nine overdoses today and this is the third death.'

'Last week was bad too,' Sophie said. 'Remember we did that group of four friends in the Cross?'

Mick nodded. 'Supply's outstripping demand. They don't cut it down so far and everyone drops from the purity.' There was a crackle from the car radio and Mick paused in his restocking, packaged syringes in his hand. 'Are they calling us?'

Sophie shook her head. 'Car fifty-one.'

'Good,' Mick said. 'So what'd you do today?'

'Home stuff, you know.' She started changing the oxygen cylinder in the Viva. 'You?'

'I got a call from Central Coast Control, wanting me for a radio shift up there tonight.'

'Another one?'

'That flu's still doing the rounds of the staff.' He shoved the kit back into the vehicle. 'I would've liked the overtime but it's kind of hard to be in two places at once.'

'Just a bit,' she said.

Mick started to say something then his mobile rang and he moved down the driveway to answer it. Sophie tightened the cylinder connection and thought about Chris.

When Lachlan had woken at six that morning, Chris got up to him. Sophie appreciated the sleep-in, especially prior to night-shift, but when she'd finally crawled out of bed at eleven she'd been surprised to find they were out. By midafternoon she was sitting by the front window with her mobile in her hand. She wasn't going to call Chris. He could call her and tell her where they were. Or come back and get her, seeing as he had the car, and they could continue the outing together. As a fucking family.

By the time she'd started getting ready for work she had herself believing he was definitely leaving her. He was that very moment signing the lease on a small two-bedder near his mum's place, picturing the smaller of the bedrooms as a nursery, planning to hire a trailer to move the cot and everything else that night. She'd come home in the morning and find the house empty, a scrawled note giving his new address, because that was only fair, but nothing else.

When the car pulled into the driveway she stayed in their bedroom, ramming the metal buttons into their holes on her shirt, yanking on her epaulettes so hard she tore the stitching on her sleeve.

Chris burst in the front door. 'Guess what!'

Sophie debated what to say.

'Lachlan walked!'

She came to the top of the stairs. In the hallway below Chris was propping Lachlan against the open front door then backing away a few steps and calling to him. Lachlan's shirt bore food stains and the knees of his trousers were filthy. He laughed at Chris, then up at Sophie, but stayed clinging to the door.

'So I missed it,' she said.

'He'll do it again.' Chris gathered him up. 'Good sleep?'

'Where were you?'

'We went to the zoo.' Chris nuzzled Lachlan's neck. 'And what did we see? Monkeys, seals, tigers — '

'Why didn't you take me?'

'You were sleeping.'

'I don't sleep all day.' She came down the stairs. 'What did he eat?'

'I took some formula, and some of those Heinz jars from the cupboard.'

'They're all desserts.'

'He liked them,' Chris said.

Sophie could smell Lachlan's nappy before she reached them. 'He needs changing.'

'I know that,' Chris said. 'I'm not totally useless.'

Sophie bent close to her son, laying her cheek to his sticky one. He grasped at her hair and she kissed the top of his head. 'I have to go.'

Now, turning the regulator on to check that the new oxygen cylinder was full, she was ashamed to think that was how she'd left things. When she'd headed out the door she'd said 'Bye' and from the kitchen where he was feeding Lachlan, Chris had said the same, but they hadn't kissed or even looked each other in the eye.

In the morning she'd buy croissants on the way home, and maybe they could all snuggle in bed for a while, and she'd ask Chris to tell her every little detail about Lachlan's first steps.

The radio crackled. 'Car Thirty-one.'

'Here we go,' she called to Mick.

★   ★   ★

They did four cases on the trot. First was a drunk who tried to cross the Cahill Expressway and got multiple fractures for his trouble; then a screeching teenage girl who'd been glassed in the face by another girl over a boy; then there was a Korean tourist who spoke no English but seemed to have chest pain, at least according to his hand gestures. The next call was 'person query dead' in bushes in Hyde Park, no other information given.

Mick eased the ambulance up the kerb from Macquarie Street and drove along the central path past the Archibald Fountain. The ambulance's sidelights illuminated the grass, shiny with damp, and the pale trunks of the figtrees. Beyond them much of the park was dark. They'd obviously arrived before the police. Mick shook his head. 'I will never understand the inconsistency of calling the ambulance but not waiting long enough to point the patient out.'

'Probably found by someone up to no good.'

'Yeah, but what do they think we're going to do? Chase after them and force them to give us their name?' Mick flicked the headlights on high and put the foglights on for good measure. A path led off to the right by a sculpture and its own small fountain. Mick drove onto the grass and in the headlights Sophie spotted two feet under the low branches of a shrub.

She called Control to say they were on scene, then she and Mick got out either side of the ambulance. Sophie crouched with a torch and Mick peered over her shoulder into the bush.

'Goner,' Mick said.

'Reckon.' The half-open eyes and the pale purplish colour of the young woman's face gave it away. Sophie touched the bare back of her wrist to the stockinged ankle between the brown leather shoe and the long skirt. Her skin was only slightly warm.

'I'll call it in,' Mick said.

Left alone with the girl, Sophie looked at her more closely. She had smooth blonde hair tied back with a black scrunchie. Above the skirt she wore a white shirt and a loose brown jacket. Her shirt had pulled out of the skirt, revealing a narrow band of tanned stomach. The left sleeve of the jacket was pulled up, exposing a fresh injection mark on the inner aspect of her elbow. An empty syringe with needle attached lay by her side. What looked like a handbag strap with its ends cut was wound around her arm. On the ring and little fingers of both hands she wore gold rings, and around her right wrist was a tight-fitting gold bracelet with a nameplate. Sophie couldn't see the name.

'Not the usual heroin death,' she said when Mick came back.

'Rich people take the stuff too.'

'Yeah, but not usually in the bushes in parks.' In her experience the rich ones took it home and did it with friends. Rumour was you could get good money by selling naloxone black market because the rich ones knew the risks and wanted to be safe, so they bought the narcotic antagonist for their friends to hit them with if the worst happened. They had profitable day jobs in places like the stockmarket and the fashion industry and they wanted to get up in the morning. 'See what she used as a tourniquet?'

Mick peered in. 'Handbag's gone though.'

'Looks like it.'

'There's your caller then. No wonder they didn't want to hang around and show us where she is. Lowlife.'

The bracelet and rings were probably too tight to get off quickly. Sophie felt protective towards the girl, sorry that she was dead and that someone had robbed her as she'd lain there. 'I guess we should be grateful they took the time to call at all.' She flicked the torch off to give the girl some peace.

'I bet the cops will be ages.' Mick leaned an elbow on the ambulance bonnet. 'Wish I had some coffee.'

Sophie rested her folded arms on the bonnet beside him. The clouds were bright with the city's glow. Somewhere out there somebody was worried about this girl who hadn't come home. Sophie wondered why she was here. If you were trying the drug for the first time, wouldn't you be with friends? And even if it wasn't your first time, why choose this lonely spot?

Bats flew overhead. There was a breeze and she could smell damp earth and leaves. Insects flew at the spotlights directed at the sculpture and the small fountain. Despite their glow it was dark under the shrubbery.

'Hey,' she said. 'How did she see to inject herself? It's pitch-black in that shrub.'

'Maybe she did it in the daylight.'

'She's not that cold.'

Mick looked again towards the body. 'Hm.' He took the torch and moved closer.

'Don't. It could be a crime scene.'

He squatted and shone the torch about. The light glinted off something in the undergrowth.

'Don't touch it.'

'I'm not touching it,' he said. 'It's one of those keyrings with a torch built in.' He stood up again. 'Hold that in your mouth, angle down at your arm, and voila.'

Sophie didn't like to think about it.

'Wow. This is what I call service,' Mick said.

Sophie turned to see two police cars crossing the dark lawns, their beacons going. 'Why two? And why the lights?'

Mick's mobile rang. 'Mick Schultz,' he answered. 'Yes . . . God, really? Are you sure?

. . . Of course. Yes, they're here now. Okay, yes.'
He hung up.

Sophie's stomach lurched at the look on his face. 'What is it?'

Mick took a moment to clip his phone on his belt. The police cars drew closer. Their lights threw alternating red and blue beams across Mick's pale face.

'Mick?' Sophie said.

'You should prepare yourself.'

She thought she'd never heard such a stupid statement from him. 'What are you — '

'It's Chris. He's been shot.'

'That's not funny.'

'Sophie, I wish I was joking.'

The police cars pulled up beside them. The whole world was now blue and red. Sophie stared at Mick then heard the car doors open. 'Mrs Phillips?'

She turned to face them. The looks on their faces told her it was true. Her mind teemed with questions — where, how, why — but two stood out. 'Is Chris alive? Is Lachlan okay?'

A sergeant came closer. It was Hugh Green from Wynyard. He took her hand. His palm was clammy. 'Chris is alive. He's in Royal North Shore.'

She waited but he didn't say any more. 'Is he okay? Is he conscious?'

Hugh's gaze was steady but he hesitated before lowering and softening his voice. 'He was shot in the head.'

Sophie couldn't breathe. 'Is — is Lachlan hurt?'

His hand tightened on hers. 'We can't find him.'

'No,' she said.

'We're so sorry,' he said, a crack in his voice.

'No,' she said again.

Another officer came forward. 'We'll take you to see Chris.'

'Where did it happen?'

'At your home.'

'Then take me there,' she said. 'I have to find Lachlan.'

'We've searched the house.'

'I'll search it again.' She hurried to the back of the police car. Hugh climbed in the front and the other officer got in the driver's seat. The crew from the second car stood with Mick, who looked stricken. Behind him was the shrub where the dead girl lay. Sophie had no room for pity now, only the tight grip of her own fear. 'What happened?'

'We don't know.' The police radio crackled and Hugh turned it down. 'Your neighbour found Chris lying in the doorway. Paramedics came and took him. Everybody searched — we're still searching — but so far there's no sign of Lachlan.'

The officer at the wheel turned on the lights and siren as they came out of Hyde Park over the kerb opposite Market Street and pushed into traffic on Elizabeth Street.

'Didn't anyone hear it?'

'Nobody we've talked to.'

The driver ignored the no-right-turn sign at Park Street and raced down onto Druitt. The beacons flashed off the shopfronts.

Sophie felt along her uniform belt for her phone and dialled a number. 'Gloria, is Lachlan with you?'

'No, he isn't,' she said. 'Why — '

'Something bad's happened. You'd better come over.'

Gloria started to say something but Sophie hung up on her. She needed to think. She sat with her phone in her hands as the car shot across Anzac Bridge and into Rozelle.

This could not be true. She was dreaming, or unconscious in a car crash, and she would wake up from this nightmare soon.

Or if it was true they'd get there and somebody would come running forward with Lachlan howling in their arms.

She pressed trembling into the corner of the seat.

Lachlan could not really be gone.

5

Sophie couldn't get warm, even after Sergeant Hugh Green lent her his leather jacket and turned the car heater up high. She wrapped her arms around herself and shivered inside the creaking leather as the car sped into Gladesville.

At her house a man and a woman waited on the driveway. Sophie was out before the car fully stopped. The woman came forward. 'Sophie Phillips? I'm Detective Ella Marconi. This is Detective Dennis Orchard.'

Sophie shook the woman's hand. She was on the short side, about forty, with dark hair and dark eyes. The male detective was taller, older, and skinny. Behind them all the lights were on in her house. 'Did you find him?'

'Not yet, I'm sorry.'

Police with torches searched neighbouring gardens and talked to residents on their doorsteps. Sophie drew a long hitching breath. 'I want to check the house.'

'Mrs Phillips, we've been over the entire place,' the female detective said. 'The best thing you can do for now is talk with us. As your house is a crime scene we've arranged to use your neighbour's, and when we're finished you can go to see Chris.'

Sophie tried to swallow. 'Have you heard any news about him?'

'I spoke to the hospital not long ago,' said the male detective. 'The doctors are looking after him. As soon as we're done here we'll have someone drive you over there.'

Sophie walked with them reluctantly. She fought the urge to get down on the ground and sniff the grass for a trace of Lachlan. She wanted to scream and grunt and moan. She wanted to roar through the shrubs and undergrowth on her hands and knees, scrabbling after her beautiful innocent son.

She squeezed her arms to her chest as they went next door to Fergus Patrick's house. When Sophie saw the retired cop his face crumpled.

'I can't believe I heard the shot and didn't realise what it was,' he said as they followed him inside. 'I was watching TV and I thought the sound was on the show. It wasn't until I went to the bathroom that I saw light coming from your place, because your front door was open.' He started to cry. 'I should know a silenced gun when I hear one. That little pop sound . . . Sophie, I'm so sorry. If I'd gone straightaway I might have stopped them. I might have saved Lachlan.'

They sat in Fergus's living room. The smell of warm dust rose from the heater in the corner but the room felt as icy as the air outside. Fergus put a tray of coffee things on the table then went out with his head down.

Sophie took short shallow breaths. She looked at the detectives. These were the people in charge

95

of finding her son. She'd already forgotten their names. The woman put her notebook on the table and flipped the cover open. Sophie examined her face, her direct gaze, and wondered if a case like this was like a code nine for a paramedic — the ultimate bringing of order to chaos. She half expected platitudes like paramedics often used, like she'd used herself, saying to dying patients that they were doing really well, that everything would be okay, because to say otherwise was inviting panic. She looked at the male detective, who dropped his gaze to the coffee cups. 'Take sugar?' he said.

Sophie could hear her watch ticking on her wrist. 'We should be out looking.' Her voice didn't sound like her own.

'We'll do this as quickly as we can, Mrs Phillips,' the female detective said.

Sophie fought against the growing terror in her mind. She put her hands by her sides and clutched the frame of the chair.

'Mrs Phillips, is there any chance that Lachlan might be with a babysitter?'

'Chris's mother, Gloria, minds him when we're both at work.' Sophie let go of the chair with one hand long enough to wipe her eyes. 'When Chris has days off he takes Lachlan everywhere he goes.'

'Where does she live?'

'She's got a unit in High Street in Epping. She's coming over.'

'Is there anyone else who could have him? Your parents?'

'Both dead.'

'Chris's dad?'

'He hasn't been around since Chris was little.'

'Does Lachlan have any aunts and uncles?'

She shook her head.

'Friends, neighbours?'

'None that would just take him.'

'Maybe Chris asked them, maybe he had something to do, somewhere to go.'

'No,' Sophie said flatly. 'Like I said, they go everywhere together.'

There were cries outside. Sophie started, then sagged back. 'It's Gloria.'

The male detective got up. 'I'll talk to her.'

The woman leaned forward across her notebook. 'I'm sorry to have to ask this, but have you or Chris ever had an affair?'

'No.' The thing with Angus was far from an affair. 'No affairs.'

It had occurred to her already that maybe this was a kind of karmic payback for cheating and lying. *Okay, I'll do anything*, she offered up. *I'll confess to Chris. I'll pay with my life. Just bring him back.*

A cup of coffee sat before her. She wrapped her hands around it. The heat from the coffee didn't spread beyond her palms, and she was afraid to take even a sip because she was sure she'd immediately vomit it up. She tried to relax her clenched jaw but her teeth started to chatter.

'What time did you leave for work this evening?'

'At four-thirty,' Sophie said. 'I caught the four-forty bus up Victoria Road to West Ryde Station, then the train to Circular Quay.'

'How was Chris when you left?'

'We weren't really speaking. We'd had an argument. He was probably over it ten minutes after I left. He would've been playing with Lachlan and they would've been happy as clams.'

'How was he earlier in the day?'

'He was out for most of it. He got up about six, when Lachlan woke up, and I stayed in bed. I didn't see him again until the afternoon. He said they went to the zoo,' Sophie said. 'That was when we argued. There's been stuff on his mind but he'll never say what it is. I think it's to do with being assaulted a couple of months ago. Though the robberies really bother him too.'

The detective studied her. 'Why's that?'

'He went to the last one and tried to save the guard, but the man died,' Sophie said. 'Then the guard's wife turned up and was screaming and sobbing. And he's hurt by the stuff the media says, about how the cops are slack because they can't catch them. That sort of stuff weighs on his mind.'

The detective tapped her pen on the table. 'You asked him specifically what was wrong and he wouldn't say?'

Sophie nodded. 'He's always saying some things can't be helped by talking about them.'

The detective made a note.

'But it's always about work. See, he wants morale to be good and police to be enthusiastic and the community to respect you all,' Sophie said. 'He hates being abused on the street, hates being hated. He's doing his diploma in Adult Ed because he wants to work in the Academy, where everyone's still keen and enthusiastic.'

'So Mr Patrick told me,' the detective said. 'Okay. Can you think of anyone with any reason to attack Chris or your family?'

'Like I said, Chris was bashed a couple of months back, while on duty — ' Sophie started up out of her chair. 'There was this man, at my work. Oh my God. How could I have forgotten? His name's Boyd Sawyer. His wife was in labour. We were called to his house but there were complications. The mother and baby both died.'

'When was this?'

'Yesterday morning. And then in the afternoon he tracked us down in the ambulance and punched my partner.' Sophie shivered. 'He told me I killed his family.'

'Can you remember his address or his car rego?'

'He drives a blue BMW, I don't know the plates. He's a plastic surgeon,' Sophie said. 'They live in Glebe Point Road, right down the end by the water. And yesterday Senior Constable Allan Denning from Wynyard arrested him for DUI.'

Sophie watched the detective go to the door and call her partner over. They had a brief conversation, then he handed her what looked like a sheet of paper in a plastic sleeve before he hurried off.

Sophie heard car engines outside roar to life and tyres squeal away. 'I keep wondering whether he's hungry now. Whether he's warm enough. He's going through a clingy stage and he'll really be screaming. They won't know how to comfort him. He needs us and he won't understand why we don't come when he cries.' Sophie wiped her eyes. The skin around them was sore. 'He's so little and so helpless.'

'Mrs Phillips, I need to show you something.' The detective slid the plastic sleeve across the table. 'This note was found with your husband.'

Sophie read: *'Keep your mouth shut if you know what's best.'*

'Does that mean anything to you?'

'Not a thing.' The letters were black and sharp against the white paper. 'If it's Sawyer, why would he leave that?'

'It might not be Sawyer.'

'Then who?'

'We don't know yet.' The detective took the note back and looked at it herself. 'We'll test this for fingerprints, and we can find out the brand of paper and hopefully what kind of computer printer it came from. Crime Scene's examining the house for evidence too,' she said. 'We've got a big team on this case, Mrs Phillips. We'll find him.'

Sophie shivered.

Thursday 8 May, 12.05 am

Sophie stared at Chris's motionless face. He lay unconscious and on a ventilator in Royal North Shore Hospital's Intensive Care Unit. The clear plastic tube was tied into his mouth with white cloth tape and his bare chest rose and fell in time with the machine's hiss and beep. His head was swathed in bandages. He had two black eyes and his nostrils were thick with dried blood.

Gloria held Chris's left hand to her forehead and muttered through her tears. Sophie gripped his right hand. Her fingers had automatically crept round his wrist to settle on his pulse. The smell of blood and antiseptic was so strong she could taste it. It reminded her of her training weeks spent in theatre, of the man who'd also been shot in the head, the way the surgeons sweated and swore over him. He'd died.

A doctor in surgical scrubs came into the room. 'I'm Pete Jones.' He held out his hand to Sophie. His eyes behind his glasses were tired.

Sophie introduced herself and Gloria.

The doctor nodded. 'Any word on your little boy?'

'Not yet.'

He squeezed her shoulder silently.

'How was the surgery?' Gloria said.

'It went extremely well. The entry wound was just above the bridge of Chris's nose but the bullet didn't penetrate to his brain. It deflected through his sinuses. We were able to remove it without much trouble and so the entire surgery was much shorter than we'd envisioned.' He hesitated. 'We found on the CT scan that there's a contusion to the frontal lobes. Because of this, plus our suspicion that he may have been hypoxic before the paramedics arrived, we're concerned about neurological damage. We'd like to keep him in an induced coma for the next twenty-four hours, just to give him a chance to rest and begin recovery.'

'But if he remembers who attacked him, it could help find Lachlan,' Sophie said.

The doctor pursed his lips. 'If he remains stable overnight, I'll consider starting to reduce his sedation.' He left the room.

Gloria smoothed the blankets over Chris's legs. 'I always wanted Chris to be a doctor.'

'I know.'

'He's smart,' she said, 'he just didn't want it enough. But maybe this is a sign. After all, doctors don't get shot in their own homes.'

'People get shot all the time, everywhere. No matter who they are,' Sophie said.

Gloria carried on as if she hadn't spoken. 'A doctor earns enough money for his wife to stay home with his children.'

'Chris loves his job and I love mine,' Sophie said.

Gloria turned away, inspecting the face of the ventilator. 'I don't know if these figures are right.'

'The staff know what they're doing.' Sophie raised Chris's warm hand to her cheek. She'd hoped maybe now, at a time like this, she and Gloria might actually support each other, but it didn't look like that was going to happen. A little voice in Sophie's head suggested maybe Gloria was so anxious over Lachlan she had no choice about how she behaved. A louder voice was having none of it. She had to get out. 'I think I'll go.'

Gloria dragged her plastic chair closer to Chris's bedside. 'Yes, you go. I'll keep an eye on things here.'

Sophie bent to her husband's face. His lips were open around the tube and she caught the stale smell of his dry mouth. His face was pale where it wasn't bruised. His eyes were slits in the swollen flesh. 'Wake up and talk to me soon, honey. We have to find our boy.' She kissed him. 'Love you.'

In the corridor she took a moment to wash her hands. The water splashed onto the sleeves of Sergeant Green's leather jacket. The police had let her take the car from the garage when she insisted she drive herself over, but hadn't allowed her into the house to get any clothes. She liked the jacket — its creaking bulk and leather smell reminded her of Chris. She still couldn't get warm though.

At the lift she got out her mobile and the business card the female detective had given her.

The detective answered on the first ring. 'Ella Marconi.'

'It's Sophie. Is there any news?'

'Nothing yet, I'm sorry,' she said. 'How's Chris?'

Sophie told her what the doctor had said. 'Hopefully he'll wake up in the morning.'

Ella said, 'Have you thought of anyone else who might have a grudge against you or Chris? And can you tell me more about that bashing?'

'It was a couple of months ago, when he was working with Dean Rigby. There've been no threats or anything made since, though. Well, not that he's told me.'

'Okay, thanks.'

Despairing, Sophie hit the lift button with her

fist. 'What did Sawyer have to say?'

'We're having some trouble locating him, actually,' Ella said. 'But I'll let you know the second we find anything out.'

The lift was empty. Sophie stood in the centre and sobbed.

12.10 am

The team of thirty-four detectives crowded into Gladesville Station's Incident Room. Most had been called in from home, some no doubt from bed, but Ella saw no bleary eyes and no barely hidden yawns. A missing kid, his cop dad shot: this was a case to be wide awake for.

The possibility that Chris might die, plus the high-profile nature of the case, meant Homicide was running the show. Dennis was in charge, and he looked up from the desk at the front of the room where he was shuffling papers and gave Ella a wink. She squeezed her hands into fists behind her back, hoping her excitement didn't show too clearly on her face. It was not right to be so thrilled when tragedy was unfolding, but there you had it. It was a lining up of the stars: Dennis being assigned the case *and* given the option to choose his number two, and whoever the bigwig signing the paperwork was, he'd miraculously agreed. Perhaps not everyone liked Shakespeare after all.

On a table in the corner stood three boxes full of A4 colour flyers. Lachlan's details were across the top of his photo, and a list of police phone numbers was on the bottom. Fergus Patrick's son ran a print shop and he had had them ready before Ella and Dennis had left the old man's house.

Behind Dennis was a TV on a stand. A digital camcorder was connected to the TV. Along the other walls stood blank whiteboards and desks with phones. A computer hummed in a corner, its screen showing the investigation coordination program desktop.

'Okay, folks,' Dennis said. He introduced himself and Ella. 'We're going to make this briefing short but thorough so we can get out there and find who did this.'

People had notebooks and pens ready.

'Around 2200 hours Senior Constable Chris Phillips was shot in the face by an unknown assailant in the doorway of his home in Easton Street, Gladesville,' Dennis said. 'His ten-month-old son is missing, believed taken by that same person. Phillips was found by a neighbour at 2215, unconscious. He's had surgery and the bullet's on its way for examination, but of course it will be some time before we know anything definitive there. The doctors believe he'll remain unconscious for some hours yet. We're hoping when he does wake up he'll remember something.'

Dennis passed some flyers around. 'The baby's name is Lachlan. There's no sign in his room or elsewhere in the house that he's been injured. Crime Scene found a lot of fingerprints and hair and fibres they have to compare. We also have this note.'

Ella handed out copies.

'We don't know what this is about,' Dennis said. 'Phillips's wife, Sophie, says that he's been upset by the gang robberies and the bad press we've received over them.'

'Any chance Phillips was the person who called the TV stations yesterday?' a detective asked.

'Makes sense,' another detective said. 'The caller promised to tell more. 'Keep your mouth shut' could be a warning to zip it.'

'That's a possibility we're going to look into,' Dennis said. 'Also, Chris was assaulted while on duty two months ago. We're not aware of any threats since.'

'Now,' he went on, 'Lachlan's mother Sophie's whereabouts for the evening have been confirmed — she's a paramedic and was working. The only other family is Chris's mother, Gloria, and she looks to be in the clear too.'

'Chris or the wife not having an affair?'

'Not as far as we know,' Dennis said. 'Two days ago when Sophie was at work she had a mother and baby die in an emergency birth. The father, a man by the name of Boyd Sawyer, later threatened and assaulted her and her work partner. We're looking for Sawyer now.'

'Why abduct the baby?' a detective asked with a frown. 'If you wanted to wipe out her family in revenge for the loss of your own, why not just kill the child there?'

'We have to hope the baby is still alive somewhere,' Dennis said. 'If it was Sawyer, he might have dumped the child or passed him on to somebody. Same applies, of course, if the abductor is someone else. Babies are easy to hide but can be tricky to disguise. One possibility is that they cut all his hair off, or perhaps dress him as a girl. Keep these points in mind when you're out there.' He looked around. 'Questions so far?'

They shook their heads.

Dennis turned on the TV and started the video. 'Okay. Here we have the front of the Phillips house.' The screen showed an open front door. In the hall beyond it a flight of stairs was on the right side, a passageway leading to the kitchen on the left. The light in the hall shone down on the blood-stained carpet. 'There's no sign of damage to the door so we believe that Senior Constable Phillips opened it in response to a knock. You can see there is a peephole, so he may have known the person, or he may simply have been unconcerned about whether the person posed a risk.'

The camera moved up the stairs and across a landing to the baby's room and rumpled sheets in a cot. 'We believe a blanket was taken along with the baby,' Dennis said. 'Possibly to muffle any crying.' The camera went closer. In the corner of the cot lay a small, soft toy duck.

'The rest shows the layout of the house.' The camera moved through the main bedroom, a spare room with a made-up bed, a tiny study, and the bathroom, then went back downstairs and briefly showed a living room, dining area and kitchen. The screen turned to snow and Dennis turned it off. 'Okay. We have a lot to do, a lot of people to talk to. It's the middle of the night, so some might not be too happy about being disturbed, but just remind them of the urgency of the case.'

'Tasks,' he said, looking at a list in his hand. 'Kemsley and De Weese, I want you to look into that assault on Chris, and check out his work generally, see if anyone's been released recently who held a grudge against him, what cases he's done lately.'

The men nodded.

'Eliopoulos and Lunney, get in touch with the Strike Force Gold people, find out if Chris's name has ever come up in any of their investigations into the robberies, and whether they've found out anything about the caller to the TV stations. Eddington, Rossi, Tranter, Clark and Curtis, back to the scene and the canvass of neighbours. McAlpine, you go with them but first check out the neighbour, Fergus Patrick. Ex-Victorian copper, apparently. He found Chris and raised the alarm . . . Just in case, you never know.'

The detective nodded.

Dennis continued. 'Sugden, get in touch with Telstra and set up a trap and trace on the Phillips phone. If you have any trouble, call me. If someone rings with a ransom demand, we need to know. Kim and Herbert, check for known sex offenders in the area. Fenwick, you're on the computer. I want every last detail logged in.'

There was a knock at the door and a uniformed officer opened it and looked in. Dennis motioned for Ella to go.

108

In the corridor she pulled the door to. 'What is it?'

'They've found that doctor.'

'Sawyer? Where is he?'

'He was overdosed in his car near the Meadowbank Wharf. Paramedics revived him then took him to Ryde Hospital. Ryde general duties officers attended and realised who he was. He wants to make a complaint about someone drugging him.'

Ella thought quickly. 'His car's still at Meadowbank?'

The officer nodded.

'Send Crime Scene,' Ella said. 'Tell them we'll be down shortly. Call the uniformed officers and ask them to keep him at the hospital until we get in touch. We don't know yet if he's involved in this but we've got to play it safe.'

Back in the room Dennis was saying to a pair of detectives, ' — for recent baby deaths, especially any possibly unbalanced parents.' He looked around. 'Okay, is everyone clear on what they're to do? Take a wad of these flyers as you go. We want this city plastered.' He looked at his watch. 'Call in with developments, otherwise we'll meet back here at five am. Let's get to work.'

Detectives grabbed handfuls of the colour flyers then hurried from the room.

Ella told Dennis about Sawyer and what she'd arranged. 'So we can check out the scene before we talk to him.'

'Good thinking,' he said, taking a sheaf of flyers for himself. 'Let's just hope he didn't drop that baby in the river before he took the overdose.'

12.40 am

Even though the fan in the Commodore's heater rattled when switched to high, Sophie couldn't stand anything less. She clung shivering to the wheel with her chin tucked inside the zipped-up leather jacket. She reached down to adjust the seat again, then up to the mirror. Nothing felt right. She'd found a bottle of water in the glovebox among a bunch of paper towels and receipts and tried a sip, but it was as if she'd forgotten how to swallow and she'd had to cough it out.

The driver's window was halfway down in a balance between keeping warm air in the car and listening for a baby's cries. She kept the high beams on despite oncoming cars flashing theirs because she needed to see every gloomy alcove on every building, every dark alleyway entrance and every hidden stairwell. It was illogical, irrational, to think she might find him this way, but at least she was looking.

She'd left the hospital and gone back to Gladesville to drive around the empty suburban streets, seeing only police cars on their own search. She'd then come into the city. After years spent flogging around it in ambulances she knew it better than the back of her hand. She started at The Rocks, doing the loop of Hickson Road first, then searching the smaller sloping streets

110

on the western side of the Bridge.

In High Street she saw a man pushing a stroller. As she drew abreast of him he glanced at her with a frown. She drove past and made a U-turn then came back. He squinted in her high beams and she saw the blanketed form and the dark hair of the infant in the stroller, and in a second she yanked on the handbrake and leapt from the car. 'Let me see that baby.'

'What?'

'Show me the baby.'

The man put the stroller behind him. He looked at her car then back at her jacket. 'Are you really a cop?'

'What's it look like?'

'Show me some ID then.'

Sophie stepped closer, craning her neck. She could see the shock of dark hair again. Her skin prickled and she reached out.

The man jerked the stroller further away and the baby started to cry. 'Don't you — '

'Just let me see it.'

'Get away from us.' His eyes were wide, his face pale in the streetlight.

'There's been a report of a child abducted,' Sophie said, 'so I need to see that baby's face.'

'Where's your police car and your partner?'

'If you want me to call for back-up I will.'

The man started to run awkwardly, pushing the stroller. The baby cried out.

Sophie ran after him. 'Stop right there.'

A couple of lights went on in nearby houses.

The baby's cries were muffled by the blanket but Sophie was increasingly sure it was Lachlan.

Why else would the man run? 'Stop! Police!'

'Help!' the man cried. 'Help!'

More house lights went on.

'Call the police! He stole my baby!'

'He's my baby!' the man cried. 'This chick's nuts!' He stumbled and almost fell. Sophie caught up to him and he darted sideways to a house. He seized the screaming child from the stroller and hugged him high against his chest, his back to the front door. 'If you come near us I'll kick the shit out of you,' he gasped.

Sophie stayed out of range, staring at the struggling bundle in his arms. 'Just show me.'

'No way.'

Back down the street her car idled on the roadway. People in dressing-gowns and pyjamas stood on the footpath looking in their direction.

Red and blue flashing lights revealed the approach of a police car before it turned into the street.

Sophie didn't dare go to the kerb to meet the officers in case the man ran away. They came up behind her. 'What's the problem here?'

She recognised the voice. 'Allan, it's me.'

'Sophie?' Senior Constable Allan Denning touched her arm.

She took her eyes from the man with the baby for a split second. 'You heard what happened? This man won't let me see the baby and I think it might be Lachlan.'

Allan stepped over to the man. 'Show us.'

'Why the hell should I?'

'Listen,' Allan said. 'This woman's husband was shot and her baby kidnapped tonight. I can

112

understand she frightened you but I'm sure you in turn can understand her behaviour.'

The man looked at Sophie. After a moment he lowered his arms so the baby's face became visible. It wasn't Lachlan. Sophie felt a wave of nausea and turned away.

She'd left her driver's door open and it was cold again in her car. She turned the heater down one notch to ring Ella.

The call went to voicemail. 'Please tell me you have some news,' Sophie said after the beep.

Allan crouched by her window. 'I'm sorry it wasn't him.'

'Me too.' Sophie wiped her eyes.

'The guy's okay,' Allan said. 'Told me the baby was crying so he came out for a walk. Said he's sorry, but he thought you were a nut in a stolen uniform wanting to take his bub.'

Sophie held onto the steering wheel. 'I told the detectives about Sawyer.'

'I know, they rang me,' he said. 'We charged him with low range PCA yesterday and he's due in court in six weeks.'

'Did he say anything else about us? About me?'

Allan looked down the dark street then back at her. 'He kept saying you killed them. At least he did until his solicitor arrived and made him shut up.'

'I have to go,' Sophie said.

'What are you doing — just driving the streets, looking?'

'Yes.'

'Us too,' he said. 'But you shouldn't tell

people you're a cop.'

'I didn't. He just assumed I was.' The lie came so easily. 'I don't have another jacket with me but I'll give it back as soon as I get one.'

'Okay.' He reached in the open window and put his hand on her shoulder. 'Be careful.'

On the eastern side of the Bridge approaches she drove back and forth, covering the grids of the streets, slowly moving south. She shone a torch from her window along the buildings for any places her high beams missed, and prayed aloud, 'Please, God, please, God, please, oh please, God.'

12.47 am

The wind off the Parramatta River was cold. Ella hunched her shoulders as she and Dennis crossed the Meadowbank Wharf carpark. On the black water two police boats motored about in the current, spotlights reflecting off the surface. She guessed there were divers out there, searching in the dark by feel, the object of their hunt worth the danger of diving at night. She wondered how they coped with the tide hauling at them, and for that matter how they thought they'd find a baby's body close to the area where he might have been thrown in. Turning upstream she saw more lights. Well, okay. So maybe they were looking all over.

'Sharks in there,' Dennis said.

'Thanks.'

The carpark was divided in two by a concrete

railway bridge. The larger area contained only three cars. Dennis wrote down their plate numbers. A passageway just wide enough for two cars led underneath to a second, smaller parking area. It was poorly lit and hidden from view from the wharf.

Sawyer's BMW sat in the far corner. It had been found by a woman walking her dog. She'd dragged the animal to the public phone on the wharf, screaming that a man was dead behind the wheel of his car.

The car's dark surface gleamed under the lights that Crime Scene had set up. They ran off ear-busting generators. Dennis said something Ella lost in the noise. 'What?'

He leaned closer. 'Nice Beemer.'

Crime Scene officer James Mooney came over. 'Got a few things to show you. Here's one.' He held up an evidence bag containing a baby's dummy. 'Found it down here.'

They followed Mooney around the BMW to the kerb and Mooney pointed to the gutter with a chubby finger. There was a collection of dead leaves with a pool of dirty water banked up behind it. 'Lying in that.'

Ella looked around. It was conceivable that some parent or child could have dropped the dummy while stepping off the kerb. It was simple to see how Sawyer might have dropped it too. Manhandling the baby, the dummy gets dropped at some stage, kicked accidentally into the gutter, Sawyer never sees it and gets back into his car. In Ella's peripheral vision the black water loomed.

'Looks pretty new,' Dennis said.

Mooney nodded. 'If it's not from our kid, I doubt it's lain here more than a day or so.'

'Name on it?'

'Couldn't be so easy,' Mooney said.

'No chance I can show the mother, I assume?' Ella said.

Mooney shook his head. 'I want to get testing for DNA and prints.' He went to his car and dug through a box in the back. Coming up with a battered old Polaroid camera he took a quick snap. 'Show her this.'

'Anything in the car?' Dennis said.

The navy BMW's doors were open, the interior light on. Fingerprint dust coated most surfaces. Ella imagined how it was when the paramedics pulled up, with Sawyer slumped in his leather seat behind the wheel. She wondered what the dog walker might have seen if she'd come along a little earlier.

'Found this on the driver's floor.' Mooney held up another bag.

It was a slim one millilitre plastic syringe, the kind that came with an orange cap over the short needle, the kind Ella saw on streets and in houses all over the city. Hospitals, doctors' surgeries, diabetics and drug addicts all used them. Sawyer could have taken it from his own practice or got it when he bought the drugs.

'We'll print it and see what we get,' Mooney said. 'Also found some hairs in the carpet and on the seats; none that look juvenile though. Then there's this.' Mooney pointed to the rear bumper, where a dent held traces of white paint.

'Hel-lo,' said Dennis.

'There's no report of it having been in a bingle, but I'm leaning towards the white being automotive paint rather than any other kind. We'll have to wait for the lab results to be sure,' Mooney said.

Dennis squatted for a better look. 'Nice and fresh.'

'Anyway.' Mooney didn't go on. It was his way of ending a conversation.

'Okay,' Ella said. 'See ya.'

'Thanks,' Dennis added, standing up.

Ella slipped the photo of the dummy into her pocket as they headed back under the railway bridge. The boats churned the water. 'Think Sawyer'll stick with his story?'

Dennis started the car. 'It'll be interesting to see.'

1.10 am

Sophie crawled so slowly along the empty back streets of Surry Hills, the car threatened to stall. She slipped the clutch and shone the torch out the window, scanning dingy apartment block entryways and tiny junk-stacked terrace-house patios. A grey cat sprang away from the gutter, startling her. A wavery quarter-moon gave her little help.

She turned left through a stop sign at an empty intersection. Down the street an ambulance was parked next to a small playground. The ambulance's sidelights showed the paramedics crouched beside a man who lay propped up on his elbows on the grass, and Sophie recognised the male officer as Mick.

She stopped behind the ambulance and ran across the park. Mick and his fill-in partner, a paramedic named Keeley, were washing dirt from a wound in the patient's leg. The patient inhaled methoxyflurane deeply. When Sophie reached them he smiled at her. 'Hey babe.'

Mick looked up. 'Sophie?'

She burst into tears. 'They can't find Lachlan. I've been out driving the streets, I scared some poor man half to death, I can't think what else to do.'

Mick handed the saline bag to Keeley and walked a few metres with Sophie. 'Listen. I was just about to call the cops. That patient told me he came down here from his flat to sit on the swings and drink. He couldn't sleep because someone turned up tonight at his neighbour's flat with a baby who won't stop crying.'

Sophie grabbed his arm. 'Where's he live?'

'It might not be Lachlan.'

Sophie hurried to the patient. 'Where do you live?'

He grinned at her, happy as a clam on the methoxyflurane. 'Up there. Fourth floor.'

She followed his nod and saw a tall apartment block. 'Where's the crying baby?'

'Flat four-twelve.'

Sophie started across the street.

'Wait up,' Mick said. 'Let me call the cops.'

'Do what you like but I'm not waiting.'

Sophie heard him tell Keeley to radio for police, then he came running after her. He caught the door to the building. 'It'd be safer if we waited.'

Sophie didn't answer, saving her breath as she took the stairs two at a time. She heard Mick press the timed light switch and hurry after her.

The stairwell stank of urine, cooking oil and stale cigarette smoke. Empty beer cans stood in the corners of one landing. Canned laughter came from a flat on the second floor. The timer switch clicked off, plunging them into darkness, but Sophie kept going, her feet finding each step automatically.

'How are we going to do this?' Mick panted behind her.

'Tell them someone rang about a sick kid.'

'Me tell them?'

'I'm being a cop.'

'What?'

She felt primed and steely hard. Turning onto the landing on the third floor she checked the zip of the police jacket. She could hear the baby crying now and her scalp prickled. The child was going hoarse. Was it him? Was it Lachlan?

On the fourth floor landing Mick pressed the light switch and she saw that flat four-twelve was three doors along. She knocked on the door.

A man's voice answered. 'What?'

She gestured at Mick. 'Ambulance,' he said.

A muttered conversation was just audible over the baby's cries. 'We didn't call an ambulance.'

'We got a call about a sick child at this address,' Mick said.

'We didn't call.'

'Well, someone did, and once we're here we

have an obligation to make sure everything's okay.'

'Everything's fine.'

'We can hear the child crying,' Mick said. 'How about if we come in for just one minute to check him over? Then we'll be out of your way.'

Another muttered conversation. Mick made a face and pointed back down the stairs. Sophie ignored him.

The man said, 'We don't need any help and we want you to leave.'

Sophie stepped close. 'This is the police. Open the door.'

'Police?' the man said.

'Open the door now.'

There was a long moment and Sophie thought he was calling her bluff, then a security chain was slid back and the door opened. Light flooded the landing. Sophie saw a man dressed in black jeans and a T-shirt, his arms folded, and behind him a woman lying on a worn brown velour lounge with her arms around a screaming blanketed bundle.

'Let the paramedic check the child and we'll be on our way,' she said.

'Since when do cops and ambos get about together?' the man asked.

'We do sometimes.' She walked in first. Mick followed her. The woman on the lounge stared at them with resentment. She was in her mid-thirties, with tanned skin and straggly brown hair. The pale pink blanket she held was worn and pilled. The baby faced her so all Sophie could see was a tuft of dark hair. Sophie's heart was racing. 'It's your baby?'

'Whose else would it be?'

The child cried. Mick said, 'Just let me check him quickly then we'll go.'

Sophie stood over the woman, her hands clenched inside the jacket pockets, as Mick crouched and reached for the baby.

'It's a her,' the woman said. She turned the baby around and Sophie saw that it wasn't Lachlan. This baby had a squinched-up face, and was younger than Lachlan, probably by a couple of months, and there was a portwine birthmark on her chin.

Sophie glared around the flat while Mick ran through the motions of checking the baby's pulse and feeling her forehead for fever. Her anger at these people swelled in her throat. Their delay in opening the door had built her hopes up and now she'd crashed and burned. Who but people with something to hide would behave in such a way? There was a sleeping bag piled on one end of the lounge and clothes thrown on the back of it. The grimy bench between the tiny kitchen and this living area held an open packet of homebrand biscuits, the end of a loaf of bread, a full ashtray, a baby's bottle still one-third full of milk, and a pile of newspapers. No sign of any weapon or stolen goods, but Sophie was certain there'd be some somewhere. She glanced at the way the man shifted from foot to foot, and decided what she'd do.

'Happy now?' the woman said.

Mick smiled at her. 'You know how it is, we have to follow procedure or we get in trouble.'

'Thank you,' Sophie said, wanting instead to scream and punch someone.

They met three police officers on the stairs. Sophie said, 'It's not Lachlan, but there's definitely something odd going on.'

The police thanked them and moved faster up the steps.

On the street Mick said, 'You said that on purpose, so they'd go up and roust them.'

'Didn't you notice how reluctant they were to let us in?'

'It's after one in the morning,' Mick said. 'Someone comes knocking at my door when I haven't called for help, I'd be suspicious too.'

Sophie didn't care. All that mattered was finding Lachlan.

6

Dennis opened the door to the interview room and Ella went in first. Boyd Sawyer got quickly to his feet and shot his hand out, ready to shake theirs. He was gaunt, like a long-distance runner who trained too hard and too often. His palm was cold and clammy, his eyes red and his face lined. He wore dark pants and a grey shirt with the sleeves rolled up, and he smelled of sweat and spilled alcohol and somewhere in there Ella caught a hint of vomit and maybe even urine. She put her hand behind her back to wipe it on her trousers.

Dennis introduced them. Tears ran from Sawyer's eyes. 'Finally someone's taking me seriously.'

Dennis motioned for him to sit down. 'Mr Sawyer, we're sorry about your family.'

'Thank you.' Sawyer took a folded white handkerchief from his shirt pocket and carefully wiped his eyes. The skin around them looked red and chafed.

'We'll do this as quickly as we can then have someone take you home.' Dennis leaned forward and put his hand on the man's arm. 'You need to be with loved ones tonight, not sitting about here.'

Sawyer wiped his eyes again then put the

123

handkerchief down on his thigh, straightened his back and drew a deep breath, the very model of a man deciding to forge ahead as best he can. Ella narrowed her eyes.

'We heard just a little about what happened tonight,' Dennis said. 'Would you mind going through it again?'

'I was abducted and drugged,' Sawyer said. His speech was well mannered and his gaze direct. He looked like a person who had high expectations of the police.

'How did this come about?'

'My wife and daughter died two days ago, after my wife gave birth at home. The paramedics . . . well, I find it hard to be in the house since.'

'And tonight?' Ella said.

'Tonight I went out in the car, just to drive around. Get out of the house.'

'Where did you go?'

'I don't remember. I think I was at a pub or bar somewhere in the city, but that's all I can recall until I woke up in my car surrounded by paramedics. They told me they brought me round with naloxone, so I'd obviously been given some kind of narcotic. Later I vomited and it smelled strongly of alcohol. The doctor took bloods so no doubt those substances will show up, as will the sedative I suspect I was given.' He ticked these points off on his fingers.

'Why do you think you were sedated?'

'I would have resisted the abduction otherwise. Also, many sedatives have an amnesic effect, which explains why I can't remember anything.' He pulled his right sleeve up higher and held out his arm. 'I expect you'll need to take some pictures of the injection site they used.'

Ella saw a puncture mark and a bruise inside his elbow. 'Are you left or right handed, Doctor?'

'Left.'

He could have injected himself. Ella went on, 'Were you injured in any other way?'

He blinked. '*Apart* from the attempted murder with the drugs?'

'Was anything stolen? Your wallet? We know they didn't take your car.'

'No, nothing.' Sawyer looked puzzled. 'Surely that hardly matters, in this context?'

Dennis bumped Ella's knee with his own under the table.

'You don't recall meeting anyone while you were out?' Dennis said. 'No memory of a face, a name?'

Sawyer shut his eyes for a moment then shook his head. 'It's all blank.'

'Doctor, we checked your record before we came in here,' Ella said.

He looked at her for a long moment before picking up the handkerchief again. 'I knew that would come up.'

'It's just procedure,' Dennis soothed.

Sawyer pressed the folded cloth to his eyes. 'It's irrelevant.'

'I'm sure it is,' Dennis said. 'We need to clarify things, that's all.'

'It was a short-term thing and I've touched nothing since,' Sawyer wept. 'It was a mistake, I got caught, I was punished, and that's that.'

'It's okay,' Dennis said.

'Morphine and pethidine. Nineteen ninety-one, wasn't it?' Ella asked.

'Ninety-two,' Sawyer said.

Ella softened her voice. 'It makes sense to me, actually. I understand that you were having personal problems when you took the drugs before. The drugs stopped the pain. And tonight was the same. You were so full of rage, so angry that this woman who had a hand in the deaths of your wife and baby should still have her own family, that you were drawn back to the needle. You can buy the stuff in bars, everybody knows that, so you were there, buying the drugs and drinking, and with a bit of alcohol under your belt it suddenly seemed there were other things you could do. Before you knew it you were at the Phillipses' door.'

Sawyer looked up, teary-eyed and puzzled. 'Who?'

'Sophie Phillips is the paramedic who attended to your wife.'

'What's she got to do with anything?'

'Her husband was attacked tonight and their child kidnapped.'

Sawyer stared open-mouthed. 'You think I had something to do with that?'

'Did you?'

'Of course not.'

'You told her she killed your wife and daughter, and said you wanted to kill her.'

He shook his head. 'I was drunk and grief-stricken.'

'And tonight you weren't?'

His mouth was a thin white line. 'I came here to make a statement about a crime committed against me, not to be accused.'

'We understand,' Dennis said, 'and nobody's accusing you. Like I said before, it's procedure that we check into a person's background.' He reached to touch Sawyer's arm again. 'Do you remember driving to the wharf? Can you remember anything about the bar you think you were in?'

Sawyer dabbed the handkerchief to his eyes. 'Nothing.'

'Do you recall your car being hit by another?'

'My BMW's damaged?'

'It's quite minor but if we can find out when and where it happened, it may help us find the people who drugged you.'

'I would certainly remember that. If I hadn't been drugged, I mean.'

Ella folded her arms.

'Okay,' Dennis said. 'Well, I think we have enough to go on with at the moment. Come with me and I'll take a picture of your arm there, and a hair sample, too.'

'What for?'

'We found some hairs in your car. They might be from the people who drugged you but we need to exclude yours first,' Dennis said. 'We already have your prints on file, and are examining the car for any your assailants may have left.'

'Oh. Okay.'

'Then I'll find someone to give you a lift home.'

Sawyer followed Dennis into the corridor and Ella stayed back in the empty room. It had gone exactly as planned. Sawyer hadn't backed out, hadn't called his solicitor, and now they'd have his hair and his prints. If he left either in the Phillipses' house or on the note, they had him.

1.45 am

Sophie sat in the car with one hand on the steering wheel and the other over her face. It was cold and the night pressed in on her. She was hyperventilating but she couldn't stop. The tingling grew in her fingers and it was hard to swallow and the city was so huge, she could feel it stretching out around her, she felt tiny and ineffectual and so, so alone.

She was just off Cleveland Street. The traffic was busy even at this hour. The network of streets in her mind spread out like veins in a body and she could no longer decide which way to go.

She lowered her hand and looked out the windscreen. A car passed, slowly. Its brakelights came on and she hit the door lock with her elbow. When at work on these streets she felt safe, confident. Now there seemed nothing out there but threat.

The car moved off and she took her foot from her own brake. Nothing was gained by sitting here. She held the wheel in both trembling, tingling hands and turned towards Randwick.

She pulled into the driveway of the familiar

128

house. The building was in darkness. She almost tripped up the step, then knocked on the door. A light came on deep inside and she knocked again. There were footsteps, fast and anxious, then a light went on over her head. She looked at the peephole and heard a male voice say, 'It's Sophie.'

The door opened a moment later. Cynthia was on the stairs in a dressing-gown, looking alarmed. Her husband, Ray, stared out at Sophie. 'Are you okay?'

Sophie burst into tears.

Their kitchen was warm but Sophie still shivered. Cynthia sat rubbing Sophie's cold hands with her own warm ones while Ray made coffee and toast. Sophie told them what had happened and tears welled in Cynthia's eyes. She leaned forward and folded her arms around Sophie, who wept into her shoulder, glad of the comfort.

When she sat back Ray put a plate of toast before her then rested his broad hand on her shoulder in sympathy. Sophie moved the plate away a little. Coffee she could maybe manage. Toast, no way.

'Do you want us to drive you back to the hospital, to be with Chris?' Cynthia said.

Sophie shook her head. 'I can't stay in there, I need to be out looking.'

'But it's dangerous,' Cynthia said. 'It's a job the police can do best.'

'I can't just sit and wait.' Sophie raised the coffee cup to her lips then lowered it again. 'Doing nothing lets the thoughts flood in.'

'And you've seen too much already, haven't you,' Cynthia said softly.

Sophie remembered the time early in their friendship when Cynthia, a midwife, had had a problem with her pregnancy. She'd appeared at antenatal class, pale and shaken, determined as ever, but said to Sophie that at a time like this it might be better to know less rather than more. Sophie wondered whether the same applied now, whether her own experiences with bereaved mothers and dead children meant she could too easily picture herself in their situation. But the job gave her good and important things too: she knew the streets, she knew how things worked in the hospital, she wasn't scared by the tubes and machines that surrounded Chris.

What it didn't give her was knowledge about specific places to look for Lachlan.

Cynthia rubbed her shoulder. 'Would you like to stay here for the night?'

Or did it?

'Or if you want, if you give me a minute to get dressed, I'll come with you, stay with you there,' Cynthia said.

Sophie was already on her feet.

'Sophie?'

She had a plan. She couldn't carry it out until daylight but its mere existence made her feel that she had direction again. She would continue her crisscrossing of the suburbs until the morning and then the real search would begin. 'I have to go.'

'It's not safe,' Cynthia said. 'Ray.'

Ray put his hand on Sophie's arm. 'Soph,

sweetheart, you're not thinking straight. Let me drive you to the hospital, or stay here tonight and in the morning we'll help you do whatever you need to.'

Sophie twisted out of his grip. 'I have to go,' she said again, and headed for the door.

1.47 am

Ella came out of the tea room and almost walked into Acting Commissioner Rupert Eagers. 'Detective,' he said.

'Sir.'

Eagers was dressed in a navy suit, white shirt and tightly knotted light blue tie. Ella couldn't decide whether he was on his way home from some late-ending dinner or had dressed up to come in. He carried his dress uniform on a hanger, covered by a plastic bag.

He hooked the hanger over the top of the tea-room door. 'I'd like an update on the Phillips case.'

Ella explained the night's events and why they were looking at Sawyer. 'He's got no record of gun ownership however,' she said. 'That note doesn't exactly fit in with him either.'

Eagers nodded.

'It's been suggested that Chris Phillips may have been the caller to the media about the robbery gang being police officers,' she said. 'If it was him, the shooting and kidnap and note might have been to silence him. Though, of course, we haven't been told whether the caller

131

was for real or a hoax.'

Eagers rubbed the back of his neck. 'Did the wife have any ideas about it?'

'She said Chris had been distracted lately and upset about the bank guard's death. She couldn't say whether Chris actually knew anything.'

The Acting Commissioner studied her. Ella met his gaze straight on. His eyes were light brown, his hair a shade paler again, and the overall effect was one of sallowness. Then again, nobody looked their best at this time of day.

'The caller is real,' Eagers said. 'He phoned me before he rang the television stations. I advised him not to but he was determined.'

'So who is he?'

'He wouldn't give his name but he knew enough about the internal workings of the service to persuade me he is, or has been, a serving officer,' Eagers said. 'He was meant to call back but hasn't.'

Ella wasn't satisfied. Any ex-officer with a gripe against the service could've made up the story. With the books available and the information you could find on the Internet, practically anyone could learn how the job worked. Without a name to confirm the caller's identity, nothing was certain.

Eagers went on. 'What protection do you have on Phillips?'

'None.'

'You can't rule him out as the caller,' Eagers said. 'If he is, and if the gang members found out and set out to stop him, they might strike again once they learn he's still alive.' He cleared his throat. 'I'm sure I don't have to tell you what a precipice we're standing on here. The community will be looking to me — to us — to lead the department out of the mire of corruption and chaos Dudley-Pearson left behind. I want you to impress on your team the importance of being above reproach in every possible way. Everyone will be watching. If things go bad and that child turns up dead, I don't want people saying it's because of corruption or that we should have worked harder or we shouldn't have gone so softly on a witness.'

That child?

'This could be the big one for the service,' he went on. 'We play it right and we can shuck off some of the grime. Play it wrong and we not only look worse than ever, but I also have to explain to the government why we should keep our budget.'

And he wouldn't get the big chair. Ella kept quiet.

Eagers shot his cuffs and looked at his watch. 'Media Liaison are arranging a press conference here at six. I'd like both you and Detective Orchard to be present, and Mrs Phillips too.'

2.29 am

Sophie's mobile rang. She grabbed it up off the passenger seat. Detective Ella Marconi's number was on the screen and Sophie braked hard in the middle of the road. 'Did you find him?'

'I'm sorry, Sophie, not yet,' Ella said. 'Where are you?'

A truck blasted its horn as it went round her on the wrong side of the road. Sophie edged the car to the kerb. 'I'm in Waterloo.'

Ella had a brief muffled conversation with someone. 'There's an all-night cafe on Broadway, near Victoria Park; can you meet us there?'

The café was warm and well lit. Sophie ordered tea then asked the man behind the counter if she could sit outside. He took a table and chairs out for her. She sat with her back to the building and called the hospital on her mobile, but Chris's condition hadn't changed in the ten minutes since she'd last rung.

She wrapped her hands around the steaming cup and stared out at the street, thinking about her husband and son, her family. Last year they'd come to watch the lighting of the big Christmas tree in Martin Place. Chris had held sleepy Lachlan high against his shoulder and Sophie had slid her arms around them both, watching Lachlan's face as he stared open-mouthed at the coloured globes. Chris had taken his tiny hand into his big one and sung the Christmas carols softly to him, and Sophie had watched with tears in her eyes.

The streetlights blurred. So many times she'd looked after people who'd been through devastating situations, tried to help and comfort them. She knew now there was no comforting.

Ella and Dennis walked up. Ella pulled her coat around herself and sat down. 'How's Chris?'

Sophie's mouth was dry. 'Still unconscious.'

Ella nodded. 'I need you to look at something.' She placed a photo of an orange and blue dummy on the table in front of Sophie.

Sophie grabbed it. 'That's Lachlan's.'

'Did you ever scratch his name into it?' Dennis said. 'Or did it have any other identifying marks? A manufacturing defect, something like that?'

'No, nothing, but I swear this is his. Where did you find it?'

'How can you tell it's his?'

'Same brand, same colour, same pictures on it,' she said. 'And you must think it's his too or you wouldn't be showing me.'

Ella said, 'Our problem is that if there's no name or other mark on it to say it definitely does belong to Lachlan, maybe it really belongs to some other child.'

'So what are you telling me?' Sophie felt as though they'd given her hope and now were taking it away again. 'You never thought it was his? You just wanted to show me to test out some theory?'

'It's not like that,' Ella said.

'You could have asked me on the phone what his dummy looked like, you could have asked me that along with a whole lot of different things so I wouldn't have got my hopes up,' Sophie said. 'I could be out there looking instead of sitting here wasting time.'

'It's not wasting time,' Dennis said. 'Every little piece of information brings us closer to the answer.'

Sophie let the photo drop to the table. 'Lachlan has one the same as this, he sleeps with it. There's no name on it. Was there one in his cot, or anywhere in the house?'

Ella shook her head.

'Then the kidnapper took it with him.' Sophie tried to swallow back her nausea. 'Where did you find it?'

'Near Doctor Boyd Sawyer's car.'

'So you've found him? What did he say?'

'He said he's not involved.'

'Can he prove that?'

'We're looking into his alibi.'

Sophie ran her tongue along her dry lips. 'Where was his car?'

'Next to the Parramatta River at Meadow-bank.'

The river. Sophie shrank inside the police leather jacket.

'People are searching,' Ella said.

Sophie abruptly got up. 'I have to keep looking.'

Ella followed her along the street. 'You're out looking, on your own?'

Sophie unlocked her car and got in.

'Let me get an officer to go with you.'

'I'd rather be alone.'

'It'd be safer — '

'I'm fine.'

Ella put her hand on the car door. 'Sophie, there's a press conference at six at Gladesville Police Station. Do you think you can speak?'

Sophie started the car. 'I'll do whatever it takes.'

5 am

The Incident Room fell silent as Dennis walked in. 'Let's get started. Street canvass first.' He looked at Detective Eddington.

The young woman checked her notes. 'Nobody in Easton Street remembers seeing anything unusual. While Fergus Patrick next door to the Phillipses believes he heard the sound of a silenced gun going off, nobody else recalls any such sound. The family who live directly behind the Phillips house is overseas at the moment and it's possible the abductor accessed the Phillips yard through there, parking in that street. A search has turned up no physical evidence, however. One resident thinks she heard a car stop in the street near that house but didn't notice the time, or the time at which it left. That was it.'

'Nothing came up on Fergus Patrick himself, either,' McAlpine said. 'Solid work record, couple of honours, moved to be near family four years ago. Sees the Phillipses like family too, apparently. He's just brought in a new batch of posters.'

'Good,' Dennis said. 'How'd Crime Scene go?'

'They have prints and hairs and fibres from the house and will need samples from Chris and Sophie to match.'

Dennis nodded. 'Sugden, how'd you go with the phone?'

'Trace is set to go. No calls yet.'

'Kemsley, De Weese?'

'There are no recent complaints or threats

against Phillips, no suggestions of corruption. Two months ago he and Senior Constable Dean Rigby were assaulted by a suspect, Paul Houtkamp, after a chase in Surry Hills. Houtkamp is currently on bail. We found him at home and he said he was visiting a relative in a nursing home last night. The staff there confirm that,' De Weese said. 'Another man, Shane Brayfield, was paroled last week after eighteen months for various PCA and driving while disqualified offences. Phillips caught him three times. We're looking into Brayfield now.'

'Herbert, Kim?'

'There are two known sex offenders in the Gladesville area,' Kim said. 'One has a penchant for ten-year-old girls, the other for six- to eight-year-old boys. Both have alibis. One was at work as a cleaner and his supervisor confirmed they were together the entire night. The other was picked up early in the evening by officers in the Cross and was in custody at the time.'

Dennis looked at the line of detectives sitting with Lunney. 'How's that robbery angle look?'

Lunney sat forward. 'The strike force detectives we spoke to said that Chris Phillips's name hasn't come up in any of their investigations to date. A check of his rostered days off shows they coincide with all but the last of the five hold-ups, but with a few thousand officers in the city it'd be a fair bet that many would be in Chris's situation.'

Dennis nodded.

'On Tuesday the sixth, the day the calls were made to the TV stations, Phillips was off duty,' the young detective said. 'His wife was on day shift so he was caring for their baby. Checks of their home phone records showed he made a call at eight thirty-three to the recruitment section in HQ. Phillips left the house some time after that and drove to his mother Gloria's unit in Epping, arriving at about nine, and asked her to mind the baby. She said he seemed tired but otherwise normal. He told her he had to go into work but didn't say why, and said he'd be back in about an hour and a half. She took the child and he left.' The detective glanced along. 'Jen?'

Detective Eliopoulos took up the story. 'Phillips turned up at HQ at nine thirty-eight. Tracking him on the CCTV system we know he went through the lobby and to the lifts. Upstairs he went to the recruitment offices. There he met with Senior Constable Dean Rigby, who's worked in there since going off the road due to injury. Rigby has confirmed that Phillips called him earlier that morning. He said that they are friends and that Phillips was upset over the bank guard's death. They talked for about half an hour, then Phillips is seen on the CCTV crossing the lobby and leaving the building at ten-twelve. He got back to his mother's place at half-past midday.' The detective looked around the table. 'We don't know where he was for those two hours and twenty minutes but that period covers the time at which the calls to the TV stations were made.'

'Tomorrow we'll start the process of getting the phone records of the TV stations,' Dennis said. 'Any joy about the one in hospital? Roth?'

'Senior Constable Peter Roth,' Detective Bill Simpson said. 'The bullet entered his left hip and he has a fractured pelvis and intestinal injuries. He's on painkillers — not enough to affect his thinking, his doctor said, but he keeps saying to the strike force guys that he's in too much pain to talk. He's been told about Chris and the baby and he showed no reaction, except to deny knowing either Chris or Sophie. But he and Chris did a course together two years ago.' Simpson passed around a photo which showed a class of police, twenty strong, half of them sitting neatly along a bench with their fists on their knees, and the other half standing at attention behind them. Ella recognised Chris's dark eyes and broad smile from the photos she'd seen in his house. Someone had scratched an arrow in biro over the head of the person sitting next to him, a slim-faced man with a clipped moustache and a sharp nose and chin. He stared directly into the camera and his smile was bold.

'If Phillips was a member of the gang,' De Weese said, 'and he'd decided to quit, it'd make sense that he wasn't in the last robbery.'

'Or maybe there were more than four in the gang and they took turns on the jobs,' Herbert said. 'Chris couldn't go on the last one because he was working.'

'Did you talk to Roth yourselves?' Dennis asked Simpson.

'No, the Strike Force detectives did.'

'Ella and I will visit him later today.' Dennis gestured for the photo. 'Onto the baby.'

'I'll start,' Laurel Macy said. 'Dan and I began

140

with the bigger hospitals in the city and already have two leads to follow up. First one: four months ago, staff at St James Private in Rozelle caught a woman in her early forties attempting to make off with a newborn girl from the nursery. When spotted, she put the baby down and ran for it, so we don't know any of her details. The incident wasn't reported — something they won't fail to do next time, believe me — but they say they've tightened security considerably. The staff who got the best look at the woman are starting work in a couple of hours and we're going back to see them then.'

'The second one's a stillborn baby,' Detective Daniel Farly said. 'He was the first child of a young couple and was born in Prince of Wales Hospital six weeks ago. The mother checked out against medical advice the day after the birth, and calls made by the hospital's social workers have not been returned. Apparently there was concern because the woman had had some bleeding and might be in need of care. The nurse we spoke to made a point of saying it was peculiar that the couple had behaved this way, when the husband should've known better, being a paramedic.'

'Patient confidentiality became a problem at this point,' Laurel said. 'We whipped out the picture of Lachlan and talked at length about his poor parents, but they wouldn't come across with any details. The hospital CEO starts work at eight, so we'll go back then.'

'Nice work,' Ella said. 'Sandy?'

Sandy Kameyama folded her hands. 'Steve

and I have handed out the baby's picture and talked to people in service stations, train and bus stations, taxi stands and every shop we could find open, heading east and south from the Phillips house. Nobody saw anything odd so we collected no CCTV footage.'

Ella nodded. 'Clinton and Travis?'

'We've done the same, heading west and north,' Travis Henry said. 'Nothing to report so far.'

Ella nodded.

'About Doctor Boyd Sawyer,' Dennis said. 'He says he was drugged and abducted over the hours in question. We'll check his prints and hair against the samples from the Phillips house, and also for anything on the note that was left there. A baby's dummy was found near his car, which Mrs Phillips says is the same kind and colour as Lachlan's. There is white paint and a dent on his bumper, so there's a chance he's had an accident, but so far we've found no reports of one. If we can find it, of course, it'll help determine where his car's been. We don't have sufficient evidence to arrest him, or even get a warrant to search his house, but Miller and Lee are surveilling him now. Hopefully in time something more will come up.' Dennis checked his watch. 'Okay. Any questions?'

'Has Phillips woken up at all?'

'The doctors have him sedated but we're hopeful that will be turned off later today,' Ella said. 'In case he is a target for the gang, we've posted a guard on him.'

'Mrs Phillips has had no more insight?'

Dennis shook his head. 'Anything else?' There was nothing. He ran through the team, moving some people from the almost-finished street canvass around the Phillips house to the teams checking the shops and places that had been open overnight. Others were to look into the rest of the hospitals. 'We'll meet back here at eleven. Call in with any news. Pick up some of the new flyers on your way out. Good luck.'

Within minutes Ella was looking at an empty room.

'We've got that press conference in ten minutes,' Dennis said to her. 'Then how about we go and see Roth?'

'Oh yeah,' she said. 'Doesn't know Chris, my foot.'

7

Thursday 8 May, 6.41 am

Sophie arrived at the hospital after the press conference to find Chris's sedation turned off. The head CT they'd done that morning had showed that there was no further swelling and the contusion on his frontal lobes hadn't increased. The next hour was the test, as his body metabolised the drugs. He should then start to come round, but nobody could say if he would wake up alert, or if he might be confused — perhaps permanently — or even that he would wake at all.

She sat on the edge of her chair, staring at his face. The tube was out of his airway and he was breathing on his own. She squeezed his hand and willed him to open his eyes.

Gloria had gone home for a shower and to feed her beloved cats. Down the corridor a plainclothes cop was drinking coffee and eating chocolate croissants with the nurses. Without explaining why, Ella had said his presence was necessary. The questions posed in the press conference had left Sophie in little doubt. She rubbed the back of her neck where tension and anger had turned her muscles into hard knots. How dare they suggest such things!

She leaned close to Chris. Hearing was the first sense to return; even with no other sign that

144

Chris was aware, he might be listening. 'Chris, honey, it's me. I know you can't move or speak. That's okay. You probably feel confused too. You don't know where you are and why.'

She took a deep breath.

'Something bad's happened, honey. Someone came to the door and shot you and took Lachlan. You're going to be fine, even though you probably hurt like hell. But I need you to remember what happened so we can find our boy.' She kissed his cheek. 'Some people are saying it happened because of the robbery gang, you were part of it somehow, but I know that you weren't. You are a good man and a good cop, Chris. I trust you and I believe in you.' She laid her cheek to his. 'I know you can hear me and you're fighting your way up. The drugs are wearing off and you can feel more of your body, you feel the pain, you feel you're lying in a bed, you can hear me talking. Open your eyes, Chris. I'm right here. Look at me.'

He didn't move. His breathing stayed at the same regular pace.

She straightened the fingers of his limp hand, then rolled them into a fist. 'They had a press conference this morning. There were cops everywhere, they all send you their best.' She thought about their hugs and quiet words. Hugh Green had been there, tears in his eyes. She'd given the jacket back but she missed it now. 'I talked to the cameras about Lachlan, how much we love and miss him. They were lined up in front of me like . . . ' They were like a firing squad but she didn't want to mention guns now. 'Like a row of big round eyes. I thought, the person who has Lachlan might be watching. If I can make them see how much we hurt, then maybe they will realise that it's time for Lachlan to come home.' She flexed his thumb. 'It's funny though, I don't really remember what I said. The whole room was quiet, I remember that, and I could hear how powerful my voice was. I'd thought I'd be all quavery and nervous but I wasn't at all. I talked, I don't know how long for, but at the end I saw this man in the crowd, holding a microphone, and there were tears in his eyes.' She paused, remembering. 'I thought, good, that's what we need people to feel. Someone who feels that way will call the cops when they hear a baby crying in their neighbour's place where there's never been a baby before. They'll remember Lachlan's big brown eyes from the photo that was shown, and they'll spot him in a stroller in a supermarket or somewhere and they'll find a phone and before we know it he'll be home.'

She pressed her forehead to the back of Chris's wrist. He smelled of iodine. The tiny hairs on his arm moved to her blinking. 'Come on,' she whispered, squeezing his hand gently, trying not to show him how desperate she was. 'Wake up and tell me what you know.'

Chris didn't move.

7.00 am

On the drive to St Vincent's, Dennis said to Ella, 'I might leave you alone in there with Roth for a while.' He glanced over at her. 'He fancies himself a ladies' man, apparently. You never know, he might feel inclined to unburden himself to you.'

Fat chance. In Ella's experience, even guys who thought of themselves that way had certain criteria, usually to do with looks and age. She doubted the appearance by his hospital bed of a stocky early-forties woman with dark messy hair was going to inflame Roth's desires one little bit.

The ward was busy with staff. Dennis went through them waving his badge but nobody took any notice. Roth was in a single room tucked away in a corner of a corridor and Dennis knocked once then opened the door without waiting for a reply.

Roth was half sitting against a stack of pillows. His face was pale and skinnier than in the photo. He needed a shave and there was a smell in the room that reminded Ella of her grandfather's room when he was losing his battle with cancer. The smell of a sickbed lain in around the clock.

Roth folded his arms. 'If it's visiting hours already my watch is wrong and someone forgot to bring my breakfast.' He wore green striped hospital pyjamas with the thin cotton sleeve pulled up on his left arm to leave an IV site exposed. A clear tube snaked from his arm up to a pump and above it to a bag of clear fluid with

147

a bright orange sticker plastered on it. Ella could make out the words '*antibiotic added*'.

Dennis stood at the foot of the bed, his own arms folded. 'We need information.'

'No 'hello', no 'how you going'? Bit rude, don't you think?'

Dennis shifted his weight so that his knee bumped the bed. Roth grimaced. Dennis said, 'You think baby Lachlan has time for pleasant-ries?'

Roth sniffed and looked towards the small window. Ella looked too. She saw the edge of the White City tennis complex. Further away, over the suburbs of Bellevue Hill and Bondi, a grey smudge hung motionless.

'So early and the smog's there already,' Roth said.

This time Dennis kicked the bed. 'You said you didn't know Chris Phillips.'

'I don't.'

Dennis tossed the class photograph on the bed. 'Yet here you are, side by side.'

Roth picked it up. 'Oh, him.'

Dennis rolled his eyes at Ella. 'Lo, his memory returns.'

'Just because they sat us like that in the picture doesn't mean we were mates,' Roth said. 'Do you know the names of everyone in all your courses?'

'What can you remember about him?'

'Nothing.' Roth dropped the picture. 'I recognise his face now, and I can match his name to it, but that's it. I don't know if he came out drinking with us every night, what station he was from, even whether we ever spoke.'

Dennis put the class photograph back in his coat pocket, then tossed the photo of Lachlan on the blanket. 'Here's his son, the one who's missing.'

'Yeah, they look the same around the eyes,' Roth said.

'What do you know about his abduction?'

'Nothing. I told them that last night.'

Dennis threw up his hands. 'I'm going for coffee.'

'Bring me back one,' Roth called as Dennis went out the door. He smiled at Ella. 'You know I don't buy this.'

'Buy what?' she said.

He didn't answer.

There was a low vinyl chair against the wall opposite the window. Ella found it much less comfortable than it looked. She leaned back and pretended to be lost in thought, her elbow on the arm, her chin in her hand. Roth plumped up his pillows and closed his eyes.

There was the frequent sound of footsteps and voices in the corridor outside but nobody came in. Ella wondered how long Dennis would stay away. If he came back soon they could admit this was a waste of time and do something useful.

Then Roth spoke. 'You have no idea how high this goes.'

She turned her head, still in her hand. 'Really.'

'Those strike force Ds come around all the time, asking who else is in the gang, saying if I don't give them names I'm looking at life inside. They don't seem to realise there are worse things.'

'Like having your kid nicked?'

'Or disappearing yourself.' Roth shifted position in the bed with a grimace.

'Is that what you think will happen to you?'

Roth's eyes searched her face. She was used to this kind of examination: police got it all the time from dirtbags who thought they could get one over on you once they found your weak spot. She was good at the blank face, the bored little lift of an eyebrow, the reflection of the gaze right back at them.

'You love your job,' he said. 'I used to, too.'

Love? Hmm.

He closed his eyes and opened them again. 'I used to think I could save people. I thought that was our goal, more than catching the bad guys even. Conviction, no conviction, what did it matter as long as the innocent in the middle was safe?'

The room suddenly felt hot.

'But then you realise that most people in the job feel differently. The bosses particularly. Sometimes they're fixed on juggling the numbers so the government's happy at the end of the year and hands over more money so they can buy a new car. Sometimes they just want good press, good image.' He raised his eyebrows. 'Makes it hard, doesn't it?'

Ella managed a shrug.

'Anyway, I think it's good you still believe that even the worst things can be made right. I hope you can keep believing it when the truth comes out about all of this and you see how far the corruption has spread.'

'And how far is that?'

'How far have you got?' Roth looked at her in a measuring way, then Dennis came in, slopping coffee from a takeaway cup onto the brown linoleum. Ella could have strangled him.

'Great,' Roth said. 'Here I am, throat dry as a dead dingo's donger after telling your little mate here everything, and you forget my coffee.'

Dennis turned to Ella. 'Did he — ?'

'Of course not.'

Dennis glared at Roth. 'You understand that you can be made to talk. You can be locked up. Your pension, all your benefits can be taken away.'

'Like I haven't already heard that from the strike force,' he said. 'Why threaten me with that when I have nothing to tell you?'

'You're not still claiming to have been shot in a street mugging?'

'Do you have any evidence to the contrary? Any witnesses? Any CCTV film?'

Dennis pointed at the photo of Lachlan. 'All we want is the baby.'

'Well, I can't be one hundred per cent sure, because I can't get out of bed to look underneath it, but I don't think he's in here with me.'

Dennis's face went pinched and white around the temples. 'When that bullet they picked out of your butt is found to match the bank guard's gun, we'll be back.'

'Why don't you get out there and look for the baby instead of harassing innocent and injured people like me?' Roth picked up the remote and turned the TV on.

Dennis reached out and turned it off. The white spots on his face were spreading. Ella checked behind her to make sure the door was shut. Dennis leaned over Roth, the cup of coffee trembling in his hand. 'You make me ashamed of the job.'

Before Roth could answer Dennis stormed from the room. Ella followed. The door swung shut with a bang behind them.

'He knows more than he's letting on.' Dennis glared out the corridor window. 'I'd just hoped that because he's a cop, even a rotten one, and because Chris is a cop too . . . ' He took a gulp of coffee and grimaced. 'I hoped that the good guy in him would come through.'

Ella realised she'd forgotten the photo of Lachlan. 'I'll just be a minute.' She left Dennis frowning down at the bustle of Victoria Street and walked back up the corridor.

She didn't knock and Roth didn't appear to hear her come in. He was staring blankly out the window. Lachlan's picture was in a different position on the bed, as if he'd been looking at it then put it down again. The expression on his face was one that Ella had trouble labelling: a combination of anxiety, fear, worry and some-thing else. Terror?

She backed out of the door and closed it quietly behind her.

Dennis was waiting by the lift. 'Did you get it?'

She shook her head. 'Maybe it'll work on him.' The lift doors opened and they got on board.

'He definitely knows something.'

They were getting in the car when Ella's mobile rang. 'Marconi.'

'It's Clinton. We've got something.'

Ella fumbled for her notebook. 'Go.'

'The checkout chick in the Ampol on Epping Road said a woman in her fifties came in early this morning and bought nappies. She came back about ten minutes later, saying the nappies were the wrong size and could she swap them.' His voice rose with excitement and Ella had to move the phone away from her ear. 'We watched the CCTV tape and you see the woman's face pretty clearly. Plus she's driving a light-coloured VK Holden Commodore and we've got a partial on the numberplate. It ends in 487. Travis is still on the system checking for cars but we've got a possible hit: one's registered to a fifty-six year old woman named Sylvia Morris. She's got previous convictions for assault and resisting arrest when police and DOCS workers took her kids into care, and she lives on Herring Road, close to both the servo and the Phillips house.'

Ella covered the mouthpiece and briefed Dennis. He started the car and pulled into the traffic.

To Clinton she said, 'Get a couple of uniforms. Watch the place but stay out of sight until we get there.'

'Will do.'

Dennis hit the lights and sirens and they accelerated through the city, Ella's pulse rising even faster than their speed.

Lachlan had been missing for ten hours.

Sophie stood on the kerb in Royal North Shore's ambulance bay and looked out across the green lawn towards the Pacific Highway, measuring out the time. Two feeds. Three, maybe four nappies. Seven hours of sleep, and the nice half-hour in the morning when Chris would bring Lachlan into their bed. They'd smile over his head as he rediscovered his toes. Then he'd have playtime after breakfast when he'd pull everything out of the toy box before deciding the squeaky book was still his favourite.

Sophie's chest hurt. If whoever had him didn't change his nappy as soon as it was wet, he'd get nappy rash. And they wouldn't know how much zinc cream to put on, or that after he was dressed again he'd expect a game of peek-a-boo before being lifted off the change table. He'd be scared and confused. He'd be screaming for her.

She only dared to think of him being inadequately cared for like this, keeping a tight hold on her imagination to stop it wandering into the realms of actual harm. That was straying too close to losing control. If she slipped into that territory she'd be no help to him at all.

She closed her eyes. She'd always thought that if anything happened to him she'd drop dead on the spot. It was incredible that she was still standing, still breathing.

154

And it was still too early to start on her plan. She checked her watch again. It felt as though time had stopped.

At the sound of an engine she looked around. An ambulance pulled into the bay and she stepped out of its path. Both paramedics were in the front, which meant there was no patient on board. Sophie knew Stuart, behind the wheel, and was good friends with Yuri. He opened the passenger door and was out on the asphalt before Stuart turned off the engine.

'Has there been any news?' Yuri said. 'Did the cops charge the smackie doctor?'

Sophie shook her head. 'He says he didn't do it.'

'You know we were the ones who treated him?' Yuri said. 'He acted all confused and said he hadn't taken anything. Just like any other heroin overdose.'

Stuart said, 'There's a used syringe on the car floor, the guy's pupils are pinned, he's got the trackmark from hell in his antecubital fossa, and he's up like a rocket from a shot of Narcan. Yeah — he took nothing and I'm the Pope.'

Sophie was sweating. 'Did you see any signs Lachlan might have been in the car?'

'No, nothing. We only found out about what happened later when one of the cops at the hospital told us why they were looking for him.'

Sophie tried to think. 'But he'd definitely taken a narcotic.'

'Everything pointed to it,' Stuart said. 'He'd been drinking too. He puked it up all the way to Ryde Hospital.'

155

Sophie didn't know any of the staff at Ryde, certainly not well enough to ask the rule-breaking favour of looking up Sawyer's blood results.

'How's Chris?' Yuri said.

Sophie shrugged and scratched her head, lowering her face. Funny how you could hold things together until a simple concerned look from a friend did you in.

'C'mere.' Yuri folded her in his arms.

He smelled of sweat and takeaway food: the perfume of a long night shift. Sophie remembered when her biggest problems were dealing with drunks and psych patients and the exhaustion of a fourteen-hour night shift plus overtime. If she could go back to that, she'd be the best wife and mother, the best paramedic. She'd never complain about a boring routine transfer or an argumentative drunk or a hypochondriac bullshit call again. She'd never again wish Lachlan would stop crying when she needed to sleep. The sound would be music. She'd never again think Chris should stop worrying so much about the standing of the police service — that was him, and he was wonderful. She'd never so much as look at another man. She would never take her family for granted, not for one single second.

She clung to Yuri.

'It'll be okay,' he said.

Her mind strained at its leash. *What if it isn't?*

The Emergency Department doors slid open and someone said, 'Sophie?'

It was Angus. For the first time since The Big

Mistake she didn't feel guilt on seeing him, as if losing Lachlan pushed everything else into insignificance.

'Chris is waking up.'

8

Chris struggled out of unconsciousness as though it was a swamp unwilling to let him go. First he heard people talking around him, then he managed a moan, then he gathered the power to move his arms and legs millilitres at a time. His head throbbed. His eyes seemed glued shut. He couldn't breathe through his nose and his throat was sore. And all the time something black and nasty pulsed in his veins, something that could surely not be true.

He forced his swollen eyes open. Sophie's tear-streaked face came into focus. The black thing in his veins flooded his heart at the sight. 'He's gone, isn't he?' he croaked.

Sophie burst into sobs and sagged onto his chest. Chris struggled to slide his arm around her back. She was alive, that was one good thing, and he swore to himself he would keep it that way. He held her close, feeling her body heave.

But Lachlan was gone and that was all wrong. Chris knew that he was the one who should be dead and Lachlan should be safe at home with Sophie. Lachlan hadn't done anything. Lachlan wasn't the one who should be paying.

Sophie said through her tears, 'Can you remember anything?'

Chris turned his pounding head. The room

was full of people and they were all looking at him. Gloria wiped her eyes; beside her Angus Arendson wore civvies and an anxious look, and doctors and nurses checked equipment or just watched.

He raised a shaky hand to the aching wound on the bridge of his nose. 'I opened the front door and saw a man in a black balaclava.'

Sophie caught her breath.

'He had a handgun. It had a silencer on it.' He saw again the mouth of the barrel. 'That's all I remember.'

'Nothing else?'

He hesitated. What should he say? What was right? More importantly, what was best?

8.12 am

Sylvia Morris's house was a sprawling, shabby, lowset brick place on Herring Road in North Ryde. Clinton pulled up in front of it and Dennis parked behind him. Ella scanned the low fence, the patchy lawn, the struggling garden. There was no sign of movement. In contrast, the neighbours' curtains were already twitching.

They met at the foot of Morris's driveway. With Clinton and Travis were two uniformed officers. Ella felt for her gun in its holster. Dennis said, 'Everyone ready?'

They nodded.

'Okay.'

The uniforms headed around the rear of the house with Clinton. She and Dennis and Travis walked steadily to the front door. There were three cracked concrete steps up to a patio coated in worn pebblecrete. A dead plant in a faded green plastic pot stood forlornly in a corner. A screen door had hung in the doorway once but only the broken hinges were left now. The door itself looked flimsy and the blue paint was split and peeling. There was no peephole. Ella unclipped her holster. Travis was breathing quickly behind her. Dennis edged up to the curtained window.

She banged her fist on the door. 'Police! Open up!'

Silence.

She banged again, harder. 'Sylvia Morris, this is the police! Open the door!'

There was a shuffling sound. Ella tried to envisage what was happening in the house. Behind her Travis bounced on his toes. 'Want me to kick it?' he whispered. She held up a hand.

There was the click of a turning lock and the door opened as far as the security chain would allow. A short woman with eyes hooded like a lizard's peered out. 'It's a bit early.'

'Are you Sylvia Morris?'

'Yeah.'

'Detectives Marconi, Orchard and Henry.' Ella gave a cursory flip of her badge wallet.

Sylvia Morris closed the door and slid the security chain free. The door swung open unassisted. She stood with her arms folded, her face blank. She wore navy tracksuit pants covered in grey pilling, and a worn white top advertising the 2000 Olympics. The word

'*Sydney*' was printed in faded multicolour across her chest. She looked tired, resentful, and older than fifty-six.

'You were at the Ampol service station on Epping Road last night,' Ella said.

'Was I?'

'You're on the closed circuit TV footage.'

Morris rubbed the top of her bare right foot with the heel of her left.

'You bought nappies then took them back and swapped them for another size.' Ella could feel Travis leaning close behind her, feel his desire to get into the situation. She nudged him back with her elbow. 'Who were you buying nappies for?'

Morris glanced over her shoulder into the living room. Following her gaze Ella saw a neat room. There was a single recliner chair upholstered in once-white vinyl, and beside it an upturned milk crate with a tea towel over it held the television remote control and a folded *TV Week*. In what she could see of the kitchen the benches were clean and bare. Against one wall of the hall stood a bookcase containing six ragged Mills and Boons in a neat row. There were no kids' toys to be seen. No sign that anyone else ever came here. One chair: Ella guessed Morris didn't often entertain friends. But why had she looked back?

'Is there anyone else here?' Ella said.

Morris cleared her throat but didn't speak. Just then there was a burst of talk from the side of the house, and Clinton came running round to the front door. 'There's a baby in the back room.'

'Is it your baby?' Ella asked Morris.

Morris didn't answer. For Ella that was reason enough to go in. Travis stepped on her heel as they crossed the threshold. Dennis veered off into the living room with Clinton and the uniforms. 'Check the place over, make sure there's nobody hiding anywhere.'

The hallway was dim. The floorboards creaked. Overhead an uncovered bulb hung on a cord; Ella heard Travis flick the switch but the light didn't come on.

The first room was on the left. There was a fist-sized hole in the outer layer of the door. Ella opened the door cautiously and saw a single bedstead with rumpled purple sheets and a grubby quilt. Travis crouched to look under the bed.

The next door was open and revealed a small bathroom with blue tiles on the floor and a cracked shower screen.

The final door was closed. A sticker on it declared that someone had a great time at the Royal Easter Show of 1979. The knob was white china decorated with painted flowers. Ella turned it and looked in.

The room was small and empty except for a bare single bed mattress on the floor. On the stained surface lay a baby. It was swaddled in a beach towel and lay face down, its head turned away from Ella. Its hair was dark.

Ella held her breath as she crouched by the mattress.

'Is it him?' Travis said. 'Is he alive?'

Ella picked the child up. It was warm and

moved in her grasp. The enormity of her relief made her want to sob out loud. She brought it close to her body and as she and the baby came face to face it opened its eyes. They were blue.

'It's not him.'

'You sure?' Travis came closer. 'Don't all babies look the same?'

'Lachlan's eyes are brown.'

'Maybe they put contacts in to make him look different.'

'Baby contacts?' The child started to whimper. Ella laid it down on the mattress and unwrapped the beach towel. The baby was wearing only a nappy. It kicked its legs and cried. Ella undid the tabs on the nappy. 'It's a girl.'

'It's not hers, though, is it?' Travis said as Ella rewrapped the baby in the towel. 'A fifty-six year old woman having a baby would've been all over the news.'

In the living room Morris sat in the recliner, her feet together on the thin grey carpet, her hands grasping the chair's arms. Dennis stood beside her, his arms folded. Clinton and the other uniform were in the kitchen.

Clinton held up a plastic pack of nappies and a receipt.

Ella said, 'It's not Lachlan.'

She stood before Morris with the baby snuffling in her ear. 'You want to tell me whose baby this is?'

Morris picked at a hole in the vinyl.

Ella felt rage building inside her. 'We're looking for a kidnapped child.' Her words were clipped and hard. 'The longer we spend dealing with you, the less time we have to do that.'

Dennis's phone rang and he walked outside to answer.

Morris pulled foam from the hole in the chair, studied it intently for a moment then pushed it back in. Ella fought an urge to kick her in the shin. 'The station then.'

Morris got up without a word.

Ella cradled the baby close, feeling the soft hair brushing against her cheek as the child wriggled. She nodded to a uniformed officer. 'First call the station and get a detective who's not on the team sent over. Get an ambulance round here. Go with them to the hospital and have them check this baby out. Call DOCS too. They can meet you at the hospital.' She handed the baby over and walked outside.

Travis followed her onto the patio. 'Can't we stay with it?'

'Our job is Lachlan.'

'But what if the cases are somehow linked? What if this is, like, a baby black market, and that's why she's not talking?'

'Doubtful. She's probably helping a friend hide from DOCS.' Ella went down the steps to where Dennis stood on the lawn, putting away his phone.

He gave her a thumbs-up. 'Chris is awake and remembers the attack.'

Sophie sat on the side of the hospital bed, her fingers interlaced with Chris's. Her need for contact with him was like a thirst. She could feel it low in her throat. She wished the detectives would get their questions over with so she could climb onto the bed properly and wrap her arms around him.

'Did you notice what colour eyes and skin the man had?' Ella said.

'Don't remember the eyes,' Chris said. 'He was Caucasian.'

Ella scribbled notes. 'Height, weight?'

'About my height,' Chris said. 'A metre eighty. Average build, I guess.'

'Clothing?'

'Something dark, but all I can really remember is the balaclava.'

Dennis said, 'He was alone, is that right?'

'I didn't see anyone else.'

Sophie watched Gloria pace beyond the closed door of the hospital room. Angus had left. Passing nurses glanced through the window.

'Notice any vehicles? Hear anything strange before he knocked on the door?' Ella looked up. 'He did knock, didn't he?'

'I saw no vehicles, I heard nothing unusual at all. I was about to go up to bed. The knock came and I didn't look through the peephole, I just opened the door and there he was. He didn't say anything, just raised the gun.'

Dennis leaned forward in his chair, his elbows on his knees. 'His eyes weren't familiar in any way?'

165

'No.'

'Have you received any threats recently?'

'No.'

Sophie moved closer to Chris so their hips touched.

'Do you remember Shane Brayfield?'

'The drink-driver?'

Dennis nodded. 'He's recently been released. He never made contact?'

'No, and I'd recognise his eyes. This wasn't him.'

'What about Paul Houtkamp? He assaulted you and Senior Constable Dean Rigby a couple of months back.'

'It wasn't him either.'

'Do you have any idea who might be behind this?'

'No, I don't,' Chris said. 'Don't you think I'd tell you that straightaway? Jesus. This person has my son.'

Dennis pulled a copy of the note from his pocket. 'This was found on you.'

Sophie saw Chris turn pale as he read it.

'Any clue what it's about?' Dennis said.

Chris shook his head. 'None whatsoever.'

Sophie tightened her grip on his hand. So much had depended on him remembering what had happened, but now it was turning out to be next to useless anyway. What had they learned? A white man in a balaclava? How the hell did they find him?

Chris looked up at her with tears in his eyes. 'I'm so sorry.'

She tilted her head to his. Having him awake and knowing he wasn't brain-damaged was not only a relief, it meant she could focus more strongly on finding Lachlan.

Ella said, 'Chris, did you call the TV stations to report that the robbery gang is made up of police officers?'

He faced her. 'I did not.'

'Do you know anything at all about the gang?' Ella said.

'I've seen their handiwork but I don't know who they are.'

'Do you remember going to see Dean Rigby on the morning of Tuesday the sixth? The day after the latest bank robbery?'

'I was upset about it. I went to talk to him.'

Sophie squeezed his hand. He squeezed hers in return.

Ella went on. 'Rigby said that you left shortly after ten, but you didn't arrive back at your mother's until half past twelve.'

'That's right.'

'It was during that time that the phone calls were made to the TV stations,' Dennis said. 'Where were you for those two hours and twenty minutes?'

'I drove to Mrs Macquarie's Point and went for a walk. The pay and display parking ticket is probably still somewhere in the car.'

'You walked for all that time?'

'I sat looking at the water,' he said. 'Thinking about the guard.'

Sophie remembered how she'd feared he was planning to leave her.

'But it wasn't you who rang the TV stations,' Dennis said.

167

'No, it was not.'

Ella cleared her throat. 'I'm sorry that I have to ask this, but have you ever had an affair?'

Sophie tried to think how a guilt-free wife would react on hearing her husband asked such a thing. She was aware of the heat at the contact point between her body and Chris's and wondered if he would notice a surge.

'You think some jilted girlfriend stole our son?' Chris responded.

'You know how this works,' Ella said. 'We have to ask.'

'No,' he said. 'No affairs.'

Ella handed him a business card. 'If you remember anything else, please call us.'

'Of course.'

'We're doing everything we can to find Lachlan.'

'I know,' Chris said. 'Thank you.'

Sophie followed them to the door and closed it behind them before Gloria could come in. She put her back to the door and looked at Chris. He hung his head. 'I'm so sorry.'

'It's not your fault.' She climbed on the bed next to him and they hugged.

9.45 am

Sophie left the hospital when a police officer brought a message from Ella saying that Crime Scene was finished in their house and she could go back in. She needed to look and smell clean and tidy if her plan was going to work. Her

168

crumpled uniform from last night was not going to cut it.

Angus was coming out of the coffee shop in the hospital foyer as she walked through. Again she felt no guilt, rather a kind of comfort at seeing a friendly and familiar face.

He fell into step beside her. 'How's Chris?'

'He's awake and told the detectives what he remembers, but none of it's much use.' She could smell coffee on his breath. They emerged from the building into the morning's bright sunlight. The glare hurt her eyes and her head.

'Did the detectives say they had any leads?'

Sophie shaded her eyes, looking for her car. 'They talked to a doctor who blames me for his wife and baby dying in a case I did a couple of days ago. He was found last night overdosed in his car at the Meadowbank Wharf, but he says he had nothing to do with this.'

'That doesn't sound good.'

'And they were just asking Chris about cases he'd done, and whether he'd rung the TV stations about the gang of bank robbers.'

Angus nodded. 'They'll look into every possibility, however remote, but that doctor has to be number one on their list of suspects.' He walked with her to her car. 'Can I help in any way?'

'You can drive around looking. That's what I do.' She put the key in the ignition and turned it. Nothing happened. She tried again. 'Shit.'

'Pop the bonnet.'

She did so then got out and went to the front of the car. Angus checked the oil and water and wiggled the spark-plug leads. 'That's about all I know, I'm afraid.'

Sophie rubbed her forehead with the heels of both hands. She couldn't stand the thought of waiting for road service. In that space of time she could get home, get clean and be back out on the streets to start her plan.

Angus said, 'I can give you a lift, if you need one.'

*　*　*

She sat self-consciously in his white Magna, remembering how they'd clambered into the back seat with the breathless impatience of sixteen year olds. She wondered if Angus thought of it every time he got in the car. She glanced over at him, his broad hands on the steering wheel, his eyes straight ahead on the traffic.

He slowed the Magna as they neared her house. There were cars parked on both sides of the road, some with the insignias of newspapers and TV stations on their doors. 'You sure you want to go in?'

She nodded, then said, 'Angus.'

'Mm?' His eyes were on the media crews.

'I need a favour.'

Now he looked at her.

'I want to search for Lachlan and I can't wait for my car to be fixed.'

'I'll drive you anywhere you want to go,' he said.

It would be more complicated than that, but

she didn't want to go into it now. 'Will you wait here while I go in?'

He nodded. 'Take your time.'

He parked and she got out and met the media at the foot of her driveway.

'Mrs Phillips, how's Chris?'

'Any news on your baby?'

'Are you happy with the progress of the police on the case?'

'Has Chris been able to tell you anything?'

She held up a hand and they went quiet. 'There's been no news about Lachlan. Chris is awake and has told the police all he can. I have complete faith in the detectives but I want to appeal to every member of the public to please, please, study Lachlan's picture — even better, cut it out and carry it with you — and look closely at every single baby you see. Somebody has him. If we are vigilant enough, we will find him. Thank you.'

She hurried away from them to the front door of her house. Flowers were piled against it. Some bunches were in fancy plastic wrap from florists, and some were tied with only a rubber band or a piece of string. Sophie saw that one note read 'To the Phillipses with love from your neighbours'. The envelope attached to another bouquet carried the police crest. The ambulance insignia was on a third. There was also a small pile of soft toys: three teddy bears, a koala, a chicken and a pig.

She unlocked the door and went inside. The house smelled of other people and chemical cleaners. Chris had been shot right there in the

171

doorway but there were no bloodstains. Sophie crouched and touched the beige carpet. It was damp, and the chemical smell was stronger. Carpet shampoo.

Sunlight was coming in the kitchen window at the back of the house and, looking down the hall at its glow, she saw dust motes hanging in the still air. Upstairs the first-floor landing was gloomy.

She went up the stairs. Lachlan's room opened off the left side of the landing and their bedroom was opposite. Both doors stood wide open but the curtains were drawn in the rooms, cutting out the sun. This was how it would have been last night. At ten pm Lachlan would have been asleep in his cot for hours.

On the wall in front of her, between the bathroom and the small study they mostly used to store junk, hung a framed black-and-white photo. It was a close-up of Lachlan, just one day old, lying asleep on Chris's open hands. She remembered taking it and looking up from the viewfinder with tears in her eyes, so grateful for her family.

She went into Lachlan's room with the picture held tight in her hands. There was an odd smell, one she couldn't place until she saw the black dust lying in the cracks on the white windowsill. Fingerprint dust. They must have tested everything then cleaned as best they could.

The sides of the cot were up but the sheets and blankets were gone, leaving the plastic-covered mattress bare. It seemed an odd thing for a kidnapper to do: it would take time to loosen the fitted sheet and gather the lot together.

The black dust on the cot railings made her think again. Forensics. They were looking for a clue to the man who'd been here. A hair might have fallen from his head, or a fibre from his clothes, when he bent over her sleeping son.

With shaking hands she turned the picture over, unclipped the back of the frame, took out the photo then turned and flung the empty wood and glass frame hard against the wall.

9

Ella placed the stapled pages of test results on the table and offered up thanks for the lab folks who'd cleared the decks to do them that morning. She read again the substances detected in Sawyer's blood, then looked at the surgeon. 'Alcohol, morphine, midazolam. Heroin breaks down into morphine in the body, doesn't it?'

There was no answer. Sawyer held the same white folded handkerchief to his eyes. His solicitor, Ron Van Pelt, sat beside him, a huge lump of a man in a black suit, arms crossed over a mountainous belly.

'Doesn't it, Doctor?'

'Yes.' His voice was quiet.

'And the lab tells me midazolam's a sedative, which also reduces anxiety and causes amnesia.'

'Yes.'

'Alcohol, morphine, midazolam,' Ella said again. 'Quite a mixture. What were you hoping to achieve?'

'I didn't take it.'

'This is your name at the top here,' she said. 'This was your blood they tested.'

'I told you what happened. Somebody drugged me.'

She turned the page over to expose another

174

sheet underneath. 'But your prints are on the syringe.'

'So they put my fingers on it.'

'In exactly the places you'd hold it to inject yourself?'

Sawyer looked at Van Pelt. In a gravelly smoker's voice the solicitor said, 'I told you at the start, you don't have to say anything. You don't even have to sit here and listen. Until they arrest you, you're free to go.'

'I just want them to believe me.'

'They're cops. They believe only what they want to believe.' Van Pelt turned his beady eyes on Ella. 'Isn't that right, Detective?'

She ignored him. 'Doctor Sawyer, the sooner you tell us what happened last night, the sooner we can understand what's going on.'

'You said you had information on my case and asked me to come in and help you.'

'We said on a case,' Dennis said. 'You can see the position we're in, can't you? We need to clear things up. It's just procedure.'

'You think I give a fuck about your procedure? My wife and daughter are dead!'

'We understand — '

'No, you don't,' Sawyer snapped. 'If you did, you'd have taken me home last night. You'd have never even brought me in here in the first place.' He placed a tightly balled fist on the table. 'My wife and newborn baby are lying in a morgue, and somebody attacked me and shot me full of drugs, and you don't give a shit.'

Van Pelt laid a meaty paw on Sawyer's arm. Sawyer lowered his head and started to sob, the handkerchief in his shaking hands, tears dripping onto his rumpled trousers.

Van Pelt glared at them. 'My client has nothing more to say.'

★　★　★

Ten minutes later Ella and Dennis watched Ron Van Pelt drive his Mercedes from the station yard. Sawyer was in the front passenger seat, ranting and gesticulating.

Ella turned to Dennis. 'So now what?'

He shrugged. 'We keep working.' His tone was cool. They'd just argued about the merits of charging Sawyer with self-administration. Ella hadn't been persuaded by Dennis's stance that it would achieve nothing and that Sawyer, who might very well be innocent, had been through a tragedy and deserved a little slack. Now she saw the muscle move in his temple and knew he hadn't come around to her point of view that, tragedy notwithstanding, they needed to know the truth and a little lever like that could do a lot of good.

She leaned against the wall, trying to appear casual. 'I mean, we've got motive, we've got a crap alibi — '

'But there's no DNA on the dummy and all the prints on it are so smeared they're beyond recognition. There's no evidence to say Sawyer was ever in the Phillipses' house or that Lachlan was in his car,' Dennis said. 'You're in a hurry. These things take time.'

Ella wanted to ask how much time Lachlan

had, but pulled back. 'One little break,' she said. 'We find who he had that bingle with, or who he bought the drugs from and when, and we can at least pin down part of his evening.'

Dennis sighed and checked his watch. 'Come on. It's meeting time.'

10.40 am

Chris struggled to sit up on the side of the bed. He was dizzy and his heart and head pounded. He had to get out of here and back home. The people who had Lachlan would get in contact somehow and it wouldn't be by waltzing into the hospital. He had to be home and available to them. Sophie needed his protection, too. He could do nothing where he was.

'What are you doing?' Gloria grabbed his arm and tried to make him lie down.

'I'm fine.'

'Your nose is bleeding.' She pulled a handful of tissues from a box.

The wound on his face throbbed. He held the tissues to his nose and looked at Gloria over the top. 'Did the doctor say when I can go home?'

'Not for a few days yet,' she said. 'You need to be taken care of.'

He edged over the side of the mattress and rested his bare feet on the floor. 'If I'm up and about, what's the point in staying?'

'But you're not up and about.' She had hold of his arm again and tried to stop him standing up. 'You're too weak. You could faint.'

177

Chris forced himself to his feet. The room spun and he saw black spots. He staggered. His ears rang so loudly he couldn't make out what Gloria was saying. Then another pair of hands had him and pushed him back onto the bed. Once he was lying down again his head cleared and he saw a nurse standing with Gloria. They looked at him sternly.

Chris closed his eyes, humiliated. It made him feel weaker than ever, being flat on his back in bed while people stared at him, or talked to him, like the detectives. And having to lie to them — and to Sophie — was awful. He kept telling himself he had no choice, but still he felt guilty.

The nurse left the room and Gloria pulled her chair close to his bedside. 'How are you feeling?'

'Good,' he lied. He watched her pat his hand, and decided on a plan. If they wouldn't let him get up, he'd do it when they weren't around. He'd exercise all night if he had to. He'd get himself strong enough to leave, strong enough to go home and wait for their contact. And if it didn't come, he'd go after them.

Simple as that.

11 am

The Incident Room smelled of coffee and sweat. Detectives yawned as they waited their turn to tell about their morning's work. Ella held her own yawns down deep in her throat and made notes; a theme was emerging: the leads were fizzling out.

Shane Brayfield, the drunk driver Chris had put away, was at a cousin's wedding over the time of the kidnapping and had the witnesses and mobile phone pictures to prove it.

The hospital CEO had handed over the details of the parents of the stillborn baby. Laurel and Daniel had found them at home, the woman glued weeping to the news reports about the case, the paramedic father on the phone asking his work HQ for the Phillipses' address so they could send flowers.

Forensics had examined the note left on Chris. The paper was Reflex brand, eighty gsm, sold all over the country. The kidnapper had used a Canon printer, also sold all over the country. There had been no fingerprints or hairs found. Ella rubbed her eyes and thought of their target: a white man who owned a balaclava, a Canon printer and an all-but-complete ream of Reflex paper.

'What about the font?' a detective asked.

Dennis glanced at the report and shook his head. 'Times New Roman, standard on every computer.'

Travis Henry slid a note along the table top to her. '*You were right. Sylvia Morris was hiding that baby girl for a friend.*' Ella shrugged at him in a resigned way.

There was a knock at the door and Acting Commissioner Rupert Eagers looked in. Dennis nodded at Ella.

She went into the corridor and closed the door behind her. Eagers was in full uniform. At the press conference that morning he'd fielded questions not only about the kidnap and shooting, but also about the robbery gang, the caller to the TV stations, and the recent surge in drug overdose cases, including the apparent accidental death overnight in Hyde Park of Lily Jones, daughter of ex-State MP Zander Jones. Ella wasn't surprised that he looked distracted and harassed.

Beside him stood a young man in a dark pinstriped suit. Ella didn't know him but saw something familiar about his face.

'How's the case going?' Eagers said.

'Slowly.' She outlined their progress so far. 'The public hotline is ringing off the hook, however, so we have a lot of things to follow up there.'

'Good, good.' Eagers rubbed his forehead. 'This is Detective Murray Shakespeare.'

Ella looked harder at the young man.

'He'll be my liaison on the case,' Eagers said. 'I want to be kept completely up to speed on events, so he is to have access to all areas of the investigation.'

'Yes, sir.'

Eagers left them standing in the corridor. Murray Shakespeare smiled at her. He had the same long eyeteeth, the same slaty eyes.

She said, 'Your dad's Frank Shakespeare, right?'

He nodded. 'He said you'd remember him.'

Ella clenched her hands behind her back. Shakespeare wore a knowing look. Having a liaison was a pain in the butt; they always needed things explained to them and you'd always rather be getting on with your case. For it to be a Shakespeare — well.

'Detective?'

Ella and Shakespeare spoke at the same time. 'Yes?'

The uniformed officer from the front desk handed Ella a sheet of paper. 'This was faxed over.'

'Thanks.' Ella read it quickly. It was the report on the bullet taken from Chris's head.

'Subsonic twenty-two.' Shakespeare was reading over her shoulder. 'Makes sense. Anything bigger and faster and he'd be in the morgue.'

Ella held back a sigh.

'No rifling marks survived though,' Shakespeare said. 'That's what hitting a skull will do to you.'

Ella folded the page over and went back into the Incident Room, where Dennis was finishing giving out tasks. Detectives scribbled details of their assignments. He said, 'We meet again at four this afternoon, and decide then who wants to knock off.'

People filed out. Dennis looked at Shakespeare. Ella explained who he was and why he was there. Dennis's temples turned white.

She held out the report. He read it. 'Hm.'

She knew what he meant. It added little to their knowledge of the culprit and was as useful as the Reflex paper and the Canon printer.

Dennis gave the sheet to Detective Roger Fenwick, who would enter the details into the computer programme.

'Detective Marconi?' The uniformed officer

181

from the front desk was at the door. 'There's an Edman Hughes on the phone, asking about the progress on his arson case.'

'How's he know I'm here?'

'Someone at Hunters Hill told him, he said.'

Ella rolled her eyes. 'Tell him I'm busy with this.'

'I did,' she said.

Ella dug her hands into her pockets. 'Tell him I'll get back to him when I can.' *When this case is solved.*

The constable nodded and walked away.

'So what are we doing now?' Shakespeare asked.

'I've got some paperwork to catch up on.' Dennis cast a glance at Ella. She caught his meaning, and said, 'I'm going to look over some of the calls from the public.'

'Is there anything for me to do?' Shakespeare asked.

'Not really,' Dennis said. 'You can go on the phones if you want.'

Shakespeare looked dissatisfied. 'I guess.'

'Good-o,' Dennis said. 'We'll call you if anything happens.'

When Shakespeare was out of sight down the corridor Dennis winked at Ella. 'Let's get out of here.'

11.20 am

At the end of Glebe Point Road sunlight shimmered on Rozelle Bay. In Angus's car

182

Sophie looked in the other direction, at Boyd Sawyer's house.

Freshly showered and dressed in clean navy ambulance uniform trousers and a blue T-shirt, and with a clean ambulance shirt neatly folded in a bag, she sat taut, stretched almost to breaking point, and thought of all that had happened since she'd last been here; then she saw a figure walk past a window in the house. 'That's him.'

Angus stared. 'How come he's not in custody?'

'I don't know.'

'What exactly did the detectives tell you?'

'What I told you before, that he was found overdosed but says he wasn't involved. Plus they found a dummy like Lachlan's beside his car at the wharf.'

'They have all that plus motive and they let him go?'

It did seem wrong that Sawyer was free but Sophie didn't want to acknowledge him as the likely culprit. Doing so would force her to recognise that Lachlan might be in the river. She turned away from the house. 'Let's go.'

As they headed into the city she twisted in her seat, examining every person on the street with a baby in their arms or in a pram. Angus drove without speaking, staying in the left lane and going slowly. 'So where exactly are we going?'

She had to tell him her plan. It would be more plausible if there were two of them. But he was a cop, sworn to the law. She looked over at him. What if he refused to help? Worse, what if he stopped her from doing it herself?

Ella turned her mobile off as she stepped out of
the lift on the fourth floor of St Vincent's
Hospital. Dennis stayed in to go up to the fifth.
He was going to see Marisa Waters, whom he
knew from after-hours work functions. Ella
guessed that the Strike Force Gold people had
already asked her everything there was to ask
about why she and Duds were doing what
looked so much like a runner the very day that
the robbery gang was alleged to be cops, but
Dennis had a touching faith in the power of
friendship.

She, meanwhile, was going back to see Roth.

The door to Roth's room was open and he
was watching TV. The IV fluid bag and tubing
were gone, though the stubby plastic cannula
was still taped in his arm. 'Two visits in five
hours,' he said, turning the set off. 'Careful,
Detective, or I might start thinking you like
me.'

She sat in the low vinyl chair with a smile.
'Got anything to tell me?'

'Nope.'

'Still got that photo of the baby?'

'I think the nurse threw it out when she was
cleaning the room.'

'Want another copy?'

'No thanks.'

Ella crossed her legs. 'So how's it feel to be
shot?'

'Like being kicked really hard. First it's numb.
Later it hurts.'

'What made you think you'd be able to hide it?'

'Blind stupidity,' he said.

She nodded. 'What I figured.'

'I tried to get that damn bullet out, digging in the wound. I had tweezers and God knows what.' He made a pinching motion with his thumb and forefinger. 'Got lots of meat but no lead.'

'Bloody hell,' Ella said.

Roth smiled at her and for an instant she saw past the tough facade. His story about being mugged was complete crap and he knew they knew it. He'd been at the bank that day, he was part of the gang. Once the ballistics report came back his life would turn upside down — he'd be arrested and charged over the death of the guard, refused bail, forced to live with the very people he'd once locked up.

'We've got bugger-all decent leads on this baby,' she said.

'It's early days.'

'It's frightening.' Most cases like this were either solved quickly or not at all. Time was slipping away. 'Can't you just tell me whether Chris was involved?'

'With what?'

She looked at him. 'All we want is the baby. If we can rule out the gang angle it'll help us a lot.'

'But — '

Just then a nurse came into the room. Ella fell silent, watching the woman's gloved hands hang a new fluid flask and connect the line to the IV site in Roth's wrist. He said, 'Thanks,' and the nurse smiled at him and left.

'Even if I knew,' Roth went on, 'why would I say anything?'

'For the baby's sake.'

'Ever hear the word retribution?' Roth said. 'I've got a child as well.'

'You can understand how the Phillipses feel, then.'

'Yeah, and I know how, given the chance, they'd do anything to protect him too.'

'We can arrange protection.'

'Not the way I need it, you can't.' He put a hand to his chest.

'We can,' she said. 'Trust us.'

Roth kept one hand on his chest and raised the other to his forehead. His face turned pale and sweat broke out on his skin.

'Are you okay?'

He drew a breath between his gritted teeth. 'I feel like I'm going to pass out. Feel really bad. God, oh God.'

'What's the matter?'

'Oh shit.' His eyes were full of fear as he looked at the new IV line and the bag of fluid. 'Ella, they got me. I was never going to say anything and they fucking got me.'

Ella was on her feet. 'Hang in there, Peter. I'll get the nurse.'

'It's too late, I'm fucked.' Roth clamped both his hands to his chest. 'Listen . . . Chris.'

'Chris what?' Ella knew she should go for help but she wanted what might be Roth's last words. She could see the slowing beat of Roth's pulse in his neck. His pupils were huge. His skin was cold and clammy.

'Chris . . . '

'Chris is in the gang? Or isn't?'

'Not,' Roth gasped, his hands still to his chest. 'Not in.'

Ella saw the call buzzer hanging over the far bed rails and she launched across and grabbed it. 'Chris isn't in the gang, Peter, am I understanding you right?'

But Roth's hands fell from his chest and he went limp.

'Goddammit.' Ella dropped the buzzer. She fumbled at his neck for a pulse but couldn't find one. 'Help!' She didn't know how to make the head of the bed lie flat so she started CPR with him sitting up. He lolled from side to side with her compressions then she grabbed his head, tilted it back, pinched his nose shut and pressed her mouth over his. Was it one breath or two? Oh, Jesus, where were the nurses? She took a breath of air. 'Help!'

A male nurse came in, saw what was happening and hit a red button on the wall. He grabbed at a lever under the bed and the top fell back with a clunk. Another nurse rushed in with a bag and mask set-up that Ella had seen paramedics use. 'Okay, we got it,' she said and Ella stepped out of the way.

'What happened?' the male nurse asked Ella, compressing Roth's chest.

'A nurse came in and connected up that IV bag there, and within a minute he said he felt bad and was going to pass out. Then he went limp.'

The female nurse looked at the bag of fluid then at her colleague. 'Was he on fluids again?'

'Not that I know of.'

'Was this nurse male or female?'

'Female,' Ella said. 'Short blonde hair. Mid-twenties. Good tan. She wore a blue skirt and white shirt.'

The nurses looked at each other in confusion. 'There's nobody like that on the ward today.'

Wide-eyed, the female nurse grabbed a clamp on the IV line and shut it off.

Ella felt a surge of adrenaline. 'This could be a crime scene. I want the tubing disconnected from his arm. Nobody is to touch it. I'll bag it as evidence when I come back.'

Before she could open the door a medical team of four burst in with a defibrillator and crash cart. Ella hurried out past them and down the corridor, checking rooms, pushing open the stall doors in the bathroom, dialling her mobile as she went. Dennis's voicemail picked up and she swore, remembering he'd turned his phone off.

She shoved open the heavy door into the stairwell and listened for the sound of running feet, then hurried back to the nurses' desk, where she flashed her badge. 'I need to contact my colleague upstairs.'

The grey-haired clerk dialled a number and handed over the phone. Ella quickly filled Dennis in and described the nurse.

'Go downstairs,' he said. 'See if you can spot her. I'll get back-up.'

In the main foyer Ella stood panting at the

door, examining the faces of everyone who left the building, knowing it was an almost useless task. Precious minutes had passed before she'd realised what was going on, easily time enough for a woman in a nurse's uniform to slip outside unnoticed. There were so many exits too. Standing at this one — probably the door least likely to be used — felt futile.

Dennis stepped out of the lift, accompanied by a hospital security guard. 'No sign?' Dennis asked.

Ella shook her head.

'Describe her again.'

Ella did so. The guard repeated her words into his radio. Dennis then motioned Ella towards the lifts. 'We need to see how he is, what the doctor says.' Inside, he pressed the button. 'After all, it could be nothing more than a medical hiccup.'

'I don't think so,' Ella said. 'Dennis, he told me he was never going to say a word but they still got him.'

Dennis narrowed his eyes.

'And he told me that Chris isn't in the gang.'

'But can we trust him?' Dennis said. 'He's not exactly cop of the year.'

The lift doors opened and they walked out.

'What did he have to lose?' Ella said. 'He was sure he was about to die. Telling me that made no difference.'

'Who knows what his agenda might be,' Dennis said. 'Anyway, let's hope he survives and is in a mood to clarify his words when he wakes up.'

Ella knocked on the door to Roth's room. The

female nurse peered out. She was sweating. 'Just a minute.'

While they waited, Dennis told her what Marisa had said. 'She and Dudley-Pearson were in love.'

Ella raised her eyebrows.

'She said it'd been going on a couple of months and they'd planned for a while to just up and leave. She'd sold some shares to finance the little adventure. It was only a coincidence it happened the same day as the news on the gang came out,' Dennis said. 'You should've heard her. She's like a lovelorn teenager, all naive about what would happen down the track, trying to tell me why doing it that way was better than the adult method of divorcing partners and resigning jobs. I felt embarrassed for her.'

'You think she's telling the truth?'

Dennis nodded. 'What I don't know is whether Dudley-Pearson was being honest with her when he said he knew nothing about the gang.' He looked at his watch. 'How long does it take to save a life?'

'Longer than on *ER*,' Ella said. 'Did Marisa ask him about the gang, or did Duds volunteer the information?'

'She said he told her he was upset about it and felt bad about leaving his staff at a time like this.' Dennis's mobile chimed and he looked at the screen.

'But he still left,' Ella said.

Dennis made a noncommittal noise as he thumbed through a text message. 'Jesus.'

'What?'

'Roth's ballistics results.' He slipped the phone back into his pocket. 'It was from the guard's gun all right.'

Roth's door opened and the medical team manoeuvred his bed into the corridor. One nurse hurried alongside, compressing Roth's chest. A tube was tied into Roth's mouth and another nurse squeezed the connected bag regularly. Ella found it difficult to match the slack and mottled face to the once-living man.

'Where are you taking him?' Dennis said.

The doctor jabbed the lift button. 'To the Emergency Department.'

'When will he wake up?'

'The way he's going now, never.' The lift doors opened and the nurses rolled the bed in, then the doctor put her foot against the door. 'There was no order for IV fluids and the ward staff tell me there are no nurses on duty today who match the description you gave. I'll need the test results on the IV bag and tubing to be certain, but from your account of what happened and Roth's clinical condition, it's possible he was given an overdose of a cardiac drug such as lignocaine, which stopped his heart. It's also stopping the drugs we're giving from having their effect. I'm betting there were other drugs in there too: perhaps insulin. A large enough dose can cause brain damage very quickly.' She shook her head. 'So far we've had no response whatsoever, and I doubt we will.'

10

'Park here,' Sophie said. 'I'll just be a minute.'

Angus looked at the brick front of The Rocks ambulance station. 'And then you'll tell me what's going on?'

She nodded and got out.

The day crew was on a case somewhere so she let herself into the station with her key. In the store room she found a spare red nylon kitbag. She threw in a thermometer, a paediatric blood-pressure cuff and a couple of bandages and dressings, just enough to make it appear legitimate to an onlooker. Paramedics never went about empty-handed.

Back in the car she cradled the bag on her lap. Angus eyed it, then her, but she was conscious of the chance that the day crew might return. 'Better drive off,' she said.

'Where to?'

'Just wherever, for now.'

This was one time it was good that parking in the CBD was so scarce. She didn't want him staring at her while she tried to explain her idea.

Just start. She squeezed the bag to her chest. 'I spent last night driving about looking for Lachlan.' Angus started to speak but she shook her head. 'I needed to do it.'

He closed his mouth and nodded.

192

'I know the chances of finding him that way are incredibly slim. Middle of the night, people with babies aren't out and about on the streets much. And then I realised there was a better way.' She glanced at him. 'A better place and time.'

He drove in silence.

She took a deep breath. 'If you'd taken a child, where's the best place to hide it? Not in an area where kids are scarce. You'd try to blend in somewhere where there are already heaps of kids. Where another baby crying at night doesn't even register.'

He indicated and turned a corner but still didn't speak.

'You know those big housing commission blocks in Waterloo?' She didn't wait for an answer. 'They're full of kids. Overflowing with them.'

Angus pulled into a bus zone and yanked on the park brake.

'Don't look at me like that,' she said. 'I'm not after your approval or your permission.'

'So why are you telling me?'

She stared out the windscreen. She would've liked to say 'because you have the car and I need a lift' but it was more than that. She wanted his help. She wanted him beside her.

'Have you told your idea to the detectives?'

'Police would scare people off,' she said. 'I knock on their doors in my uniform and they see a person who's there to help.'

Angus turned the steering wheel thoughtfully from side to side. 'And then what?'

'I ask to see any young children in their care,'
she said. 'I tell them some story about an
infectious disease doing the rounds. I'm a free
community service, right there on their doorsteps.'

'And you think they'll go for that? They'll let
you in?'

'Yes.' *Probably. Hopefully. Maybe.*

Angus made a face. 'It seems a lot of risk for
not much reward.'

'What risk? I'm going to get mugged for
knocking on someone's door? And maybe I don't
find him, but at least I'm looking.'

A bus braked behind them with a blast of its
horn. Angus waved and pulled out of the spot.

'Okay,' he said. 'I'll take you to Waterloo on
one condition: I come into the blocks with you.
You can make me part of your story, I don't
care, but you're not going there alone.'

Sophie hugged the kitbag tightly. 'Thank you.'

He turned south and she looked him over. He
was dressed in a light blue button-up shirt and
tan trousers. She said, 'Would you mind stopping
at Woolies first?'

He let her off in a no-standing zone outside
Woolworths opposite the Town Hall. She was
back in minutes with a bag of purchases and
tossed a dark blue tie at him. 'Put this on.' She
tore a notepad from its plastic packaging and
jammed it inside a clipboard, then added a pen,
and explained her idea as he drove.

She pulled her uniform shirt on over her
T-shirt, and fell silent as they neared Waterloo.
The odds of finding Lachlan this way were

terrible, but every baby she looked at was one she could be sure wasn't him. If she could only look long enough, eventually she'd find him. If there were a million babies in the city, then she had to look at a million faces, and the next one would be him. If there were two million, three million, she didn't care. She had only to work hard, not give up, not waver in her belief that she would find him, and sometime she would be looking into his eyes, holding his warm wriggling body, and she would never let go of him again.

A woman was coming out of the door of the first building and Angus smiled at her and caught the door before it closed. Sophie knocked at the door of the first flat and readied a smile on her face.

A rangy woman wearing jeans and a denim jacket opened the door. 'Yes?'

'Good morning,' Sophie said. 'I'm Penny Burke from the Ambulance Service and this is Brian Stevens from the Department of Health.'

Angus stood beside her with his feet apart and the clipboard in his hands. He smiled at the woman.

'We're currently going door to door in your building notifying people about a potential health risk to young children.'

The woman lost her wary look. 'Like what?'

'A child in the next building has been diagnosed with a particularly contagious strain of meningitis,' Sophie said, 'and we're letting parents know about the signs and symptoms, and also offering a free on-the-spot examination of young children and babies.'

'Come in, please.' The woman hastily opened the door wide and Sophie felt a flash of shame for making her afraid. 'I have a daughter, she's only three months old. Could you check her over?'

'Absolutely,' Sophie said. She followed the woman into the bedroom where the baby was asleep in a cot. Sophie looked down at the tiny form under the little blanket, the perfect features, the curled fist as it lay on the sheet. 'She's beautiful.'

The woman smiled. 'Thank you.'

Sophie checked the baby's temperature. 'No sign of a rash?'

'She does have this thing here.' The woman pulled up the baby's singlet, exposing a red flaky area the size of Sophie's thumbnail on her back. The baby stirred but didn't wake.

'The meningococcal rash is a distinct one,' Sophie said. 'It's dark red or purple and appears in spots or blotches.' She pressed a finger to the reddened area on the baby and it blanched. 'If you do that to the meningococcal rash it won't lose colour like this one did, even for a second.'

The woman was nodding.

'Other signs to look out for are drowsiness, fever, stiff neck and inability to tolerate bright lights,' Angus said behind them. 'Is this your only child?'

'I have a five year old, but he's at school.'

'Okay then,' Sophie said. 'Your baby looks very healthy. Thank you for your time.'

'Thank you,' the woman said.

In the corridor Angus said, 'You sure you want

to do this at every flat?'

Sophie's answer was to knock on the next door.

11.59 am

Dennis took charge of the IV stand and drip and put Ella in the ward staffroom to wait for the Strike Force Gold investigators. She was looking out the window at the junkies sleeping in the park when the detectives came in.

Hollebeck was a balding man in his fifties who'd been part of the team on the homicide where Ella had told Shakespeare off. He sat at the table and looked in the biscuit barrel labelled 'Nurses only', took out a milk arrowroot and said, 'Roth's dead. We heard as we came through Emergency.'

Ella sat down, feeling weak. She'd seen bodies, she'd seen people in the process of dying in car wrecks, but she'd never seen anyone killed in front of her. She felt for Roth, and his ex-wife and child.

'I hear you're working with Murray now.'

Ella focused on Hollebeck. 'Are you going to take my statement or not?'

Draper, a soft-featured woman in her twenties, opened a notepad. 'So what happened?'

Ella went through it while Draper scribbled shorthand.

'Describe the nurse.' Hollebeck got another biscuit.

Ella repeated the phrases she'd used earlier. 'A

woman in her mid-twenties with short blonde hair and a good tan. She wore a blue skirt and white shirt.'

'That's it?' Hollebeck said. 'How'd she behave?'

'Like a nurse setting up an IV.' The woman had been so matter-of-fact, so routine in her actions, that Ella hadn't noticed anything more about her. If there'd been some edginess the situation might be different. What kind of nerve did it take to do a thing like that while someone watched? Ella remembered something else. 'She smiled at Roth before she left.'

'Did she speak?'

'No.'

Hollebeck and Draper looked at each other. 'Okay, that'll do for now,' he said. 'We know where to reach you if we need you. Little old Hunters Hill, isn't it?'

'I'm on the Phillips case at the moment, out of Gladesville.'

'Of course. I forgot.' He took a handful of biscuits and slammed the lid back on the barrel. 'Say hi to Murray.'

Ten minutes later she was in the car with Dennis, heading back to Gladesville. 'I hate that bastard Hollebeck,' she said. 'Rubbing it in about Shakespeare.'

'Senior or junior?'

'Whichever,' she said. 'They'll never let me forget that homicide.'

'People know you bite, that's why. If you forget it, so will they.'

She rolled her eyes. 'Yes, Dad.'

'Your statement didn't take long to do.'

'Nice change of subject there.'

He inclined his head.

'They only took notes. I get the feeling they're not really that interested in who got to Roth.'

'But if they figure that out, they'll have a lead to the people with a vested interest in his silence,' Dennis said.

'Unless they themselves are those people.'

He looked over at her.

'Hey, I'm just saying.' She shrugged.

As they crossed the Anzac Bridge she looked southwest to Glebe Point. Boyd Sawyer's house was hidden by blocks of flats and a spreading figtree. 'If Roth was telling the truth, and Chris wasn't in with the gang, where does that leave us? Just with Sawyer?'

'And the unknown kidnapper.'

Ella was silent for a moment. 'Remember that assault on Chris and his partner, a couple of months back?'

'Dean Rigby was his partner.'

'Wasn't he the guy Chris went to see the day before he was shot?'

'Yep. They're friends.'

'And the assailant had an alibi,' Ella remembered. 'But I wonder if that's worth looking into further. I mean, the guy's got a case pending against him; maybe he figures if he knocks out a solid witness he's got a better chance.'

'He's got no chance at all,' Dennis said. 'That one's cut and dried. My mate Figgis worked it.'

'The famous Figgis,' Ella said.

'You wouldn't be so mocking if you met him.'

'I have met him.' She hadn't been impressed. Darnell Figgis stood too close to you and kept hold of your hand too long when he shook it. He'd leaned on the bar in the Jungle and talked too loud and in way too much detail about a woman whose death he was investigating and what he'd found in her chest of drawers.

'If you worked with him, then.'

Ella raised her eyebrows. 'Get me the file on the assault and let me see his work on the page, maybe I'll change my mind.'

12.20 pm

Chris sat in the hospital bed with his hands on his thighs under the blanket, pinching his skin to stop himself passing out. 'I promise you I'm right to go home.'

The doctor shook his head. 'You're not even one full day post-op.'

'I feel fine. I want to go.'

'Out of the question,' the doctor said. 'There could be swelling, you could have an intracranial bleed. You need to be monitored here.'

Chris pinched harder. There was a roaring in his ears and the doctor was disappearing behind a wall of black dots. 'What about tomorrow?'

'Next week at the earliest.' The doctor's voice came down a long tunnel. 'Do you want to lie down?'

'I'm fine.'

'You don't look it.'

Chris drew a deep breath. 'Thank you for coming to see me.' As he'd hoped, the doctor took it as an indication to leave. Chris slumped back on the pillows, sweat trickling down his face. Of course the doctor would have been able to see how pale and clammy he'd turned, but with Lachlan's life at stake Chris would die before admitting how weak he really was.

He sucked in lungfuls of cold hospital air. He'd told Gloria he wanted to put on pyjamas from home instead of the hospital gown he was wearing, and estimated he had half an hour before she returned. He reached for the call button looped around the bed railing.

The young male nurse stuck his head into the room. 'Wassup, Chris?'

'Can I use the phone please?'

When the cordless handset was in his grasp and the nurse out of earshot, he dialled the number he knew by heart.

'Recruitment,' a female voice said.

'Is Dean Rigby there?'

'He's in a meeting at the moment, I'm sorry,' she said. 'Can I take a message?'

'Tell him that Chris Phillips called, and ask him to ring me back as soon as he can. I'm in the ICU in Royal North Shore Hospital,' Chris said. 'Tell him it's urgent.' He hung up and sat with the phone in his lap. A message like that would surely get handed to Dean straightaway. With any luck he'd call back in minutes, Chris would be able to say what he needed to say — or arrange a meeting if Dean was reluctant to talk on the phone — and it'd all be over with before Gloria arrived back.

2.15 pm

As the door of the last flat in the block closed behind them, Sophie and Angus headed for the stairs. 'How many babies do you reckon we checked?' Angus said.

'Fifty-seven.' Sophie moved swiftly, her hand on the railing, the kit bouncing against her leg. The next block waited. She no longer felt bad about causing concern, and in fact seeing all those parents worry over their babies strengthened her resolve. There was nothing she wouldn't do to find Lachlan.

Angus said, 'I don't know how you do it.'

'Do what?'

'Keep going like this. I don't think I could get up off the floor if I had a child who was missing.'

'It's hard to explain.' It was more than that: it was impossible. Only somebody who'd lived what she was living could understand.

'My nephew has cancer,' Angus said. 'It's so hard watching him suffer, but at least we can be with him. I can't imagine how it would feel to not know where he was, whether he was okay.'

Sophie slowed and glanced back up at him. 'I'm sorry to hear that. How old is he?'

'Almost a year. He's been sick for a few months now. Leukaemia.' They emerged from the building and crossed a thinly grassed lawn.

'My sister Bee's on her own, so I'm the nearest thing to a dad he's got. I take a lot of pride in that.'

Sophie looked at him, striding along beside her, the tie swinging from side to side, the clipboard tucked under his arm. Of all the people she'd spoken to since Lachlan was taken, he came closest to her position. Being faced with the loss of a child was just one step — albeit a big one — from the loss itself.

She said, 'I get up off the floor because I have to. If I don't do absolutely everything I can to find him, I'm letting him down. I already have, just by allowing him to be taken.'

'You didn't do it. You weren't there,' Angus said.

'I know, but I'm his mother and it's my job to keep him safe, yet now he's not,' she said. 'And God forbid that it was Sawyer, because then I'm even more to blame.'

2.35 pm

Ella told Dennis she was going home for a couple of hours' sleep but really she wanted to be away from the noise and bustle of the station when she read the assault file. Roth was on her mind too. She kept seeing his stricken expression as he looked at the IV bag.

The afternoon sun streamed through the living-room window of her half-a-house and she pulled her armchair around to take advantage of the warmth. She put a cup of coffee on the floor next to her and rested the closed folder on her knee.

The smile on the fake nurse's face was what got to her the most. Such an ordinary smile. Ella would have liked to think the woman didn't know what she was doing and that was why she was so calm. But if she really was an interloper then she was there for one reason only.

It frightened her to imagine that the same people were behind the shooting of Chris and the kidnapping of Lachlan.

Enough.

She opened the folder and began to read.

The assault had happened two months before, on 8 March. Chris Phillips and Dean Rigby started their shift at Wynyard Station and answered a call to a violent domestic argument in Surry Hills. When they got there things had quietened down. They spoke to the occupants, who said they were fine, they didn't want to make complaints against each other, it was just a bit of a disagreement which had got out of hand. When Phillips and Rigby headed back to their car, Rigby spotted somebody he recognised on the street. Chris's statement said:

Senior Constable Rigby told me the person was Simon Leeman and there was a warrant out for his arrest on rape charges. I didn't know Leeman but once we started running after him, the man ran away. Senior Constable Rigby continued the pursuit on foot while I went back and fetched the car. I saw the suspect run into a small laneway, followed by

Senior Constable Rigby. I entered the laneway about two minutes later. The lane is straight for about seventy metres, then bends to the right and dead-ends about fifty metres further on. When I entered this section I saw the suspect had his back to a fence and was swinging what looked like a metal pole at Senior Constable Rigby. I saw the officer duck then slip over. The pole struck him in the neck and shoulder and he fell to the ground. By this time I was approaching the suspect. I had my OC spray at the ready. I told him to drop the pole. He lunged at me, and as I side-stepped, Senior Constable Rigby tried to get up. We collided and I fell too, and lost hold of my OC spray. I grabbed the suspect's legs and pulled him off balance. The three of us fought on the ground. Senior Constable Rigby and I managed to cuff the suspect, then I went to the car to call for assistance and paramedics.

Ella picked up her coffee. It was odd that Chris Phillips hadn't sprayed the suspect immediately, and also that he'd be so close as to get tripped up when Rigby tried to climb to his feet. Second-guessing was a dangerous habit though. She'd talk to Chris and see if he could make things a bit clearer.

The bigger problem was that the man turned out not to be Simon Leeman at all but a man named Paul Houtkamp. Ella looked at his sheet. He was thirty-six years old, he lived at 5/39 Banks Street in Waterloo, he held a truck licence, and had a history of convictions for assaults and minor robberies. A small-time guy really. There was nothing listed for the past two years — not that that meant a whole lot, only that he hadn't been caught doing anything.

The mug shot taken after the assault showed a clean-shaven man with his dark hair brushed back. His left cheek and jaw were bruised, consistent with a good hard belt from a right-hander. Ella expected to see defiance in his dark eyes but instead recognised fear. Had he expected another wallop? A visit from Rigby's friends when he was in the cells?

Before she left Gladesville she'd looked up Houtkamp on the computer file of the Phillips case. On the night of the kidnapping he claimed to have been at the Bower Brae Nursing Home in Randwick. The detectives who had investigated him said he'd signed in to the visitors' book at eight-forty pm and out at ten, and had been seen to come and go by two of the nightstaff, both of whom knew him. Ella sipped her coffee and looked out the window. Fergus Patrick, the Phillipses' neighbour, believed he'd heard the shot that injured Chris Phillips at about ten pm, then found him unconscious fifteen minutes later. Paul Houtkamp couldn't have left Randwick at ten and made it to Gladesville in much less than half an hour.

Unless Chris had been shot much earlier. She put the coffee down. Just because Houtkamp had been seen to come in, and leave, didn't mean he was there the entire time. Fergus Patrick said he first thought the sound of the shot was on the TV show he was watching.

Maybe it was, and *nobody* had heard the actual shooting. Houtkamp could have signed in to the nursing home, sneaked out, done the job, dumped the baby off somewhere, and sneaked back in to sign out for ten pm quite easily. His poor demented mother or whoever he was visiting probably didn't even know who she was herself, let alone who was sitting next to her.

It was a drastic action, however, for a guy who hadn't done too much big stuff before.

That we know of, she reminded herself.

Even so. What could he really hope to achieve? On a quick flip through the file, Figgis's work looked solid. What crack could Houtkamp possibly hope to widen by putting a witness out of the picture? Even if Phillips had died, Rigby remained alive to stand up there with his neck brace and his records of surgery and the workers' compensation directive that put him behind a desk for the rest of his career.

Still.

Ella looked at the photo of Houtkamp again.

Maybe there was more to this than met the eye.

3.17 pm

Chris's hospital room was empty. Ella looked at the rumpled bedclothes then around at the nurse who came up behind her. 'He's in the bathroom,' the young man said.

'He's walking?' Ella said. 'So soon?'

The nurse nodded. 'Some people will do

207

anything to stay clear of a bedpan.'

The detective who was meant to be minding Chris came out of the lift, carrying a newspaper. He saw Ella and frowned, then put the paper behind his back. She raised her eyebrows. He turned away, heading for the staffroom. Ella made a mental note to mention him to Dennis.

'You can wait in Chris's room if you want,' the nurse was saying. 'And let him know his friend Dean still hasn't called, and Mrs Schlink in room four will have the cordless phone for the next half-hour or so, but if Dean does ring, switch will divert it to one of the other numbers.'

'Oh, you mean Dean Rigby?' Ella did a quick bit of creative thinking. 'He's been tied up with a case.' It was a fair bet the nurse had guessed Dean was a cop but didn't know he was off the road.

'That'd explain why he hasn't rung.' The nurse looked at his watch. 'It's been almost three hours now.'

Ella sat in the plastic chair by Chris's bed. So Chris was keen to talk to Dean. Super-keen, in fact, by the sounds of it. They were friends, and it was plausible Chris just wanted his mate's shoulder to cry on, but hearing about it so soon after reading the Houtkamp file made Ella wonder. Was it possible that Chris suspected Houtkamp was involved in the kidnapping and wanted Rigby to find out? But why wouldn't he have told her and Dennis? She thought back to the conversation they'd had with Chris that morning. Nothing had struck her as odd.

Perhaps she needed to power up her antennae a little.

Chris came slowly into the room then stopped when he saw her. 'Is there news?'

'Not yet, I'm sorry,' Ella said.

He was pale and as he climbed into the bed his nose started to drip blood. He pulled a bloodstained tissue from his pyjama pocket and jammed it into his nostrils.

'How are you feeling?' she asked.

'Fine.'

Ella let the obvious lie pass. 'The case is progressing well.'

'Then where's my son?'

Okay, not that well. 'We're getting loads of calls on the public hotline. Everyone in the city is on the lookout.'

His face softened a little. 'That's good.' His voice was dulled by his blocked nose.

'I've been reading the file about the assault on you and Senior Constable Rigby,' she said. 'Which reminds me: the nurse said he hasn't rung yet.'

A flicker of some emotion crossed his face too quickly for Ella to recognise. Then he said, 'Why are you looking into the assault?'

'I wondered if Houtkamp might have had reason to want to hurt you.'

He shook his head. 'It wasn't him. He's taller than the guy who shot me.'

'Nevertheless,' Ella said, 'I was curious about the case.'

'In what way?'

Practising in the car on the way over here it

had been easy to ask aloud, 'Why did you wait so long to spray him? How did you manage to trip over Rigby? And how the hell does a lone bad guy get the upper hand over two experienced officers?' But now she was faced with the man whose son was missing and they felt like cheap-shot questions. The second-guessing thing again. She would take it more carefully. 'Could you describe what happened?'

He told it almost exactly like it was written in the statement. Not quite word for word — but close. Ella sat rubbing her chin, thinking as she listened. Rehearsed lies sometimes came out this way but so could a statement repeated numerous times to various investigators.

'And then I called for urgent back-up and for paramedics,' he concluded.

She sat up straight. 'But Houtkamp was cuffed by that time, wasn't he? So why *urgent* back-up? He was no longer a threat.'

Chris studied her over his tissue. 'Both Dean and I were hurt, and I didn't know how badly. If something happened to the prisoner, I couldn't guarantee we'd be able to look after him.'

'If something happened,' Ella said.

'Yeah, like if he had a fit. He was face-down in cuffs.' Chris shrugged. 'I was trying to help Dean, too. I had my hands full just with him.'

Ella nodded. It was a plausible answer. 'Have you thought of anyone who might have done this?'

'It's all I think about, but I really have no idea.' He was calm and collected. They watched

210

each other for a long moment.

She said, 'Why are you so eager to talk to Dean?'

He gave her a puzzled look. 'He's my friend. Do I need a reason?'

'Not really.' She brushed at the knee of her trousers. 'You know Peter Roth, don't you?'

'We did a course together a couple of years ago. Why?'

'He's dead.'

Chris looked shocked. 'From the gunshot wound?'

'At this stage, we're not sure,' Ella fibbed. 'The PM will find out.'

'But . . . ' Chris hesitated. 'It wasn't foul play, anything like that?'

'Like I said, we're not sure.' She watched him closely. He lowered his chin to his chest and appeared deep in thought. 'Chris, are you sure it wasn't you who rang the TV stations?'

'I told you before, no.'

'And you know nothing about the gang.'

'That's right.'

Ella leaned forward. He wasn't meeting her gaze. Her antennae quivered. 'Chris, if you know something, you should tell me. I can help you. I can protect you.' The thought sneaked into her mind: *Like I protected Roth?*

Now he looked at her. 'How can you think that I would hold back any information when my son's life is at stake?'

'Perhaps for exactly that reason,' she said. 'You think you can save him and we can't.'

He pointed at himself. 'We're the victims here,

211

me and my family. Is it easier for you to suggest I'm hiding something than to get out there and bloody work?'

She placed another of her cards on the bed. 'Ring me when you want to talk.'

11

Angus drove towards Glebe.

'The car's at North Shore,' Sophie said.

'I just want to see something.'

Sophie had no energy to argue. They'd looked at another seventy-three children and each one caused a little rise then crash of hope. She was exhausted and close to breaking point. Her chest ached. Her eyes and the skin around them hurt and when the tears began again she let them run down her face unimpeded.

At a red light on Broadway Angus reached over to squeeze her shoulder and she looked at him, desolate. 'What if we can't find him?'

His hand tightened on her shoulder. 'We'll find him.'

He slowed outside Sawyer's house. Cars were crammed in along the street and a man and a woman leaned talking against the balcony rail at the front of the sandstone house. 'He's obviously still here,' Angus said, driving past. 'Not in custody.'

Sophie craned her neck back to look again. 'You think he should be?'

'It's hard to say without knowing more about the case against him.' Angus continued around the corner then into a parking space near the sportsground. 'There's the birth and the way he

213

threatened you, which makes a pretty good motive in my book. Plus you said they found him overdosed in his car at the wharf, and they found a dummy like Lachlan's there too.'

Sophie nodded, feeling sick.

Angus turned in his seat to stare at the back of Sawyer's house. 'It just seems weird the detectives don't have him in the station, under pressure, getting him to talk.'

Sophie couldn't look any more. *If it was Sawyer . . .*

'I'm going to ask around about it,' Angus said with resolve. 'There must be a reason why they let him go. I just can't figure out what.'

Sophie sank her face into her hands. *If it really was Sawyer . . .* She swallowed back bile.

4.15 pm

When the meeting was over Ella and Dennis were left at the table in the Incident Room, sipping coffee and staring into space. Before Dennis was the information from the surveillance team, stating that Sawyer hadn't budged from his house, hadn't phoned anybody to talk about the missing baby, hadn't stepped outside the law a fraction of an inch. Relatives had arrived in preparation for the funeral tomorrow, and, like yesterday, a number of floral arrangements had been delivered. The team had also reported that Sophie had been at his house twice that day, with an officer named Angus Arendson. They pulled up in Arendson's car, sat there for a few minutes in the morning and again in the afternoon, then went on their way. It didn't appear that Sawyer had seen them. Ella imagined that in Sophie's shoes she, too, might want to keep Sawyer under her own surveillance.

'I've met Arendson before,' Dennis said. 'I think I'll ring him, see what they're doing.'

Ella nodded, rubbing an eye.

Dennis said, 'You don't look like you had that nap.'

'I read the Houtkamp file, then I went to see Chris.'

'You should let the man rest.'

'I had some questions about the assault.'

'Like what?'

She held up a hand. 'I'm not criticising Figgis's work.'

'Good.'

'But how does one unarmed man get the better of two officers?'

'He wasn't unarmed, he had a metal pole,' Dennis said.

'And how did the officers manage to trip over each other so neatly?'

'Do you think they're lying?'

'I'm not sure what's going on.'

'Either you think they're telling the truth or you think they're lying.' Dennis raised his cup to his mouth. 'From the things you're asking, I know where my money lies.'

'It's just a little hard to believe, you know? And I was thinking maybe something else was going on, maybe something that gave Houtkamp a good solid reason for wanting to hurt Chris.'

'Houtkamp's alibi checked out.'

'I've been thinking about that too.' She told him what she'd worked out. 'I reckon he's worth talking to.'

Dennis sighed and rubbed his forehead, then there was a knock at the door.

A young uniformed constable held out a sheet of paper. 'A man made a report this morning about damage to his car. He drives a white Ford Falcon and he said he was parked outside a pub on Wednesday night and someone backed into him then drove off. It left blue paint on his car.'

Dennis sat up straight. 'He's sure it happened then?'

'Yes. When he rang his insurance company they told him to report it to us and to ask the pub people about CCTV. Apparently there is footage of the incident.'

Ella took the piece of paper from the constable. 'Do we have that tape?'

'The manager wouldn't give it to the complainant,' the constable said. 'It's the Red Pheasant, in Newtown. The licensee lives upstairs.'

'Ah, that charming establishment,' Dennis said. 'Let's go.'

★　★　★

The pub was dark red on the outside, cool and dim and stinking of spilled beer on the inside. Groups of patrons in their twenties and younger sat drinking around tables while music pounded from huge black speakers. The licensee, James

216

Bartrim, was a short nuggety man who rubbed a hand across his bald head when Ella told him what they wanted.

'Don't you need, like, a warrant or something for that?'

'Sure, we can go and get one,' Dennis said. 'Out of interest, when was the last time you were raided for drugs?'

'There're no drugs here,' Bartrim said.

'Not now, no,' Ella said. 'We'd do the raid late in the evening. Probably a Saturday evening, I'd think. About eleven.'

Bartrim blew air out of his mouth and led them behind the bar to a tiny office. A small television and a VCR system sat high in one corner above shelves full of piled paperwork and unlabelled folders. Bartrim scratched through a box of video tapes and located one which he stuck into the VCR. He pressed the button to turn the TV on and leaned against the desk.

The screen showed a grainy black-and-white view of a laneway. The tape had been filmed at night. The screen was dark. A date and time counter in the lower right corner read '*Wednesday 7.5, 9.25 pm*' and the seconds whizzed by. Someone walked down the footpath past a line of parked cars. Then the door to the pub opened and two people stepped out.

'That's them,' Bartrim said. 'Hey, if you don't mind me saying, this all seems pretty dramatic for a parking bingle.'

'Ssh,' Dennis said, though there was no sound. He and Ella stared at the image on the screen.

It looked like Sawyer to Ella. Same build. It

was hard to tell from his walk because he was staggering. The person with him supported his arm. They moved to a dark-coloured car, which Ella thought she recognised as Sawyer's BMW though she couldn't make out the plates. Sawyer held out his hand, the hazard lights flashed as the car unlocked, and he got in. The other person — Ella was sure it was a woman — went around to the passenger side. Headlights and brakelights flashed up then the reversing lights lit as the car lurched into the car parked behind him.

'He doesn't even get out to look,' Bartrim said.

'Ssh,' Ella said.

The car drove out of the parking space. Ella caught a glimpse of the numberplate but it was hard to decipher with the car moving. The brakelights disappeared at the edge of the screen. Bartrim shrugged. 'That's it.'

Dennis reached up and ejected the tape, tucking it under his arm. 'Do you recognise either of those people?'

'You've got to be joking. This is a student pub. The place is packed every night of the week.'

'Not many students drive cars like that,' Ella said.

'I don't look outside to see what they drive,' Bartrim said. 'I just try to keep up with their thirst.'

'Just yes or no'll do. Do you recognise them? Are they regulars?' Dennis said.

'No.'

'We'll need to talk to the staff who were

working that night.'

'That'd be Nicki and Luther and Farouk. They're all on later tonight.'

'We'll need their addresses so we can speak to them before then.'

Bartrim pulled a folder off a shelf, causing a pile of papers to cascade to the floor. He found a page and turned the folder around for Ella to see. She wrote the names, addresses and phone numbers of the three staff in her notebook. 'Can you show us where the camera is?'

Bartrim jammed the folder back onto the shelf and they walked out through the noisy bar. He pulled open a side door and fresh evening air poured in. Ella and Dennis stepped into the street.

The side of the pub was as red as the front. The camera was high on the wall. The street was narrow. A rusting red VW Golf was parked in the spot where Sawyer's car had been. Behind it, gumleaves collected in the gutter. The wind blew and the spindly tree in a backyard across the street lost more leaves.

Bartrim watched them look around. 'Anything else you want?'

'No.'

Bartrim didn't have to hear it twice. No sooner had Dennis spoken than he'd disappeared.

'Well,' Ella said. 'That looks like our man to me.'

Dennis nodded slowly. 'I agree.'

'With a woman,' Ella said. 'What kind of man comes to a bar and picks up a woman the day after his family dies?'

'A lonely and sad one,' Dennis said.

Ella snorted.

'Give the man a break,' Dennis said. 'Everyone copes with grief in their own way. He said himself he was out driving around. So he comes here for a drink, then some friendly and kind person starts to talk to him. More people would appreciate the sympathetic ear than not.'

'If he wants to drink, why not take a bottle home? Or just park somewhere quiet?'

Dennis rubbed his forehead. 'What matters is that this happened half an hour before Phillips was shot. This woman might be his alibi.'

'Or maybe she saw him do it.' Ella paced the footpath. 'If she's a local drug dealer people here might know her. We have to bring more people tonight and canvass everyone.'

'Or,' Dennis said, 'if we show him the footage he might remember and be able to tell us.'

Ella looked at him. 'You don't think he knows exactly what he did?'

'Maybe he really doesn't.' Dennis flicked a gumnut onto the road with his shoe. 'Those drugs were in his blood.'

'So what?'

Dennis shrugged. 'Also it's convenient that just after the guy's wife and baby die, this happens to the family of the paramedic who was called to them.'

'That's called a motive, not convenience.'

'I mean it works well as a red herring. It's such a good motive we latch onto him straightaway.'

'You're suggesting that somebody set all this

up?' Ella said. 'That in some magnificent lining-up of the planets, a birth gone wrong happened to occur around the time persons unknown decided to act against Chris Phillips, and that same birth was in the hands of Chris's wife?'

Dennis picked up a gumleaf and crumpled it between his fingers. 'Not exactly.'

'Then what?'

'Maybe the birth was convenient cover. Maybe the rest was already planned and they've been fortunate that this happened and threw us off.' Dennis paused. 'I know how that sounds.'

Ella placed the flat of her hand on the roof of the rusting Golf. 'What would they have done if the birth hadn't happened?'

'Gone ahead anyway,' Dennis said. 'If they leave no evidence, and nobody talks, we have no case.'

'How about the fact that Chris survived?'

'Nobody shoots another person in the head and expects them to live.'

'But anybody who's familiar with guns and wanted him dead would hedge their bets and use something other than a twenty-two subsonic,' she said. 'And still the question remains: why take the baby?'

'Okay,' he said. 'I told you that I know how it sounds.'

Dennis had developed an incredible scenario but was it any more incredible than her musings about Houtkamp? Yes, she decided after a moment, it was. 'This is out there.'

Dennis dropped the leaf and brushed his

221

hands together. 'It doesn't really matter at the moment. Until we know more about what Sawyer did that night, we can't say for sure whether he was involved.'

4.45 pm

Chris asked for the phone again, and dialled another number. 'Hi Angela, is Dean home yet?'

He wasn't but Angela said she'd pass on the message. In the background he could hear their kids yelling.

'Perhaps he could come and visit me?' Chris said.

She'd tell him. She had to go. She was always abrupt on the phone — because of the kids, Chris guessed. He couldn't tell from her tone whether she knew what had gone on between him and Dean or not. He suspected not: if Dean had told her about that, she naturally would have asked the reason why, and that was a place Dean would never have wanted to go.

He pulled his pillow higher so he was sitting more upright. The room turned and the black spots appeared but he needed to overcome his dizziness. The nurses kept telling him to rest, to save his strength for getting better, that was the best way he could help Lachlan, but none of them understood. Even Sophie didn't get it. No matter how bad she felt, it wasn't her fault that Lachlan was gone.

Chris shut his eyes against the black spots. After the bank case he hadn't been able to shake off the memory of the guard's still chest, his limp hands, the way his head lolled to the side whenever Angus released his grip. Worst was the terrible knowledge that it had not had to happen. He could have done something earlier if he'd wanted, if he'd had the *guts*, and that red-haired woman and her twins would not be alone. Instead, guilt-stricken, he'd done it after the fact, calling the TV stations to tell them what was going on, hoping to make it up to the dead man in some small way. Now his head held more images that wouldn't go away: the last time he'd seen Lachlan, asleep on his back in his cot, as safe as any baby could be; then the man with the gun on his doorstep.

And now Sophie was running around out there like some kind of vigilante, so caught up in her search that she would never know if she was being followed, and Ella was starting to snoop about the Houtkamp case. It scared him half to death. He needed to make contact with the people who had Lachlan and let them know he was sorry, he'd made a mistake, he would never ever do such a stupid thing.

He picked up the phone again.

'Recruitment.'

'Is Dean available?'

'I'm so sorry, he's left for the day,' the woman said. 'I did pass on all your messages.'

Maybe he would drop in on his way home. Chris sat biting his lip, feeling his head throb. He would make it all clear to Dean. He would tell him that if they wanted his life in return for Lachlan's and Sophie's safety, then that was the price he would pay.

'There's another department for our Christmas card list,' Dennis said as he and Ella got back in the car with the pictures the Photographics Unit had processed from the CCTV tape. The unit had been near to closing for the day when the detectives hurried in, but like so many other sections they'd pulled out all stops to get the work done immediately. Another cop's child missing was like their own child missing.

They pored over the pictures.

'It's definitely Sawyer,' Ella said.

'And his car.'

The photos weren't as clear as shots taken in daylight, but the unit techs had been able to zoom in and enhance and God knew what, to the point where the BMW's numberplate was clear and Sawyer's face was recognisable. The woman was another story however. Ella said, 'It's as if she knew the camera was there and was being careful to hide her face.'

'She's shorter than him, and has a slim build,' Dennis said. 'Short dark hair. Wearing dark trousers and a dark shirt.'

All fine and true but it wasn't going to help them find her.

'Let's go and visit Sawyer,' Ella said.

'He's not going to talk without his solicitor.'

'Let's just knock at his door and see what happens,' she said. 'Like you said, looking at this might bring his memory back. He might recognise her. She might provide an alibi for the time of the shooting.'

'I thought you thought he was guilty.'

'I just want to know one way or the other,' she said. 'If we can cross him off, I don't have to think about him any more.'

They drove through the lengthening shadows to Sawyer's house. A for sale sign stood outside the block of flats across the street and Ella figured the surveillance team were probably comfortably ensconced in the empty unit.

Dennis knocked on Sawyer's door. A dark-haired woman with red eyes answered. 'Not interested,' she said, and started to close the door.

Dennis showed his badge. 'We're police.'

Her eyes widened. 'Have you found out who drugged Boyd?'

Dennis said, 'You are?'

'Helen Sawyer, Boyd's sister.' She glanced behind her. Ella could see shadows of people moving about, and hear the clink of cups and teaspoons. The conversation was low, sombre. The woman went on, 'I think he's upstairs. Just a minute and I'll fetch him.' She started off then turned back. 'I'm sorry. My mind this afternoon . . . Would you like to come in?'

Dennis shook his head. 'We don't want to intrude.'

The woman gave a small smile and went up the stairs.

In the house somebody began to weep. Ella and Dennis exchanged a glance and Dennis made a face. 'We had to come,' Ella whispered.

Sawyer came slowly down the stairs. Ella was shocked to see he looked even thinner than before. She hadn't thought that was possible.

Sawyer looked at Dennis. 'Have you found the man who drugged me?'

Ella was fine with being ignored. Just fine.

'Would you mind looking at some photos for us please?' Dennis said.

'Do I need my solicitor?'

His sister tucked her arm through his. 'It's okay, Boyd.'

'We just want you to tell us whether you recognise someone,' Dennis said.

Ella held the picture out. 'That's you, isn't it? So who is this?'

Sawyer looked at the photo for a moment then back up at them. His face was blank. He said, 'I'm saying nothing without my solicitor present,' and shut the door in their faces.

5.20 pm

The last of the sun's rays streamed in the tow truck's window but Sophie couldn't feel them. She wrapped her arms around herself and looked down into every car they passed. Some of them had pale blue ribbons tied to their aerials. She felt as if she'd worked three night shifts in a row with no sleep between them and drunk enough espressos for ten people. Her skin was sore, her eyes red and painful. Thoughts of Lachlan filled her head. She'd give her life to be able to hold him again and know he was safe.

At Royal North Shore, while Angus had waited with the car for the tow truck, she'd gone into the hospital to see Chris. He was silent. She'd hoped to lie next to him, comforted by his arms around her, his face close to hers, but he grumbled when she started to get on the bed. Instead she sat in a chair with her hand on his knee and tried to get him to talk. When she told him what she'd been doing all day he got angry. Didn't she know the danger she was putting herself in? Apart from the fact she and Angus were breaking the law by lying to these people? Wondering for a second whether he was jealous because of who she was with, or simply angry over what she'd done, she'd said she had to do *something*, she couldn't simply sit around. Then he'd gone all defensive, saying he was doing the best he could but he was injured. She'd felt like shouting about her own needs, her own loneliness and grief, but in the end she'd pecked him on the cheek and left. Now all she wanted was to sink into a hot bath and think of ways to look at more children.

The tow-truck driver let her out at the end of her driveway and she walked to the house with her head down, the kit slung over her shoulder, the ambulance shirt rolled up in the plastic bag in her hand. Sounds of children playing came from the houses nearby but she didn't want to look up and see the parents, didn't want to listen to their sympathy, didn't want to go through what the police thought and where they were up to with the case. The answering machine in the house would be full of the same queries, no doubt many from Cynthia and her other friends from the antenatal group, but she wouldn't call anyone back. She just couldn't face anyone now. She needed to be alone and think.

The doorstep was empty and she paused. That morning it had been full of flowers and soft toys, and she'd left it that way. Now the step was clear and there was a pale blue ribbon tied to the door handle.

Next second the door opened and Gloria pulled her into a hug. The house was bright and smelled of cooking. 'Where have you been?'

Sophie stepped inside. The living room was full of the flowers and soft toys from the step, and cards hung on a string across the wall. Fergus Patrick smiled uneasily from an armchair, a photo album open on his lap. A radio played softly somewhere. Rage swelled up inside Sophie's chest and she turned on Gloria. 'What have you done?'

'Just tidied up a little,' Gloria said. 'Did you see the ribbon? It was Cynthia's idea. They're even talking about it on the news. And Mr Patrick is looking for another picture of Lachlan, to print on the posters.'

Patrick cleared his throat. 'I might use this one, if that's okay with you?' He held up a recent picture of Lachlan sitting outside on a rug in the sun. Sophie remembered taking it, how she'd made silly faces to get him to smile, the sound of his laughter.

She pulled away from Gloria and ran upstairs. There were vacuum marks on the carpet. Her and Chris's room was neat, all the clothes gone from the floor, the bed made with fresh sheets. Lachlan's room smelled of Mr Sheen and his toys were lined up tidily on his dresser.

'Don't you think it looks better?' Gloria said behind her.

Sophie bit down hard on a scream. How could she explain her need to keep everything exactly as it had been the night Lachlan was taken? That freezing time in this little world when time outside marched on made her feel more able to bring him home?

'The milk was off, in the fridge,' Gloria said. Sophie whirled to face her. 'I mean, things needed doing,' Gloria added lamely.

Sophie said, 'I'm having a bath.' She went into the bathroom and slammed the door.

'Dinner will be about half an hour,' Gloria said through the crack.

'I'm not hungry.'

'You need to eat.'

'I am not hungry.'

Sophie ran the bath deep and hot. She poured in some of Lachlan's baby wash then sank into the water, breathing in his smell, her tears mingling with the bathwater.

The ringing of her mobile made her sit up, and she grabbed it from her pile of clothes on the floor.

'It's me,' Angus said. 'I've found out some

229

stuff about Sawyer but I don't know if you'll want to hear it.'

'Tell me,' she said, her voice cracking.

'They've got surveillance on him and they only do that when they're pretty sure about a suspect.'

Sophie closed her eyes.

'But they're not positive that he went to the river to, um . . . You know.'

Sophie knew. 'So what do they think happened?'

'They think he may have dropped him off somewhere. Given him to someone.'

'Like to a friend?'

Angus hesitated. 'Like the baby black market.'

'I thought there was no such thing.' Her head was spinning, from the hot water or the news or both.

'That's what people like to think,' he said.

'So why don't they haul him in and hammer him to find out?'

'He won't speak to them any more and he's got one hell of a bulldog for a lawyer,' Angus said.

There seemed to be steam in her mind as well as in the room. 'And they're letting that stop them?'

'There are rules about what they can do.'

'He's my baby,' she said.

'I know it, and they know it. They're doing as much as they can but there are legal lines they can't cross.'

'Why hasn't Ella told me these things?'

'They worry about letting out information,

firstly in case the wrong person hears about the progress of the case, and secondly in case people take it on themselves to act.'

Sophie rubbed her face with a wet hand.

'I only found out because I've got friends in there and they know I can be trusted.'

'But you can't. You just told me everything,' Sophie said.

'But I know that you can,' he said. 'If you ask Ella about this she'll deny it, you understand. But she'll know someone leaked information, and that could mean trouble.'

When he'd hung up she dropped the phone back onto her pile of clothes and sank into the water. All her life she'd trusted and believed in the police, and this had only increased when she'd become a paramedic and worked so closely with them, then married one. If they thought Sawyer was the one, then he must be.

It's my fault.

Nausea struck her and she leapt out of the bath to stand dripping over the toilet, retching up bile.

She should've done more, she should've worked harder at saving Sawyer's wife and child. She should've shown more compassion. If he'd seen her holding back tears at the scene maybe he would've known how much she wished for them to be okay. She shouldn't have hidden outside at the hospital but gone to see him, talk to him, show him the effect it had had on her.

There was a tap at the door. 'Are you okay?'

'Leave me alone.' Sophie glared into the toilet. She was furious with herself. She was furious with Gloria for coming in and changing the house. She was also furious with Ella for not telling her everything — what did the detective think she would do, kidnap Sawyer and torture the truth out of him herself?

9 pm

Music thumped from the monstrosity that was the Red Pheasant. Dennis looked in at the crush of people. 'This is not going to be easy.'

They had no choice. Van Pelt refused to meet with them unless Sawyer was under arrest. Not tonight, not tomorrow, the day of the funerals. Maybe the next day. Maybe.

Inside the pub the noise was deafening. A DJ bounced on a small stage at one end, and red and green lights flashed fast enough to give you seizures. Ella spotted Farouk, the barman they'd spoken to at home earlier in the evening. Neither he nor the other two staff had recognised the people in the photo.

Ella followed Dennis to the far end of the room, took a deep breath of humid air and put her hand on the shoulder of a young man in torn jeans and a black T-shirt, with a black goatee beard. He turned with a smile that shrank when she opened her badge in his face. She then held out the photo. 'Do you recognise either of these people?'

'What?'

Ella shouted it louder.

He screwed up his eyes over the picture. The girl with him leaned over to look too. They both shook their heads. 'Sorry,' he bellowed.

Ella smiled her thanks and moved on.

When she held out the picture and yelled the question for the eighth time, the man she was showing it to nodded. 'I know him, yeah.'

'You know him?'

'What?'

Ella pointed to the door. She grabbed Dennis on the way. Outside they stood under a streetlight. The air was cool and smelled of car exhaust. 'You're sure you know him?' Ella said.

'Yeah, he's a plastic surgeon. His name's Sawyer.' The man was in his late twenties with brown hair cut short and spiked up. He wore black jeans and a grey T-shirt with the words 'Crazy Mofo' across the chest. 'He did my girlfriend's tits. Did a really good job too,' he said. 'She's a stripper. Tax deduction, you know. Enhanced her earning potential no end.'

Ella said, 'Have you ever seen this man here at the Red Pheasant?'

'Yeah, I saw him last night.' He looked at the picture again. 'I'm pretty sure he was with this chick. I remember cos she had no tits and I wondered if she was his girlfriend, if he'd do hers for free.'

'You're certain you saw this man here in this pub last night?' Dennis said.

'Yes,' the man said.

'Had you seen the woman before?'

He shook his head.

'Can you describe her?'

'She had no tits,' he said. 'That's really all I remember.'

'Was she tall, short, thin, fat?' Ella said.

The man shrugged.

Dennis said, 'What was her height in comparison to Detective Marconi?'

The man looked her over. Ella resisted the urge to fold her arms. 'I only saw her sitting down so I don't know how tall she is. Oh, but I remember she had skinny arms. I saw those arms and I thought, yeah, that's why she's got no tits.'

'So she's skinny.'

'Skinny arms is all I saw.'

'What about her face?'

'Don't even remember it.' He shrugged again. 'Say plain. Average. Forgettable, you know.'

'Would you recognise her if you saw her again?'

'Probably not.'

Dennis took his name and contact details and said he'd get him in for a proper statement in the morning.

'No sweat. See ya.' The man wandered back into the pub. Ella thrust her hands into her pockets. 'A real charmer.'

'At least now we know something.'

'What do we know?' Ella said. 'We already knew Sawyer was here, and left with this woman. The only new bit of information is a fragment of a description, but how do we find a woman with no tits and skinny arms?'

'The description might help Sawyer remember her,' Dennis said. 'Or if she's a drug dealer the Local Area Command might know her. We should get onto that tomorrow.'

Ella pressed a thumb into her right eye, trying to ease the growing headache there. 'Let's just go back in there and get this over with.'

The rest of the pub was a bust. Ella got sick of seeing people shake their heads. It was after ten when she finally beckoned Dennis outside. They had to squeeze through the door past the stream of people entering the building. Almost as many were leaving.

'We can't keep up with this,' she said into Dennis's ear. Someone bumped into her and she turned ready to snap, but they'd already slipped away into the crowd.

'You want to call it a night?'

She gestured at the crowds jostling at the door and started to speak, then a strong male arm snaked around her waist. 'Hey, babe!'

Without a second's hesitation she seized the wrist and bent it back and sideways, causing the Crazy Mofo to drop to the footpath with a yelp. She kept the tension on, twisting his arm over, making him scrabble drunkenly to keep up and save his arm. People stopped to look and someone giggled crazily.

'He probably needs that arm,' Dennis said mildly.

Ella kept the pressure on for a moment. The man grimaced up at her. 'I'm sorry.'

She held up one warning finger then let go of his arm. The Crazy Mofo scrambled to his feet and disappeared into the watching crowd. Ella felt like crying. Her head throbbed with the music and fatigue and the sheer bloody misery of the case; she felt it would never be over, they would never find Lachlan and reunite the family, and she would spend the rest of her life calculating his age and staring into the faces of dark-eyed boys.

12

Dean Rigby didn't show up and he didn't call. Chris lay awake most of the night thinking, and when the day-shift nurse came in to check his pulse and blood pressure he told her his decision.

'You're joking,' she said.

'You can get all the doctors in here, you can even bring the hospital CEO, but I won't change my mind.'

She did get the doctor. He listened as Chris explained again what he wanted. The doctor said, 'I can't stop you but I am advising in the strongest possible terms against it.'

'Understood.'

'You could die.'

'I'll sign all the waivers you want,' Chris said.

Gloria arrived as he was filling in the paperwork. It was way before visiting hours so he guessed one of the nurses had called her.

She stabbed a finger at the forms. 'This is proof that you need to stay. Only a man with a brain injury would want to leave hospital so soon after being shot.'

'I'm fine,' he said, signing his name in haste. It was taking some effort to sit up and talk to people and read and write, and there was more

236

to be done before he could collapse on the lounge at home.

The doctor insisted he go downstairs in a wheelchair. Chris agreed, if only to keep Gloria from getting any further on his back. She maintained a stony silence in the lift then through the hospital foyer and carpark. He climbed into the front seat of the car. She took the wheelchair back to the building then got in the driver's seat.

As she put the key into the ignition he said, 'I need you to drive me into the city.'

'No.'

He opened the door. 'Then I'll get a taxi to the train and go in by myself.'

She considered him for a long moment, her gaze moving over the wound on his face and the bruising around his eyes. Then she turned the key and revved the engine. He closed the door. 'Thank you.'

When they were on the Pacific Highway in North Sydney she said, 'So where are we going and why?'

'The Headquarters building. I have to see someone.'

'But why?'

'To sort out some things.'

'Can't you do it over the phone?'

'No, I can't.' The glare from the windscreens of oncoming cars made his head hurt. He closed his eyes, then felt dizzy.

When they were over the Bridge and in the CBD he directed Gloria to the Headquarters building. 'Stop here. I won't be long.'

She looked anxiously about. 'It's a no-standing zone. I'll get booked.'

'If a grey ghost comes, just go around the block.' He got out of the car, ignoring his mother's protests.

Inside the building he took the lift up to the Recruitment Office. People bustled in the corridors. Someone said 'Hi' to him but he didn't take his eyes off the door to the office.

A young female constable with her arm in a cast looked up at him when he walked in. 'Can I help you?'

'I want to talk to Dean.'

The door to the inner office opened and Dean looked out. 'Chris?'

★ ★ ★

They sat on opposite sides of the desk. 'I can't believe you're out of hospital so soon,' Dean said, adjusting the wide foam collar around his neck.

'You never called me back.'

'It's been crazy in here.' Dean waved towards the boxes of mail stacked in a corner of the room. 'We've got a drive going on, the phones are ringing off the hook all the time, people requesting packages and sending in applications and asking stupid questions like will a rape conviction stop them from becoming a copper.' He smiled but Chris didn't smile back. Dean turned serious. 'Any news on your boy?'

'You should know.'

'Huh?'

Chris leaned forward over the desk. 'You tell the others that I'm no longer a threat, okay? You tell them I'll do whatever they want.'

'What are you talking about?'

'What I did was wrong, I know that now,' Chris said. 'But nobody else knows I did it. I won't say another word. All I want is my son.'

'Chris, mate, you've lost me.'

The ringing started in Chris's ears. The room was so hot. He took a deep breath. 'What do they want? They want me dead?'

'Chris — '

He tried to blink away the dark spots. 'Talk to them, tell them what I said, then call me.' He lowered his head to his knees. 'That Detective Marconi's looking into Houtkamp, you know. It's not a huge jump from one thing to another.'

There was silence from across the desk. With a little more blood in his head Chris was able to look up. Dean was staring at him.

'Tell them what I said.'

Dean suddenly smiled. 'I think you've come out of hospital too soon. Something's wrong with your head, making you paranoid.'

'I won't wait forever,' Chris said. 'Bring him back today. You tell them.'

Dean gave half a laugh. 'How about I get an ambulance, get you back to where you should be?'

Chris stood up unsteadily and moved towards the door. 'You tell them.'

Mercifully, the lift was empty. He leaned his forehead against the cold steel doors and fought back tears. He'd known Dean wouldn't admit to anything but he'd hoped that there'd at least be some sign that the message was getting through, that things would be fixed. Instead he'd seen no response at all — only a glimmer of fear when he'd mentioned Houtkamp.

10.12 am

There was nobody home in the top-floor flats. Sophie took a moment to lean on the landing's windowsill. The glass was broken and she looked out over the southern suburbs and felt the breeze come across all those houses, all those families, to touch her face.

'You're different this morning,' Angus said.

It was true. While she hadn't yet decided to go ahead with her idea, she could feel herself coming to believe it was the only way she'd find Lachlan. Going flat to flat now felt pointless, little more than a time-filler while she decided how to do it.

She watched Angus from the corner of her eye, wondering how much he could be trusted. He'd kept The Big Mistake a secret from Chris, and hadn't ever embarrassed her over it. He'd come along with her so far, had even given her information she wasn't meant to have, but what she was considering next was much worse than a simple con. Finally she said, 'Have you ever done a case where the law didn't do what it was supposed to? Where someone didn't pay for their crime?'

'Lots of people get shorter sentences than they deserve.'

'I mean a case where the culprit walked completely free. Or where maybe he was never even charged.'

Angus nodded. 'They're unfortunately not that rare.'

'Don't you ever wish you could do something more?'

He brushed at his tie. 'I did, once.'

She faced him.

'When I was working out Bankstown way, this guy grabbed a twelve-year-old girl off the street. The girl had been on her way home from dance class. She wanted to be a ballerina. After she'd been on the stand and had to answer questions about the exact details of the man's anatomy and actions, after the case got binned on technicalities, she took an overdose of her mother's newly prescribed depression medication. She spent a week in ICU and came out brain-damaged enough to no longer dance or cope with school, but not so brain-damaged she didn't know about it or had forgotten the entire sequence of events.' He kicked the wall. 'I saw the mother some time later; she told me they put their place up for sale and the guy came along to an open house under a false name and took a picture of the girl's bedroom then mailed it to them.'

'What did you do?'

Now Angus studied her as if measuring her trustworthiness. 'I followed him for a while.'

She waited.

'And one night he came out of a pub drunk and started walking home, and when he staggered into a dark street I was waiting.' Angus lowered his gaze. 'I kicked the crap out of him.'

A week ago Sophie would have disapproved. 'Did he live?'

Angus nodded. 'Bruises, scrapes, a few cracked ribs, bit of internal bleeding.'

'Did it do the job?'

'His name hasn't popped up on the system since.' Angus shrugged. 'I don't know if people like that can really change, but I like to think he got a bit of his own medicine.'

Sophie looked out the window again. There was a message in what Angus had just told her: the way to do it was on your own. There was no need to tell him what she was thinking. It was safer that way too, because he might be happy to pretend he worked for the Health Department, he might beat up a child rapist in a dark alley, but what she was considering was a whole different matter.

'Better get moving.' She bent to pick up the red kit then heard a noise. She froze.

'What's the matter?'

'Listen.'

Angus frowned. 'I can't hear . . . ' He stopped. The sound was faint but distinct.

'That's a baby crying,' Sophie said. She went to the nearest door and pressed her ear to the wood. Angus checked the next one. At the third one Sophie found the cry was louder. 'It's in here.'

Angus put his ear against the door while

Sophie stood back and surveyed the area. There had been no signs of life in any of these flats when she and Angus knocked. There were no peepholes in the doors, no windows along the landing.

The baby wailed.

'I can't hear any other sounds,' Angus whispered. 'Maybe there's nobody here with it.'

'Or they're taking great care to sneak around.' Either meant something was wrong. Sophie tested the doorknob and found it locked.

Angus went to the end of the landing and leaned out the window. 'There's one window that might be within reach.'

'We're six floors up.' Sophie tapped a knuckle across the wood. She'd kicked flimsy doors down before, getting to critically ill patients. This one sounded solid.

In the flat the baby howled.

'Maybe between us we can kick it in?' she said. 'If we find him, or we save someone's life, nobody's going to be too fussed about asking why we were here.'

They stood side by side, holding each other for balance. Angus counted down and they hit the wood simultaneously with their heels.

'Again.'

This time Sophie reeled back, her foot throbbing. 'It must be deadbolted top and bottom.'

Angus crouched and rubbed his ankle. 'How the hell are we going to get in?'

Inside the flat, the baby screamed.

Edman Hughes waved at Ella from the station doorway as she drove into the yard.

He came down the steps to meet her. 'Hello, Detective Marconi.'

'I'm sorry but I can't talk now,' she said, going past him, the manila envelope of photos in her hand.

'It's just I've heard nothing about my case,' he said. 'I was wondering what you'd found out about the, um, accelerant?'

'The samples are still being processed.' Had she even sent them in? God only knew. 'I'll let you know when I hear anything.'

'I can't find work,' he said, looking up at her from the bottom step. 'All my money was in that business.'

'I'm sorry for you, Mr Hughes, but I have other cases going on, and I have important things to do.' The station door clunked shut behind her and she hurried away. Just before she turned the corner in the corridor she couldn't help glancing back, and she saw he was still there, peering in like a lost dog. She felt like shouting, *Hey, I'm trying to find a baby here! Let's get our priorities right, shall we?*

Around the corner she ran into Detective Hollebeck, who was leaning against the wall. He checked his watch. 'Part-timer?'

She went to move past. 'If you don't mind, I have things to do.'

'I know.' He pointed her down the corridor. 'Top of your list is talking to us.'

When they were seated in an office Hollebeck leaned forward on his folded arms. Draper, the quiet achiever, opened her notebook. Ella put the envelope on the table and waited.

'There's been some interesting developments in the Roth case,' Hollebeck said.

'How so?'

'Your prints weren't on the IV bag or line.'

'I wore gloves.'

'We know,' Hollebeck said. 'Dennis told us.'

'When did you talk to Dennis?'

Hollebeck ignored her question. 'In fact, nobody's prints were on the bag or line.'

'The nurse wore gloves too. I told you that.'

'We know.' Hollebeck smiled at her.

Ella smiled back. 'Can we get to the point?'

'Preliminary tests on the IV set show traces of lignocaine and insulin. Whoever went for Roth knew what they wanted and knew how to cause it,' he said. 'We've spoken to the staff on Roth's ward and none of them saw any strange nurse. We checked the hospital's security footage. The woman you describe does not appear.'

'So she changed her clothes and wig in a bathroom somewhere,' Ella said.

'Oh, was she wearing a wig?'

'I don't know, I'm just making suggestions.'

Hollebeck turned to Draper. 'Might have worn a wig. Write that down.' He looked back at Ella. 'See, we don't know any of these things because nobody else saw her. Except Roth himself, of course. But he's dead, so no help there.'

His tone pissed her off. 'I'm surprised you

didn't have a guard posted for precisely this sort of event.'

'Oh, but we did.'

'I never saw one.'

'He was cunningly disguised as a patient in a room across the hall.'

'So what did he see?'

'Nothing,' Hollebeck said.

'Too busy watching TV?'

'He was asleep.' He leaned further forward. 'Because he'd been drugged.'

Ella had been about to suggest he pick his team a bit better. 'That nurse again?'

'He didn't have an IV. All he'd done was eat the meals brought to him.'

'Sounds like you've got your work cut out for you, finding someone with access to the meals as well as a fake nurse,' Ella said.

'I want you to think very carefully,' Hollebeck said, 'about whether anyone walked past the room when this nurse was in there, whether anyone at all may have seen her. Because otherwise . . . '

She folded her arms. 'Otherwise what?'

'Otherwise we have to consider the possibility that you may have done it.'

She snorted laughter. 'I was trying to get information from him about the Phillips case. Why would I want him dead? That's even if I knew how to connect an IV line, which I don't.'

'Just so you know where we stand.' Hollebeck leaned back in his chair. 'You can go.'

Ella grabbed up the manila envelope then slammed the door as she went out. The nerve of him! She knew what this meant: people would be looking into her, searching for links to Roth, the robbery gang, anything out of the ordinary. There was nothing to find — except maybe that thing about Shakespeare — but it was a nasty feeling.

In the Incident Room she slapped the envelope down on the desk. Dennis turned from the computer. 'What are you all wound up about?'

'Hollebeck just asked me if I killed Roth,' she said. 'Not in so many words, of course.'

'They're only barking up every tree they can find. They don't really think it was you.'

'So long as they don't suspend me from duty while they make up their mind.'

'How'd you go with the photos?'

Ella was still thinking of Hollebeck's stare. 'If only you'd been in Roth's room with me, you could confirm that woman was real.'

'Ella,' he said. 'The photos?'

She focused. 'No good. If she is a drug dealer, none of them knew her.' Nobody at the police stations around the pub even thought she looked familiar.

Dennis leaned back in the chair and stretched his arms above his head. 'I talked to Arendson last night. He's Chris's current partner. He said Sophie can't stop searching and he's going along to make sure she's okay while Chris is crook.'

'That's good,' Ella said. 'So does she think Sawyer did it?'

'Apparently not. Arendson said Sophie told him about the birth and everything else, how we looked into him, and he simply wanted to see if the guy was in custody or not.'

Ella sat down and nodded at the computer screen. 'So what are you doing here?'

'Just rereading some stuff.' He moved the mouse desultorily. 'I feel like we're in a holding pattern. We can't show those photos to Sawyer because the funeral's on today, we're still trying to get access to the TV stations' phone records, everyone's out chasing down baby leads and getting precisely zip.'

Ella knew what he meant, especially about the photos. She aligned the envelope with the corners of the desk. 'You don't think we could duck around this afternoon, when the funeral's over, take some flowers or something — '

'No, I don't,' he said. 'He's not so major a suspect that he deserves that.'

She put her palm flat on the envelope. 'Tomorrow, then.'

He nodded, eyes on the screen.

'Hey,' he said, looking up after a moment. 'Did I tell you that the money found with Marisa Waters and Dudley-Pearson was really hers? She actually had sold a bunch of shares.'

'So it was true love after all.'

'Nothing dodgy at all.'

'That's so sweet.'

He grinned at her.

Sophie watched the paramedics emerge from the block of units with a female patient wrapped in blankets on the stretcher. She lay on her side with an oxygen mask on. The drip stand was up and a bag of Hartmann's ran through the IV line. The paramedic at the woman's head bent down and spoke to her. Sophie nodded to herself. *Conscious but drowsy, and hypotensive enough to need fluids: probably a drug overdose. Prescription tablets. Maybe antidepressants.*

The paramedic at the foot of the stretcher glanced around and Sophie slid lower in the passenger seat of Angus's car. The red kit, clipboard and tie were on the floor. She'd come up with the idea of having Angus in the block to visit a friend who wasn't home, when he thought he heard a cry for help so called an ambulance.

Now he emerged from the door of the block carrying a baby. The baby was blond, and red in the face, and flailing its arms in his grip. Angus hurried to the ambulance and a slim arm snaked out from under the blanket towards the baby as the paramedics loaded the stretcher into the vehicle. The paramedic climbed in beside the stretcher then reached back out for the baby.

Angus waited on the street until the ambulance was gone, then came to the car. 'Lucky for her we came along,' he said.

'Tablets?' Sophie said. 'And alcohol?'

Angus nodded as he started the car. 'When the three of us were kicking at that bloody door she actually woke up enough to come over and unlock it.' He put the car into gear, then slipped it back into neutral. 'Where to now?'

'Home, I think.'

'Really?'

She nodded. She'd made her decision and she had some serious planning to do. Gloria would be at the hospital all day, so the house would be peaceful and quiet; and if she wavered, Lachlan's empty cot would spur her on.

★　★　★

Gloria's car was in the driveway, its aerial a mass of pale blue ribbons. 'Damn.' Sophie recalled Angus sympathising when she'd bitched about Gloria that night at the Jungle. She wondered how well they'd known each other. It would be odd having him in the house, but maybe he and Gloria would sit around reminiscing and she could retreat into her head and scheme. 'Do you want to come in?'

'Why not.'

Gloria opened the front door.

'Gloria, you remember Angus?' Sophie said.

Gloria glanced at him and nodded, then reached for Sophie's arm. 'Chris signed himself out of hospital. He needs to go back. You need to tell him so. To make him.'

Sophie motioned for Angus to go in past her. 'I'm sure he knows what he's doing.'

'He doesn't.' Gloria slammed the door. 'That's the problem.'

'He always was stubborn,' Angus put in.

Gloria looked at him, and Sophie took the

opportunity to run upstairs. As she reached the landing she heard Gloria ask about Bee. Angus started telling her about Bee's sick son, Ben.

Chris lay on his side on the bed, his mobile phone on the covers next to him. 'I hope you haven't been running around the streets again.'

So that's how it's going to be. She kicked the kitbag into a corner and started changing out of the uniform. 'I hear you signed out against advice.'

He said, 'It's not safe for you out there, and anyway are you allowed to be in uniform if you're not on duty?'

'It's not safe for you here,' she said. 'You could have a cerebral bleed, and what can Gloria and I do about it?'

'Are you trying to control me again?'

She threw the clothes onto the floor. He'd been badly injured, she reminded herself. He could have died. His son was missing. He needed understanding. And so did she. 'It's going to be okay.'

He looked at his watch. 'Says who?'

'Says me. I'll find him.'

'Because I can't?'

'No, not because you can't,' she said. 'Because it's my fault, and I'm going to fix things.'

'It's not your fault.' But he didn't look at her as he said it, and she suddenly saw all his anger, his silence, even his resistance to her wanting to get on his bed in the hospital, for what it was.

He blames me.

She didn't know why it should hurt so much, because he was right to blame her. But the two metres of space between them suddenly seemed like miles and his back looked like that of a stranger. When she spoke the words fell into dead air. 'I'm going downstairs.'

He didn't reply.

13

Detective Murray Shakespeare was leaning in the doorway watching officers take calls on the public hotline. Ella pulled Dennis into a corridor before he could spot them.

'Do you a deal,' she said. 'You keep him for the next couple of hours and I'll take him all weekend.'

Dennis frowned.

She put her hands together in prayer. 'Houtkamp's not going to talk if he's there.'

'He also won't talk if he doesn't know anything.'

'An hour. Just give me one hour.'

Dennis rolled his eyes and held out his hand. She shook it with glee.

She was heading out of the station carpark when Shakespeare ran from the building into her path. She braked. 'What?'

He opened the passenger door and got in. 'Dennis said he was going home for a break and I should find something else to do.' He shrugged. 'So here I am.'

Oh, great. 'That's really nice, Murray, but I've got something I need to do on my own.'

'Like what?'

'I can't say.'

'Acting Commissioner Eagers said I'm to get full access.'

253

'To the case, yes. But I'm not sure yet if this is related.' She smiled at him. 'So you'd be better to go back inside. Read through the computer log. You might see something we've missed.'

He seemed to consider this for a moment. 'Thanks, but I'll stay.'

She couldn't think of a way to get him out, short of opening the door and kicking him, and that'd no doubt end in someone else kicking her. *Goddammit*.

They drove without speaking to Banks Street in Waterloo. Ella tried to clear her mind of anger and concentrate on what she'd say to Houtkamp and how she'd say it, but Murray's nose whistled when he breathed and made it impossible to think.

When she parked outside number thirty-nine, Murray narrowed his eyes at the eight-storey block of flats. 'Who lives here?'

'The person I'm going to talk to alone.'

'It might not be safe.'

'It's broad daylight,' she said.

'Like nobody gets killed in the day.'

'I'll be fine.'

He shook his head. 'I'm coming with you.'

She'd have dearly loved to order him to sit down and shut up but they were of equal rank. She slammed the door and stalked across the footpath.

Flat five was on the second floor. Ella knocked on the door and waited. Behind her the nose whistled. 'Have you got a cold?' she said.

'No, why?'

She knocked again.

'Doesn't look like your secret squirrel's home.'

'He might be in the shower.' She pounded on the door with her fist.

Across the landing a door opened and an old man looked out. 'You after Paul? He's at work.'

'Right, right,' Ella said. 'Of course. I asked at the nursing home but they said he wasn't there. I should've realised he'd be at work.'

At the mention of the nursing home the old man smiled. 'Do you want the address of his site?'

Site? 'That'd be great, if you have it handy.'

'It's on Mooramie Street in Kingsford. Going to be big, he told me, penthouse at the top and all.'

Ella thanked him.

He nodded. 'If you're going there now, would you mind taking this to him?' He reached back inside his flat and brought out a floral arrangement in a basket. 'I'm leaving for a few days' fishing up the coast. Paul goes straight to the nursing home after work on Fridays, so I won't be here when he gets home. Can't leave it in the hall: who knows who might pinch it.' He held it out with a smile.

Ella handed it on to Murray then smiled at the old man. 'Thanks for your help.'

In the car Murray balanced the basket on his knee. 'You bluffed that old guy.'

Ella pulled out into the traffic.

'You should've identified yourself and asked him straight out.'

'And get some poor old bloke in a tizzy about

255

why his neighbour's got detectives at his door? This way's kinder.'

'Easier, you mean,' Murray said. 'It saved you figuring out what to do if he wouldn't give you the information.'

Oh yes. Dennis was going to pay.

Utes and trucks were parked along the kerbs near the site in Mooramie Street, and dirty tyre tracks led out onto the asphalt. The builders were having lunch, sitting on their eskies with a radio playing and a fire going in an empty drum. They watched with interest as Ella approached. Behind her Murray stumbled over a clod of earth and almost dropped the flowers. One of the builders laughed.

'Paul Houtkamp?' Ella said.

The builders' heads turned towards a dusty-faced man drinking chocolate milk from a carton. He wiped his mouth and put the carton on the ground between his feet before looking up. 'Yes?'

'Can I have a word please?'

He got up and came over. The fact that he didn't ask who she was meant he'd probably already figured it out and didn't want to talk in front of his work mates. He wore dirty work boots, stained khaki shorts and a navy T-shirt. He walked past her to the footpath so she had to follow. He leaned against the side of a grimy ute, waiting for her to speak.

'I'm Detective Ella Marconi. I want to ask you about the assault two months ago.'

Houtkamp studied Murray. 'Who's the flower-boy?'

'I'm Detective Murray Shakespeare.' He put the basket on the ground.

Houtkamp said to Ella, 'You could've read the file instead of coming out here.'

'I've read it,' she said. 'I wanted to hear about it from you.'

'I confessed. What more do you want?'

'How did you get the upper hand on two experienced officers?'

'Just lucky.'

'One of those officers, Constable Chris Phillips, was shot and his child abducted two nights ago.'

'I've already been questioned about that. I was at the Bower Brae Nursing Home.'

'You told the investigating officers you were there from eight-forty until ten pm. Were you there the entire time?'

'Of course I was.'

'Can you prove it?'

'Ask the staff, check the visitors' book.'

'I know the staff saw you arrive and leave. Did either of them come into the room while you were there?'

Houtkamp folded his arms. 'No.'

'And I don't suppose the person you were visiting would remember, would they?' Ella said. 'Or they wouldn't need to live in a nursing home.'

Houtkamp stared at her with anger. 'Am I under arrest?'

'No.'

'Then I don't have to talk to you.' He started to walk away but Murray grabbed his arm.

'When a detective wants to talk to you, you listen,' he growled.

'Whoa,' Ella said. 'Let him go.'

A couple of the builders got to their feet. Houtkamp wrenched his arm free. Murray glared at him, red-faced. Houtkamp muttered something and turned to go, then Murray picked up the basket of flowers and thrust it at his back. Houtkamp spun around at the touch. When he saw what Murray held out he put his hands in his pockets.

'Fer Chris — It's not a bomb,' Murray said. 'Your neighbour said these were delivered to your place.' He dropped the basket on the ground and stalked away.

Houtkamp pulled the envelope from the handle. He tore it open, read the card and turned white.

'Are you okay?' Ella said.

Houtkamp kicked the basket into the street. Petals flew as a passing four-wheel drive tried to swerve around it.

'What's wrong?' Ella asked.

Ella reached for the card but Houtkamp crumpled it in his fist. She lowered her voice. 'Tell me. I can help you.'

He ran to the fire in the drum and threw the card and envelope into the flames. Ella put her hands on her hips. Houtkamp glared at her from the midst of his work mates.

Murray came back. 'What's going on?'

'Nothing,' Ella said. 'We were just leaving.'

Sophie stayed out on the driveway after seeing Angus off. The media watched her in silence from a distance, and she was risking having a neighbour coming over to inquire about the case, but going inside was worse, with Gloria fussing about and Chris's accusatory silence radiating from upstairs. She kicked a pebble into the street. She didn't blame him for blaming her, but the burden of her guilt would be easier to bear if he'd take her in his arms and kiss the top of her head and lie.

An ambulance approached and parked at the kerb. A pale blue ribbon fluttered from the aerial. A photographer raised a camera. It was her truck, number thirty-one. Mick got out of the driver's seat and she ran to throw her arms around him.

'Hey, Soppers.'

The affection in his voice made her throat ache. When she could speak she said, 'I've realised what number one is.'

'You found something worse than the shooting and the steamroller?'

'It's being alive and suffering,' she said, tears in her eyes, 'not knowing where your baby is, wondering what happens if you don't find him, how you're going to endure the rest of your life in despair and grief. You're dead inside, forever.'

He blinked back tears, hooked an arm around her neck and pulled her close again. The metal paramedic badge on his shirt pressed into her cheek as she clung to him. This was what she needed so badly from Chris. Plain old comfort.

'Don't the police have any leads?'

'Boyd Sawyer denied it and they let him go. The law says they need evidence.'

'Law,' he said. 'Shit.'

That was her feeling too. She closed her eyes and breathed in the smell of hospital disinfectant from his uniform. The smell of her old life.

'Hi, Mick,' Gloria called from the house. 'Want a cuppa?'

'Can't stay long, I just brought some forms for Sophie to sign.'

She let him go and wiped her sore eyes.

'It's your leave paperwork,' he said. They leaned on the bonnet of the truck while she signed the pages. The return-to-work date was blank. 'The boss said for you to take as long as you want.' Mick looked at the media. 'They always here?'

She nodded. 'They keep their distance though. Anyway, I don't mind, as long as they keep printing Lachlan's picture.' She gave him back the forms. 'Thanks for bringing them out.'

He smiled at her. 'Mind if I borrow your loo?'

'Careful Gloria doesn't bully you into that cuppa.'

When he disappeared into the house Sophie opened the side door into the rear of the ambulance and climbed up the steps. Sitting in the seat beside the stretcher she looked around at the labelled lockers on the walls, the oxygen masks in the netted compartments, the flow meters and the resus bags. She opened the bottle of antiseptic handwash and sniffed at it. A few days ago this had been her second home; now the whole environment felt distant and strange.

She pulled open the drawer at her knees. The drugs and needles were in colour-coded packets. Sophie studied them, her mind ticking over.

She glanced at the house. There was no sign of Mick. She looked the other way and saw the photographers had got back into their cars.

The drugs kept here were replaced as they were used, sometimes after each case, or sometimes, if the shift was busy, at the end of the day. It wasn't unheard of for them to sometimes be forgotten altogether, and the next crew to use the truck would find the drawers short. Sophie calculated that she could take two boxes of adrenaline, two of atropine and one of lignocaine without raising suspicion. She shoved the boxes into her bra then slipped in a vial of midazolam too.

She glanced up at the house. Mick was in the doorway talking to Gloria. Sophie grabbed an assortment of needles and syringes. She was pushing them down her shirt when Angus appeared in the ambulance doorway. She froze.

Angus said, 'You'd never make a criminal with that guilty face.'

'I was only — '

He held up a hand. 'Don't let me stop you.'

Mick came down the driveway. Angus went to meet him and they stood talking. Sophie took a moment to breathe, then slammed the drawer shut. She patted herself down, making sure nothing stuck out too much, thankful she was wearing a loose shirt. She climbed out of the

ambulance feeling bulky and guilty but determined to hide both.

'Reminiscing?' Mick said.

'Something like that.'

He put out his arms to hug her again and she
froze. He would feel the boxes! But just as he
reached her the portable radio on his hip
crackled. 'Thirty-one for a code two.'

'You'd better go,' Sophie said, taking a
surreptitious step back.

He leaned to kiss her cheek while unhooking
the radio. 'Keep me posted.'

'I will.'

He raised the radio to his mouth as he ran
down the driveway. 'Thirty-one's ready for
details.'

When Mick drove off, Sophie turned towards
Angus, wondering if he'd raise what he'd seen.

He smiled at her. 'I just came back because I
left my mobile in your lounge room.'

He went into the house and came out clipping
it onto the waistband of his trousers. 'Just be
careful, okay?' he said, before crossing the street
to his car. She saw that it, too, now flew a light
blue ribbon. She watched him drive off and
wondered if the warning was an invitation to
trust him and tell him what she planned. Once
upon a time she would have liked the comfort of
sharing her thoughts. Now, however, she found
strength in keeping things to herself. In a way,
Chris's holding her at arm's length helped,
because his affection would make her want to
open up and tell him everything. As it was, she
felt single-minded and focused. Purposeful.

Powerful. Nothing was going to stand in the way of her getting Lachlan back.

12.25 pm

'This time, if you don't stay in the car, I'm calling up Eagers,' Ella said.

Murray shrugged. No doubt he knew she was bluffing but would play along to keep his position with the investigation.

She got out of the car and walked along the busy street in Erskineville to the florist's. Their logo and address had been on the basket. It was a long shot that they'd give her the name of the person who ordered it but she had to try.

She was back in the car in minutes.

'No go?' Murray said.

'Rebuffed with extreme prejudice.' Ella started the car and headed towards Gladesville. 'Woman was a lawyer in a previous life.'

'Ouch,' he said. 'Think you'll try for a warrant?'

'For what? I have no evidence of anything.'

When they arrived at Gladesville Station, Dennis was smoking in the carpark. He glanced at the car, stepped on the butt and started off inside.

'Not so fast,' Ella called. She parked and caught up to him at the door. 'Time to pay for your bad deeds.'

'I didn't tell him to find you.'

'But you brushed him off after promising you'd take him,' she said. 'He stuffed up my

263

conversation with Houtkamp.'

'He was the reason it fell over, huh?'

'Why else?' she said. 'You owe me, you know. You should have to look after Murray all weekend.'

'If you'll keep him this afternoon.'

'If that's what it takes.' As Murray came up the steps, she smiled at them both and said, 'Well, I'm off home for a couple hours' kip.'

* * *

At home she dozed in the armchair by the window then woke at three with plenty of time to get ready. By three-thirty she was in the car heading for Randwick.

The Bower Brae Nursing Home was set back off the street. She walked between well-kept flowerbeds to the door.

A young nurse looked up from the desk. 'Good afternoon.'

'Hi, I'm Ella Marconi, I'm an old friend of Paul Houtkamp's.'

The woman smiled. 'You've come to see Jane, then.'

'There's not much chance she'll remember me,' Ella lied valiantly.

'I'm sure she'll be delighted to see you.' The nurse walked along a corridor and Ella followed. 'Paul shouldn't be long.'

Ella had figured the building site probably knocked off about four. Fifteen, twenty minutes to clean up a little and drive on over, and he'd walk into the room to find her and

Jane nattering away like old pals.

The nurse opened a door and ushered her in. 'Jane, this is Ella. Do you remember her?'

The occupant of the single room shook her head. She was a chubby woman in her early thirties. She sat cross-legged on the bed. She wore a Snoopy sweatshirt and had a plastic flower stuck behind one ear. She held a fat red crayon over a giant colouring book and beamed at Ella. 'Hello.'

'Hello to you.'

'Have a seat,' the nurse said. 'Like I said, Paul won't be long.' She pulled the door to and walked away.

Ella sat on the plastic chair by Jane's bed and looked around the room.

Jane held out the book. 'Do you want a turn to colour in?'

'Maybe in a moment.' Ella spotted a framed photo on the wall and got up to see. It was a wedding picture of Houtkamp and a woman. Ella looked closer. 'Is this you?'

'That's me,' Jane said. She held up her hand and Ella saw a gold ring. 'I love Paul and he loves me.'

She looked different in the photo. 'When did you get married?'

'A while ago.' Jane scribbled in the book.

'How long have you lived here?'

'A while.'

Ella glanced again at the picture then sat by the bed. 'You're really good at colouring-in.'

'I can do one for you to take home,' Jane said.

'That'd be great.'

The door flew open and Paul Houtkamp stormed in. 'Get out.' He carried a paper-wrapped parcel.

Ella smelled hot chips. 'We're just talking.'

'You lied to the nurse about being a friend of mine and you didn't identify yourself as a cop.'

'Chippies!' Jane said. 'Ella, is it okay if I finish your picture after afternoon tea?'

'Absolutely.'

Paul smiled at his wife then leaned close to Ella's ear. 'You have no right to be here.'

'I just want to talk to you.'

'Paul, I'm hungry.' Jane reached for the parcel he held.

He gave it to her. 'And the only way you could manage it was by lying?'

Ella spread her hands. 'You were obviously embarrassed to have us at your work.'

'I wasn't embarrassed,' he said.

'Who sent the flowers?'

He looked at Jane, who was unwrapping the paper. The smell of vinegar filled the air.

'Is somebody threatening you?' Ella said.

He stayed silent.

Ella didn't take her eyes off him. 'I just want to find the baby.'

'I like babies,' Jane said. 'I like potato scallops too.'

'I had nothing to do with that and it's up to you to prove otherwise.'

'Ella, do you want a scallop?'

'I don't know if Paul will let me,' Ella said.

'Paul, can she have a scallop? I have four here,

so that's one for Ella, one for Paul, and two for me!'

'She can have one,' Paul said after a moment.

Ella tore off a scrap of paper to hold it. Jane patted the side of the bed and Paul sat down. She offered him a chip. 'Aren't you hungry?'

'Not really.'

Ella said, 'If you want me to go, I will. But I know there's something odd going on, and while there's even the slightest chance it involves the Phillipses I won't stop looking into it. So you can tell me now, or you can wait till you're sick to death of the sight of me knocking at your door, sitting outside your work, following you in your car.'

'I know who'll get sick of it first, and it won't be me,' he said.

Ella ate the rest of the scallop and wiped her fingers on her jeans. 'Bye Jane. It was nice to meet you.'

'What about your picture?'

'It doesn't matter,' Ella said.

'Yes it does, yes it does! I'll finish it now.' When she handed it over the red-crayon picture of a kitten was marked with grease stains.

'Thank you,' Ella said. 'I'll put this on my fridge at home.'

Outside, evening was falling. Ella rounded the garden beds and almost ran into the nurse who'd shown her in. This time Ella got out her badge.

The nurse looked at it carefully in the gloom. 'I knew you weren't really an old friend of theirs.'

'But you still let me in,' Ella said.

'It's a nursing home, not a jail,' the nurse said. 'People can visit whoever they want.'

Ella put her badge away. 'Did you work on Wednesday night?'

'Yes, and the other police already asked me about that.'

'I know,' Ella said. 'Is it possible that Paul Houtkamp wasn't here the entire time he said he was?'

The nurse frowned. 'I didn't actually see him, but the doors are locked after hours. To get out you have to press a buzzer and the other nurse or I come and let you out. To stop patients wandering, you know. And we only let Paul out once.'

'There's no other way he could've got out? A window, maybe?'

She shook her head. 'They all have security screens.'

'Thanks,' Ella said.

'Jane do that for you?' The nurse pointed at the picture she carried. 'She's my favourite.'

'Why is she here?'

'About three years ago she left her car in neutral and forgot the park brake and it started to roll. So she tried to jump back in to stop it, but she was crushed against a tree. She suffered brain damage and now has a mental age of five.'

'That's awful.'

'She used to be this big-shot hairdresser, had her own salon in the city and everything.'

Ella said, 'Paul seems dedicated.'

'You know why he brings the chips on Fridays? Well, it used to be fish and chips but

Jane won't eat fish any more. They started the tradition on their honeymoon, and he keeps it going.'

'Incredible.'

'He really is,' the nurse said. The phone started to ring inside the building. As she walked away she said over her shoulder, 'If only there was a man like that for each of us, hey?'

6.05 pm

Chris sat on the bottom stair, tissues to his nose. Gloria turned at the front door to face him. 'Families should pull together at times like these, you know.'

'We're just not hungry.'

'It's not only the meals,' she said. 'You don't talk to each other, or to me. A family should share its burdens.'

'Like — ' He stopped himself, and pressed the tissues harder to his nose.

'Like what?'

He looked up at her then away.

'Like what?' she said again, her voice a little harder.

'Like our family did?'

She folded her arms.

'I'm just saying,' he said.

'So say it.'

He wiped his nose, refolded the tissues and applied the clean area to his nostrils. 'A little more gentle conversation in our house and maybe Dad wouldn't have gone.'

She was staring at him, he could feel her gaze burning the top of his head. After a long moment, she turned on her heel and stamped out the door.

After her car pulled away, Sophie came down the stairs. 'She's gone?'

'Yes.' Chris didn't look around.

She sat a couple of steps behind him. Her foot nudged his back. He heard her breathing and felt the tentative touch of her hand on his neck. He wanted to turn and smile at her, take that warm foot in his hand, but in the same way he'd got Gloria to leave he needed Sophie gone too.

He leaned slightly forward, leaving her foot touching nothing. She moved it in pursuit. He shifted on the step, out of reach again. Her foot stayed still and she took her hand from his neck, and he blinked back tears. He would explain later. For now nothing was more important than getting Lachlan back.

He was aware of time ticking by. Soon, he needed her out soon. He'd wasted the whole day staring at the screen of his mobile. The house phone had rung frequently but he always let someone else answer. That line was tapped and Rigby and his mates would know it. There'd been no contact, and it was time to make his move. 'What are you doing tonight?'

'Now the car's back from the garage, I thought I might go looking again.' The garage had found the lead had come off the starter motor. It happened occasionally, they said, and had been simple to fix. 'Do you want to come along?'

'My head's too bad,' he lied. 'The car would make me sick, too.'

Sophie said nothing. Chris sat for a moment, hands clenched between his knees, trying to summon the strength for what he needed to say.

He turned on the step to look up at her face. 'You know you'll never find him that way.'

The hurt in her eyes was like a knife sliding into his already shredded heart. 'What are you doing that's so much more successful?'

'I was shot. What do you want me to do?' He felt cruel but the words had the effect he wanted. She leapt to her feet and stormed up the stairs, then seconds later pushed roughly past him without a word, the jacket she carried whipping him in the face. He watched her, wishing he could say something comforting but knowing that might make her stay. She grabbed the car keys and slammed the door on her way out. The car screeched backwards out of the garage and onto the street, then she was gone.

Chris wiped his eyes then pulled his mobile from his pocket. 'I need a taxi please.'

14

Ella burped as she turned in to Easton Street. The Subway sandwich wasn't sitting as neatly in her stomach as it had when she'd scoffed it while parked in a no-standing zone in Newtown. The scoffing was the problem, not the pepperoni or the onions, she was sure. She took another sip of milkshake and slowed as she neared the Phillips house.

A taxi was in the drive. Chris came gingerly out of the house and climbed in the back. He was holding a wad of tissues to his nose. Perhaps he was going back to hospital. But then why wasn't Sophie or his mother driving him?

Ella slid low in the seat as the taxi backed towards her then drove off. She put the milkshake down on the passenger seat and followed.

Down Pittwater Road, then left onto Epping Road. They went slowly with the evening traffic. Through Epping itself, into Cheltenham, Beecroft, Pennant Hills. Ella kept the taxi's red tail-lights in view but would've bet money their destination was Dean Rigby's house.

Sure enough, fifteen minutes later the taxi braked on Wright Street in Hornsby. Ella parked some distance back and watched through the steering wheel as Chris got out and the taxi

272

drove away. Chris moved slowly from light pole to light pole, resting against each one. Ella felt for the man but to go to him and reveal her presence was out of the question. Nevertheless, what he did or said when he knocked on Rigby's door could answer all the questions buzzing around her head.

She knew from looking into Rigby's file that he lived at number sixty-three. She put her headlights on again and drove past the lurching Chris down the dusky street, turned around and came back to a spot near Rigby's single-storey brick house. The light was on over the door but the streetlights were far enough away that she could slouch in the seat and see without being seen. She reached over and lowered the passenger window, then watched Chris stumble into Rigby's yard.

The door opened before he knocked. Rigby stepped out and pulled it shut behind him. Chris lowered himself onto the small wall to the side of the porch and put his head in his hands, and Rigby crouched beside him, looking awkward with the foam collar around his neck.

They talked too softly for her to hear. She wanted to thump the steering wheel and swear. Instead she surveyed the surroundings, looking for shrubs that might provide cover for her to sneak closer. But the foliage on the few bushes was thin and the streetlights revealed too much of the footpath and gardens of the houses.

She leaned towards the open passenger window and held her breath.

' . . . all day,' Chris said, his voice rising.

Mutter mutter from Rigby, and he put his hand on Chris's shoulder. Then — hello — Chris was on his feet, his finger in Rigby's face. 'Don't you dare act like you're still my friend.'

Rigby stayed crouching, his hands spread wide. A reasoning tone.

Chris shook his head. 'I told you what I wanted, what you had to do.'

Mutter.

Chris reached into the pocket of his jacket and pulled out a handgun.

'Holy shit,' Ella whispered.

Rigby stayed where he was. His voice dropped even lower.

Ella swallowed nervously. Chris wasn't pointing the gun at Rigby yet. If she got out and ran over there he might be prompted to do so, or to aim at her, in which case she'd be forced to draw her own gun at him. She sat tense and taut, gripping the wheel.

'You're not listening to me.' Chris raised the gun and pressed the barrel to his own temple.

Rigby eased up to his feet, his hands wide to the sides.

'Is this what you want?' Chris yelled.

The door opened and a woman stuck her head out. She took one look and slammed the door closed. Ella guessed her next action would be to call the police, and knew she had to move.

She got out of the car as stealthily as she could. There was a line to tread between being so quiet she startled them when she drew close, and being so loud they stopped talking too soon. She edged along the footpath, keeping in shadow as much as possible.

Chris was trembling. His nose streamed blood down his face and onto his shirt. 'I promised you I'd never say anything about Houtkamp. Why couldn't you believe me?'

'I did believe you,' Rigby said. 'It's not me doing it.'

'You or one of your mates in the gang. It's all the same.'

The gang? Ella crept closer.

'I haven't heard anything there either,' Rigby said.

'I'll do whatever it takes.' Chris was pale and starting to cry. 'You want me dead, to prove I won't talk again? Okay, I'm dead.'

'It's not us!'

Chris drew a long hitching breath, then Ella's movement must have caught his eye. 'Who's that?'

Rigby whirled. He shielded his eyes from the porch light.

Ella moved out onto the footpath. 'Put the gun down, Chris.'

'It's not an offence to kill yourself.'

'I know that, but if the boys turn up in droves, as I suspect they will any second, you'll scare the shit out of them waving that thing around.'

Chris lowered the gun to his side. Ella slowly approached him, her left hand out, her right on her own gun in its holster. 'Give it to me.'

Shakily he put it in her palm. It was his service Glock. She checked it while Rigby spoke to his wife.

'She didn't call anyone,' he reported back. Chris sat on the low wall, his head in his hands again.

The Glock safely under her folded arms, Ella looked both men up and down. 'Care to tell me what that conversation was about?'

Rigby swatted a mosquito. Chris sniffed, a wet sound.

'I heard you arguing about Houtkamp and about the gang. About you, Chris, not talking again,' she said. 'Spill it.'

Chris spoke in a low voice. 'I came here because I was upset. Dean was comforting me.'

Rigby nodded.

Ella took a step closer. 'I heard what you said.'

'You must have misunderstood,' Chris said.

'I heard you say Houtkamp.'

'I was telling Dean how upset I was. I said I felt like killing myself.'

'I was trying to comfort him,' Rigby put in.

'You pair of bastards,' Ella said. 'I'm trying to find your son, Chris — how the hell can I do that if you keep lying to me?'

The men were silent.

'Which one of you sent flowers to Houtkamp with some kind of message?'

They didn't reply.

She took another step closer. 'Sooner or later I'm going to find out what's going on, so you may as well tell me now.'

After a long moment Chris looked up at Rigby. 'Mind calling me a taxi so I can get home?'

'Sure.' Rigby turned to go inside but Ella said, 'I'll take you.'

Chris considered her. 'Okay. Thanks.' He got to his feet and walked slowly across to the street, pulling a handkerchief from his pocket. Ella gave Rigby a long hard look then followed.

At the car she found the milkshake had fallen over and the front seat was wet. Chris got into the back and sat with his head against the window, his eyes closed and the handkerchief to his nose. Ella put the Glock into the glovebox, angled the rear-view mirror so she could see him, and started the car.

After they'd gone a few kilometres he said, 'I know what you're going to say. 'Now that we're away from him, why don't I tell you what's going on.''

'That's pretty much it.'

More kilometres went by. He refolded the handkerchief. 'Mum says that I should go back to hospital because I'm bleeding all the time.'

'She's probably right,' Ella said. 'Why don't you?'

'Because of Lachlan.'

'What can you achieve being out here? Apart from supporting Sophie, I mean.'

'Sophie.' He cracked the window a little. The sound of traffic came into the car. 'She's off on her own thing.'

'The driving around?'

He nodded.

'You didn't want to join her?'

'She blames me for what happened, and she's

right to, but searching the streets won't bring him back.'

Ella looked at him in the mirror. 'So what will?'

He closed his eyes against her gaze.

'Okay then, let's see if I can figure it out,' she said. 'You think you know who has him and why but you can't tell me because . . . because you think that will jeopardise your chances of finding him.'

Chris said nothing.

'Meanwhile Rigby covered for you back there because you are friends. No, that's not it: you said, 'Don't you act like you're still my friend.' So if he's got no interest in protecting you, maybe his caginess is because he could lose something too. Is it a risk to himself or his family? Or perhaps his career?'

No answer.

'I'm guessing it all revolves around Hout-kamp,' she said. 'Something happened at that assault, didn't it?'

'You can guess as much as you like,' he said. 'I've got nothing to say.'

'Were you expecting trouble? Is that why you took your gun home? You wanted to be prepared?'

'If that was the case, don't you think I would have kept it handy and used it when that guy knocked at the door?' he said. 'I took it home accidentally.'

That sometimes happened. Ella drove through Ryde and into Gladesville. As she turned into Easton Street she said, 'How can you be so sure that Houtkamp will stay silent too? Or was that a death threat attached to the basket of flowers?'

'There are worse things than death.' He opened the door to get out but she reached over and grabbed his arm.

'What do you mean by that?'

'Exactly what I said.' He pulled free and got out.

She watched him go into the house. No lights came on. Her mobile rang and she checked the screen. Dennis. She let it go to voicemail. She had to go into Wynyard to put Chris's gun in the station safe where it should be, and then she wanted to think for a while, and drive — not talk.

7.30 pm

Sophie parked in Maxwell Road in Glebe and walked across Jubilee Park in the darkness. She pulled her jacket close against the cold air. She'd spent the last hour driving aimlessly about the city, trying to resist the pull of this place. She wasn't surprised that she'd lost.

At the edge of Rozelle Bay she looked at the black water lapping against the stone wall, then went right, walking along the edge towards the lights of the city. In Pope Paul VI Reserve she stood under a spreading figtree and stared at Sawyer's house. It was brightly lit and she could see people moving about near the windows. She clenched her fists in her pockets, her whole body taut with fury.

When she could breathe again, she went around to the far side of the tree, took her mobile from her pocket and dialled. When Angus answered she said, 'I think he's having a party.'

'Sawyer?'

'Of course Sawyer.'

'Where are you?'

'In the park.' She shivered.

He was quiet for a moment. 'Do you know that cafe on George Street, the art deco one with the old paintings in the front window? Near the — '

'I know it.'

'Go there and wait for me.'

'Okay.'

'I might be an hour. Don't leave. Just wait.'

'Okay,' she said again. Angus hung up and she slipped the phone back into her pocket. It would be good to talk with Angus. If she couldn't release her rage with him she didn't know what she might do.

8.12 pm

Ella parked the car outside Houtkamp's block then listened to the voicemail message Dennis had left on her phone.

'*Sawyer's sister persuaded him to call me about that picture from the pub CCTV. He says he remembers nothing, doesn't recognise the woman, continues to have no idea whatsoever. Um — you missed this afternoon's*

280

meeting. Give me a call sometime so I know you're still alive.'

It came as no surprise that Sawyer remembered nothing. *Claimed* to remember nothing, that was.

However, this thing with Houtkamp and Rigby and Chris made her reconsider her judgement of the doctor. Maybe he really was drugged and abducted. But why? And was it just a coincidence that it happened two days after the death of his family, which served as such a neat motive, and the same night Lachlan was kidnapped?

Ella entered Houtkamp's building and climbed the stairs. Stewing about Sawyer was pointless. If things went to plan here she'd be able to forget him entirely.

The lights were on in Houtkamp's flat: she could see the glow through the peephole. She knocked on the door. The peephole darkened and she smiled at it.

The door stayed shut.

'I know what's going on,' she said.

The peephole turned bright again. She imagined him moving to the side of the door, standing there, listening.

'I heard Rigby and Chris Phillips arguing. Your name came up. And Chris told me there are worse things than death.'

No sound from inside.

She lowered her voice. 'I know what they have over you.'

No response.

'Five minutes,' she said. 'You can give me that,

281

surely. I don't want you as a witness, I don't plan to investigate any further than to find the baby. That's all I want.'

Finally he spoke. 'You don't plan to.'

'That's right.'

'You're not the only copper in the force. What about your bosses?'

'They only know what I tell them,' she said. 'Look, nobody knows I'm here. Nobody knows I'm even looking into this.'

'Flowerboy knows.'

'He doesn't know about Rigby and how it all ties in with Chris Phillips.' She shivered. It was cold on the landing. 'Five minutes and then I'll go.'

A chain slid back, a lock turned and Paul Houtkamp opened the door. 'I must be an idiot.'

She was grateful for the warmth of the small, sparsely decorated living room. He waved a hand at a chair and sat on the lounge opposite.

'Here's what happened,' she said. 'That assault was not the simple incident you're all pretending it was. Something took place, either then or beforehand, and you and Chris ended up with information Rigby wishes you didn't have. Now Chris thinks his son was taken because of it, and you're keeping mum because you're scared for your wife.'

Houtkamp seemed to think about this. Then he leaned forward. 'Stand up. Lift up your shirt and turn around.'

'I'm not wired.'

'Lift up your shirt and turn around.'

She got to her feet. This was humiliating,

infuriating, but might get her the answers she needed. She did as he said, sat down, crossed her legs and folded her arms. 'Happy?'

'I'll never repeat any of this in court or to anyone else,' he said. 'If I'm asked, I'll deny this meeting ever happened.'

'Fine.'

'And I'm only helping you for the sake of the baby.' He pressed the heels of his hands into his eyes. 'God, what am I doing?'

'It'll be okay,' she said.

Just like it was for Roth?

Man, she hated that smart-arse voice in her head.

Houtkamp shook his head for a long time then spoke in a low voice. 'After the thing with Chris Phillips, when I was lying cuffed on the ground, Rigby sat there clutching his neck and told me that Jane would pay if I ever told what was going on. He said he and his friends know which nursing home she's in, and you've seen yourself they have no security at all, and he said they'd get to her like this,' he clicked his fingers, 'and they wouldn't just kill her. You met her, she's like a little kid. She understands nothing. She loves everyone. She'd be all excited about visitors.' He held out his hands. They were shaking. 'There are things *way* worse than death, you know?'

Bile rose in Ella's throat.

Houtkamp drew a deep breath. 'I went to that alley to meet Rigby and give him some information. I did that sometimes, when I needed money, but it wasn't your regular help, to catch crims. He wanted to know about particular people. People who worked in competition to some business he and his friends — some cops, some civilians — and before you ask, no, I don't know who they are — had going.'

'What kind of business?'

'Some gambling scams, though I didn't know much about that. It was mostly drugs. They were trying to take over areas of the city. I heard they got some purer stuff, they were selling it cheaper, all that kind of thing.'

Ella thought of the rash of recent accidental overdose deaths, of Lily Zander cold and stiff under a shrub. 'And what happened then?'

'That guy Chris was there too. I'd seen him around but never met him. He wasn't in on it. Rigby made him wait in the car while we talked, but finally he got out and came over. He wanted to know what was going on. They got into a big argument, and from what Chris said I guess he'd figured out a few things. He accused Rigby of being dirty, being corrupt, said was he in on the robberies, said he was totally sick of cops like him. Rigby threatened him, and went for him, and they got into it. There was nobody around. Rigby had Chris on the ground and was saying, 'I'll kill you, I'll kill you, don't you know how much money this brings in?' I wanted to run away but I was scared he really would kill him, so I grabbed this metal pole and belted him across the neck.'

He'd probably saved Chris's life. 'You deserve an award, not an arrest.'

'Yeah, well, Rigby went down for a moment then he leapt up and grabbed me. Next thing

I'm in cuffs and he's standing over me holding his neck and kicking the crap out of me. Chris called for back-up, I guess knowing Rigby wasn't going to listen to him, and just before they arrived Rigby backed off.'

'Was anything else said between them?'

'Nothing that I heard. Just lots of glares.'

'And then you got charged, and the story is that you hurt them both,' Ella said. 'And you'll probably get locked up.'

'If that's the price to pay to keep Jane safe, I don't mind,' Houtkamp said. 'Who would listen to me anyway?'

'I am.'

'I mean officially. What boss would take my word over two cops'? And even if Rigby got slammed straight in jail, he's still got friends.'

'There's witness protection — '

'Where can you hide a thirty-year-old woman with a mental age of five?'

He was right. All Ella could do was use what he'd told her to solve her case. For the moment anyway. She put out her hand. 'Thank you for trusting me.'

He held onto it. 'Don't let me down.'

★   ★   ★

Ella threw her mobile phone on the passenger seat. There was no way she could ring Dennis about any of this tonight. She needed time to decide what to say and how to say it.

She started the engine and turned the heater up high, rubbed at the goosebumps on her arms.

She now knew exactly what the robbery gang was capable of. If Rigby was involved with them, as Houtkamp claimed, and if the gang had taken Lachlan, the odds of finding him alive were not something she wanted to consider.

9.07 pm

Sophie was sitting bolt upright when Angus burst into the cafe. He stormed to the booth and sat down opposite her. She waited for him to speak. He put his clenched fists on the table and pressed the knuckles together, then leaned forward. She leaned forward to meet him.

'This job,' he said softly, 'is fucked.'

She stared at him. 'What did you find out?'

'They've gone completely hands-off on Sawyer,' he said. 'It is such bullshit. Guy's a big-shot doctor, surgeon, whatever; looks after rich and important bastards; so he knows people and obviously they know people and the detectives do nothing but wait for him to step out of line. Which he won't.'

'They're doing nothing?'

'Oh, they have this piss-weak surveillance on him, but all that is is watching his house and seeing if he goes out,' Angus said. 'But if it's already all been done, he doesn't need to go out, does he?'

'But Lachlan is an officer's child,' Sophie said.

'I know. It should count for something.'

'It should count for a lot,' Sophie said.

Angus's knuckles were white. 'I knew there'd

be a day when I'd have to leave the job. When we can't even look after one of our own any more, I don't see the point in struggling on.' His voice cracked.

Sophie felt cold and hollow. 'So what will they do?'

Angus wiped his eyes with his sleeve. 'In a few days they'll call off the surveillance, then they'll cut back the team working the case. They'll say the leads have dwindled out, they don't have the work for all those people any more and they're needed elsewhere. Soon there'll be just a couple still on it, but they can't do much.' He lowered his gaze. 'Then it'll be marked unsolved and filed away.'

Sophie stared at him but was seeing instead the moment when Sawyer's daughter was born, remembering how she'd cradled the tiny body in her hands, feeling the heat of the baby's skin, the slippery texture, the smell of the blood and vernix. She had done her absolute best for that child, she had worked so hard and willed her to live as strongly as she'd ever willed it for anyone. Couldn't Sawyer understand that? How could he have done what he did, knowing that Sophie and Chris had gone through a delivery just like he and Julie had?

Angus was shaking his head. 'This friend of a friend, on the surveillance team, he said they are having a party, of sorts. Lots of people there, they can hear the glasses clinking from across the street. And apparently Sawyer's going back to fucking work tomorrow. Jesus.'

287

Sophie focused. 'Work? On a Saturday? Where?'

'St Helens, in Camperdown.' Angus rubbed his red eyes. 'He's saying he's got paperwork to catch up on, and needs to get out of the house. You ask me, he wants to try to give surveillance the slip.'

Sophie thought for a moment, then started to talk.

15

Dennis was smoking in the carpark when Ella arrived for the morning meeting. She locked her car and leaned on the wire fence beside him.

He said, 'Seems like Sophie was outside Sawyer's house again last night.'

'With Arendson?'

'Nope. All alone.'

'Doing what?'

'Standing, staring.' He stubbed out the butt on the top of a post. 'Surveillance spotted her in the streetlight but they don't think Sawyer did. He had people over, an after-funeral type thing. She was there for about five minutes then she left.' He looked at Ella. 'That's two days in a row.'

'I'll go and see her after the meeting.'

Dennis nodded. 'So where were you yesterday? Did you get my messages?'

He'd left one on her landline as well, she'd found when she got back home. 'I was out and about. Looking into things.'

'You're supposed to let me know what you're doing.'

'Yeah, sorry.' Last night she'd thought at length about what to say and whether she could keep Houtkamp's confidence. 'Briefly, Chris Phillips argued with Rigby about Houtkamp,

289

and then I found out that Rigby might be involved with the gang or, at the very least, something else dodgy.'

'You found out how?'

'I can't say.'

'Houtkamp told you.'

'His family's been threatened. I promised him nobody would know we talked.'

'You can't promise stuff like that,' Dennis said.

'The end justifies the means if we find Lachlan.'

'But you can't pick and choose,' Dennis said. 'Follow up some allegations, some cases, and not others.'

'He'll never testify, so what can I do?'

'Maybe he won't testify because he knows it's all lies,' Dennis said. 'And anyway, you said Roth said Chris wasn't involved in the gang.'

'I don't think he is,' she said. 'I think he found out something about it. I think he rang the TV stations and now he believes his son was taken as payback.'

'Chris told you this?'

'Not exactly.' She explained what she'd overheard and the men's reactions.

'So you've got a man with a criminal history who may be lying, but who you believe, and two officers who you claim are lying though you have no evidence to say so.' He shook his head. 'This is why you should always take me along on your excursions.'

'If I can get a warrant I can find out who sent the flowers to Houtkamp, maybe prove a link between him and Rigby.'

'Murray told me about the basket.'

'All I need is that first crack. I jam in the crowbar and away we go.'

'You've got no grounds for the warrant though,' he said. 'And listen, there are other things happening. We got the phone records from the TV stations. I've had people going over them half the night and with any luck they've found the origin of the calls.'

'Maybe we can prove it was Chris who rang, then.'

'Crowbar mark two,' Dennis said. 'Let's go in.'

Before they reached the station door a uniformed constable came out. 'You were on an arson case?' he said to Ella. 'A guy named Edman Hughes?'

'Don't tell me — he's made a complaint against me.'

The constable shook his head. 'He was found hanged at home this morning. Left a note about having no future, according to the officers called there.'

He went back inside and Ella leaned on the railing. 'Shit.'

'Sorry,' Dennis said.

'It's only been five days,' she said. 'Who gets their case solved in five days? How could he expect me to run around on that when we've got this missing kid?' She didn't want to tell Dennis how she'd brushed Hughes off the day before, on these very steps. She stuck her fists on her hips. 'Oh shit.'

Sophie sat in her car up the street from The
Rocks ambulance station, her mobile in her
hands. She'd seen the tired night-shift crew
wander out to their cars a minute after eight, and
the day-shift crew power out of the building just
a couple of minutes after that. They turned left,
the siren wailing and beacons flashing as they
went under the Bridge. Saturdays were busy
— hell, every day was busy. They wouldn't be
back for hours.

Her phone rang.

'It's a go,' Angus said. 'See you soon.'

When she entered the station she went first to
the store-room and put back the drugs she'd
taken the previous day from Thirty-one. She
went next to her locker and changed into her last
spare uniform. Someone had left a portable
radio on and the voices echoing through the
empty building put her on edge. From above the
roof came the constant sound of traffic crossing
the Bridge. She went into the station manager's
office and searched through the desk drawers for
the spare locker keys. In the men's change room
she opened the locker of Joe Vandermeer, a nice
guy who was the closest to Angus's height and
build of any of the men on the station. She took
one set of uniform then replaced the keys in the
drawer.

The plant room had space for three
ambulances. This was the minimum they could
have on a station of their size — one for day
shift, one for night shift if the day shift wasn't

back yet, and one spare in case of breakdowns. On the whiteboard was a log of mileage and service due dates for each car. Beside car thirty-three Sophie scrawled 'workshop' then took down a set of keys. Mechanics and vehicles came and went all the time. Nobody would wonder about Thirty-three.

In the ambulance she put Joe Vandermeer's uniform on the passenger seat and activated the roller door. Sunlight streamed in. She drove out of the building, closed the door and was on her way.

* * *

Sophie slowed on Carillon Avenue in Camperdown. There was the phone box on the corner, but where was Angus? An older man standing there raised his hand as she drew level and she realised with a start that it was Angus.

His hair was grey and combed back, and he wore tan slacks and a plain jacket and carried a plastic shopping bag. His face was different, even his stance. She pulled over and he climbed into the passenger seat. Even close up she had trouble recognising him until he smiled. 'Holy shit.'

'Good make-up, good dressing-up and good acting. That's what working undercover teaches you.' He put the bag on the floor, took the uniform and scrambled into the back of the vehicle. 'How are you feeling?'

'Fine,' she lied. 'Good.'

His face appeared in the rear-view mirror. He was buttoning the paramedic shirt. 'I've been

293

around and into the hospital. There's one guy watching his car, and two inside, I'm pretty sure, on the exits. I don't know any of them but they're easy to pick when you know what to look for.'

'And Sawyer?'

'With a judicious flower delivery and a story about my dear departed wife and her breast reconstruction after cancer, I found out from a sympathetic receptionist that he should be on the fifth floor for the next hour or so.'

'Good.' Sophie's hands were sweaty on the steering wheel. 'No problems getting the stuff?'

'None at all.' He climbed back into the passenger seat and smiled at her. She was struck for an instant by the absurdity of life, how just days ago she had squirmed with guilt every time she saw him, and now they were about to commit a serious crime together.

Angus said, 'We're going to find Lachlan today. I know it.'

She knew it too. A fire burned in her chest, fanned first by the plans they'd made last night, then the thoughts that had come when she'd lain in bed at home, unable to sleep.

She drove further along Carillon Avenue then turned right into Milson Road. St Helen's Private Hospital lay directly ahead.

She took a deep breath as they approached the hospital driveway. They could do this; she just needed to control her nerves. The key to the entire operation was to hide in plain sight — to make no attempt to sneak about but to be fully visible at the same time as looking like they belonged. If things went to plan, no witness would recall more than the uniforms.

9.00 am

Chris opened the door to find Ella standing there. 'No news, I'm sorry,' she said. 'May I come in?'

Behind him Gloria clanked pans in the kitchen. He said, 'If you want.'

They sat in the lounge room. 'Is Sophie home?'

'No.'

'Driving around?'

Chris nodded. He had no idea where she was, really. She'd gone off in the car at seven without saying a word.

'Was she here last night when I dropped you off?'

It went quiet in the kitchen. Chris's skin tingled. 'Yes.'

'That was about seven-thirty, wasn't it?' she said. 'And did you or she go out later?'

'No.'

'You slept in the same bed, you would've known if she went out, right?'

'Of course,' he said. 'Why are you asking?'

'Someone matching Sophie's description was seen outside Boyd Sawyer's house last night. I want to talk to her, find out if it was her. Explain what a bad idea it is to be doing that.'

Chris shook his head. 'We were both definitely here.'

Ella looked doubtful, but she leaned forward, her elbows on her knees. 'The other thing is, we're tracing the calls made to the TV stations about the robbery gang.'

'How does that help our case?'

'I thought you should know. So you can be prepared.'

'You won't find my number there,' he said. He'd started to sweat and he hoped she couldn't see it. He was safe, he told himself. There was no way they could link that public phone to him.

Ella lowered her voice. 'It would be best for you to tell me what you know now.'

'What I know about what?'

'The robberies and the gang,' she said.

'I know nothing.' He badly wanted to wipe his forehead.

'I don't believe you.'

His nose started to drip blood and he grabbed a handful of tissues.

Ella said, 'When the facts come out, and we can prove you chose not to tell us what you know, do you think people will believe you weren't involved?'

Chris's blood rose. It didn't matter what people thought. Finding Lachlan was all he cared about. 'If you've got no news on our case I'd like you to leave.'

When Ella was gone, Gloria came in from the kitchen, wiping her hands on a dish towel. 'You shouldn't lie to the police.'

'I am the police,' Chris said. He was tired of talking, of trying to stay mentally one step ahead when his head ached and he was dizzy.

'You told that detective Sophie was home when you got home, but you told me she didn't get in till midnight.'

'Sophie's trying to deal with her grief. If she has to be out there driving on her own, then that's fine with me,' he said. 'The last thing she needs is to be accused of stalking somebody.'

'What if she is?'

'Come off it, Mum.' He squeezed his pounding forehead. He wished she'd go back into the kitchen so he could lie down. If he did it now she'd say he was sick and should go back to hospital.

'It's a mother's instinct,' she said. 'You don't know what you might do until your child is threatened.'

'He's my child too!'

'It's different for men.'

'That's old-fashioned crap.'

'Oh really?' she said, eyes flashing. 'When your dad and I broke up, who was it that left? Who never had any contact with you again?'

Chris shut his eyes. 'Here we go.'

'Don't take that tone,' she said. 'You have no idea how it was. You were just a baby.'

'I was four and I remember more than you know.'

'Four,' she said. 'So what do you remember, Christopher?'

'I remember you yelling at Dad. You told him to get out. And he went.' Chris blinked back tears. 'Without saying goodbye.'

'So why was I yelling? You know so much, you should be able to tell me that.'

'You were just fighting,' Chris said. 'Like you always fought. Shouting and screaming.'

Gloria's mouth was a tight line. 'Yes, he was always careful to keep the actual punches behind closed doors.'

Chris looked at her. 'Dad didn't hit you.'

'You think because you didn't see it, it didn't happen?' She was trembling.

'But — '

'But what?' she said. 'You thought you knew how it went and now you're learning the truth. Your dad was nobody worth looking up to, and the reason I finally got the courage to kick him out was that he'd started to turn on you.'

Chris was speechless.

'That day.' Gloria started to cry. 'You were playing outside. He took his belt off and hit me once, and you walked in. He rounded on you and raised his arm. You were looking at me, you didn't even see him.'

Chris shook his head. 'I don't believe you.'

'He left us with nothing, and for your sake I didn't try to get child support, I decided it was best to live our lives alone, just us, with nothing to do with him.' Her voice was rising. 'All my life I've protected you and sacrificed for you. I put myself at risk to help you. How can you sit there and accuse me of lying, when I was the one who stayed with you, getting up to you in the night, helping with your homework, encouraging you, loving you? Who held the bucket and washed the sheets when you had that awful gastro for days on end? Who gave up a promotion because it would have meant more hours away from you?

298

Who took care of things when your sixteen-year-old girlfriend turned up at the door pregnant? You think your no-good father would have done all that for you?'

'What?'

Gloria paled under his stare.

'You got Bee an abortion? Is that what you just said?'

'You were away at cadet camp.' Gloria wiped her eyes with her palms. 'Bee didn't want you to know. She didn't want her own mother to know, or Angus. She said as a nurse I must have friends who could help her.'

'How could you do it?'

'It was for the best,' she snapped. 'You were both sixteen! There's no future for a family that starts like that. And how could you have gone to medical school with a wife and child?'

'She was underage. You didn't have her mother's permission.'

'I did what I thought was best, and maybe Sophie's doing the same,' Gloria said. 'Like I said, it's a mother's instinct.' She came around the end of the lounge to sit with him but he turned away.

'I can't talk to you,' he said. 'You need to go home.'

She sat down anyway.

'Mum, I mean it.'

'It was for the best,' she said again. 'You think it hasn't hurt me? That I didn't think about that baby when Lachlan was born? You think it hasn't been a burden, knowing what I did to my own first grandchild?'

'Oh, now you feel sorry for yourself?'

She started to speak but he cut her off.

'Just leave, okay?'

She slammed the door on her way out. Chris lay on the lounge, his face in the crook of his arm, his heart peeling away from the wall of his chest like a piece of dead dry paint.

9.10 am

Sophie's heart pounded with anxiety and hope as she wheeled the stretcher through St Helen's. Angus walked beside her, the Oxy-Viva backpack slung on one shoulder, the contents of the plastic bag tucked inside it. They waited for the lift then squeezed on board along with three chattering nurses and a grumpy-looking wardsman. Sophie resisted the urge to reach up and touch the ten millilitre syringe of midazolam in her shirt pocket and instead stood as though she were bored, as though this were a normal day of ferrying patients from one place to another.

On the fifth floor she and Angus got out and parked the stretcher against the wall. The floor had two wings that met in the lift foyer. One wing was a ward, the other was full of doctors' consulting rooms. Sophie leaned casually against the stretcher and looked down the corridor. She felt conspicuous, like there was a neon sign above her head flashing '*CRIMINAL, CRIMI-NAL*', but nobody ever looked twice at a pair of paramedics and a stretcher in a hospital corridor. Patients weren't ready to go, or the doctor wasn't finished writing some report, or you were just having a bludge. You were part of the furniture. She breathed in the familiar hospital smell and consciously lowered her shoulders.

Angus heaved the Oxy-Viva onto the stretcher. 'That's his office there.' He nodded. 'Third on the right.'

The blue door was closed. Sophie stared at it. She ran through the plan one more time in her head. Worries crowded in on her: what if he wasn't there, or wasn't alone? What if he called for help?

'Ready?'

Sophie gripped the stretcher frame and tried to breathe. Sawyer could not hold out against them, surely. He would reach a certain pain threshold then tell them everything. When she imagined it, the time afterwards was a fog. She didn't care about what the police and courts might do. She didn't care if she was sent to jail for years. Once they found Lachlan, she'd get to see him when Chris visited. She'd know where he was, that he was fine, and that was all that mattered. Despite her fears of the previous night, she couldn't imagine any result other than Sawyer telling them where Lachlan was hidden, alive and well. She worked up a bit of saliva so she could speak. 'Ready.'

They wheeled the stretcher towards his office. Angus opened the Oxy-Viva and pulled out the plastic zip bag containing a cloth soaked in chloroform. He tucked it under his arm then used a tissue to open the door. It closed behind him, and Sophie waited in the corridor, sweating, acutely aware of the sound of voices in the lift foyer and a radio playing in an office further along. She pulled the syringe from her pocket and shoved it under the pillow, and waited for Angus's signal.

After long seconds she heard his low whistle and pushed her way into the rooms. The first room was an empty waiting area. An open door led into Sawyer's actual office, where she saw an upturned chair and Angus standing over Sawyer's limp body. The air smelled of chloroform even though the cloth was already back in its plastic bag by Angus's feet.

Sophie was dizzy, looking at Sawyer lying there. She could almost believe this was a case, this man unconscious on the floor her patient, and she had to protect his airway, check through the possible causes of his loss of consciousness, think which hospital was closest, which had neurosurgery perhaps. Because she surely was not really doing this; she wasn't really about to kidnap a grown man and force him to tell the truth.

'Sophie,' Angus hissed.

She looked at him. It was hard to breathe.

'We have to get moving.'

She was close to crying. She looked down at Sawyer again then Angus leaned over and grabbed her arm. 'He knows,' he said in a low voice. 'Don't forget that.'

Sophie bit the inside of her cheeks.

'It's him or Lachlan.'

Sophie rubbed a shaky hand across her eyes, then picked up the syringe and squatted by

Sawyer's side. 'Hold his arm like I told you.'

Angus wrapped his hands around Sawyer's forearm and squeezed till the veins stood out. Sophie tried to breathe deeply as she uncapped the needle and slid the tip into a vein on the back of his hand. 'How did you do it?' she croaked.

'He was staring out the window,' Angus whispered. 'He never heard me come in.'

She injected three millilitres of the drug then withdrew and recapped the needle. 'Okay.' Angus lifted the Oxy-Viva off the stretcher then grabbed the unconscious man under the shoulders, while Sophie, trembling, grasped his belt with one hand and slid her other arm under his knees. 'One, two, three,' she whispered, and they heaved him up onto the stretcher. They rolled him onto his side, and while Angus arranged the pillow and blanket to cover as much of him as possible, leaving only part of his face exposed, Sophie set up an oxygen mask and slipped it over his head. It was another cover, distorting the appearance of his face for anyone who happened to glance at him. She clipped in the stretcher's seatbelts, pulled the blanket a little higher over the side of his head, hung the Oxy-Viva on the side of the stretcher, then nodded at Angus.

Angus peered out of the main door then opened it wide. Sophie manoeuvred the stretcher into the corridor with sweaty hands. They walked to the lifts. Angus pressed the button with a knuckle and they waited, Sophie gritting her teeth, staring at Sawyer's motionless form,

303

willing him to stay unconscious, wondering if she should have given him more midazolam but knowing that could have stopped him breathing. She watched his chest rise and fall under the blanket. Her own breathing was twice as fast. A couple of nurses came towards them along the ward corridor; she looked anxiously at Angus but the women turned into the stairwell.

The lift gave a ping, the doors opened, and Sophie pushed the stretcher in so that Sawyer was facing the wall. She was trembling.

'Almost there,' Angus said.

The lift opened on the ground floor. Angus walked by the stretcher's head, an additional shield for Sawyer's face, and they moved along the passageway to the Emergency Department. With great effort Sophie controlled the urge to run, the desire to be safe inside the ambulance. The surveillance officers would be looking for an upright and walking Sawyer, not one unconscious on a stretcher, but any oddity could stick in their minds. Not wanting to know where or who they were, fearful of even making eye contact with them, Sophie kept her gaze on Sawyer's chest, counting his breaths for distraction as they walked through the ED and out into the sunshine of the ambulance bay.

Angus took the keys from his pocket and clicked off the ambulance's central locking. He opened the back door, and together they lifted the head of the stretcher inside. Sawyer didn't move. Sophie went to the foot of the stretcher and pulled the release handle to collapse the legs as she pushed the stretcher in fully. Any second she expected a nurse to wander out of the ED for a chat, or another ambulance to pull in and the paramedics inside to recognise her, and as soon as she could she climbed into the back with Sawyer and motioned for Angus to shut the door.

He started the engine. Sophie peered out the rear window as he drove from the bay. Nobody was looking after them curiously. Nobody was looking after them at all.

'We did it,' she said.

'Did what?' Sawyer mumbled.

She clipped a tourniquet around his arm, found a vein and injected another half-millilitre of midazolam. She didn't want him awake until they reached their destination.

16

As Angus drove west, Sophie rolled the unconscious Sawyer onto his back. She made four limb restraints from triangular bandages and tightly tied his hands to the stretcher rails and his feet to the stretcher frame. She watched him carefully and when he started to snore she inserted an oral airway. Having come this far, the last thing she wanted was him dying from an airway obstruction before she learned anything.

'Five minutes,' Angus said.

Sophie clipped the tourniquet around Sawyer's arm again and this time inserted a cannula into his vein and connected an IV line. She taped it down well, knowing he would be struggling later, trying to pull it out. She connected up a bag of Hartmann's fluid and hung it from one of the hooks screwed into the wall.

'Two minutes.'

Sophie watched out the window as Angus took a winding route through an industrial estate. Being Saturday many of the businesses were closed, but here and there roller doors were up and she saw sparks from welders and heard music playing. Nobody stood on the street and watched them go by, but that didn't mean they weren't noticed. Well, if the police knew to come here and ask if anyone remembered the ambulance, they'd already know the rest.

Angus rounded a bend, turned into a driveway and circled around the back of a deserted warehouse. He got out to open a door then drove in.

Sophie drew a shaky breath. She looked at Sawyer, flat on his back with the plastic airway in his mouth. It wasn't too late, she thought, they hadn't done anything really bad yet. They could take him back, make up some story about what happened.

'Sophie?'

'What?'

Angus was watching her in the mirror. 'You okay?'

She felt sick. She looked at Sawyer again. *We have to do this for Lachlan.* She imagined holding him in her arms, rubbing her cheek on the top of his head. She pictured herself taking him home to Chris. *We have to.*

'Sophie?'

'I'm okay.' She made herself look out the window, away from the man on the stretcher. 'How big is this place?'

'Come up here and see.'

She went forward and leaned into the front as Angus drove through the enormous space. The concrete floor was cracked and littered with smashed bottles. 'How'd you find this?'

'Good cops have contacts,' he said.

'Isn't that just in movies? Chris has never mentioned any.'

'Oh, he'd have them too.' He turned behind a wall in to a smaller sectioned-off area. It was the perfect size for the ambulance and the extra walls would muffle any sound even further. It was exactly what she'd asked for. Angus said, 'Seriously, if you have the money you can get anything.'

'That is from the movies.'

'I'm not kidding,' he said. 'I could get you a fake passport, driver's licence, birth certificate — a whole new identity if you wanted one.' He turned off the engine.

Sophie looked back at Sawyer. She was drenched in a cold nervous sweat. But they were here now, and maybe he would be reasonable. 'Let's get him out.'

Angus opened the back door and they pulled the stretcher out onto the concrete floor. Sawyer didn't move. Sophie felt under the stretcher mattress for the metal drip stand and stuck it in its hole on the stretcher frame, then hung the IV bag from the top.

Angus was staring at Sawyer. 'How long till he wakes up?'

'Not long.'

Angus reached out and flicked Sawyer's cheek with his fingernail. 'Hey.' He flicked again, leaving a red mark.

Even this ran against the grain of everything Sophie knew and believed in. She stood in the cavernous warehouse, shivering and afraid. How could she threaten to seriously hurt a man if he didn't tell them the truth, when she knew she couldn't really hurt him at all?

Ella sat at the computer, her chin in her hand. Since getting back to the station from the Phillips house she'd been looking up information on Chris, Dean Rigby and Peter Roth, trying to find links between them. All she found was what she already knew: that Roth and Phillips had attended the same in-service course, and Rigby and Phillips had worked together at Wynyard.

She yawned. Her head ached. The bustle and noise of the station washed around her as she tried to think of what to do next. She could wander down and see how Dennis was progressing: the calls to the TV stations had been traced to a public phone in Raglan Street in Waterloo, and he had people checking for CCTV and any parking tickets given out in the vicinity. She yawned again. Maybe in a few minutes, after she rested her eyes.

'Wakey wakey,' Dennis said. 'We struck gold on the parking tickets.'

She woke up smartly. 'Chris's car?'

'No — Angus Arendson's.'

'The guy who was with Sophie outside Sawyer's house?'

'Booked in a no-standing zone almost opposite the phone box at the time the calls were made.' He offered her his hand. 'May I take the dozing nanna for a drive?'

Sawyer gagged on the airway and Sophie pulled it from his mouth. She had to resist the urge to talk to him reassuringly as she'd do with a patient, biting her cheeks to keep from speaking. Sawyer blinked groggily and tried to raise his hands but the triangular bandages held him tight. The stretcher shook as he struggled to move his arms and legs. He grunted and coughed.

Angus slapped his forehead. 'Time to wake up, dumbo.'

Both Sophie and Sawyer flinched at the assault. Sawyer peered at Angus, then at Sophie. Recognition spread over his face and he raised his head and stared wildly around the empty echoing warehouse. 'Are you nuts?'

Sophie said, 'I want my son.'

'What did you — you kidnapped me to ask me where he is?'

'Smart man,' Angus said.

'I don't know anything about him.'

'I think you do.'

'Well, I fucking don't!'

Sophie checked the flow of the IV bag. She was shaking and hoped he didn't see it.

'Oh, I get it,' he said. 'Next you're going to inject me with something. Threaten to kill me if I don't tell you.'

'Did we say anything about killing?' Angus said.

'You think I'll promise not to tell the cops if you don't?'

'See, now, you're smart in some areas and not in others,' Angus said. 'You need to realise that we don't care. Getting Lachlan back is all she wants. If the price we pay is jail, then that's fine.'

Sawyer struggled against the arm restraints with renewed vigour.

Sophie collected her strength. 'I've tied up violent psychotics with those,' she said loudly, hoping to conquer the waver in her voice. 'You'll never get free.'

'I don't know anything!'

Sophie climbed into the back of the ambulance and opened the drug drawer. The cardboard boxes were colour-coded. Her hand shook as she reached for them and she closed her eyes for a moment. Lying in bed last night she'd imagined having Sawyer at her mercy, and he always gave in before she had to act. The scenario was always in her control. How could she proceed, now that he wasn't giving in? She looked around the ambulance interior as if the answer might be written on the walls.

Bluff. That was what it boiled down to. When she had a patient she wasn't sure what was wrong with, she never let it show. It was the same here — Sawyer had to believe that she was willing to hurt and even kill him. If he saw that she had doubts, it was all over. She'd have no chance.

She took out a box and climbed down from the ambulance. Sawyer nervously craned his head around to see. She stood by his side and showed him the grey-striped box of adrenaline, fitting her thumb to the indented line at one end so the cardboard tore. Inside the box lay a glass vial and a plastic tube with a needle inside it. Both were sealed at one end with yellow plastic caps. She held one in each hand and flipped the caps off with her thumbs, then fitted the exposed ends of the glass vial and the plastic tube together and twisted. The needle in the tube ruptured the seal inside the glass and the drug was drawn up, ready to be injected. She attached a needle to the end and pressed the plunger until a glistening bead appeared on the point. A couple of millilitres injected into a vein was enough to reverse a severe asthma attack or kick a too-slow heart rate into a good solid rhythm. It also had the potential to shoot your heart rate through the roof and kill you. Sawyer, a surgeon, would know that. She held up the syringe so he could see it held ten millilitres.

'Untie me and let's talk about this,' he said.

'Where's Lachlan?'

'I don't know.'

Angus stepped close. 'Tell us where the baby is and all this will stop right now.'

'I don't fucking know!'

Sophie concentrated on hiding her shakes as she brought the needle towards the IV line. Was he really going to let her do it? The second he felt the drug hit his system, accelerate his heart beat, would he shout out where Lachlan was?

The needle slid into the plastic port. She fitted her thumb to the base of the plunger. 'Last chance.' *Please, tell me*.

'If I knew where he was I'd tell you, but I don't!'

'Wrong answer.' Sophie braced herself. *For Lachlan*. She pushed the plunger in. One millilitre: enough to produce a reaction yet still be safe. In seconds his skin turned cold and clammy as his peripheral blood vessels shut down. He broke out in a pungent sweat, his pupils dilated, and Sophie saw the racing pulse in his neck.

'You bitch!' He was crying and retching.

Sophie felt like crying herself. Why wouldn't he just give in and tell them?

Sawyer retched again and spat a gob of mucus at her. Angus punched him in the stomach. Sawyer groaned and Sophie felt sick. She wanted to scream at Angus for hitting him but Angus had told her it was important to appear united, that if Sawyer saw a gap between them he wouldn't tell them the truth. She tried to breathe deeply, evenly. If she could keep control of the situation Angus might not hit him again. *It's Sawyer or Lachlan*, she told herself, and gathered her courage to take hold of the syringe again.

10.25 am

During the drive to Angus Arendson's house in Enfield, Ella and Dennis discussed the possibility that he was the person who had called the TV stations. It was the first time

313

they'd had a particular person other than Chris to consider in that role.

'There's nothing else to suggest it was him, though,' Ella said.

Dennis rubbed his chin. 'We've got very little to say it was Chris.'

They pulled up outside his house in Flax Street and Ella said, 'Well, it'll be interesting to hear him explain why he was there.'

The house was a small, plain fibro building, painted grey with darker grey trim. The lawn was cut short and there were no garden beds.

'Carport's empty,' Dennis said.

They approached the front door and knocked. The house was silent. Ella looked at the collection of dead leaves along the bottom of the door. 'Try the back?'

The back yard was almost as stark as the front. A lone mango tree stood in the far corner, its dark green leaves shivering in the breeze.

Dennis held open the screen while Ella knocked on the door. There was no answer. 'You did check he's not working today?'

'I thought you did.' Dennis let the screen go. 'Kidding. Of course I checked.'

Ella knocked again. She could hear no sound in the building. 'I guess he's out.' She wrote '*Pls contact me*' on the back of one of her cards and stuck it in the doorframe.

Dennis let the screen slam shut and they walked back to the car.

Sophie crouched in the back of the ambulance, trying to catch her breath. She'd twice more injected small doses of adrenaline and Sawyer was still crying that he knew nothing. Angus had hit the doctor three more times in the stomach, once hard enough to make him vomit for real, and they'd shouted at each other so much Sophie was worried somebody outside would hear them. The situation was completely out of her control. She needed time to think, time to breathe, but while Angus was yelling and punching she had neither. He was like a madman and Sophie was afraid of where he was taking them.

'You can't let him be for too long.' Sophie looked up to see Angus leaning into the vehicle. He said in a low voice, 'If he gets his equilibrium back he'll be harder than ever to break.'

'You don't have to hit him so much.'

'People like this are tough targets,' he said. 'Softly softly will get us nowhere.'

She stared at him, and it suddenly seemed odd that he would go to such lengths for someone else's child. She thought of his story of the young girl and his revenge on her attacker. Maybe he enjoyed violence and this way was able to do it for a reason?

Behind him Sawyer started a fresh struggle with the bandages that held him down. The stretcher rattled with his movements.

'A little more and we have him I reckon,' Angus said.

She faced the drawer but knew Angus was still there. She tried to think. Why was Sawyer holding out? A thought crept into her mind — *What if he really didn't do it?* — but she forced it away. Of course he did it. He had motive and opportunity. The police just hadn't been able to prove it yet.

But maybe . . . maybe . . .

No. She grabbed needles at random and jumped out of the ambulance. The small dose wasn't enough, that was all. It was time to get serious with the bluff.

Sawyer was saying to Angus, 'I know why the bitch is doing this, but why are you here? Just getting your kicks out of watching someone suffer? I'm memorising your face, you know. She can fill me up with whatever drugs she likes. I'll remember you and you'll be in the deepest shit.'

Sophie steeled herself. 'You're assuming I'm still going to let you live.' Shaking, she stuck the needle of a new syringe of adrenaline into the IV port and depressed the plunger slowly. One millilitre, two, three. Any more was too risky.

Sawyer gasped. 'Oh God, oh God.' He panted for air. He looked on the verge of cardiac arrest.

Sophie grabbed his arm, terrified he would die. 'Tell me where Lachlan is,' she begged.

He gagged, choking on a mouthful of vomit. She seized his chin and turned his head to the side. 'Cough,' she told him. 'Cough it out.'

Crying, he managed to clear his mouth and throat. 'I don't know anything about your little boy,' he wept.

Sophie started to cry too. She looked up at

316

Angus, shaking her head. It was time to stop. They had to take Sawyer to hospital. Any more and he would die, and then they'd know nothing.

'Liar,' Angus said.

'I don't,' Sawyer groaned.

'LIAR!' Angus launched himself across Sawyer and grabbed the syringe still attached to the IV line, slamming the plunger down and emptying the syringe. Sophie gasped and grabbed for the IV line to crimp it off and stop the flow of adrenaline into Sawyer's bloodstream but it was too late. Sawyer turned white, took a short sharp breath then went limp.

'Shit.' Sophie leapt into the ambulance and grabbed the defibrillator. She tore open Sawyer's shirt and slapped pads onto his chest. The screen showed the wriggling line of ventricular fibrillation, the state when the heart muscle was quivering uselessly. A shock was their best chance of restoring a natural rhythm. She charged the machine to two hundred joules. 'Stand back.'

'Sophie — '

Sophie hit the shock button. Sawyer's body jumped as far as it was able with his feet and hands tied down. The screen still showed VF. 'Shit!'

'He was lying, Sophie.'

She charged the machine, shocked him again. Still VF. 'Why the hell did you do it?'

'I wanted to frighten him, make him realise we could see through all the crap, and he'd finally have to tell the truth.' Angus clasped his head. 'I

317

didn't know this would happen.'

'Jesus, Angus.' Sophie charged the machine to three hundred and sixty joules. Sawyer's body jolted but his heart stayed in VF. 'Jump in there and grab that resus bag.'

She started chest compressions while Angus climbed into the vehicle. 'Where is it?'

'There, on the wall.' She felt a rib crack in Sawyer's chest and lightened up. 'Right there in front of you.'

'I don't — '

'There!' Sophie grabbed Sawyer's face. She pinched his nose shut, raised his chin and blew into his mouth. His chest rose and fell. She breathed into his lungs again then began compressions.

'This thing?' Angus held out the bag.

'Hold it on his face when I tell you. No, not now.' She charged the machine and hit Sawyer with another three-sixty joules. No change from VF. 'Okay, press the mask to his face. Tilt his chin up a bit. Hold it on with one hand and squeeze the bag with the other.'

She kept on with the compressions, trying to think what drugs she should give him. Basic treatment of an arrest included frequent doses of adrenaline, but what did you do if that was the cause?

She shocked him again. Angus squeezed the bag and she heard air leaking from the sides of the mask. 'Press it on tighter.'

'I am,' he said.

'Change places.'

She worked hard with the bag to get plenty of

air into Sawyer's lungs. She stopped for seconds to inject lignocaine, hoping to settle the heart down, then sodium bicarbonate to reverse the metabolic acidosis. But the monitor continued to show the irregular rhythm of VF and Sawyer's skin turned from purple to mottled. Sophie wept as she worked, and her tears fell onto the resus bag and rolled down its curved sides then dropped to the dusty floor below.

Angus took his hands from Sawyer's chest.

'Don't you dare stop,' she snapped. She heard another rib crack as he pressed down again. *Oh God, what have I done?*

She charged up and delivered a shock. The smell of singed chest hair filled the air. She forced the mask tighter on his face and squeezed the guts out of the bag.

'Sophie, he's gone.'

'Not until we stop he isn't.' She charged the monitor again. It reached two hundred joules then stopped, the words '*low battery*' flashing on the screen. She hit him with the two hundred and charged up again. This time the machine made it to a hundred then the screen turned black. The batteries were dead. There were spares in all the cars except the spare one itself, this one.

'I'm calling for back-up,' she said.

'You can't.'

'I have to.'

'He's dead, Sophie. Look at him.'

The surfaces of Sawyer's half-open eyes were dry. His forehead and nose were turning bony white as the blood drained towards his back, the lowest point of his body. The skin of his neck and chest was cooling, the mottling turning pale. She'd seen more people in this state than she could recall. It was the point at which you got out the body bag.

The enormity of the situation fell on her like a monstrous cresting wave. She dropped the resus bag on the warehouse floor and slumped onto the ambulance's back step, her head in her hands. Shock and grief engulfed her and she felt she might collapse. *What have I done? What have I done?*

After a moment she croaked, 'How will we find Lachlan now?'

'We can't.' Angus jabbed a finger into Sawyer's motionless chest. 'He killed him.'

Sophie shook her head.

'You've seen all the cars out there with the blue ribbons.' His voice was hoarse with emotion. 'All those people looking out for Lachlan, yet nobody's found him. Soph, what do you think that means?'

Sophie stared at him, unable to speak.

He lowered his voice. 'Can't you see there was only one reason he was parked at the river?'

Sophie couldn't get her breath. She collapsed on her hands and knees on the cracked concrete floor, her vision blurry, her stomach roiling. She hung her head and her tears dripped onto the floor. Everything in her chest dried up and blew away in a grim and icy wind.

Gone. Lachlan was gone.

17

Sophie sat on the cold concrete floor, her hands over her face. She felt like going home and killing herself.

'Get up,' Angus said.

She couldn't move. He crouched before her and grasped her upper arms, pulling her to her feet.

'Ow,' she said. 'Stop it.'

'You should go home and rest.'

'For what? My time in jail?'

He shook his head. 'That won't happen. I'll take care of it all.'

She looked at Sawyer's cooling body, the mess of vomit and drug boxes on the floor, the IV line that still slowly dripped fluid into the dead veins. 'How?'

'Just go home,' he said. 'Don't think about it. Think about you and Chris. Look after yourself.'

Her head hurt. Wind whistled through a crack in the building's wall somewhere. 'The ambulance,' she said.

'Tell me how to put it in the station, what to say if I meet anyone.'

She sat on the ambulance's back step, weak and sick. It didn't seem possible that they could get away with this, she wasn't even sure she wanted to, but her mind was so muddled that

321

she couldn't think it all through. 'The remote for the station roller doors is attached to the dashboard,' she said. 'Reverse in, close to the wall.'

'And if I meet anyone?'

She tried to think. 'Say you're new to the city. Say that Control told you to bring the truck back from the workshop and your mate's getting code twenty at the Quay. Then get away as quickly as you can.'

'Okay,' Angus said. 'Now, to get you home.' He looked around, then went to a pile of rags and rubbish that lay against the wall and fished out a tattered and dirty blue shirt. 'Put this on, then go outside. Back down the road was a public phone. Call a taxi.'

She held the shirt at arm's length. There was already grease on her fingers from it.

'It's better than your uniform shirt,' he said. 'I'll take that and get rid of it along with mine.'

'The taxi driver will remember me anyway, won't he?'

'He's guaranteed to if you're in full uniform.'

Sophie pulled her ambulance shirt off and yanked on the grimy blue one. Angus turned away while she did so. 'Need phone money?'

She patted her pockets, thought of her wallet in her car at The Rocks. 'I do.' He gave her some coins. 'My car keys are in the front of the ambulance,' she said. 'Maybe you can use my car to get home yourself.'

'Thanks, I will if nobody's around.' He came close and put his hand on the side of her neck. 'It's going to be okay.'

She looked past him at Sawyer's body, feeling certain that nothing would ever be okay again.

12.15 pm

In the carpark Ella watched Dennis light a cigarette. 'Have you noticed that any opportunity you get now, you have a smoke?'

Dennis tilted his head up and exhaled smoke. 'Your point being?'

She ignored that. 'Angus Arendson rang. Said he was at golf earlier. I gave him the spiel about how the calls to the TV stations about the robbery gang were made from a phone box across the street from where he was booked in Waterloo, right around that time. I asked if he was the caller or if he'd perhaps noticed somebody in the box. He said no.'

'Why was he there?'

'Apparently there's a vintage record shop on that stretch and he was looking through their collection. Thought he was in an hour zone but when he found the ticket he realised he'd looked at the wrong sign.'

'Buy anything? Got receipts?'

'Yep,' Ella said. 'Well, so he says.'

Dennis finished his smoke and stepped on the butt. 'We might go and have a look after the meeting.'

When they entered the station the desk officer waved them over. 'Call for you, Detective.'

Dennis took the handset she held out. 'Orchard.' He listened for a moment then

323

motioned for Ella to pick up another handset.

' — searched the hospital grounds and found no trace,' she heard a man saying. 'He was last seen in his office about eight-thirty this morning. His car's still there and none of us saw him go.'

Dennis rubbed his forehead. 'Are there other exits?'

'Well, if he'd gone out with the laundry he might've managed it,' the man said.

Dennis looked at Ella, then said into the phone, 'Keep us posted, will you?' He put the handset down. 'Sawyer's done the bolt.'

'I knew it.' She clenched her fists in glee. 'He was hiding something from the start.'

'Put his description out,' Dennis said to the desk officer. 'We need to find this guy.'

12.33 pm

Chris opened the door when Sophie knocked. 'Where have you been?'

She pushed past him, got some money and paid the taxi driver, then went inside the house again. Chris followed, an icepack held to his forehead, bloodied tissues in his nostrils. 'I need to talk to you.'

'Just don't,' she said.

'Are you crying?'

'Does it matter?' She tore off her clothes and threw them in the washing machine.

'Whose shirt is that?'

She left him in the laundry and went upstairs to shower.

Chris came into the steam-filled room. 'Sophie.'

She didn't answer. Her skin burned under the hot water and the scrubbing brush. It didn't make sense, she hadn't been in close prolonged contact with Sawyer's dead-man sweat, but if she inhaled deeply enough she still caught a whiff of it.

'Sophie.'

'Not now.' She turned the shower off but stayed in the cubicle. The last of the water trickled down the drain between her feet. She stared into the little holes and wished she could slip away with it.

He opened the cubicle door. 'I've got to talk to you. Something's happened.'

She shivered and he handed her a towel. She couldn't look him in the eye.

'Soph?'

She felt sick and faint, and crouched down, hands hard against the tiled walls. Despair over what she'd done overwhelmed her. Great racking sobs rose up from deep inside her chest.

'Jesus, Sophie.' Chris crouched beside her, his arm over her back, pulling the towel up to cover her goosepimpled shoulders, hugging her to him.

She sank even lower on the shower floor. *Oh God, I didn't deserve him before. What will he say when he finds out what I've done?*

12.40 pm

In the meeting Ella sat with her elbows on the table, barely listening to people reel off their lack of success. Her mind was on Sawyer. Where was he? What was he doing? Did he have Lachlan hidden somewhere and was in the process of moving him? If so, was the baby dead or alive?

Dennis's mobile rang. 'Orchard,' he muttered. He blinked then started to scribble on a notepad. Ella peered over his arm to see an address in the inner western suburbs. He said, 'Thanks,' ended the call and stood up. 'Meeting adjourned, folks, we've found a body.'

Ella felt a sharp pain in her chest and the detectives sighed and slumped down in their chairs.

'It's not Lachlan,' Dennis said. People brightened.

'Who then?' Ella said.

'Not sure yet.'

In the car she said, 'But obviously you have some idea?'

'A real estate guy arrived at this warehouse and found a dead man in it.' He accelerated out of the carpark. 'He was in a state when he rang triple 0, saying something about an ambulance being there but nobody else around, but his description made it sound like Sawyer.'

'An ambulance.'

'Yes.'

She put a hand on her head. 'That's bad.'

'First we make sure it's him,' Dennis said. 'Then we know.'

Chris walked Sophie to the bed, sat her on the side and pulled the quilt up around her. She couldn't stop shaking. *I killed a man.* The thought went round and round in her head. *I killed him.*

Chris wrapped his arms around her and pulled her close. She felt simultaneously comforted and guilty in his embrace. She laid her head on his shoulder, looking at the side of his face, as every bad thing she'd done rose up in her memory from the cheating to the events of today. At Mrs Macquarie's Point they'd kissed while fireworks shot from the Harbour Bridge, and she'd felt his heart beating against her chest, and now they were so separate. When all this was over she had to live differently, holding nothing back. She should start now.

'I need to tell you something,' he said. He looked down at her with tears in his eyes. 'Lachlan being taken was my fault. I'm so sorry.'

'No, it was mine.' Sophie started to cry. 'Sawyer took him because I couldn't save his wife and baby.' She drew a long faltering breath. 'And today I killed Sawyer.'

Chris looked horrified. 'What?'

'Angus and I kidnapped him. I wanted to make him tell me where Lachlan is. He wouldn't say, then he got an overdose and died and I couldn't get him back.'

Chris started to cry too. 'You killed an innocent man.'

'No, we didn't. The detectives think it was him too.'

'You did,' he said. 'Lachlan being taken was my fault. I rang the TV stations about the robbery gang being all police. I wasn't completely certain that they were, really, but I found out that officers like Rigby were doing some bad stuff and I thought this way the government would be pressured into a general investigation into corruption. But people in the gang somehow found out I did it, and they shot me and took him as payback.'

'That's wrong,' Sophie said. 'I know it was Sawyer. Angus said so too. He kept me up to date with the things Ella wouldn't tell me, like how she felt Sawyer might have got rid of Lachlan on the baby black market.'

'He said that? Are you sure?'

'Positive.'

'But there's almost certainly no such thing,' Chris said. 'Ella would never seriously suspect that's what happened.'

'Then why would he say it?'

Chris was silent for a moment. 'Where's Sawyer's body?'

'Angus is taking care of it.' She explained what he was going to do.

'So your getting away with killing Sawyer depends on Angus's carrying out his part of the plan.' Chris suddenly stared at her with such a fire in his eyes she felt afraid.

'What is it?'

'Mum told me today that she arranged an abortion for Angus's sister, Bee, when we were

328

sixteen,' he said. 'But the baby wasn't mine. We never had sex.' He grabbed her arms so tightly it hurt. 'Do you see what I'm saying?'

1.05 pm

Four uniformed police waited for Ella and Dennis outside the warehouse. Two local area detectives stood inside, some distance from the ambulance. Ella and Dennis approached slowly, careful not to step on any drug boxes or syringes. It was all evidence and would be photographed in situ before being logged in, packaged up and taken away for analysis.

The body was tied to the stretcher by both wrists and both ankles. The once-white shirt was torn open and what Ella guessed were defibrillation pads were stuck on his chest. She walked parallel to the stretcher, studying the body's face. 'It's him.'

Dennis nodded. 'I agree.'

Sawyer looked even skinnier than before, perhaps an effect of being dead and flat on his back, though Ella remembered he'd looked more gaunt each time she'd seen him even while alive. There was dried vomit around his mouth and on the floor. His eyes were half-open and an IV bag hung from a metal pole on the stretcher, its tubing connected to his arm. A needle and syringe stuck out of it. Ella twisted her head to read the printed label: '*Adrenaline*'.

'Look at that.'

Ella turned to where Dennis was pointing and

saw a crumpled ambulance uniform shirt thrown partly under the ambulance.

'Detective Orchard?'

Ella looked towards the door, where a uniformed officer and a detective stood with a man in blue workman's clothing. 'This man has information.'

The man worked as a welder in a factory down the road. 'I was on my break,' he said, 'about eleven, when I saw a woman come out of the building and walk to the public phone down there. She was almost staggering, so I watched her, thinking she was maybe sick. She stayed in the phone box for a while, I could see she'd sat down in there, then about five or ten minutes later a taxi pulled up and she got in. I didn't think anything else of it until I saw all you guys here.'

'What did she look like?' Dennis said. 'What was she wearing?'

'She was tall and slim, and she had long hair tied back in a sort of bun thing. She was wearing a really raggedy-looking shirt, a blue one. And dark trousers. Blue or black, I'm not sure.'

'Which taxi company was it?'

'The red and blue one, I can't remember their name.'

'Thank you.' Dennis turned to the detective. 'Get his statement, track down that taxi and then call me.' He headed outside, Ella right behind him.

He tossed her the car keys then pulled out his phone and dialled a number. 'I need a warrant for Sophie Phillips's house.'

18

When she knocked on the door Ella heard running footsteps then the door was almost torn off its hinges. 'Chris?' Gloria Phillips's eyes were red and her face tear-streaked.

'Mrs Phillips, we have a warrant to search these premises,' Ella said. 'Are Chris and Sophie home?'

'No, I don't know where they are. When I got here I found the back door unlocked and windows open, and they never do that,' she said. 'It's as if they took off in a big hurry. I thought maybe you'd called and said you'd found Lachlan.'

'I'm sorry, we haven't,' Ella said.

Dennis squeezed past them and started upstairs. Ella went into the living room and looked around.

Gloria followed, sniffling. 'I'm sorry to be in such a state but Chris and I had a big argument today.'

'It's a stressful time,' Ella said, peering into the kitchen. 'Perhaps you'd like to sit in the living room while we take a look around?'

Gloria took a box of tissues with her.

Ella went upstairs to Dennis. 'They're not here, are they.'

He shook his head. He was standing in the

main bedroom. There were piles of clothes on the floor. An ambulance uniform lay in a corner. It looked as though it had been there for a few days. 'Just like she said, seems they left in a hurry.'

The sliding door of the built-in wardrobe was open. Ella looked in, expecting to see clothes and suitcases missing, thinking now they were on the trail of a fugitive murderer. Instead she saw an open shoebox on the floor, its contents tipped out among black work boots and men's running shoes. She knelt for a look. 'Eight years and under, 50 metres backstroke,' she read from a small faded blue ribbon. 'Boys' junior soccer, runners-up.'

'Funny what some people keep.' Dennis went into the next room.

Ella stood up and saw a collection of letters on the bed. She smoothed out the top one. '*Dear Chris,*' it began. '*I will always love you.*'

'Got some love letters here,' she called. She scanned down to the bottom of the letter. 'To Chris, from someone called Bee.'

'New or old?'

'Undated.' Ella shuffled through the pile but there were no envelopes, no helpful postmarks. They didn't look recent but it was important she find out. They could be evidence that Chris was having an affair after all.

'Distinctive name,' Dennis said. 'Mrs Phillips might know.'

Ella took the letter downstairs. Gloria was sitting on the lounge, rocking back and forth, twisting a tissue in her hands.

332

'Do you know a person named Bee?'

Gloria looked up. 'That's Angus's sister.'

'Angus Arendson?'

'Well, not really his sister,' Gloria said. 'Angus was adopted by Bee's mother when he was small. His mother and Bee's were friends, but his mother was a bit of a no-good, well, I mean, she took off with this bloke, to India or somewhere, and never came back. Bee's mother took Angus in and after a while she adopted him.' She dropped shredded tissue on the floor. 'None of the other kids knew and Bee's mother asked that we never tell them. I don't think Chris ever knew. Well, unless Bee told him. She might have done. I don't know.'

Ella tried to keep it straight in her mind.

'And Bee and Chris used to go out when they were teenagers. Now she has a little boy and he's sick, he's got cancer, poor little thing.' She started to sob. 'Life isn't fair when such bad things happen to such little babies.' She pulled another tissue from the box. 'Why do you ask?'

'I found some letters from her upstairs,' Ella said.

'Chris must have been reading them after I left.' Gloria wiped her eyes. 'She was the reason for our argument.'

'Had she been around? Was Chris seeing her again?'

'No, nothing like that.' Gloria covered her face with her hands. 'I helped her get an abortion when she was sixteen. Chris didn't know until today.'

Ella stared at her.

'He was furious,' Gloria went on. 'He hates me now' Her voice cracked. 'I don't blame him either.'

Ella went out in the hall to read further in the letter. *'I'm sorry that I was nasty yesterday. Sometimes I feel so bad, so ugly, about things going on in my life. Things I can't tell anyone about, they are that bad. But at the same time it feels so nice! I don't understand that. If it's all so wrong, shouldn't it feel bad at the time, not just later?'*

Ella struggled to get her thoughts in order. Angus and Chris knew each other years ago; Chris went out with Angus's adoptive sister, Bee; Chris's mother arranged a secret abortion for Bee when the girl was sixteen.

Chris obviously thought the letters were relevant because he'd got them out of the box, either today or very recently, and he and Sophie had left the house so quickly they hadn't even locked up. It was possible that they'd rushed out because of what Sophie had done, but Ella didn't think that was the reason.

It was a long shot, but she pulled her phone out and called the Incident Room. Murray answered. She said, 'Grab a piece of paper.'

There was a shuffling sound. 'Okay.'

'Woman by the name of Bee Arendson.'

'Bee's short for Belinda,' Gloria said from the doorway.

'Belinda Arendson,' Ella said into the phone. 'Put her in the system, see what we've got.'

'System's down,' Murray said. 'All the metro

computers are offline. They're working on it, but — '

'As soon as they're back up, then,' Ella said. 'Meanwhile, call Births, Deaths and Marriages and check for registered births. A son.'

'Named Ben,' Gloria said.

'Ben,' Ella told Murray, then covered the phone. 'Have you ever seen him?' she asked Gloria. 'Or a picture?'

Gloria shook her head.

'Call me back when you know anything,' Ella said to Murray, and hung up. 'Dennis!'

'Why are you asking about Bee's little boy?' Gloria said.

Dennis came halfway down the stairs. 'What?'

'A lead.'

'What is it?'

Ella nodded at the door.

Gloria followed them outside, clutching at Ella's sleeve. 'What are you thinking? Do you know where Lachlan is?'

'We'll call you the second we know anything,' Ella said. 'I promise.'

2.10 pm

'I don't know,' Dennis said, frowning in the passenger seat. 'I can't see it.'

'It is a lead, though,' Ella said.

'Absolutely. Just not one strong enough to get us a warrant.'

'We'd better start hoping he's home then,' Ella

said. 'Try Murray again, see if things are working yet.'

Dennis did so. After a short conversation he closed his phone. 'No go, and so far nothing back from Births, Deaths and Marriages.'

Ella braked to a halt in front of Angus's house. The carport was empty. 'Shit.'

They got out anyway and went to the back door. Ella opened the screen and was about to knock, then stopped. 'Hello.'

'What?'

'Door's open.'

Dennis leaned in to see the centimetre gap between the door and the frame.

They looked at each other.

'Could be somebody injured in there,' Ella said.

'Could be,' he said, pulling his gun out. 'We'd better go and see.'

She got her own gun out, pushed the door open with her foot and waited a moment. 'Police, coming in.'

The house was silent. Ella shivered, then stepped inside, listening hard. A car droned past outside. She could feel Dennis's breath on the back of her neck as she started down the narrow hallway.

The first doorway on the right was the bathroom, painted green, small and unrenovated. Opposite was a tiny laundry with a dented washing machine and a sink.

At the end of the hall was the small kitchen. The sink and cracked linoleum benches were bare.

The living room contained a worn lounge and small TV. There were two bedrooms, one obviously kept as a spare with a mattress leaning against the wall, the other with a double bed made up with flannelette sheets and wool blankets. A rug was pushed up close to the bed and Dennis almost tripped on the folds when he went to check under the bed. 'Place is empty.'

The dresser drawers stood open and held just a few crumpled T-shirts. Dennis looked into the wardrobe as he reholstered his gun. 'Someone's packed and left in a hurry.'

Ella put her gun away then stood in the hall with her hands on her hips. 'But where's he gone, and why?'

Dennis didn't answer. He was smoothing the rug's worn pile with his shoe.

Ella went back to the kitchen. Magnets held two photos to the fridge door. One showed Angus and a young woman sitting smiling on a lounge, the other the same young woman holding a baby wrapped in a blanket. Ella looked closely at it. The baby was hardly visible. It could be anyone. She focused on the woman, noticing skinny arms and small breasts. 'Do you think this could be the woman from the pub CCTV?'

Dennis came to look. 'She's a similar build.'

Ella thought she looked a little familiar from somewhere else too, but couldn't place her.

'Next stop Bee's house, once we get the address, right?' she said. 'Dennis?'

'Mm.'

'What is it?'

'Just thinking.' He was walking through the

rooms, hands in pockets, staring at the walls.

Ella headed down the hall. 'I'll ring Murray.'

Dennis followed, frowning.

She was on the step at the back door, starting to dial, when she saw him whirl and charge back up the hall. She ended the call before it went through and ran after him.

He was in the bedroom, tapping his knuckles along the wall, then he grasped the corner of the dresser. His eyes were bright when he looked up at her. 'Help me with this.'

They dragged the dresser away from the wall. Its legs came to rest against the folded rug. 'I knew it,' Dennis said.

'Knew what?'

He pointed at the rug, then at the corners of the room. 'There's a false wall here.'

Ella squinted at the walls. 'Really?'

He ran his hands across the wall and pinpointed a crack in the paint. 'He closed it up but forgot about the rug.'

'If you say so,' Ella said. 'You want me to ring for a warrant?'

'Take too long.' Dennis went into the kitchen and started opening drawers. He came back with a screwdriver, and slotted the tip into the wall. 'I don't care any more about the rules of evidence. I just want to find this kid before something bad happens.' He managed to lever off a panel. Behind it was a small dark space. Dennis grabbed a lamp and turned it on, and they peered in.

The place was tiny but organised. A laptop, printer and digital camera lay on a bench to one side, below a sheet of cork to which colour photos were pinned.

'Canon printer,' Ella said. 'And look, half a ream of Reflex paper.'

The other walls were covered in shelving. The equipment the shelves had once held was now mostly in a jumble on the floor. Dennis raised the lamp higher and Ella saw pages stapled in bundles, labelled audio tapes, photocopies of maps with particular routes highlighted, and newspaper articles spilling from torn cardboard files on the floor. There was a clear plastic disc and microphone, and a small directional 'gun' microphone, the likes of which Ella had seen used in surveillance operations. A tangle of wires and a pile of small black listening devices had tumbled from an upended cardboard box. There were three cameras with long lenses, and four boxes of different ammunition. Ella's gaze fell upon one open box. 'Twenty-two subsonics.'

'Can't see any guns but we'll pull up the floor, go into the roof space,' Dennis said.

'He might have them with him.' Ella took the lamp to examine pictures on the corkboard. It was a series of colour shots of Chris, Sophie and Lachlan out shopping somewhere, a close-up of Lachlan sucking on a dummy the same as the one found by Sawyer's car, a shot of Sophie talking on the radio in an ambulance, and one taken through a window of Sophie feeding Lachlan in a highchair. The dates printed in the corners ranged from two weeks to three months ago.

Dennis picked a photo up by its corner.

'Here's the phone box in Raglan Street.'

The shot showed Chris on the phone looking anxious. In the background was a shop awning that read '*Raglan Street Drycleaners*'. In the bottom corner of the photo was a time and date stamp.

''*May 6, 10.22 am*'. I guess we know who the caller to the TV stations was,' Ella said.

'So Angus or Bee followed him, took this happy snap and — ' Dennis poked the directional microphones lying on the floor with his foot ' — listened in as well?'

'Looks like it.'

'So they heard Chris call the stations and say the robbery gang was all police.' Dennis pinched his chin between his finger and thumb. 'And then what?'

Ella was about to answer when she spotted a couple of bills in the mess on the floor. 'These are addressed to Bee. Lot 37, Marshall Road, Palm Glen.'

'And look at this.' Dennis pointed to a twin pack of dummies lying on the floor. One was missing. The one that remained had a sun and moon pattern Ella recognised from the dummy found next to Sawyer's car at the river.

Ella's phone rang. She handed the lamp back to Dennis. 'Marconi.'

'It's me,' Murray said, excited. 'Belinda Arendson's had four registered births but they were all stillborn. Apparently once the pregnancy gets over twenty-eight weeks and the baby's born dead it has to get registered as a birth, but it's not registered as a death because — '

'Four dead babies. We get the picture,' Ella said. 'No live ones?'

'Nope.'

She punched Dennis's arm. 'Let's go.'

In the car she accelerated hard, while Dennis fumbled with her phone, trying to put it on loudspeaker. 'That button there,' she said.

Suddenly Murray's voice came through. 'Hello?'

'We hear you,' Dennis said.

'Okay. Record-wise Bee has a good behaviour bond from eleven years ago. She was a nurse and worked in a nursing home and this old guy died from a drug overdose. She said it was an accident but the family said he'd told them he wanted to die and that a nurse was going to help him. Old guy dies, family kicks up stink, in come the cops.'

'What was that drug that came up on Sawyer's tox screen?' Ella asked Dennis. 'The one that knocks you out and makes you forget stuff?'

'Midazolam.'

'We need to find out how closely that's controlled in hospitals, especially anywhere Bee's worked.'

Dennis gripped the door as she took a bend at speed. 'You're thinking Bee and Angus are behind the entire scheme?'

'Maybe,' Ella said. 'Bee wants a baby. She can't have one. She sees Chris and Sophie with Lachlan, she feels cheated, she decides she'll just take what she wants. Angus, being the helpful adopted brother, goes along, spying on the family, plotting out how they'll do it.'

'And Sawyer?'

'Maybe Angus found out about Sawyer's wife and baby dying and how Sophie was involved, perhaps after Sawyer was arrested for that DUI,' Ella said. 'He sets Sawyer up so we'll find him unconscious by the river. Bee picked him up in the pub and gave him the drugs so he wouldn't remember any of it, which in turn increases our suspicion of him.'

Dennis murmured something incredulous.

Murray jumped in. 'Angus could've done the actual shooting of Chris and kidnapping Lachlan. He left the *keep your mouth shut* note because first of all it would cost us time to look into it and then if we found out Chris had indeed called the TV stations, we'd believe the kidnapping was tied to that.'

Ella started, realising where she might have seen Bee. 'I think it was Bee who killed Roth, too.'

'Really?'

'I'd have to see her in the flesh to be sure,' Ella said, 'but what I've seen so far fits.'

Dennis rubbed his eyes. 'I'm too old for this.'

Murray said, 'You think Angus is involved with the gang as well as being behind the kidnapping?'

'Maybe he's planning a quiet life for the three of them and his takings from the robberies were making a little nest egg.' She was all excited. 'Even the cancer story fits. You said there weren't many disguise options for babies, but one was to shave his hair off. They could tell everyone he's being treated for cancer, that's why he's got no

342

hair, and they keep shaving him to keep him that way.'

Dennis was still frowning. 'You have some imagination.'

'It works for me,' Murray said.

Ella smiled at the phone. Maybe he wasn't so bad after all.

'But where does Sawyer getting killed fit in?' Dennis said.

'I guess that was Sophie believing he was behind the kidnapping,' Ella said. 'We know that Angus spent some time with Sophie the last few days, including driving past Sawyer's house. Perhaps he egged her on. Perhaps he even helped kidnap him, maybe even kill him.'

'But why, if they just wanted the baby? Why not take him and disappear?'

'Good question.' Ella sped through an intersection.

'Maybe it wasn't just the baby,' Murray said.

'What?'

'Maybe they were out for more than the baby,' he said. 'If Bee's got trouble with her upstairs wiring, as sounds increasingly likely, what if she blamed that first abortion for all her stillbirths since?'

A light went on in Ella's brain. 'That's it!'

'Eyes on the road,' Dennis said.

'Gloria started it all by arranging that abortion, right?' Ella said. 'Say things went to plan for Bee and Angus. Chris ends up brain-damaged, maybe really badly. If Angus helped Sophie today he's probably arranged things so that all evidence points to her and not

343

him, and she winds up in jail. He even told us his alibi on the phone, remember? Meanwhile Lachlan is never found. So what happens to Gloria?'

'She's lost her family and she's all alone,' Dennis said.

'A fate worse than death, some might say,' Ella said. 'I reckon Chris and Sophie have reached the same conclusion about Angus and Bee and that's why they left their house in such a hurry.'

'Without letting us know?'

'Sophie may have just killed a man,' she said. 'I'm guessing she thinks we'd arrest her first and ask questions later.'

Murray put in, 'And maybe they think if the Arendsons get away now, none of us will be able to find Lachlan.'

Dennis put down Ella's phone and pulled out his own. 'I'm arranging back-up. If Angus and Bee have guns and we've got an unarmed paramedic and an injured copper going up against them before we get there, they're going to need a hell of a lot of help.'

19

'Okay.' Chris scribbled as he listened into the phone. 'Got that. Yep. Thanks, Mick.'

Sophie glanced over from behind the wheel at the little map he'd drawn. They were almost at Palm Glen. When Allan Denning at Wynyard had told him that all the city computers were down, Chris had called a friend on the South Coast to look up Bee's address; then, because they had no map of the area, he'd rung Central Coast Ambulance Control for help on the location of Marshall Road. Mick was the controller on duty and he had looked up the computer-aided dispatch map for them.

Now Chris held the phone out. 'He wants to talk to you.'

'Hold it up to my ear,' she said.

'I don't think you should go in,' Mick said, his voice tinny on the phone. 'Wait for the cops. There's a siege in Gosford at the moment, so response might be a bit down, but they'll come when I tell them what Chris said.'

'This guy can get passports, fake ID, anything. If they get away from us, how will we know what name they're going under? How could we stop them at the airport if we don't know that?'

'But how risky is it, you just charging in? What

345

happens if you both get shot? Then where will Lachlan be?'

Mick made good sense but Sophie had no choice. She was a churning mess of emotions: fear that they might get away, or that Lachlan might be harmed; guilt that she'd had a one-night stand with the man who'd taken her child (and was that part of his plan? Had he been manipulating her even then?); the roaring fury of the betrayal of his 'assistance' to find Lachlan while all along he was actually steering her further in the wrong direction; and the awful sinking knowledge that she had been involved with him in the torture and death of an innocent man.

'The exit's coming up,' Chris said.

'I have to go,' she said to Mick.

'Please don't do it, Soppers.'

'I have to.' She moved her head away. 'Turn it off.'

They were on the exit. 'Head up here then turn left onto Palmdale Road,' Chris said. 'Travel along about a kilometre then Marshall turns off to the right. Lot thirty-seven is on the right, a couple of clicks along, past a creek.' He held up the map, his finger on a crosshatched section. 'See this?'

She glanced over.

'It's State forest. Full of four-wheel drive tracks that come out all over, Mick said. Their house backs right onto it.'

'We can't let them get in there,' Sophie said.

'We won't.'

They shot onto Palmdale Road. 'So what are

346

we going to do? Just drive through the front gate?'

Chris pored over his scratch map. 'Mick told me there's a right-hand bend around a hill and their house is on the other side of that. I think our best bet is to try to take them by surprise — go through the forest and come at the house from the back.'

Sophie hurtled onto Marshall Road, taking note of the speedo. A couple of clicks, he'd said. She tried to look everywhere at once: the letterboxes on the roadside with 'Lot 12' and 'Lot 17' painted on them, the road ahead in case they met Angus coming out, the speedo again. They covered the few thousand metres quickly and crossed the creek. 'Right-hand bend,' she said, slowing the car. On their right was a tree-covered hill.

'Along here would be best.'

She pulled over and popped the boot. From it she took a tyre lever and a jack handle. Chris wiped his nose, which was starting to bleed. 'You okay to go?' she said.

'Don't even ask that.' He took the tyre lever, grabbed her hand, and crossed the road.

They climbed a fence into a paddock. The grass was long and caught at their feet, and it hid hollows which made them stumble. The paddock was a narrow strip running along the lower slope of the hill below the forest. Sophie looked up at the tree line as they neared it. She was breathless with nerves and exertion. The afternoon sun was hot on her back and she felt conspicuous in the open.

They clambered through another wire fence into the forest. It was cooler here and the ground sloped more steeply and the undergrowth was thick and spiky. Branches of shrubs scratched their arms and faces. Chris slashed at bushes with his tyre lever but they sprang back at him.

Adrenaline and effort made Sophie's heart pound. What would happen when they found the house? She had to assume Angus would have at least one gun. He was a trained cop, while the best defence strategy she knew as a paramedic was to run away. They'd need to take him by surprise, but how could they do that? What if he had seen them coming and was lying in wait? What if he held a gun on them, put Bee and Lachlan in the car, then left? What if he told Chris about her cheating to throw him off, even momentarily? She smashed the jack handle into a tree trunk. She couldn't think like this. If it cost her her life she would do everything in her power to stop Angus getting away.

Chris struggled through the scrub beside her. His nose streamed blood and he didn't bother wiping it away. His legs were trembling, and sweat soaked his shirt. She reached out to stop him and briefly feel his racing pulse, measure his gasping breaths. He took her hand from his neck. 'I'm fine.' He tugged her forward.

'How are we going to do this?'

'Find the house first,' Chris panted. 'Then see what we've got.'

They crested the hill together. Going downhill was easier but the undergrowth was thicker. Sophie looked ahead for the glint of a farmhouse roof or for movement of any kind. 'There,' she said. 'Something reflecting.'

They worked their way ahead more cautiously. The scrub thinned, then the trees thinned too, and they could see a small unfenced dam full of brown water, three cows lying in the shade of a eucalypt, and a grey weatherboard house. It was a Queenslander, elevated two metres off the ground, the underneath area fenced in with wooden slats. Angus's white Magna was parked at the side of the house. There was no sign of any people.

Sophie only realised how much she had been hoping that the police would be here when she saw they weren't. She gripped the jack handle and stared down at the little house.

Chris whispered in her ear, 'See how some of those slats are broken? I reckon we should get under the house itself then attack from there.'

A cry broke out in the house and the hair stood up on the back of Sophie's neck and she grabbed Chris's arm. It was Lachlan!

They both burst into tears. Chris slid his arm around Sophie's neck and hugged her tight. Sophie wrapped her arms around Chris's body and pressed her face into his sweaty bloodied shirt and wanted to scream out her relief and joy. *Thank God, oh thank God!*

But there was no time to waste. She turned her head to speak. 'We've got to get down there. If they make it to the car, we won't be able to stop them.'

Chris wiped the tears from her cheek with his thumb. 'We approach from different angles so there's less chance he'll spot both of us. You go from here. I'll work my way around there a little and then down to the house.' He raised the tyre lever in a warrior pose. 'See you under the house, okay?'

They hugged briefly then he was gone. Sophie tightened her grip on the jack handle and started down the slope. She moved from tree to tree, trying to be quiet as the scrubby bushes caught her legs. Crickets chirped and birds called in the bush around her, and a breeze rustled the leaves. She stared at the house as she crept forward, searching for gun barrels protruding from windows, but saw nothing. Lachlan's crying subsided and the house was silent. She wiped her tears away. It was time to be strong.

The trees stopped ten metres from the house. Sophie eyed the open area of grass she had to cross and the single window that overlooked it. A tattered blind hung from the top. Further along the back of the house six concrete steps with no railing led up to the back door. It was open. A wooden-framed screen door banged in the breeze.

Chris peered from behind a tree at the other end of the house. He scanned the windows then gave Sophie a thumbs-up. She checked her window again, took a deep breath, fixed her eye on a gap in the slats and ran.

Under the house was gloomy after the bright sunlight outside. Sophie stood panting on the bare earth floor, listening for any sounds above her that would indicate she'd been seen. She could hear footsteps and the murmur of voices, but none were panicked. She allowed herself a couple of deep breaths. She'd made it — this far, anyway.

Chris squeezed through a break in the slats and came towards her, past old farm implements and a dusty workbench. A beaten-up and rusty Landrover was parked facing out. He glanced at it then crouched by a rear tyre.

'We don't have time,' she whispered.

Air hissed from the tyre as he depressed the valve. 'I'm cutting down their options. We should do something about the Magna too.'

'He'll spot us for sure.'

Chris peered out through the slats, then around at the jumble of tools on the workbench. 'I could cut the fuel line, stop them going anywhere.'

'I'll do it,' she said.

'No way.'

'You need to fix your nose and have a rest, even for thirty seconds,' she whispered. He was ghostly pale and clammy to touch. When she moved close to look at his pupils she could hear his breath rasping in his throat. He was shaking hard, and she pressed her hand on his shoulder to try to make him sit down, but he shrugged out from under it.

'Tell me where the fuel line goes and I'll be out and back before you know it,' she said.

He started to speak but was interrupted by a voice from the house.

'Hurry up, will you?' It was Angus. Sophie looked up at the floorboards over her head. He sounded curt and angry. There was a murmured

351

reply. He said, 'I told you to always be ready.'

'I usually am,' a woman's voice said. Bee.

'I don't care about usually,' he said. 'I rush up to take the two of you away and you're not even here! You're over at that bloody creek!'

'Ben wanted a swim.'

Sophie's blood surged.

'Just pack, would you?'

Sophie felt a fresh burst of rage at Angus. She leaned close to Chris. 'I'm going.'

He was silent for a moment. 'The fuel line runs along underneath the chassis. Cut it, crimp it, do anything, then get back here.'

She found a dusty pair of pliers on the bench. She stood at the slats, eyeing the Magna, wishing she could see the windows above her. There were footsteps across the floor in a far corner of the house and she took a deep breath and squeezed through the gap. She ran to the car and dived underneath.

The chassis and engine were hot. She burned her shoulder trying to get on her back, but she hadn't been shot and there were no shouts from the house. She looked at the slats and saw Chris's bloodied face peering out. The underneath of the car was filthy with road grime and dirt and she searched for a moment before locating the small pipe. She grabbed it with the cutting edge of the pliers and with a great effort snapped it in two. *Take that, you bastard.*

She wriggled to the edge of the car. Lying right at the border of the sun and shade she tried to look upwards to the windows but could see no higher than the slats. Chris stared at her fearfully.

She offered up a little prayer then rolled out, leapt to her feet and bolted.

Chris caught her as she came through the gap in the slats. There were no shouts from above, no shots. She whispered, 'He doesn't know we're here!'

'Come *on*!' Angus was right overhead.

The air smelled of smoke. Sophie sniffed at it. 'He's surely not burning the place down?'

'Let's not wait to find out,' Chris said in her ear. He had a strange light in his eyes. Bits of bloodstained rag were twisted up his nostrils. He held her tight. 'You know that we could die.'

'If they get away with Lachlan it's all over anyway.'

'I love you.'

'I love you too.' *If Angus tells you what happened you might not believe that, but I do, I swear on my grave I do.*

'Follow me.' He squeezed out through the gap in the slats and edged along the wall to the front steps. Sophie hunched her shoulders, frightened to think that Angus might lean out of a window above them, but desperate to save Lachlan. Chris put his finger on his lips then started up the steps. Sophie got it — as long as Angus didn't know they were here they had the upper hand.

The front door was open. There was nobody in the first room, a mangy sitting room with a tatty cane lounge and a threadbare maroon rug. A cloth nappy lay on the back of the lounge.

Sophie's heart hammered in her chest. The back door banged and she jumped. Chris squeezed her arm reassuringly but his forehead poured sweat and blood was making its way around the rags in his nose.

The smell of smoke was stronger. Someone sneezed and a shadow passed the doorway to the next room. Chris raised the tyre lever. Elsewhere in the house Angus said, 'You want these bottles?' and Bee appeared in the doorway with Lachlan in her arms. He was bald but Sophie recognised her son in a heartbeat and she grabbed for Chris's arm, terrified he'd accidentally hit him.

Chris's blow glanced off the side of Bee's head onto her shoulder. She screamed and heavy footsteps thudded their way. Chris raised the lever again as Sophie dropped the jack handle and reached for Lachlan.

An explosion almost deafened her. Splinters floated from the ceiling and she realised Angus had fired a shot. Lachlan was screaming as Bee spun and ran. Chris ducked backwards into Sophie and she braced herself, expecting to see Angus come through the doorway, gun in hand, to shoot them both. Instead she became aware of him shouting to Bee — 'Go! Go!' — and realised they were more focused on getting away.

Chris peered around the corner. Sophie heard the back door slam and Lachlan's cries recede. His dummy lay on the floor. She was crying and she started forward but Chris grabbed her arm. 'Better we set ourselves up here. Once they find the car won't start they'll have no choice but to deal with us. I'm going to look for a gun.'

Smoke was visible in the house as she ran to a window. Bee was climbing into the front seat of the Magna, Lachlan squirming and crying in her arms. Angus glanced up at the house and she pulled back momentarily then peered out again to see him slam the door and start the car. It headed off, bouncing over the grass. The three cows scrambled to their feet and ran.

'The car's going!' she screamed at Chris. He rushed to her side, clutching a burned and still smoking fragment of paper. The Magna jolted in a wide circle and picked up speed.

'You cut the line!'

'I cut something.' She sprinted for the back door, Chris so close behind her he kicked her.

The grass on the slope was uneven and Sophie tripped and almost fell. The car swerved and there was a loud report. Angus was shooting at them. She could see him, half out the driver's window, aiming a black handgun. Judging by the way the car was all over the place, Bee had the wheel from the passenger seat. Ahead of the car was the dam.

There was another shot and Chris fell.

Sophie looked back. He lay still, on his face in the grass. She was torn but could not push aside the thought of her baby son in that car. She put on an extra burst of speed. There was another shot then Bee screamed something. Angus dropped the gun and started to slide back into the vehicle. Sophie saw the brakelights go on but the car didn't slow. The front wheels slewed sideways but it was too late: the car ploughed over the dam wall with Angus still partway out the window.

It hit with a bang and a splash. Sophie heard

herself screaming as if from a distance as she leapt over the top of the wall. The car was already sinking, the water up to the doorhandles. She struggled through the brown water towards the passenger door, crying and screaming Lachlan's name. The driver's seat was empty, the door open. Bee was slumped half on the passenger seat, half in the footwell, blood running from a fresh cut on her forehead as well as from the one on the side of her head that Chris had caused. Muddy water lapped across her legs and over the struggling Lachlan. Sophie wrenched at the door but it was locked. Bubbles rose from Lachlan's mouth. Sophie screamed his name. There were rocks further along the bank but the water grew deeper over him as the car sank in the mud and she balled her fist and punched the window with all her strength.

The glass shattered into hundreds of tiny cubes and pain shot up her arm. She grabbed Lachlan with her good hand and yanked him out the window, clear of the water and the car. He coughed and gasped. She fought her way to the bank, holding him up to her face, brushing glass from his clothes, patting his back to help him bring up any swallowed water. On the dirt she lay him on his side and knelt over him, crooning wordless sounds, her tears dripping onto his soaked clothing, ready to do mouth-to-mouth and delighted to see his colour turn pinker by the moment. She smoothed her hand over his hairless head and he opened his mouth and screamed. She laughed with joy. A baby who could make that much noise was far from death.

Suddenly an arm wrapped around her neck. She was jerked backwards into the water. She tried to elbow her attacker but couldn't make contact. She thrust her fingers back over her head but caught only hair. From the corner of her eye she saw Lachlan lying on the dirt kicking and wailing. She couldn't breathe from the pressure on her neck and her head started to buzz with a sound like distant sirens.

From all his kicking, Lachlan started to roll. The water was too close, he was going back in. Energised by her rage, Sophie brought her good fist around in an arc into her attacker's face. Something crunched under her hand and pain flashed through it, but the grip on her neck loosened a little. She somehow found a foothold in the mud and twisted her body to come face to face with Angus. His nose streamed blood and he was blinking. She rammed her palm upwards into his nose and he cried out, grabbing her and falling backwards, pulling her underwater.

The world was brown and full of bubbles. Angus's face was a pale blur below her and his left hand clawed at her throat. She found his neck and squeezed, thinking of Lachlan on the bank, trying to get her head up for air and to see where he was.

Angus's hand was crushing her throat and he straightened his arm, forcing her away, loosening her hold on his neck. She realised his right arm must have been hurt in the crash, as he wasn't using it, and struggled harder, trying to break free. Black dots appeared before her eyes. She jerked her head backwards and could feel the warmth of the sun on her hair, knew she was so close to the surface and the beautiful wonderful air, but Angus's hand closed tighter and tighter on her throat. Gathering every ounce of her waning strength she hit with her elbow at his straightened left arm. She felt his elbow give way and she launched herself forward, taking a fresh grip on his neck.

She could feel the tendons in Angus's neck against her palms. As her mouth opened involuntarily and filled with water she slid her thumbs closer together and found the bony structure of his larynx. She rammed her thumbs sharply inwards, the pain sharp in her injured hands, feeling the larynx crush, feeling the spasm in Angus's hand on her neck. But he kept his grip. The black dots grew and merged, filling her vision, obliterating the pale shape of his face. She struggled, once feeling air against the side of her face, aware of the growing weakness in her body, the pounding pain in her head and in her hands as she kept squeezing his neck, the wrenching desire to inhale even if it was water she'd take in, until finally Angus's hold weakened enough that she could jerk herself backwards and out of his grasp, and burst up out of the water.

Lachlan lay red-faced and screaming at the edge of the water. Sucking air in deeply she scrambled to him and lifted him clear, cradling him to her chest as he cried. She stumbled up the dam wall, putting her ear against his back to listen to his lungs, hearing no rasps when he took a breath that would indicate he'd inhaled water. She nestled him against her as she clambered over the wall, feeling she could never get her fill of simply gazing at him. On top of the slope she glanced away for a second to see Chris trying to crawl towards her.

In seconds she was at his side. 'Chris, it's okay. Look, he's here and he's fine.'

Chris raised his head to see his son. Tears ran down his pale, blood-streaked face. Sophie put Lachlan on the grass next to Chris's chest and he managed to loop an arm around him. 'Thank God, thank God.'

'Where are you shot?'

He half rolled so she could see the wound in his lower left abdomen. 'I can't stand up.'

She tore the sleeve from his dry shirt to make a firm pad against it. There were sirens in the distance.

'Thank God,' he said again, weeping and cradling Lachlan to him.

Sophie bent low, kissing them both. Lachlan was flailing his beautiful chunky little arms and legs but she felt every inch of them anyway, searching for bruising, watching his face to see if he grimaced over any particular spot. He seemed sore along his left arm but he moved it freely. She smoothed her hands over his head and found only a scratch from the glass, no lumps or cuts. In the nape of his neck she found a line of stubble as if they'd missed that area on the most recent shaving. She kissed him and kissed him.

'Thank God,' she echoed Chris, then she heard a bang and dirt sprayed up over them. She looked up and saw Bee on the dam wall, sodden and bloody, a silver gun shaking in her hands.

Oh Jesus, no.

Chris curled himself around Lachlan and Sophie wriggled forward to shield them both. Chris coughed once then raised his voice. 'Bee, I know why you're angry. Mum only told me today about what happened, what she did. She was wrong to do it. She knows that now.'

Sophie saw Bee shakily adjust her aim. She saw the fingers contract, the knuckles turn white. She shut her eyes.

There was another bang and something kicked Sophie in the thigh. At first there was no real pain. The blood running down her leg was warm in contrast to the cold dam water in her clothes. She clamped her hand over it but it didn't stem the flow much. The sirens seemed no closer. Lachlan was gazing up at her.

'I'm sorry that I didn't know at the time, Bee,' Chris went on, squeezing Sophie's arm. 'I understand now why you broke it off with me and I'm sorry I wasn't more sympathetic.'

Bee's silence was eerie. Sophie watched her from the corner of her eye, hoping to avoid agitating her. The sirens stopped.

Chris lowered his voice. 'What else should I say?'

In a unsteady voice Sophie called, 'You're obviously a very good mother. Lachlan's in excellent health. Thank you for taking care of him.' It hurt her to say it when she would have preferred to scream abuse. Lachlan put his tiny hand on her arm. Chris stroked the baby's little bald head. Her leg was throbbing now.

'We'll tell them how well you looked after

him,' Sophie said. 'We'll make sure they know that.'

Bee stood there, the gun out in front of her. Sophie heard cars speeding up the slope. 'Drop the weapon!' someone shouted.

Bee made another adjustment in her aim.

'Bee, drop the gun!'

Sophie recognised Ella Marconi's voice.

'Drop it now!'

Sophie couldn't help it, she was drawn to look at Bee. The end of the barrel was a round black spot, aimed directly at her. A shot rang out and Sophie flinched. Bee crumpled in a heap then rolled backwards out of sight down the dam wall.

20

Sophie lay shivering on the stretcher, her leg throbbing, as one paramedic connected an IV fluid bag to the cannula in her arm and another wrapped Lachlan in a warm dry blanket. The woman handed him back to Sophie with a smile and she tucked him in beside her as best she could with an icepack strapped to her injured hand. He yawned and sucked his thumb.

On another stretcher nearby, Chris was also receiving IV fluids. A bulky dressing was strapped to his abdomen and he propped himself up on his elbow as he handed Ella the burned fragment of paper he'd found in the house and talked through the events. Dennis scribbled in a notebook, flipping page after page. Sophie watched as Ella read the piece of paper and clapped Chris on the shoulder.

Three police officers stood on the top of the dam wall. Sophie knew what they were looking at: Bee lying dead from a gunshot wound to the chest at the water's edge and Angus floating face-down in the brown water near the half-submerged Magna with its drooping blue ribbon. She thought with grief about Sawyer. She'd told Ella all the details already, and knew she deserved everything the courts would throw at her, and more.

362

The paramedics wheeled Chris's stretcher over. 'Give us a minute?' he asked them.

Sophie looked at her husband's face. The blood had been cleaned off. He was pale but his eyes shone with a light she hadn't seen for weeks. He stroked Lachlan's arm with his fingertips.

'Do you remember when he was born?' he said.

Sophie's throat thickened. 'Of course.'

'Holding him, looking into his face, it was like I'd been given the world again,' Chris said. 'All mistakes were gone, and there was nothing to regret, because we were at the start of a new life.'

Tears welled in Sophie's eyes.

'That's how I feel now,' he said, and leaned over and kissed her.

She clutched at his arm. 'Chris.'

He kissed her again, and looked into her eyes. 'What?'

But she couldn't do it. To say the words, to release the secret that she'd slept with another man — and not just any man but the one who'd shot him and taken their son — would steal that light from his eyes forever. This was a pain she would have to learn to live with. Maybe Chris was right, some things could not be helped by talking.

'What?' he said again.

She said, 'I love you.'

21

Home at last, Ella opened the window and leaned on the sill. The night was chilly, the sound of traffic on Victoria Road carrying clearly on the cold air, and the cloudless sky was bright with the city's glow. She yawned and rested her shoulder against the frame and watched the red and green lights of some high plane cross the sky, heading north.

The case was over. Tonight Lachlan was sleeping in a cot in Sophie's hospital room, and Ella imagined the paramedic pulling the cot right up by the bed and keeping the light on to watch her son. She was having surgery on her leg tomorrow. In another room, down the hall perhaps, Chris was sleeping off the anaesthetic from the operation to remove the bullet from his abdomen.

Bee and Angus — their bodies, anyway — were in Gosford Hospital's morgue, awaiting the van that would move them to Glebe in the morning. Nobody would ever know now if that first aborted baby was Angus's, though Chris was certain. Ella thought about the twisted adoptive sibling relationship, losing a baby in their teens and it perhaps charting the course of their lives, a strange little family trying hard to have children and losing so many that they

364

turned both desperate and vengeful.

Sawyer was already in Glebe. She wondered what the post mortem would show as his cause of death, and thought about the case that homicide detectives would build against Sophie. If Sophie got a good lawyer who argued some kind of temporary insanity due to her son being missing, Ella thought she probably had a reasonable chance of avoiding a long sentence, even though she'd confessed every little detail in the statement she'd made at the hospital.

The fragment of paper that Chris had saved had turned out to be part of a roster. The station name was gone but you could see the surnames Wilson and Battye, and Battye was circled, with the word '*Civic*' and the date '*5 May*' scribbled next to it. Between that and the bag of money and the foreign bank records showing large deposits found in Angus's car, Strike Force Gold would be wetting themselves. Ella wished she could be involved with that case rather than going back to the suburbs, but couldn't see herself getting the call, especially with the marks she felt she had against her name now. Poor Edman Hughes was dead; she'd more or less allowed Roth to be murdered; and they'd been lucky to solve this case, stumbling across Chris and Sophie's trail rather than working it out for themselves. Not to mention the investigation into her shooting of Bee.

The investigators were on their way back to Sydney tonight with her gun and the transcripts of the initial interviews with her, Dennis, and every other cop that arrived on scene, whether they'd witnessed the shooting or not. They'd all had blood taken for drug and alcohol tests, and there would be more interviews to come, and a full-blown investigation, and at some point in the future — maybe not for months — she would be told whether her actions had been justified.

Whatever the official verdict, she knew she'd done the right thing. She'd been over and over it in her mind, reliving the rush up the hill in the car, seeing Bee standing on the top of the dam wall with a handgun trained on something in the grass, and how the closer she'd got the clearer she could see Sophie and Chris huddled together. She saw blood on them, saw they were moving, and that was all. She hadn't even known then whether they had baby Lachlan. Dennis told her later she'd leapt from the car, hadn't even put it into neutral, and it had stalled with him still fumbling with his seatbelt while she'd gone racing across the grass. She didn't remember getting her Glock out, only seeing Bee at the end of the barrel, and her own voice shouting at her, so loud. 'Drop the weapon! Drop it now!' Bee hadn't even glanced her way. It gave Ella a shiver to think of the way the woman had kept her focus on the Phillipses. There they'd been, the sun shining on them all, and Ella saw, *saw*, the movement of Bee's hand on the gun, the tightening of the tendons and muscles, and tightened her own, heard the bang, felt the recoil, and Bee had fallen. Ella ran again, first to see Bee motionless at the edge of the water, then to Sophie and Chris, where she'd looked down to see little Lachlan cradled between them. Sophie and Chris had been laughing, hugging, crying, and then Chris handed Lachlan up to her. She'd taken him in her arms like he was the Holy Grail, the water in his clothes soaking through to her skin, and he sighed and lurched and his head came to rest against hers. He was alive, he was fine. They'd done it. It gave her goosebumps now to think about it, and she clung to the sill with tears in her eyes.

This.

This was plenty.

We do hope that you have enjoyed reading this large print book.

Did you know that all of our titles are available for purchase?

We publish a wide range of high quality large print books including:
Romances, Mysteries, Classics
General Fiction
Non Fiction and Westerns

Special interest titles available in large print are:
The Little Oxford Dictionary
Music Book
Song Book
Hymn Book
Service Book

Also available from us courtesy of Oxford University Press:
Young Readers' Dictionary
(large print edition)
Young Readers' Thesaurus
(large print edition)

For further information or a free brochure, please contact us at:
Ulverscroft Large Print Books Ltd.,
The Green, Bradgate Road, Anstey,
Leicester, LE7 7FU, England.
Tel: (00 44) 0116 236 4325
Fax: (00 44) 0116 234 0205

BEAT THE REAPER

Josh Bazell

Peter Brown is a young Manhattan emergency room doctor with an unusual past. His real name Pietro Brnwa, and he is on the FBI's protection programme. After finding his grandparents dead, murdered by the Mafia, he's become proficient in Martial Arts and using a handgun. His goal: to find and despatch those who committed the crime. He fortuitously befriends, and is assisted by, a Mafia lawyer, who discovers their identities. But when he reveals them to Pietro, is there an ulterior motive? Then a new patient visits Peter who knows him from his other life, when he had a different name and a very different job. Now, whatever it takes, he must keep his patient alive so he can buy some time . . . and beat the reaper.

THE DARKER SIDE

Cody Mcfadyen

FBI Agent Smoky Barrett and her team are called in by the Director himself to investigate a murder committed on a flight from Texas to Virginia. They find that they are dealing with a serial killer who has already struck a truly horrific number of times. He kills people with the deepest, darkest secrets and is using them to target and destroy his victims. The case is about to go public, with all the accelerated power of the internet behind it and public hysteria is not far behind. Smoky is under intense pressure to get results, yet the team has never been faced with such an apparently insoluble problem. Who will the next victim be? Everyone in the world has secrets. Even Smoky.

TOO CLOSE TO HOME

Linwood Barclay

When the Cutter family's next-door-neighbours, the Langleys, are gunned down in their house one hot August night, the Cutters' world is turned upside down. That such brutal violence could be visited on an ordinary suburban family is as shocking as it is inexplicable — but at least the Cutters can comfort themselves with the thought that lightning is unlikely to strike twice in the same place. Unless, of course, the killers went to the wrong house . . .

THE DECEIVED

Brett Battles

Jonathan Quinn is a professional 'cleaner': he disposes of bodies and ties up loose ends; he doesn't get his hands dirty; he doesn't ask questions. But when Quinn is hired to vanish all traces of Steven Markoff, a rare friend in his line of work, all that has to change. Determined to avenge Markoff, Quinn embarks on a trail that snakes from the corridors of power in Washington to the bustling streets of Singapore, along with his quick-witted apprentice Nate, and the brilliant, beautiful Orlando. But events spiral dangerously out of control. The pace quickens as the bullets get closer . . . and to trust is to be deceived . . .

BLOOD BROTHER

J. A. Kerley

Detective Carson Ryder's sworn duty is to track killers down. He's never revealed the fact that his brother, Jeremy, is one of America's most notorious killers — now imprisoned. Now his brother's escaped and is at large in New York. With Jeremy the chief suspect in a series of horrifying mutilation-murders, a mysterious video demands Ryder be brought into help. What should be a straightforward manhunt couldn't be more different — or more terrifying. A dangerous cat-and-mouse game develops between Jeremy and the NYPD with Ryder in the middle, trying to keep his brother alive and the cops in the dark. But it's a game of life, death and deceit, a game with an unknown number of players and no clear way of winning . . .

HOLD MY HAND

Serena Mackesy

During the Second World War, Lily Rickett, a nine-year-old urchin from the Portsmouth docks, is evacuated and sent to the unwelcoming arms of the dysfunctional Blakemore family . . . It's the present time, and to single mother Bridget Sweeney and her daughter, it seemed like an answer to their prayers; a residential job in a part of the country where no one would know them. With reasons of their own for leaving London, it would mean a fresh start, with new names and hope for the future. But Rospetroc, the Bodmin manor-house Bridget has agreed to caretake, has secrets of its own; a history of high staff turnover and a certain reputation in the village. Soon Bridget suspects that she and little Yasmin are not alone there . . .